FOR US
THE LIVING

Antonia Van-Loon

FOR US THE LIVING

St. Martin's Press   New York

Library of Congress Cataloging in Publication Data

Van-Loon, Antonia, 1940-
  For us the living.

  I. Title.
PZ4.V26Fo [PS3572.A459]   813'.5'4   75-10002

To my husband, Clifford,
our children, Jennifer and Christopher,
and my parents, Bernadine and Frank Smith

FOR US THE LIVING

She would always remember the music. The war and the aftermath had been sprinkled with its golden notes. Now, as the veterans sang, it seemed to her that all they could see was the glint on the dark, splintered years. Only once did she hear her brother's singing falter. She wondered what he was thinking about.

Events had been accompanied by tone and rhythm; by words that had different meanings for each person here in the parlor. She listened, and disconnected images floated in and out of her mind: a soldier black with battle smoke; the mob on Third Avenue; violets in the back yard; the ride down to Gettysburg; a carriage clattering along Broadway; Kent walking toward her; Greg reaching for her hand.

She was settled now and knew approximately where she was going. But there had been a time when she had not known, could not even have guessed. The war had coincided with her own transition from adolescence into adulthood. And the music was all the more poignant.

ONE

... they dressed me up in scarlet red
And used me very kindly.
Still I thought that my poor heart would break
For the girl I left behind me.

Her name was Mary Elizabeth, but most people called her
Beth, and she did not mind the reduction of six syllables to
one. There were more important things to object to, and at
the moment she was objecting to nearly everything. It was five
thirty and already dark, and she had been waiting too long for
the creaky omnibus that would take her home. She was annoyed too because it was raining, she had no umbrella, and
her drenched bonnet was beginning to sag over her forehead.
She had been mad at the world all day. This morning one of
her students had laughed (laughed!) at a Wordsworth poem
she had read to the class, a poem, about a forgotten young
woman named Lucy, that always brought tears to her eyes.
And since then everything had seemed to go wrong.

There were many things in life to be angry about, not the
least of which was the fact that she was expected to suppress all
such anger with a gentle smile. *Gentle* was the adjective of the

1

day. Everyone was a gentleman, a gentlewoman, a gentle reader—gentlefolk. And Beth Shepherd, who was feeling almost violent, bitterly resented the fact that she had to stand here serenely on the corner of Broadway and Reade immersed to her ankles in mud and slush, suffering the racket of carriages on cobblestones and police roaring directions to drivers and drivers crackling whips over their horses when what she really wanted to do was howl like an animal. Gentle! Her countrymen were slaughtering one another in Virginia, and everyone ran on about gentility.

Something was wrong with the world, Beth thought. People ought not live in this unnatural way; pouring pretensions over one another, piping platitudes, acting as though everything were fine when it wasn't, thinking that the future would be better when it wouldn't.

She had had negative feelings about life before, and after a while they had been replaced with acceptance or even positive feelings. What had caused the change?

Her friends told her that she ought to be married. She was already twenty-two. But in January, 1863, there were so many men away at war that there were few left in New York. The officers she had met during their furloughs had bored her. Besides, she wasn't certain that marriage would solve anything.

Last year two men had proposed to her. One had been a businessman fifteen years her senior who seemed more enthralled with the world of finance than with her. Had she married him, he would have paraded her out for dinner parties and then sent her scurrying back to the sitting room. The other had been a young officer whose eyes glazed over when she offered her profound observations on life but became piercing points of brightness when gazing upon her basque, which was well-shaped by ample breasts. She had coolly turned him down because she had hoped to be able to *talk* to a husband.

In all her life there had only been one man she had wanted

2

to marry. She had met him three years ago. He had read poems to her in the garden and told her how beautiful she was and how clever she was and how whenever he was with her he felt better about himself. She had loved him for that. She wanted to be needed—truly needed by a man. And she had hoped to walk through life beside him, their minds blending together in sweet unity. Then suddenly, without any warning, he had sold his soul for the dowry of a smug young heiress, leaving Beth so dejected that she wondered if she could go on. To her surprise, she had recovered from him very quickly (youth is resilient) but she had not been in love since.

At last an omnibus drawn by six horses came to a halt in front of her. By daylight these conveyances were garish, but after dark the intense colors were softened by amber gaslight and they warmed the dismal winter streets. Beth, gathering up her skirts, stepped into the bus, dropping her coin into a hole at the roof behind the driver, and wove down the narrow aisle, filling its width with her hoop-fortified skirts. She sat down in one of two empty seats, glowering at the straw on the floor which was supposed to insulate passengers against the cold but never did. A few people looked at her. She was pretty—not beautiful or exotic, but pretty, vibrant even in her sodden state—with large dark eyes, a straight nose, and a well-shaped mouth, which at the moment was distorted in a scowl. She turned her head to look outside. There wasn't much to see. The street lights illuminated spots of buildings and left other parts in darkness. There was an advertisement for a dental preparation called Sozodont and a recruitment poster that said, "Attention! Young men who wish to avenge their country . . ." She turned around again as the omnibus lumbered to a halt and picked up a passenger who looked like Daniel Webster.

When she was a child, she had wanted to be an orator. She would make speeches in the Senate that sent chills through the spines of her fellow senators. Then she would run for the Presidency and win by a landslide.

3

"President!" her older brother had roared. "Women can't even vote, Beth."

"They will some day. If Victoria can be a queen, I can be a president."

"Be sensible, little sister. Perhaps you could be a president's wife . . ."

The bus creaked along in the traffic at a rate slower than that of brisk-paced pedestrians. More passengers ascended, until the vehicle was filled to the bursting point. One man, forced to stand, kept weaving back and forth against her skirts. He could not help it, and she realized that, but she was angry all the same. Tears stung her eyes. Taking deep breaths, she tried to pinpoint a reason for her mindless rage. On other days—even the dreariest days—she could sail through her routine with a smile on her face. She could laugh with her students, sympathize with her weary fellow teachers, and enjoy the sights and sounds of this city of marvels. She did not understand what was wrong tonight. She knew only that it had something to do with her age, the war, discarded child-hood dreams, and a longing for love. And the emotions were sharpened by this moment in a bus that moved too slowly in a predetermined direction while damp humanity lurched helplessly inside it and pressed itself against her heavy skirts.

The bus dropped her off at Sixteenth Street, and she began to walk the block and a half home. Food would improve her spirits, she decided, and it was almost time for supper. Her street was lined with brownstone buildings. Many were not true brownstones at all but brick houses with brownstone facades, for every fashionable home had to display a front built from that sacred mineral, and hers was one of these. She walked down the stairs to the ground floor, holding fast to the railing lest she slip, and opened the heavy door. Home smells drifted toward her: roast beef, her father's cigars. But the mixed scents, while not aromatic, were comforting to her. She began to feel a little better.

The house had four stories but the living center was on the

ground floor just below street level. To the left of the long hallway were three rooms: the family room, dining room and kitchen. Upstairs on the main floor was the parlor, its furnishings dating from the Shepherds' wealthier days. It was used when the family was entertaining. Behind the parlor was the library, a marvelous place to spend rainy afternoons. The top two floors contained bedchambers for Beth, her parents, and her three brothers. There was also a room for guests and small servants' quarters. Beth loved her tiny room. She valued privacy.

From the hallway she called a greeting to her father, who was seated in an armchair in the family room reading the *Tribune.* He waved at her, smiling, then turned back to his paper. Her fourteen-year-old brother Sean, sitting on the floor examining a map of Virginia, also looked up and waved with a lead pencil. Sean loved to plan war strategy and was hoping that the war would last long enough for him to join his two older brothers.

Sheilah, their maid, came into the hallway as Beth was removing her bonnet. She spoke in a heavy brogue. "Mother of God, look at you! You'll catch your death. Quick, up the stairs with you and into some dry clothes."

Sheilah was a portly woman of fifty-five with small bright eyes and a florid face. Her white hair was pulled severely back and she never wore a cap to soften the effect except when the Shepherds were entertaining. She had been with the family for ten years. In the past the Shepherds had had as many as four servants living under their roof, but Sheilah was the only one remaining. She needed the assistance of the family for some of the daily chores and relied on outside help for laundry and heavy cleaning.

Beth hung up her coat. "I *am* drenched. I didn't think I'd need an umbrella today. When is supper?"

"Ten, fifteen minutes."

"Good. I'm awfully hungry. Is Mother home?"

"She's in the kitchen."

"Oh, do please keep her there, Sheilah! If she sees me

looking like this, I'll have to suffer another lecture about how I ought to stay home and do embroidery like a proper young lady."

"Then you'd better scoot up them stairs straightaway. I hear her coming."

Beth couldn't very well "scoot" up the stairs, but she did move with as much dispatch as possible within the confines of her cumbrous outfit. Though the money was needed, Mother disapproved of Beth's teaching. But Beth vastly preferred working to staying home day after day with nothing to do but clean house, gossip with her mother's friends, and knit or embroider—two arts at which she had failed utterly. She actually felt sorry for girls wealthier than herself who had no excuse whatever to venture out into the world and therefore had to spend the dreary winter isolated in prim sitting rooms. They could never go far without a chaperone, whereas she, Beth, could walk all over the city by herself after school and explain to the family that she had been delayed with a student or at a meeting.

In her room she discarded the drenched navy poplin, throwing it carelessly over the silk coverlet of her bed, then hastily hanging it up lest the water ruin the silk. She put on a white basque and a brown wool skirt. Then, smoothing back her dark brown chignon and poking hairpins into place, she walked down the hall to the bathroom to wash her hands. The bathroom's function was as its name suggested: One only bathed or washed there. The boiler, which was connected to the bathtub and to the range downstairs by pipes, had been lit earlier this evening. She filled a bowl with hot water and added some cold water from a pitcher. She washed her hands, dabbing lightly at her face, then poured the water into a copper ladling can which would be carried out later.

Feeling cheerier now that she had freshened up, Beth walked down to the dining room where her mother was placing napkins on the table. Kate Shepherd was still an attractive woman, despite the changes that age had wrought. Her hair,

6

now gray, had once been a striking blond, and she missed those long golden tresses that had captured the attentions of many a beau. But her eyes were still a crystal blue, and her plump figure seemed somehow no less fragile than it had once been. In appearance, mother and daughter bore little resemblance to one another. Beth, taller than average with dark hair and eyes, favored her father. And her figure was in no way fragile. A beau of hers, known for his indelicate adjectives, had once called Beth voluptuous.

"Good evening, Mother." Beth preferred "Mother" and "Father" to the more informal "Ma" and "Pa" used by her brothers.

"Hello, dear. You look awfully tired. Do sit down. We'll be eating in a moment." Kate bustled about the table, now arranging water glasses. She always fluttered like a bird, doing things in quick little movement and even speaking in a voice that rippled like the swoop of wings. "Is there anything new, dear?"

"Not a thing. And you?"

"Well, I called on the Kendalls this afternoon and met Diane's new beau."

"The war hero?" Beth asked.

"Have you met him?"

"No, but Diane mentioned him when I passed her on the street the other day. There wasn't time to talk."

"I think this is serious," Kate said. "Diane adores him."

Diane Kendall, Beth's next-door neighbor, was a year younger than Beth and dazzlingly beautiful. She had wavy blond hair, and the most delicate of features, with beguilingly slanted eyes of sapphire set in a face of pure ivory. The relationship between the two went back to early childhood and had passed through three phases. At first Diane had been Beth's best friend. They had played together in their rooms on long winter days telling one another their secret thoughts. Summers had been spent in the Shepherds' garden. Diane, an only child, had played with Beth's brothers too, and one of them had loved Diane ardently for many years. Before enlisting in the army, he had informed Beth that he could no longer handle the unremitting competition of other men.

Beth couldn't tolerate the situation either. When Diane began to glow, Beth—quite attractive in any normal gathering of women—felt plain by comparison. Men had gravitated toward Diane at party after party, and only when Diane had too many to handle did they turn to look at her brown-haired, brown-eyed friend. At sixteen Beth had hated the girl, loathed her with all the passion of her being. Diane had not known this, of course, and had been hurt when Beth airily informed her that she was too busy with studies to call on her friend. Beth was also at pains to keep her own beaux from meeting Diane, for she was certain that they would defect to "Golden Girl"—Sheilah's nickname for Diane—as soon as they laid eyes upon her.

At eighteen Beth found that she had been mistaken. One beau of hers had told Beth bluntly that no man could love a woman so perfect as Diane. He could admire her, but he could not love her, for such women were always spoiled and lacked depth. Beth could not in conscience let that remark pass. To her surprise, she found herself defending her beautiful neighbor. "She has a great deal of character," she told the man indignantly.

And so began Phase Three of the friendship, in which Beth neither loved nor hated Golden Girl. As Mr. Kendall began making money in tremendous amounts and Diane was lavished with clothes, jewels, and social opportunities that were far beyond Beth's reach, she began seeing Diane as she might see a heroine in a *Harper*'s story who traveled in Newport society. Diane was no longer of Beth's world. She was a fictional character—too beautiful, too wealthy to be real. Beth no longer felt a sense of competition with her, and her only interest in Diane's latest alliance was to determine whether or not there would be a wedding in the spring. Lord knew she needed a wedding to pick up her spirits. She could taste the champagne already.

Kate described Diane's latest beau as Sean and his father came into the dining room and took their places at the table.

"He's a modest young man, for all that he's a war hero and rich as a Croesus besides."

Sean looked up. "A war hero? Who's a war hero?"

"A friend of Diane's," said Kate. "You'll meet him next week. I asked the Kendalls to the dinner party we're having and I thought it only proper, since he was in their parlor when I issued the invitation, to invite him also."

"What did he do?" Sean asked his mother.

"Excuse me?"

"To become a *hero*, Ma."

"Why, I never thought to ask him."

"Never thought to—" Sean broke off, shaking his head.

"I'm sorry, dear, but I wouldn't have understood even if he'd told me. I do hate descriptions of violence." She paused. "But I know his name. Gregory Allister."

No one at the table reacted.

"His father's the banker, James Allister."

"No, I've never heard of him," said Beth.

"Gregory suffered a severe wound under his left shoulder," Kate said to her daughter, "so he's been sent home for a while. He has a nice face. Brown hair and blue eyes. He's quite tall and thin—disconnected almost, as though his limbs were tacked on as an afterthought. And he's quiet. Somehow one expects war heroes to come thundering into a room shouting, 'Glory hallelujah!' "

Beth wasn't especially interested in a detailed description of the man. She was merely curious about Diane's marital plans. "Did you say they were engaged, Mother?"

"No, I said that Diane seems especially fond of him."

"Oh." Beth's visions of champagne bubbled away. "Then he's just another beau?"

"Yes, but he's most unusual. He's . . ." Kate talked on while Beth's mind drifted elsewhere. She would meet the man next week and learn all about him soon enough—if there was anything worth learning. War heroes did not impress her as they did Sean. Her patriotic fervor had died with the soldiers at First Bull Run. As Kate stopped to catch her breath, Beth heard her father say, ". . . the Black Plague." Kate's eyebrows shot up, and Beth looked toward her father.

"Sean asked me what I'd done at the library and I told him I'd helped someone research the Black Plague," said John.

"Oh! I couldn't imagine—" Beth began to laugh, remembering the men standing in their black greatcoats on Broadway this afternoon. What a splendid way to describe them. She began to laugh louder. Her father tugged at his beard and smiled quizzically, and Kate said, "Whatever has come over you, dear?"

"I'm just visualizing—here we were all sitting here and suddenly Father dropped this phrase onto the—"

"I didn't suddenly drop it," said John. "There was a preface that you obviously missed."

"It's—it's—Oh I know the plague is nothing to laugh about but—" She broke off in peals of mirth, holding her sides.

No one shared in Beth's laughter, least of all John Shepherd, who had read gory contemporary accounts of the cursed plague that had swept through medieval Europe. John Shepherd was a librarian. At one time he had been a publisher in partnership with his brother, and the Shepherds had been comfortably situated. On his brother's death, John had taken in a partner and begun losing money immediately. The two men were of one nature in their skill at evaluating books and in their total inability to balance books, a sad fact which contributed to the demise of the company and ultimately its sale to a more mathematically inclined publisher. John had, with the guidance of his nephew Bill Shepherd, invested his share of money in real estate and stocks before taking a position as a librarian. Beth had finished normal school and secured a teaching position. The boys had been able to attend Columbia, and Sheilah had stayed on with them too. But the Shepherds could no longer live the good life on the scale demanded by up-and-coming New Yorkers.

This had caused Kate no end of grief, though she was fond

of her husband and pleased that he seemed to thrive amid the dusty library books. Nevertheless, there was their status to consider, and Kate, especially after the war started, was adept at enhancing it. At the sewing and bandage-rolling parties she would comment favorably on the "old wealth" and "good families" in New York, Boston, Philadelphia, and Washington who felt that showiness in wartime was vulgar. Allied thus with the sober leaders of the nation, she could make their financial predicament sound modest, patriotic, and dignified. When she was in certain company, she let it slip that their considerable monies from various investments were being held in abeyance for the splendid country home they planned to build after the war. In reality, these investments were barely enough to keep their city house functioning.

As Beth's hilarity subsided into hiccups and finally into silence, Kate, looking a bit annoyed, resumed her account of Diane and her latest young man.

"As I was saying, he's most unusual. I can't imagine why Diane would be attracted to him. He's rather serious. One might almost call him morose."

"Oh?" Beth said politely, still thinking of how well "the Black Plague" described her dismal afternoon.

"No. *Intense* would be the word. He's intense and very intellectual. And we all know that cleverness is not one of Diane's attributes. I rather think he's dazzled by her appearance."

Beth sipped her soup, vaguely irritated that the entire dinner conversation was being monopolized by a man who wasn't even present.

"What battle?" Sean asked his mother.

"What *battle?*"

"The war hero. Was it Antietam or Fredericksburg?"

"I didn't ask him."

"You didn't ask him *that* either?" Sean looked incredulous.

"You know how I hate to discuss the war," Kate said, more firmly than was her custom. "Ask him yourself when you meet him next week."

Kate was almost obsessed with the fear of her sons' being harmed. Left an orphan, after seeing her parents and one surviving brother wiped out in a cholera epidemic three months after they arrived from Ireland, she had been taken in by a family friend who was a maid for a wealthy childless couple. The pair had loved Kate to distraction, adopted her, and ultimately delivered her into the hands of the handsome publisher from England before permitting themselves to die, one soon after the other, of consumption.

Without any other family, Kate clung to her husband and children. She hoped that each would marry well and have a flood of offspring, establishing a "clan" like the one in Dublin she had learned of as a little girl. With John's sympathetic indulgence, she had named all her children after members of her lost family. Her first-born had been named Patrick, symbol of her homeland.

She also remained attached to the Church. Her adoptive parents, not Catholics themselves, had seen to it that she retained her religion. John had magnanimously permitted her to save the souls of her four children, and she had taken them to Mass every Sunday, but to little avail. Of the four, Pat and Beth had already lapsed into agnosticism, and Joseph and Sean were beginning to question sacred truths. Kate placed the blame on John, who considered himself a pantheist and didn't care who knew it. But she was convinced that all of them, John included, would see the Truth revealed some day. She worried over whether the boys would be given extreme unction on the battlefield, should the Lord see fit to claim them. There must be priests enough in the army. There were so many Irish in the regiment. Every evening, kneeling by the bed, she prayed that the priests would be there.

Sean, his mouth full of mashed potatoes, asked his mother, "Is this man of Diane's in the same regiment as Pat and Joe?"

"I don't *know*, Sean," Kate snapped. "I don't know anything about Gregory's role in the war except that he was wounded. Nothing else. If you like, I'll have the dinner party tomorrow

12

night so you can assault him with questions." She paused, looking guilty. "Oh, I'm sorry, Sean. It's just that—"

"It's all right, Ma," said Sean. "I'm just interested. I can't help it."

"No, I suppose you can't. I never will understand men and their fascination with war." Kate looked up at the maid. "The roast beef is delicious, Sheilah. Could you make it again next week for our guests?"

"I'll make it better."

The one luxury the Shepherds permitted themselves in these lean years was the informal dinner party. John was always meeting new people at the library, and Kate liked to invite wealthy friends to their "intellectual" dinners and watch them squirm when John and his friends dropped quotations they didn't recognize or made references to Greek deities or medieval morality plays to which they couldn't respond in kind. The dinner party Kate was planning for next week, however, was to include only close friends of the family, the one stranger being Diane's young man.

Kate chatted on about her afternoon with the Kendalls. Diane's mother and Kate were neighbors and friends; thus Kate was close enough to Diane to be her aunt. This fact irritated Beth. As Kate's voice rippled on, Beth began to wish that Diane and this man of hers would marry and move to California. She could tolerate Diane at a distance, but she did not look forward to spending an evening with her and this wealthy war hero who sounded awfully full of himself.

"Her face is transformed whenever she looks at him," Kate said.

"Whose face?" asked her husband absently.

"Diane's face," said Kate. "I take it you haven't been listening, John."

No one had been listening, thought Beth. Her mother did have a habit of running on and on, as though failure to fill a void of silence was a mortal sin. Beth had sometimes wondered if her mother and most women talked this way because it was in their nature to do so, or if they babbled because all interesting avenues of life were closed to them and there was no other way in which to affirm their presence. She had frequently found herself talking in this same rushed way.

John Shepherd stared glassy-eyed at his wife and nodded every so often, tossing out an occasional "Indeed?" to assure Kate that he was listening.

John was a distinguished man, London-born and Oxford-educated, who had come to America with his only brother twenty-six years earlier. His black hair was almost all gray now, but he was still attractive, despite the slight puffiness of his face—the effect of excellent brandy, fine cigars, and rich cuisine. He wasn't a practical man, for he saw in life not what was there but what he wished to be there. "The world is too much with us," he would proclaim from time to time, while his earth-bound sons nodded respectfully and went about their practical lives. His daughter Beth, despite her realism about many things, was more impressed with her father than were her brothers, Beth being literary and somewhat philosophical. But Beth received little of John's attentions. She was a girl, and society had dictated that a girl was her mother's province. He saw her as something of a tragic figure, blessed with brains in a world that rarely permitted women's minds to be used. He could think of nothing to teach her (except possibly an appreciation of the arts) that would be of any use in the life she was fated to live. He loved her as he loved the others, perhaps a bit more because of the problems he guessed she would have.

John had moments when he could deal with the world on its own terms, but he usually looked at life through the eyes of a poet. Even his wife was a poem: the fair-haired daughter of Erin, embodiment of that proud land; wild, free, and driven by distant dreams. Thus he had seen her in the beginning, thus he still saw her, and staid, conventional Kate forgave him his foggy vision. A close friend of his—a Negro teacher who often stopped at the library—also forgave him. John found a richness in the African heritage and ran on at length about the thick, tangled jungles from which the man's ancestors had burst, possessed of a fire for life unknown to the Northern white people. Philip Weatherly, who was portly, middle-aged, and hardly able to bound through a jungle without risking a heart attack, would nod distantly, thinking of the morning's news or a paper he was planning to write. Only when John touched earth (in discussions of politics or current literature) did he fully engage his friend's interest. But, however astigmatic, John was sincere, and most of his friends realized that. People of his own cultural background frankly bored him, and when he was fortunate enough to acquire a friend like Phil, he marveled at his good luck.

With two parents so different—the mother dogmatic in religious beliefs and therefore decisive in everyday decisions ("The Commandments tell us . . .") and the father rather vague about what Ultimate Truth was and not certain of anything—the children grew up questioning things, as those whose parents were in accord rarely did. Beth had indicated an interest in every new social idea from the Oneida Colony to the Women's Rights movement and had asked older friends of the family to accompany her as chaperone to the lyceums where such groups and their ideas were discussed. She had also read her brother's copy of *Origin of Species by Means of Natural Selection,* published in 1859 by an Englishman named Darwin, who had shaken continents by boldly contradicting the teachings of Scripture and so subjected himself to threats of murder (hanging was the preferred method) by irate citizens the world over.

Kate did not always approve of the interests of her children, but she was accustomed to John, a charming eccentric in her opinion, and tolerated her children's interests while wondering aloud whether many similar social reforms and scientific theories had been revoked or disproved with the passage of time.

All members of the family, though, were to some extent at variance with the prevailing morality. They lived in a city where refugees from all over Europe were now converging.

15

Manhattan, in 1863, was a continent of tiny nations, a stewing pot of new ideas. There were intellectuals here who had lived through the European revolutions of 1848. Accounts of their experiences found their way into native-language newspapers, and from there they were picked up by the New York press. One could question the habits, religions, and attitudes of the "furriners," but it was impossible to escape their influence or, if one were conscientious, to deny some of their assertions.

It was an era of industrial as well as political revolution. While most agreed that the new inventions, from the reaper to the sewing machine, were making people's burdens easier, there were some who could sense problems as an arthritic senses the impending rain. With railroads and steamboats whisking people too quickly from one way of life to another and with a transatlantic telegraph cable almost completed, where would it all end? How would the next generation live? And what hidden perils would these marvels spawn?

Beth had heard all these subjects—revolution, the impact of science, the changing morality—discussed in the lyceums and in her family's parlor. She was a well-informed young woman, but a confused one. It would be easier, she sometimes thought, to be told what was right, what was wrong, what the future would probably bring, and how to behave in any given situation. Perhaps if she knew less about the world, she would not be so angry about so many things. Yet she did want to know. There was nothing for it but to suffer the unfortunate side-effects of that knowledge.

On the evening of the dinner party, Beth had effected a temporary truce with the world and was feeling much jollier than she had on that dismal evening in the omnibus. She stood in the hallway with her father, greeting guests, while Sheilah prepared dinner and Kate fussed with place settings in the dining room. The first to arrive was her Aunt Louise, John's widowed sister-in-law, who didn't have to pause for social amenities (they saw her every other day). She patted John's arm, kissed Beth's cheek, and then swept briskly downstairs to the dining room to chat with Kate.

Next to arrive was John's former publishing partner, Nate Klein, and his wife. Nate, who had opened a bookstore after the demise of the publishing company, was still losing money steadily. But Louise's son supervised his investments as well as John's and so managed to keep the Kleins solvent.

Philip Weatherly, the third member of what Beth called The Triumvirate, followed the Kleins. Scarcely a week went by without John, Nate and Phil getting together for an evening of brandy and good talk. Phil was the principal of a "colored" school and a frequent contributer to the *Weekly Anglo-African*. Since Phil had become a friend of the family, some of the Shepherds' acquaintances, anxious to illustrate their belief in equality-for-the-Negro, hastened to invite him to their own social affairs. One hostess had trilled to Kate, "Isn't it wonderful? Our very own Frederick Douglass!" But at many of these parties Phil was gazed upon as a curiosity and some guests actually spoke to him in simple words, raising their voices as though he were deaf. Hosts and hostesses would color with embarrassment but Phil would usually laugh and answer them in words selected from a grammar school primer, measured out in slow, loud cadence. Most of these guests came to realize that they were being mocked.

John, Nate, and Phil, standing together, looked much alike. They were all of the same height, all had beards, and all wore black frock coats, silk waistcoats, and bow ties.

There was no Mrs. Weatherly, for Phil was a widower, so Beth talked in the hallway with Ruth Klein, a woman of quiet dignity. She had grown children, and she answered Beth's polite inquiries after them, her eyes reflecting pride.

At last the Kendalls came in. Beth, who did not like either of Diane's parents, marveled that Diane had reached adulthood as sane as she was with these two serving as her models. The father seemed interested only in making money. He was piling up fortunes selling munitions to the army, and he had once remarked that if the war would only last long enough, he would be a millionaire. "Of course I'd as soon not make another penny if only our brave boys could come home again," he had added hastily. Beth guessed that he didn't care a whit about the "brave boys," and she frankly detested the man. His wife was little better. She was petty, catty, and as greedy as her husband. Kate remained her friend merely out of habit. They had been neighbors for twenty years.

Behind Mr. and Mrs. Kendall stood Diane. She kissed Beth with a warmth that Beth scarcely noticed. She was gazing curiously at the stranger who had dominated Kate's dinner conversation the previous week: Gregory Allister. He was dressed in uniform—a caped overcoat and an officer's hat— and he looked much as Kate had described him: tall and thin, dark, clean-shaven, and very serious. He had an awkward stance that one did not associate with either wealth or heroism.

"Beth, I'd like you to meet Gregory Allister," Diane said, smiling. "Gregory, this is Elizabeth Shepherd. Beth as we call her."

He bowed formally, his eyes quickly taking in every curve of her body. Beth was wearing a sedate dark green silk that seemed dowdy alongside Diane's blue velvet, the skirt of which could be seen beneath a white fur wrap, but Mr. Allister's expression indicated that form intrigued him rather than color. A blush stole over Beth's cheeks as she took his coat and turned away from him.

Most of the people were, by this time, moving toward the parlor, and John urged Gregory in that direction so that he might be introduced around. Diane lingered in the hall until everyone had gone and then said in a breathless voice to Beth, "What do you think of him?"

"I've scarcely met him, Diane."

"Oh I do hope everyone likes him." Diane twined her hands nervously.

"I've no doubt they will. But what matters is the way you feel." Beth felt like a mother advising a daughter. It was a strange sensation, trying to reassure a woman who already

18

had everything. For a moment it was as though they were children again, sharing their secret thoughts. Diane's wealth and beauty could not be denied, but she had retained the vulnerable personality of the eight-year-old who had once said to Beth, "You're not as afraid of things as I am."

"They'll like him," said Beth with genuine warmth.

Beth went down to the kitchen to help Sheilah. When she returned to the parlor, her father and Gregory were standing near the fireplace discussing the war, while the other guests sat on chairs and couches listening.

"I daresay you're very modest, Mr. Allister. Or do you prefer Captain Allister? I understand you were promoted."

"Greg would be fine, Mr. Shepherd."

"Greg, then. But false modesty is not a virtue."

"It isn't false, sir. I acted in self-defense."

"And you attacked them all with a bayonet? That's quite remarkable."

"It was either them or me, sir. I would have preferred that it had been none of us."

John's expression changed. "Well yes, of course, it was a difficult—uh—situation." His voice trailed off. In a corner of the room, Sean's face fell. Clearly Mr. Allister did not wish to discuss the great battle.

John was annoyed with what he considered Greg's sullenness and turned awkwardly to another guest, leaving Greg standing alone for a moment. His arms fell loosely to his sides, his expression blank. Diane was on her feet immediately and Kate too rushed to join him. Though it was rude, Beth stared at him from her position at the door. In his face she could see a side of the war she had seldom thought about amid the bands and badges that had marked her acquaintance with the brave boys in blue. Even the funerals had been clean, dramatic, musical affairs that never called to mind bullets and blood. Impulsively she longed to take away his pain as she had pulled splinters from Sean's finger or bolstered Pat's spirits on being rejected by a woman. Such instincts came automatically to a sister of three brothers. Of course Greg had Diane, whose vivaciousness could pull anyone out of the doldrums. But how had Diane come to choose such a man? They seemed quite different in temperament. Diane had had many dashing beaux that complemented her better. It couldn't be his money either. Diane was not mercenary. To the contrary, she was romantic and had given her parents many a scare when she proposed eloping with men who looked as though they'd originated in the Five Points, a notorious New York slum. Speculation about this newly mismatched couple would no doubt constitute the mainstay of gossip in the dreary months ahead.

At dinner, the quiet Allister was seated next to Aunt Louise and across from Phil Weatherly, either of whom could keep up a steady, entertaining monologue. Aunt Louise, who with her husband and son had taken the overland trail to California "just for the fun of it" back in '51, actually coaxed a smile out of Greg with accounts of her misadventures. Phil had once been involved in the Underground Railroad and never tired of telling the hair-raising stories of those dangerous days when slaves were smuggled into the North. He too succeeded in keeping Greg diverted.

The conversation at John's end of the table was literary, as it always was when he and Nate came within quoting distance of one another. At the other end of the table, Kate spoke animatedly with the people seated near her. Their conversation covered fashions, furnishings, and the ideas espoused by the editors of and contributors to the periodical *Godey's Lady's Book.* Beth usually preferred men's subjects, because normal school had emphasized rigorous academic training instead of the ladies' arts that constituted the curriculum of the expensive women's academies. While her wealthier friends were learning how to paint on velvet and drop a phrase in French, Beth was struggling with Latin, mathematics, and the basics of government. This was not because normal schools were anxious to educate women; it was because women, who increasingly entered teaching for the meager wages that men were beginning to scorn, had been vested with the sacred obligation of educating little boys.

Beth had therefore been deprived of formal instruction in social graces—a fact which disturbed Kate, who was disappointed that Beth had few opportunities to meet girls from the best families. But the boys' university education had been the important thing, and there was little money left over for Beth. Kate's only hope was that her daughter would marry one of those rare species of men who liked intelligent women, even those ignorant of household matters. In the meantime, Kate had done her best to educate her daughter.

"Beth, pay attention," she had said years ago during one of her lectures in the feminine arts. "You must use porous, pulpy paper so that the flower will adhere to it. Then you place each piece on opposite pages of the book and lay the flower on it thus."

"Excuse me, Mother, but did you hear what Father just told Joe? There's been more trouble in Kansas. A man named John Brown—"

"Haven't you been listening to me?"

"I'm sorry, Mother, but I want to hear what they're saying. Could we go back to it in a few minutes?"

Kate never gave up. She did manage to teach Beth a few things about household décor and basic etiquette, and considered that an accomplishment. As time went by, she became proud of her daughter's conversational skills. For all that Beth thought like a man (and growing up in a house full of them had influenced her), she did attract her fair share of beaux. That was the important thing.

The dinner was splendid. Sheilah's roast beef was flavored to perfection with her own special spices (she never would reveal the recipe), and her baked-apple desert was a cinnamon-studded work of art. As they were enjoying the latter, while conversation flowed around the table, Phil Weatherly's voice swirled into a rare vacuum in the conversation in a response to Gregory Allister.

21

"My son plans to join the Massachusetts colored regiment. He hopes he sees serious action soon, so he can prove that Negroes are as brave as anyone else."

John looked up. "Don't be so sensitive, Phil. Negroes can fight and you know it."

"I know it, but who else knows it?"

Greg replied, "Obviously the state of Massachusetts does or they wouldn't have approved the regiment, sir."

Phil shrugged. "Well, they're getting desperate. To avoid conscription, they've finally pulled black lackeys out of the trenches and put them in uniform."

"Sir, conscription will be approved anyway," said Greg.

"I've heard," said John, "that anyone who doesn't want to fight will be able to hire a substitute."

"It's true," said Greg, "and the wealthy will take every opportunity to do so. There are enough starving Irishmen in this city who need the money badly."

The group at the table looked at Greg, who was himself very wealthy, and wondered why he would admit this.

Beth said, "But the poor who are selected and don't want to go—what will they do? *They* won't be able to hire substitutes."

"I suspect they'll protest," said Greg.

"Oh, certainly," Phil agreed. "They're up in arms about it already, and the law hasn't even been passed. I hear them at night in the saloons shouting, 'Rich man's war and a poor man's fight.' "

Phil Weatherly, himself comfortably well-off, was nevertheless segregated in a slum area where Negro and Irish scrambled over one another for the stale bread and decaying fish that kept them from starvation.

Phil continued, "In any case, it's heartening to know that in Massachusetts, at least, black men are being accorded the dignity of taking up arms against the oppressors. Negroes with rifles." He shook his head. "Amazing."

Beth asked, "Why don't they have Negro regiments in New York?"

"There aren't enough young men to form a full regiment,"

22

said Phil. "And even if there were, I doubt New Yorkers would approve."

"Well, can't they join white regiments?" asked Sean.

"White regiments!" Phil began to laugh. "Sean, you are very young."

"But aren't we fighting for freedom? And doesn't that include the freedom for a man to join any regiment he pleases?" asked Sean.

John said, "We're fighting to free the slaves. Unfortunately, that does not mean that segregation will end."

Greg smiled.

"Am I amusing you?" John asked him.

"Sir, do you really believe that the Union cares about the fate of the Negro?"

"Well, of course." John straightened up in his chair.

"I see."

"And what do you think the war is about?" asked John.

"Money."

"Only money?"

"Money and power. We want tariffs; they don't. We want industrial representation in Congress. They want agrarian spokesmen. Both sides are struggling for control of the West. If the South—"

John waved his hand impatiently. "I do read the papers, Mr. Allister. But tariffs and the like are minor reasons for the war. Why for thirty years the issue of slavery—the moral outrage over the institution—has been moving our countrymen toward the brink of battle. And now that the battle is joined you tell us that slavery has nothing to do with the war?"

Greg replied, trying to keep his voice even. "Sir, I did not say that. I said the Union does not care about Negroes. Our leaders may wish to abolish slavery but their reasons are economic, not moral. They hope to cripple the Southern aristocracy. Once they have succeeded in that objective, most leaders, including President Lincoln, would prefer to ship the Negroes off to some colony rather than deal with them as human beings. As for the men in the ranks, they don't think

23

about the slaves when they march into battle. Most of them consider Negroes their inferiors. They would howl with indignation if the freed slaves actually came north to settle in their communities."

John's eyes blazed. "Well, if this is true, then why were so many Northern men fired with outrage over the scenes depicted in Mrs. Stowe's book? They deplore the institution of slavery. And on *moral* grounds, Mr. Allister. Not economic ones, as you suggest. I'm amazed that you would—"

Greg interrupted. "Many of the people who wept copiously over *Uncle Tom's Cabin* never gave a thought to the poverty of Negroes in their own Northern cities—to the segregated schools and transportation systems. Why you stated the facts yourself, sir, when you told your son that we're fighting to free the slaves but that prejudice will continue. Doesn't this contradiction disturb you?"

John sighed, closing his eyes briefly. Then he said in a weary voice, "But the fact remains that the men *are* fighting. Surely they must have a reason! And I doubt that it's something so abstract as a desire for industrial representation in Congress."

Greg said, "Most young men consider war a great adventure. They are not especially concerned with the cause. They go to war in order to escape their monotonous farm lives and most hope to return as heroes." He paused and leaned forward, glancing around the table briefly and then fixing his eyes upon John. "There are of course some humane men who will risk their lives for the dignity of their Negro brothers but their numbers are few, sir. But let us assume, for the sake of argument, that our soldiers truly wish to see the slaves freed. And let's suppose that we do, after half the nation, North and South, is slaughtered, attain this objective. If the South then treats Negroes the way they are currently being treated in the North will we have accomplished anything at all?"

John nodded towards Phil. "Mr. Weatherly leads a better life than the Southern slave."

"Granted, Mr. Shepherd. There are some token exceptions like Mr. Weatherly, but then there are free black plantation owners in the South, too. However, most black men are slaves in the North *and* South, the only difference being that here they receive a dollar or two to give the illusion of freedom."

Beth asked Greg, "If war is no solution for the injustice, what is?"

He looked at her intently as he answered, "To pass laws in the North that will give Negroes full equality. *Full* equality in every sense of the word. When we in the North have done that, the South will capitulate. Until then, they may rightly look upon us as hypocrites."

Diane's father protested. "But our own people haven't achieved full equality yet."

"Your own people?" Greg repeated. "Who would they be, sir?"

"Why the white immigrants, the—" He stopped abruptly, giving Greg a withering look for having trapped him into an admission of prejudice, and in front of a Negro besides. Phil either didn't notice the remark or chose to ignore it, for he said to Greg, "You're very optimistic, Mr. Allister, if you believe that we could ever possibly be considered the equals of white men."

"You'd be a good deal closer to that day, sir, if the right government were in power and if a new constitution were written."

"New constitution?" John repeated. "Are you suggesting revolution?"

"I can't suggest anything while I'm wearing the uniform of the United States Army," Greg answered evasively. He sipped his coffee and looked down. Kate exchanged a quick glance with Diane's mother. Diane blushed and studied a spoon. And Beth stared across the table at this fascinating stranger.

John glared at Gregory. "Then why, if the war is such a useless bloodbath, do you fight in it? To protect your father's fortune?"

"No, sir. I fight because everybody fights. By that I mean the poor. I can't permit them to carry that burden alone."

"Ah, a humanitarian."

"Mr. Shepherd, please don't mock me."

"I'm sorry," John said lamely. He hadn't meant to be sarcastic.

Diane's parents exchanged alarmed looks. Her mother, Rose, sighed aloud. And this was the man Diane hoped to marry? If it weren't for his wealth and social position, they would put an end to the alliance immediately. He didn't even care for money, it seemed. Would he give his fortune away to charity? The man was a dreamer. An impertinent dreamer as well. How dare he embarrass his future father-in-law! How dare he argue with so distinguished a man as John Shepherd! And would he stay home and pamper Diane, or would he always be off fighting causes and making speeches? Perhaps Diane would tire of him as she had all the others. How long would it take her to come to her senses?

With conversation now at a standstill, Kate suggested that the ladies adjourn to the parlor. They sat stiffly silent for a while, studiously avoiding any reference to Greg in Diane's presence, but none of them thinking of anything else. Diane, however, was not to be put off.

"What do you think of him?" she asked Aunt Louise.

"An interesting young man."

"I think so too. He's very—well—deep, don't you think?"

"Yes. That would be the word to describe him."

Diane looked uneasily at Louise. What had she meant by that? But she continued, "I hope that some day soon we'll have an understanding."

Diane's mother had her eyes fixed on a Hogarth engraving. The room became very quiet.

"None of you seem impressed," Diane said petulantly.

"Well I am," declared Beth. "How and where did you ever meet such a man?"

Diane smiled. "At the Martins' ball for the Christian Commission." She looked suddenly embarrassed. Beth had not been invited to this ball. "He was so different from the other foppish officers, and he asked me to dance." Beth grinned at Diane's easy dismissal of men she had once adored.

"Have you met his parents?" Beth asked her.

"Not yet. But I'm not afraid of them. They're very nice people, I hear. They don't care if Greg calls on someone who's not in society."

"That's true," Louise agreed. "The Allisters are neighbors of mine over on Washington Square. Not in the least snobbish."

"Does he come from a large family?" Beth asked Diane.

"He has two married sisters. Neither lives in New York."

"How old is he?"

"Twenty-seven."

"Does he work for his father?"

"He did before the war. Now he plans to write or teach."

"Or incite a revolution," murmured her mother.

Diane looked at Rose. "What was that, Mother?"

"I was clearing my throat."

Diane turned to Beth. "Greg doesn't want his father's money."

Louise said, "It's easy to abhor money when one is already wealthy. So many of these visionary types have never known a day's hunger. All the same, he has to be admired. He didn't have to fight, after all."

"Well, I admire him," said Diane defensively.

"Yes, and so do I," said Beth.

Kate looked at her daughter. "You will allow that some of his remarks were out of place?"

"A bit, yes. But he was only being honest."

Rose Kendall fidgeted, anxious to speak her mind on the subject of Gregory Allister, but afraid to do so. She was undecided. The man was rude, self-righteous, an iconoclast too. And yet—and yet there was all that money. Money and character warred in her mind. By the time the gentlemen left the dining room to join the ladies, she had decided to urge her husband to let Diane herself make the final decision.

In the parlor, Diane, grateful to her ally, motioned Beth to sit beside her. Greg was already seated there, looking awkward and uncomfortable.

"Have I told you how talented Beth is?" Diane seemed anxious for Greg to know that she had intelligent friends.

"No, I don't believe so," Greg replied with a half smile.

"She's a teacher, you know." She named the school where Beth taught.

He nodded, and Beth squirmed uncomfortably in the silence.

"She also plays the piano quite well, and she writes poetry."

"Do you?" He seemed genuinely interested. "So do I."

"You never told me that," Diane said.

"Well I don't write too often. I can never seem to get my lines to scan properly."

Beth smiled. "That's wicked, isn't it? By the time you find a word that fits or rhymes, the whole meaning of the poem is changed. Then you have to go back and change the concept."

"You can always switch to Whitman's style," he said.

"Whitman," Diane repeated. "Louise knows him. Beth's aunt. The one you were talking to."

"Indeed?"

"Yes. He's a friend of one of her boarders. Louise has several Bohemian boarders."

"Ah," he said, trying to appear interested in Louise's literary alliances. But Beth could tell that he was not impressed. He turned to Beth. "Do you like Whitman?"

"No, I'm old-fashioned. I can't stand poets who dribble every last emotion all over the page. Some feeling is fine, but goodness!"

Greg laughed at this, and people turned. It was the first time anyone had heard him laugh. "You prefer stately iambic, then?"

"Yes—or at least some sort of control. Aunt Louise likes Whitman, though. And Father would have *Leaves of Grass* embossed in gold if we could afford it. If you're interested in Whitman, talk to him."

"No, I don't care for his style either. And I don't relish the prospect of another conversation with your father."

"Don't fret about that. It was nothing."

Greg did not respond.

Beth felt uncomfortable with this subject and also with the fact that Diane seemed left out. She turned to her friend. "I love your dress. Is it new?"

"Yes it is. I did the embroidery at the neckline myself."

"It's very delicate work."

"Why, thank you," Diane blushed modestly.

"And now I'm afraid I must leave. I promised Sheilah I'd help her." She nodded uneasily at both of them. She hadn't meant to monopolize the conversation.

The Shepherds were not game-loving hosts. In lieu of whist and parlor games, John and Kate preferred conversation or entertainment after dinner. Usually they asked their guests to perform or read poetry. Some had been lecturers at the lyceums, and they often rounded out an evening at the Shepherds' with an impromptu speech, inviting discussion afterward. Tonight Louise was asked to sing some Schubert songs. She was a small, lively woman in her late fifties, but she looked much younger. She had a delicate soprano voice that had long ago delighted the pioneers gathered around the campfire during the trip to California. As always, she ended her singing with a folk song of the overland trail, the title of which had since become her nickname. The actual words were as follows, but Louise was forced to use several substitutes:

Oh do you remember sweet Betsy from Pike,
Who crossed the wide prairie with her lover, Ike,
With two yoke of cattle and one spotted hog,
A tall Shanghai rooster, an old yeller dog?

Sing too ra li oo ra li oo ra li ay
Sing too ra li oo ra li oo ra li ay

They swam the wide rivers and crossed the tall peaks
And camped on the prairie for weeks upon weeks.
Starvation and cholera, hard work and slaughter,
They reached California spite of hell and high water.

29

She sang verse after verse, omitting words or verses in questionable taste, substituting *husband* for *lover* and *pain* for *hell*. The audience sang the refrain. Even Greg seemed relaxed, singing in a pleasant bass and grinning at Diane. When Louise had finished, she was breathless. Despite the audience's entreaties for more, she sank gratefully into a downy chair. They then urged Phil Weatherly to sing.

"Would you like to hear some plantation songs?" he asked the group.

"Plantation songs?" John looked disappointed. Phil usually sang operatic arias. He had a rich, resonant voice with a great range that had the power to produce chills in his listeners. No one was enthusiastic about hearing Phil sing something like "Way Down upon the Swanee River," which they considered a typical plantation song.

Phil walked over to the piano and struck a few chords. But he didn't sing the sunny tunes they had been expecting. He sang a song they had never heard before, one that clashed harshly with the image of Stephen Foster's happy darkies:

> When Israel was in Egypt's land,
> Let my people go!
> Oppressed so hard they could not stand;
> Let my people go!
> Go down, Moses,
> Way down in Egypt's land.
> Tell old Pharaoh
> Let my people go!

His voice filled and shook the room as he sang several verses. The power and pain of the song left people too moved to applaud. Some cleared their throats, and John wept. Then Phil sang another song that bore no resemblance whatever to Foster's music:

> Nobody knows the trouble I've seen,
> Nobody knows my sorrow,

30

> Nobody knows the trouble I've seen,
> Glory hallelujah.

John asked Phil where he had learned these songs.

"Some slaves we helped escape to Canada sang them for me. An Ohio family hid them for three weeks. The farm was far from civilization, and they were able to speak aloud and sing. I wrote down the words and notated the music." He paused. "Ironic that these songs should sound as strange to me as to all of you." Greg looked puzzled, and Phil, noticing this, said to him, "I never lived in the South nor did any of my ancestors. My grandparents were New England slaves, but all four of them were eventually manumitted."

He concluded his singing with a ballad that was almost a sustained cry:

> Sometimes I feel like a motherless child
> Sometimes I feel like a motherless child
> Sometimes I feel like a motherless child
> A long way from home.
> A long way from home.

The lyrics of these songs were poetic in their simplicity and in the irony of the imagery. The melodies were extraordinary, making striking use of the minor key and evoking moods effectively. Beth found it sad that music so moving was the by-product of monstrous pain, as was so often the case with fine works of art. It was as though an oppressor, in attempting to crush the passion out of an individual or a people, succeeded only in channeling it into their music or literature or painting, so that the work of art ultimately produced was more than one or two symbols; it was the artist's life.

After this, Louise went over to the piano and demanded that everybody sing. Her selections were patriotic songs and sentimental ballads. Some people, including Beth, gathered around the piano. Others remained in their chairs, singing or humming along. They were well along into the third stanza of

"When Johnny Comes Marching Home" when Beth noticed that Greg, sitting in a chair facing her, wasn't singing. She continued to watch him as she sang, glancing alternately at him and at the sheet music she held.

> The laurel wreath is ready now
> To place upon his loyal brow
> And we'll all feel gay when—

Beth's voice trailed off as she noticed Greg blinking back tears. Why, he's very patriotic, she thought. She never would have guessed that after what he had said to Father. But as he lowered his head so that his face was inclined away from Diane's, she realized that he was distressed rather than moved by the song. She could guess why. He had been at Antietam and had probably seen good friends blown to smithereens. After a while he glanced up briefly to find Beth staring at him, her eyes wide with concern.

"Aunt Louise," Beth commanded, "do play something else. I'm tired of marches."

"For someone who's tired, you were singing loudly enough."

"Please, Aunt Louise!"

"Very well, dear." She looked hurt, but after a while the spirited singers plunged gamely into "The Last Rose of Summer," a mawkish piece, as were "When This Cruel War Is Over," "Sweet and Low," and most of the others that followed. Aside from Louise's folk songs, there was scarcely a jolly melody to be found. Beth sang along dispiritedly. The incident had upset her. In the chair near the window she saw Greg nod Thank you, and she inclined her head.

It was getting late, and the voices were becoming hoarse. The Kleins were the first to say good night, followed rapidly by the rest of the group. As they gathered in the hallway putting on wraps, Greg came over to Beth.

"I'm sorry I embarrassed you," he said. "I can't explain it now, but—"

"You needn't. I think I understand."

And then he said softly, studying her face, "Somehow I feel I've always known you."

Diane had come up to them, so Beth couldn't reply. But the words echoed in her head long after he had gone, for she realized that she felt the same way.

Michael had given a flawless recitation of his nines-tables and Beth had praised him and, on impulse, canceled all homework for the night. While the cheers resounded in the chilly classroom, she walked over to the window to see if it had begun to snow. She caught her breath sharply: Down at the corner, standing in the wind, was the lanky, blue-uniformed figure of Gregory Allister. She wondered why he was standing there like a Bowery vagrant on this bitter day. But she shooed the children to the coat closets and hurriedly slipped into her own jacket, hoping that he'd still be there when she left.

As the children poured through the door ahead of her, Beth, looking over their heads, noticed that Greg had begun walking with studied casualness across the street and down toward the school. She knew at once that he had planned to meet her "accidentally." She remembered Diane's mentioning the name of the school to him. Guilty thoughts of Diane swept through her mind, but she quickly banished them as she came face to face with Greg.

"Why, Beth! What are you doing here?"

"I teach here." She couldn't hide a smile at his poor acting.

"Oh? Are all these children your students?" He gestured toward the mob of shouting urchins.

"Only the rowdies chasing that boy in the brown jacket."

He smiled. "You look frozen. Could we stop somewhere for a chocolate?"

Yes, he was a poor actor. How could she look frozen after being out in the cold only three minutes? But his awkwardness touched her. If he weren't so involved with Diane, she might easily fall in love with a man like this. Beth knew she must not appear too eager. She forced her face into doubtfulness and said, "Very well. But only for a little while. I'm expected home."

They walked down toward Broadway, not speaking because the clatter of iron wheels on the cobblestones was too noisy for civilized conversation. Once seated in the chocolate-scented booth, she noticed that he had become shy. They ordered chocolates and cakes and sat looking at one another in silence. She wanted to ask him questions: Why had he come to meet her today? Why did he feel he had known her all his life? Was he still seeing Diane? But she said nothing.

Finally he blurted out a sentence. "I'd like to call on you."

"I'd like that too, Greg, but Diane—uh—"

"Yes, I know."

"She's very fond of you."

"As I am of her."

"I believe she loves you."

He brushed at his forehead. "She thinks she does, Beth."

"I don't understand."

"She loves an image. It's a play she's acting out. I don't quite know what the play is all about, but I'm certain her feelings will never last." He paused. "I'm not explaining this very well, am I?"

"I'm afraid not."

"Diane and I are not alike. She's sweet and optimistic; I'm not. We aren't made to understand each other, yet I find her straining to understand. She doesn't need to, Beth, and some day she'll discover that she never wanted to."

"I see. But I must be honest and tell you that I find this situation disturbing."

"I'm sorry. My feelings can't be helped."

"What are your feelings?"

"You know them."

"Do I?"

"You know me. I think each of us sees something of himself—herself—in the other."

"Yes," she said without pause, for she had been thinking the same thing.

"To like a person because you see yourself in her—is that vanity, Beth?"

"Perhaps. And perhaps it's understanding."

They gazed at one another for a long moment, and at once Beth felt the lightheadedness of infatuation. The world was slipping away and Greg was filling all the vacant places. But all too soon her practical voice asserted itself, warning her that they were speaking only words. Only words. She must not lose sight of that.

He stirred his chocolate and looked down. "I like Diane very much. I've been seeing her for two months. She's a fine human being, and a very beautiful one. But—" He hesitated a moment, then continued—"but when I met you I realized what it was I wanted in a woman."

She was stunned. He was telling her that she, and not Diane, was the woman he wanted—though what he meant by "wanted" she did not know. Courtship only? Courtship with the hope of marriage? Would Greg ever marry a woman of limited means? But of course he would; he disliked the wealthy so much.

"Did you hear what I said, Beth?" He was staring intently at her.

"Yes. I'm very—flattered." The wrong word, but she'd almost been fool enough to say thrilled, and that would have been worse. She did not look at his face but concentrated on his left shoulder as though fascinated by the captain's shoulder straps.

"I shall have to speak to Diane," he said.

"What—what will you tell her?"

"I won't deny that it will be difficult. We are not betrothed, however, and—"

"Does she want to marry you?"

He looked away. "I believe she has had the thought."

"And you?"

"I too."

"And?" Beth was aware that she sounded like a lawyer doing a cross-examination, but she had to have an explanation.

"And it would be a mistake. There's no point in entertaining any thoughts of marrying Diane."

He had said it, and suddenly she knew he meant it. Words had become fact. Outwardly her expression was cool. She must appear relaxed as though men were continually spurning wealthy and beautiful women like Diane in order to court Elizabeth Shepherd.

But what *of* Diane? The thought was like a chunk of ice in a warm bath. Diane was her next-door neighbor, her childhood friend. Every time Greg came to call on the Shepherds, Diane would see him from the window and burst into tears. Beth sighed. It was her luck that the most romantic and triumphant moment in her life must be ruined with feelings of guilt. If Diane were sitting here now, would she be fretting over Beth's feelings? Yes, Beth had to admit. Yes, she probably would.

"What will you tell Diane?" she asked again.

"I'm to see her this Sunday. I'll try to be honest."

"Will you tell her about—about me?"

"Do you want me to?"

"Oh, no. Not for a long time."

"Then you won't let me call on you?"

"How can I, Greg? We're neighbors. If she sees your carriage—"

"But I want to see you again!" He looked very upset.

"Then you shall. We could come here after school and talk."

He sipped his chocolate. "Yes, I suppose that's best. Would you mind if I called for you in my carriage? We could take drives."

"Not long ones, though. My parents become frantic if I'm not home by dark."

"Short drives then."

"I don't suppose there's harm in that—" she smiled—"if your intentions are honorable."

36

"As honorable as Mr. Lincoln's," he grinned.

"Who tramples all over the Bill of Rights."

"But he does it to save the Union."

"Indeed? And what do you propose for my salvation?"

"Whatever you suggest."

"Ah, so you place the burden on the hapless woman, giving me no recourse but to remain hopelessly respectable."

"Caught in my own trap!"

Her expression changed. "I like you when you joke. You're usually so serious."

"I haven't seen many amusing diversions in my recent travels."

"So I've gathered. Nor have I. But it's hard to face the serious things in the world."

"It's sometimes better if one chooses not to. Although I think you saw the truth the night you stopped the singing."

"I saw only that you were upset."

"That song is a recent one, isn't it? I've only heard it once before."

"I think it is, yes. 'When Johnny Comes Marching Home.' "

"There was a lad in my platoon named Johnny. He had bright red hair, so at first we called him Red. But he didn't like that. It wasn't distinguished, you see. He insisted on being called John, but the men called him Johnny and he had to be content with the compromise. He was eighteen years old and his dream was to be a hero. He came from the Sixth Ward. The Dead Rabbits Gang was his only model and that depressed him." Gregory sat up straighter in his chair and rubbed his hands together. "Would you care for another chocolate?"

"No thank you. But I'd like to hear more about Johnny."

"We were in the woods. We'd just attacked a band of rebels and lost many men. Johnny and I went forward to where there was an opening in the trees. Suddenly he was hit in the chest, and as he fell, four of them came charging toward me. I shot the first one, but there was no time to reload. I had to use my bayonet on the other three."

"That's what you were telling my father. How did you do it?"

"One of them was out of ammunition. He was not a problem. The second one was reloading. The other had shot me in the shoulder, but I was able to attack him before he could shoot again."

"You attacked while you were wounded?"

"There was no other thought in my head. Not even pain."

"No wonder you were given a decoration."

"As it happened, I diverted a regiment by killing some of their scouts. My 'heroism' was an accident, and I have no feelings about it." He paused. "After that someone dragged me into a thicket and laid me beside Johnny. I watched him die. It took a long time. He never did have his chance to be a hero."

"Oh Greg." Without thinking, she reached across the table and grasped his hand. He held hers and brought it up to his cheek.

"That's why I don't care for that song." He continued to hold her hand on his cheek—a gesture that both touched and excited her. They sat this way, saying nothing, until the waiter came for the payment. Then they rose and walked out into the afternoon. It was snowing.

"I'll take you home."

"No, don't do that. The Kendalls—Diane—might see us."

"Then I'll ride with you as far as your corner." He hailed a hack and assisted her into it. "Sixteenth Street and Fifth," he told the driver. Settling back against the seat, he said, "Beth, I won't be in New York much longer."

She wasn't surprised, but she was disappointed. "The wound is fully healed?"

"Long since. I would have returned long before this, but the doctor told me to convalesce for a while. I'll be leaving in two or three weeks."

"You'll write to me?"

"Of course."

"You're not in my brothers' regiment, are you?" She named the regiment.

"No, but I'm in the same corps."

"Do you know Pat Shepherd, my brother? He's a doctor."

"I don't know Pat, but I do know the regimental surgeon over there—Kent Wilson."

"Yes. He's Pat's superior officer."

"Kent has an extraordinary cure rate for amputations."

"Does he? I know nothing about him other than his name. Pat doesn't write, and when he's home he rarely talks about the war. Joe doesn't say much either."

"He's not a doctor, is he?"

"No. He's an infantry lieutenant. Do stop by and say hello to them when you get to Virginia."

"I certainly will." He took her hand in such a way that she could feel a communication of spirit between them—a transmission, one to the other, like telegraph operators exchanging messages in code. At first there was no pressure at all. And then he pressed his palm down, moving his fingers against hers with varying intensities and finally openly caressing her hand until she responded in the same manner. By the time they arrived at her street she was unexpectedly aroused. Reluctantly, she disengaged her hand and prepared to leave.

"May I see you tomorrow, Beth?"

She smiled. "Yes."

"I'll pick you up at school."

"That would be fine." He helped her out of the hack and she turned to leave. "Good night, Greg."

"Good night." He squeezed her hand tight, then turned back to the hack. The driver gave him a strange look. What sort of gentleman was this who would not see his lady to her door? A disgrace to the army, certainly. Greg climbed back into the hack and the driver jerked the reins sharply. Beth, looking on, could not understand why the man was so abrupt.

She watched the hack move on down the snowy street and walked slowly toward home. Things Gregory had said and done tumbled around in her mind, leaving her with a feeling of intense desire. As she watched the snow falling in the encroaching darkness of late afternoon, she was filled with an expectation of sweet, warm things she couldn't name and her throat tightened with longing.

Beth went up to her room early that evening and lit the stove. She removed the clips and hairpins that held her hair and watched in the mirror as the brown hair tumbled luxuriantly over her shoulders. There was no outstanding feature in her face, she told herself. Her eyes were large, brown, and oval in shape. She had often wished they were round or slanted or otherwise unusual. Her nose was perfectly straight, like her father's, not turned up as her mother's was. The structure and coloring of her face were satisfactory, if not unusual. She envied women with delicate high cheekbones like Diane's or with sharp contrasts in coloring: blue eyes and pink lips, or raven hair and creamy skin and rose highlighting the cheeks. The best she could do was to redden her full lips with coralline salve and use a trace of rouge on important occasions. Beth's overall coloring could best be described as tawny: a mingling of browns, tans, and olives that was striking when set off by the right shades in her dress. But she rarely wore the vibrant colors that made her look exotic. For one thing, they were inappropriate in the classroom. And even outside, she didn't believe she had the personality to complement such flamboyant costumes.

Slowly, still carefully observing her image, she unbuttoned her brown poplin dress, slipped it off, and tossed it on the bed. Now she stopped and contemplated the foolish hoops and stays. Though these body-distorters had been in fashion for years, Beth had always hated them. Here were the monstrous hoops—they seemed to get wider every year—which served no purpose except to impede progress, insure clumsiness, and require twelve yards of material for every skirt. And the tight stays, the main cause of swooning, summer and winter, were

40

oppressive. Someone in the women's rights group had described them as a symbol of women's bondage, and Beth heartily agreed. Their supposed aesthetic appeal fooled no man. A fat girl in stays was still relatively fatter than a thin girl in stays. If everyone discarded them, the relationship would still exist. All would have larger stomachs, certainly, but who cared, if they could all breathe again? As for the petticoats and pantalettes, they were warm in winter, but surely some other garments could be substituted in the summer.

After struggling out of her underclothes, she contemplated her nude body. She knew she had a good figure, though if she had to find fault, she would say that it was perhaps too well-developed. One more inch at the bustline and she'd look like one of those women of easy virtue who padded themselves.

She turned away and slipped into her nightgown. There was for Beth, as for most girls, a shame of indulging in such self-scrutiny. It was wrong to do this, said the Church, and her withdrawal from her religion and its rosters of sins to be avoided had not totally changed that view. She remembered the halting conversation she had had with Aunt Louise at the onset of puberty nine years earlier. They had been sitting in the garden under the oak on a warm August afternoon while Kate nervously fanned herself and Louise stammered out the facts of life that her sister-in-law was too embarrassed to divulge. Beth had been shocked to discover that certain covered-up, shameful parts of the body were used in making babies. It was easy for her to understand that sex was dirty, for the organs involved in the act had always been considered dirty. But she failed to comprehend Louise's assertion that the whole picture changed once a woman was married. The act suddenly became sacred—as though the hand of God swept over these parts of the body and pronounced them clean.

Her next discussion of the subject occurred at normal school. One of the students was a beautiful young girl from a farm in northern Manhattan. She had confessed to indulging in "the ultimate" after sneaking into the tall grasses one balmy evening with the beau to whom she had then been promised.

"I know it was wrong," Linda had admitted, "but it was such a glorious sensation."

Several of the girls avoided her after that, but others (though properly disapproving) were overcome with curiosity and remained quite friendly. Beth was in the latter group.

"Linda," she had asked, trying to refrain from blushing, "could you tell me why it—why it was what you call a glorious sensation?"

"Oh Beth, you must be careful. It's very risky."

"But I've no intention! I was just curious."

"If you must indulge, Beth, don't ever let him enter you."

"Oh, I won't indulge until after I'm married. But Linda, how can one avoid—I mean—"

"There are many ways to achieve a release without actually having him enter—"

"A release? What's that?"

"You know the feeling you have when you kiss someone?"

"Yes."

"Wanting to do more? To have him touch you in other places?"

Beth's face was scarlet. "Yes."

"Well, that feeling grows and grows and suddenly it's discharged and you feel marvelous."

"It's discharged? I don't understand."

"You would have to experience it." Linda's tone was that of a knowledgeable professor.

"When the feeling is discharged—does that mean one is in danger of having babies?"

"No. There doesn't need to be actual completion. I made one mistake of that nature and nothing happened. The next time my beau and I worked out another arrangement."

"Oh. Are all men aware of this type of—arrangement?"

"I would assume so."

"What is it that they do?"

"A type of caressing. I'd rather not say more. The specifics are—well—personal."

42

"I see. I didn't mean to pry."

"Promise me that you'll be careful?"

Beth nodded, but she doubted that she would have much opportunity to make use of this knowledge. She was envious of Linda's pleasure. Though she told herself that such conduct was wrong, she often wondered if the only sin in sex was having the baby.

Linda's revelations continued to puzzle Beth through the years, though she never had any further discussions of this nature and dared not experiment with the proper young men who called on her. But now that she seriously wondered whether she would marry Greg, she began thinking about the sexual act. From what she understood, the man lay flat on top of her and inserted the—protuberance. That was all. Of releases and tension discharges she knew nothing. But then, women were not supposed to know of such things. And as for feeling marvelous afterward, Beth did not understand how that could be. She had once heard a friend of her mother saying that life would be a lot more pleasant if men did not subject women to certain indignities. The sexual act, Beth had gathered, was in a class of martyrdom equivalent to bearing children.

Beth slipped into bed, put her hands behind her head, and daydreamed. Indecent though it might be, she wished she were married now and could participate in this mysterious act. The tension in her body, aggravated in the past by eager kisses, was tonight growing past the point of endurance. Perhaps Greg would propose and they could marry quickly. But that was impossible, because of Diane's feelings and the fact that Kate and John had saved through the years for a grand wedding. Well, if he proposed now they could be married in June if the army could spare him for a few days. That meant waiting only six months.

She put out the lamp, burrowed under the covers, clasped her pillow to her, pretending it was Greg, and tossed restlessly until long past midnight.

*   *   *

The next few days were reasonably warm. She and Greg drove over to Madison Square and walked around smiling at the snowball-throwers and the wealthy ladies in ornate carriages who liked to display their elegant furs. Later they sat in the carriage and talked. She was surprised at the change in him since the night of the dinner party. He now seemed cheerful and relaxed.

"Why were you so quiet that night when you first arrived at our house?" she asked him.

"I'm ill at ease in a room full of strangers."

"But you seemed comfortable with Aunt Louise and Mr. Weatherly."

"I felt acceptance with them. With the others, I had the impression that I had better say the fashionable thing if I were to be welcomed again."

"What would be the fashionable thing?"

"I should say the fashionable position: that Lincoln can do no wrong, that all Southerners are despicable, that the war is being fought to free the slaves."

"I know you don't believe the last."

"No. If we care so deeply for the manhood of the Negro, why do we keep him segregated? Why can't he attend our schools, marry our daughters?"

"You approve of miscegenation?"

"Of course. It's part of the freedom we purportedly espouse. And since people in the North aren't ready to accept these things, and particularly our leaders who should be setting the example, I'm forced to conclude that this war, like most wars, is purely economic. It amounts to such things as an abhorrence of free trade with Europe, not an abhorrence of slavery."

"But consider John Brown and Harriet Beecher Stowe and—"

"I'm not saying that there aren't some sincere abolitionists. I'm saying that the war itself stems from other causes."

"But you did express that unfashionable thought."

"Yes, and you saw what happened."

44

"Well Greg, you were rather hostile. You could have made your point in a more palatable way. Perhaps you might have enjoyed the evening more."

"Some statements are not palatable. If you try to make them palatable, the meaning is lost."

She and Greg had several such discussions on the afternoons in Madison Square. But he also asked her questions about herself, and her answers seemed to delight him.

"Why didn't I meet you years ago? We think so much alike," he said.

"I should have liked that too."

"We think alike, but we're man and woman. That difference is important."

"Why?"

"Because when two men or two women have similar views, they find the relationship competitive. You and I enhance one another."

He kissed her gently on the cheek. And later, when there were no people looking, he kissed her more passionately on the lips. He did not press hard. His lips were mobile, questing, and he varied the pressure until she was very excited. She had never been kissed this way before.

"You're a beautiful woman."

"Thank you."

"From that first night I noticed your body."

She colored. "Oh?"

"A sensual body. The clothing you wear seems unimportant to you. You move as though you were wearing none."

"Greg, you must not say such things."

"Why not? They're true."

She smiled. "But such frankness is unfashionable."

"So are you, my dear."

"Unfashionable?"

"Yes. You're aware of your body. I notice that you walk without that stiff gliding gait that most young ladies struggle to perfect."

"Mother thinks my gait is clumsy."

"Only because she and other women have chosen Queen Victoria as their model. I like free motion in a woman." He kissed her again. "You should have been born in another age—an age of freedom."

"Will there ever be such a time?"

"I doubt it. But it's worth striving for."

Occasionally he recited poetry for her. His memory was even better than her father's. And sometimes they had intense philosophical discussions.

"You know," she said, "our conversations remind me of those college talk sessions my brothers were always describing."

"Yes. College men think they're very profound."

"Did you talk all night about life?"

"Oh yes. We'd get roaring drunk and assure each other that we alone could see—Truth."

"It sounds like fun."

"Fun?"

"Getting drunk and trying to figure things out. Women can never do those things. We're chaperoned from morning till night, can never take a drink, and if we ever talk about anything more profound than flower arrangements, someone comes along and asks us if we're feeling all right."

He laughed.

"What's so funny?" she asked.

"You. You're so candid about your envy of men."

"What's wrong with being envious?"

"Nothing. I don't blame you. Being drunk as a lord in a dilapidated Boston tavern and solving the problems of the world while not actually having to do anything about them *is* smashing good fun. But how did you guess that?"

"I have brothers, remember?"

"They didn't go to Harvard, did they?"

"No, but they did the same things at Columbia that you did at Harvard."

"Ah yes. And while they were out chasing women, you sat home with the fancy work, and it struck you as unfair."

"It wasn't the chasing women I envied. After all, I don't think I'd care to chase men."

"No, but you envied them their option to seek women."

"Did you—uh—seek women?"

"Must I answer that?"

"Never mind. I can guess."

She didn't care to think of him searching for prostitutes as her brothers did, but she guessed that he had. He had also told her that he had been to Paris, and she could not bear to think about the temptations he might have met in that city.

"Would you like to stop for tea somewhere?" he asked.

"No. It's too late. My parents will worry."

"So I must take you back to your sheltered life?"

"Alas."

Sitting in the parlor that evening, trying to correct papers, she wondered what it was about him that she loved so much. Was it his uniqueness—his marching, like Thoreau, to a different drummer? She had always been fascinated by such men, who failed, as she did, to find fulfillment in the tedious world but lived an existence, part fact and part fantasy, that was inspirational. She would love to have known Keats or Byron, and she doted on everything Wordsworth had written. That was it: Greg was poetic. He had all the characteristics of the romantic poet, even that dark, bitter side of him that made her want to console him, protect him from blatant reality. Yet there had been those bold remarks about her body that did not quite square with her knightlike image of him. Perhaps he was more like the Cavalier poets who tossed words like "breasts" and "virginity" all over their verses. If she were going to be fair about it, she too had wondered, though not aloud, what he might look like without his clothes.

Being in love wreaked havoc with her life. She couldn't concentrate on anything for more than a second and found herself smiling foolishly at the children's recitations, regardless of how good or bad they were. During arithmetic lessons, the last subject of the day, her heart began to hammer, her legs became weak, and when she wasn't laughing she found herself on the verge of crying, not from any sadness but from acute nervousness. Fifteen minutes before school was over, the children were dressed and waiting at the door. She would count the endless minutes on the desk clock that ticked like a heartbeat, and then she would follow the children out, slowly, so as not to appear too excited. Yet when she saw him, some deep instinct took over, enabling her to respond to him as a woman rather than as a flustered schoolgirl. She always marveled at the way calm reason dispelled her agitation as soon as he said, "Hello." Perhaps it was the fact that he was a man, not a god, and each time she saw him in all his mortal reality, she was struck anew by this truth.

On the fifth afternoon of their after-school meetings, it rained. They went for another chocolate and talked about a whole range of subjects. One of Greg's theories was that the wealthy, without fully realizing it, had engendered hatred between the poor whites and the Negroes. Many in the monied classes allied themselves morally with the Negroes and showed open contempt for the immigrants—particularly the Irish. In this way, he said, the poor were kept so busy fighting each other that they left the aristocracy alone. And in the South, the kindly plantation-owners praised their "darkies" and ridiculed their poor-white neighbors. They called the whites "crackers" or "white trash." The "trash" and the Negroes came to hate each other so much that when the war came, the white poor, who owned no slaves, were only too anxious to fight to maintain the institution of slavery. Effectively, the poor in the South fought the war for the rich.

He told her that some day he would like to write books about this subject or to teach—or to run for political office.

Beth said, "The other night you hinted broadly at revolution."

"It's a possibility, Beth. But we'll have years to think about these matters."

"We?" Her heart began to pound.

"I would like to marry you."

48

She had been prepared to hedge and consider and look suitably doubtful, but she smiled at him instead and exclaimed, "Oh, yes!"

He exhaled audibly. "I've been rehearsing this proposal for two days."

"Did you doubt for a minute that I would accept?"

"Well, I'm not what you'd call a typical suitor. We won't have much money. I won't accept my father's."

"I don't care about money. If you know me at all, you must realize that."

"I think I know you, but everyone is capable of revealing last-minute surprises." He paused. "I won't be here much longer. I'd like to set a date."

"When would you be ready?"

"I'm ready now."

"I think May or June would be better, Greg."

"I take it you'll want the whole circus?"

"My parents will. And there's still Diane—"

"I intend to see her this Sunday."

"Don't tell her. Let's wait till spring. By that time she will have met someone else."

"Very well. And what shall we say to our people?" he asked.

"I think we should wait. They're bound to question a five-day courtship."

"That's true." He smiled. "Then we'll wait a few weeks?"

"That would be best."

It was after dark when they left the restaurant, both of them glowing with the anticipation of a glorious future together. They hadn't discussed details of the marriage: children, where to live, what his work would be. It was too soon for details. For the moment it was enough that they loved each other, and both of them punctuated every other sentence with those avowals as they sat holding hands across the table and later as they walked down the drizzly street searching for a hack. The parting at Sixteenth Street was sealed with a passionate kiss inside the hack and mumbled words of endearment on the street. Greg stood at the corner watching

Beth walk westward. She turned once and waved at him, thinking that she would never again know a moment as beautiful as this one.

The following day was Saturday. They had planned to go carriage-riding after her morning chores were completed and to spend the whole day together. But she knew as soon as she woke up that there would be no carriage-riding today. The shrill wind penetrated the tiny cracks in the window frame, and her ears were so cold, despite her nightcap, that she dreaded getting out of bed. Once her Saturday chores were finished, however, and the fire was blazing in the Franklin stove, she felt warm enough to dress with special care. She wasn't sure where they would go in weather like this, but when they stopped to eat, she hoped he would admire the wine velvet dress that she so loved because it was elegant yet simple and warm enough to withstand the winter winds. She rubbed coralline salve on her lips but omitted rouge because the wind would bring color to her cheeks soon enough. She laced up her boots and put on her dark gray paletot jacket, pausing to appreciate how nicely the short, fitted coat flared below the waist to accommodate her huge skirts. Then Beth tied the bonnet her mother had made to match the dress and stood before the mirror. Very fetching, she decided. Very attractive indeed. And because she was engaged and looking so well, she smiled at herself with a vanity she rarely displayed and walked downstairs with the sweep and self-assurance of a queen.

The temperature was near-zero, but she didn't think about that as she walked toward Fifth Avenue, where Greg would be waiting in his carriage. The sky was a pure blue; there was not a cloud in it. And the colors of the city seemed so sharp today. Generally she preferred slightly cloudy days to take the harsh light away from the uglier things, but today she didn't care that the winter sun pointed up the mud and refuse in the streets as sharply as it enhanced the blue velvet drapes in the Kendall parlor window. Even the mud looked beautiful. It was part of nature and ought to be illuminated.

He was waiting in the carriage, shivering, and his teeth chattered when he greeted her.

"Have you been waiting long?" she asked.

"Fifteen minutes."

"I'm sorry."

"Don't be. I was early." He assisted her into the carriage. "It's too cold to go up to the Harlem River."

"Indeed it is."

He started the horse. They rode for a block. "Are you feeling any warmer?" he asked.

"I haven't been out in the cold as long as you have."

"Let's have tea somewhere on Broadway."

"Will we drink tea all day?" she asked.

He smiled. "We'll have to. What else can we do? We can't go to your house or mine or to the Central Park or to the river—"

"We can go to P. T. Barnum's or to Stewart's to shop."

"I'd rather drink tea," he said, holding the reins with one hand and tugging at his officer's hat with the other to keep the wind out of his face.

"Yes, so would I."

It was noisy on Broadway, and she couldn't talk to him. She occupied herself by looking at the people surging along the sidewalks. Everyone looked lovely to her this morning: the gentlemen in the tall silk hats and sweeping greatcoats; the laborers in the squat little caps and rough work jackets; the ladies in their fur-trimmed bonnets and matching paletots; and the poorer women in their shawls and head-scarves. All of them were beautiful from this distance. Up close there would be the deep lines of suffering that etched the faces of the impoverished. Up close were the toothless mouths and pockmarked faces—indications that many New Yorkers could afford neither dentists nor the miraculous smallpox vaccinations. The sun this morning, which had glistened on the mud in the streets, would also be playing on ravaged faces, lighting them up so that all would see. But comfortable New Yorkers didn't want to see and rarely did. Beth was unique in that her work had trained her to look closely at New York's poor. Every morning in the classroom she saw the effects of hunger and privation in the faces of her hollow-eyed young students. She heard them speak of epidemics and soothed them when they wept at their desks because another little brother or sister had died of hunger or diphtheria or because their mothers had died in childbirth or their fathers of pneumonia after a cold day on the docks. She fought her own tears when some proud little boy came up to her and announced with dignity that he was now the man in the family and would have to go to work.

Beth wondered why she was thinking of such unhappy things on the happiest morning of her life. It was a habit of hers, born of some sense of guilt, to consider that anyone who was fortunate was obligated to pay for that fortune somehow. Her feeling was akin to that of wealthy ladies who ran charities.

Looking at the crowds now, she remembered what Greg had said about the conscription laws. When the army chose its men, it would take most of them from the homes of poverty. The wealthy who were drafted would have the money to pay a substitute; the poor would not. There in the crowd she could see the silk hats and the work hats side by side. How misleadingly democratic it must all appear to a foreign visitor! She thought about this a while and decided that the foreign visitor was probably clever enough to see through the ruse. Dickens, on a visit to New York, had described some parts of the city as being far worse than London. He must have wondered what Americans meant by democracy. The foreign immigrants, on the other hand, who had committed themselves to the new land, at first refused to see the truth. No, it couldn't be! Through potato famines and wars and pogroms they had consoled themselves with the thought that everything would be fine when they reached America. Now the facts were becoming apparent. And in New York the inequities were most glaring. Millionaires in Fifth Avenue mansions lived only blocks away from dirt-poor Irish whose domiciles were flooded cellars where pigs and chickens often shared quarters with their owners; where young girls sold hot corn to earn their pennies, or, if business was bad, sold themselves.

Greg shouted to her above the Broadway traffic. "You look as though you're deep in thought."

"I am," she shouted back.

"I hope you're thinking about me."

"I'm thinking about something you said." She looked at this officer who would one day be her husband and thought: Greg sees the unfairness too. Perhaps he'll be able to do something about it. They would both do something about it, she decided, and having made that decision, she was able to turn her thoughts to the lovely day ahead of her.

A full day with Greg! What lengths she had gone to in order to experience this glory. A lie to her mother about spending the day with a school friend. A warning to the friend never to contradict the story, followed by a lie to the friend concerning the identity of the young man. ("Jim Patterson. You don't know him, Mary.") But oh it was worth it.

She had known Greg only a week, and already he was so much a part of her that she couldn't understand how she'd ever known a moment's happiness without him. That other man—that poetry-spouting turncoat she had thought she loved—what had she seen in him? What had she seen in life itself before Greg came along to gild it and make it glow?

They stopped for breakfast at a Broadway restaurant and discussed their plans for the future over pancakes, sausages, and a pot of tea. It was decided that he would teach and she would write (married women were not acceptable as teachers) and it would make no difference if they were poor in the beginning. They would both want children, of course, but they could manage without having to rely on his father's money. It all seemed so simple. They were both young and healthy. What could go wrong?

When the last drop of tea had been consumed, they sat looking at each other. Where would they go now? Beth dared not order more tea for fear of having to answer a call of nature and destroying the romanticism of this intimate breakfast. On the other hand, they could not go to his house or to hers until the matter with Diane had been resolved. Where to go in this weather? Greg had a suggestion that made her windburned cheeks redden even more.

"Why don't we take a room in the hotel across the street?"

"Oh!" She was astounded that a gentleman would suggest such a thing to his intended.

"Not for immoral purposes," he said hastily. "Only so that we can be alone and out of the cold."

"But it *would* be immoral."

"We're engaged, Beth, and I love you so much. All I want is to be alone with you."

"Oh, I love you too, but—"

"We can sit side by side on two chairs if you like."

It was on her lips to demand a promise to that effect, but she didn't speak. Of course she could trust him. She was going to marry him. She lowered her eyes and said nothing.

"Will you do it, Beth?"

She sighed. "Very well. But are you sure you wouldn't rather go shopping?"

He laughed for a long time and she noticed that his eyes crinkled in the corners. He looked so happy that she laughed with him.

"I take it you'd rather not go shopping," she said.

He stood up and walked around the table. He took her hand as she rose and he said, "Let's go."

Her heart was pounding as they entered the lobby of the hotel. She was too agitated to notice that she had narrowly escaped the projectile of a man spitting into a cuspidor. Greg clutched her arm. "Beth, be careful. You were nearly sprayed by that—whatever he is." He looked at her. "Is something wrong?"

"I'm nervous."

"I promised you I wouldn't do anything unless you—I won't even touch you."

She swallowed. "Very well."

54

"Would you rather not be here? Tell me now. I'm about to register."

"I told you I'd do it," she mumbled.

She stood next to him with her head lowered and her hand half-covering her eyes. If anyone she knew saw her here, if anyone heard Greg intoning "Mr. and Mrs. James Johnson," she would leave New York on the next train and never return. It seemed an eternity before he turned, holding the key and saying to the clerk, "We have only one small bag and we'll take it up ourselves."

"Where are the stairs?" Beth hissed.

"I can't hear you."

"Hush! Do you want everyone to see us?"

He laughed. "Do you think there's a big letter *A* tacked to your coat?"

"Oh, hush and let's hurry."

The room was expensive and beautifully furnished, but Beth did not notice this or care. She had a vague impression of massive drapes and ornate chairs and tables, but her attention was fixed on the large double bed that dominated the room like a judge. There was nothing to do but remove their coats, and this they did with somewhat more ceremony than necessary. Greg moved his chair closer to hers and facing her but maintained a discreet distance. There was a long silence during which they could hear nothing but the distant Broadway traffic many stories below. She cast about in her mind for an appropriate subject and decided that an impersonal one would be best under the circumstances—at least until she'd had time to adjust.

"Greg," she began, scarcely recognizing the sound of her own voice, "tell me how the army is organized. I've never fully understood."

"The army?" He drummed his fingers impatiently, looking at her, puzzled. "What specifically did you want to know?"

"What a corps is and a brigade. And a company. It's confusing."

He sighed. "Well, there are two theaters in this war and two major armies: the Western Army and the Army of the Potomac."

She nodded. "I know that much."

"An army is composed of a number of corps. Your brothers and I are in the same corps but in different divisions. A corps has two or three divisions and a division has three brigades. Each brigade has about five regiments. All right?"

"I'd no idea it was so complicated."

"It's quite complicated. Boring too," he added pointedly.

"You haven't explained regiments."

Exasperation was beginning to show in his face. "Regiments are composed of companies, companies of platoons, platoons of squads, and that's it. The whole army. Now—"

"Which officers command those units?"

He bit his lip. "A general commands a corps and a major general commands a division. A brigadier general commands a brigade." He took a deep breath and said in a rush, "A colonel commands a regiment and second-in-command is a major. A captain commands a company, a lieutenant a platoon, a sergeant commands a squad, assisted by a corporal, and a private commands no one." His sigh this time was very loud.

"You're a captain and Pat's a captain too, but he's a doctor. How—"

"He has the same rank and the same rate of pay, but he can't very well command infantry." He paused. "Beth, are you really interested in this?"

"My brother Joe is infantry, though. A lieutenant."

"Beth, I'm not going to attack you, so you can stop acting like a reporter. There are more important things to discuss than the god—the army and how it's formed."

"Very well," she said petulantly. "You begin the discussion."

"I shall. To start with, I'd like to set a date for our wedding."

"Let's wait until after the matter with Diane is resolved."

"It will be resolved tomorrow."

"Yes. Well, perhaps May or June would be a good time."

"I may not be able to get furlough then. Those are campaign months."

"March?"

"Early March. Before the spring."

She smiled. "Early March then." She looked concerned. "When Diane finds out—"

"Diane is a sensible woman. In time she will understand. Believe me. One day she may tell you that you did her a favor."

"Are you sure?"

"Very sure. She doesn't love me, Beth." He paused. "So we'll be married in about six weeks."

She nodded, smiling.

"God, but I'm impatient."

She was impatient too. He looked so attractive with his long legs stretched out and his hands resting on the arms of the chair. She wanted to be kissed by him and to have him do other things as well. Six weeks wasn't so long to wait, but now it seemed like forever.

"I like your dress," he said softly.

"I was hoping you would. It's my favorite."

Greg shook his head as if to clear it. "It's incredible how my life has changed. Just a few months ago I was fighting to stay alive in a miserable Baltimore hospital and now—"

"Fighting to stay alive? What do you mean?"

"I had blood poisoning. Septicemia."

"Oh, yes. Pat says that's almost always fatal."

"But I survived it. And I'm very glad I did."

"What was it like, being wounded?"

"I was taken to a field hospital. Those are tents near the battlefield. Pat must have mentioned them."

She nodded.

"They gave me chloroform and extracted the bullet. A day later I was sent to Baltimore in a creaky ambulance. I remember the bumps. The fever was beginning to set in then. They tell me I became delirious. I don't recall that of course. One day I woke up and I was in a hospital looking into the eyes of a kindly old nurse. I remember her gentle smile."

Beth shuddered. "How can you bear going back to the war?"

He shrugged but said nothing.

"I still don't understand why you're fighting in it, knowing how you feel about it."

"As I told your father, the poor will fight regardless. The least the rich can do is help them."

It was hard to believe that he was that unselfish. She had never known a true humanitarian before, but she knew that they existed. John Brown, a white man who had been hanged for leading a slave insurrection, was one of them.

"Oh, you're so noble, Greg," she exclaimed, aware that she sounded like one of those silly heroines in magazine stories but meaning every word.

He cleared his throat, embarrassed. "Beth, please let's not discuss my motives in this war. Most people—your father included—don't believe me anyway."

"Oh, but I do."

She thought of how exciting it would be married to him. A man who believed in truth, justice, and social reform. Most men were interested only in how much money they could accrue. In some ways Greg was like her father. But Father was passive and a tiny bit hypocritical, for he mouthed words of justice for the poor while sipping the most expensive brandies. Greg seemed ready to give up his comforts for a cause. And she would be at his side fighting with him. She looked at him, her eyes filling, and said, "I love you so much."

"I love you. And if I hadn't made you a promise, I'd kiss you right now."

She smiled. "One kiss wouldn't be so dangerous, would it?"

But it was. At first he kissed her as other men had sometimes kissed her. He held her arms loosely and pressed his closed lips against hers. But then he parted his lips slightly and held her closer. Her heart was racing and she could feel stirrings in certain parts of her body. She didn't want to let him go. When he parted his lips fully and probed at her closed mouth with his tongue she began to panic. Dimly in her memory she could recall a friend whispering that kissing with the mouth open was as bad as the sexual act itself, for once a man succeeded in making a woman succumb to such passion she was powerless to resist him.

Beth broke away from him. "Oh Greg, you mustn't!"

"I'm sorry. I couldn't help myself." He sat down quickly and she collapsed into a chair. They talked of inconsequential matters, she keeping her head lowered so that he would not notice her blushes and he drumming his fingers in an infuriatingly monotonous rhythm. At length he said, "Beth, I *am* sorry. I did ask if I could kiss you and you said—"

"I know I did. I know." She straightened up in her chair and said, "Tell me again? How is the army organized?" And they both began to laugh.

She thought that the laughter and amusing chatter would take her mind off the kiss but it did not. Just remembering it caused her to become aroused to the point where she felt slightly queasy. And to think that married girls of sixteen and seventeen had already participated in the sexual act and knew what it was like, while she, at twenty-two, must remain a virgin only because she had not married. She must at all costs avoid the sin of—but it wasn't a sin at all, really. It was a dangerous situation; that was all. Linda had said that this queasy feeling could be discharged and without a baby. Any man would know, Linda had said. But she could not ask Greg. She must not shame herself before him, reveal the extent of her lust. She must sit here demurely, hands folded, and pretend that such thoughts never entered her head.

They chatted until half past one. He asked her if she was hungry.

"No. I couldn't eat a thing."

"Aren't you feeling well?"

"I'm nervous," she admitted.

"Why, Beth? I haven't touched you."

"Oh, Greg," she blurted, "Don't you think I have feelings too? I wish—but six weeks isn't so long to wait, is it?"

He stood up, walked over to where she was sitting, bent

down, and kissed her. "We could be married next week."

"You know that's impossible."

He pulled her to her feet and kissed her deeply and for a long time in the manner she had been told to avoid. Not only did she not avoid it, but soon she too had parted her lips. They decided that it would be more comfortable to lie on the bed and still better if she removed her hoops and her boots. She demanded that he turn around while she slipped off the cumbrous hoop contraption and hid it in a corner. Then they lay side by side on the bed and kissed. It was a bitter day, and the room was chilly. Greg suggested that they follow the old New England custom of "bundling"—sleeping together under the covers, fully clothed. They remained in this attitude for over an hour kissing and clasping one another, but not caressing, and talking very little. By this time Greg was breathing hard, and she was so excited that she decided Linda's method at least deserved a try. She trusted him now. He had taken no liberty that she had not specifically granted him. But how could she convey her plan to him without sounding like a woman of the streets?

"Greg," she whispered, "you must not violate me." The word "violate" sounded absurd, but what other word was there?

"Violate? How can I? You're wearing all those clothes."

"I'm not sure how far your—your lust will take you, you know. Promise, please promise that you won't violate me."

"Of course I won't," he said, confused. "I can't. You're wearing—"

"I don't want a baby until after we're married," she interrupted, kissing him, "so you must swear to me that *whatever else you do*, you won't—violate—" She trailed off.

He was beginning to understand now. Gingerly he placed a hand on her breast, and when she did not remove it, he began to caress her. Soon his hands were all over her body and he was moaning. She did not caress him. To do so, she decided, would be unspeakably brazen. She also tried to stifle her own moans of pleasure and that was difficult. At last the frustration of having to pretend she felt no desire when she was almost exploding found release in tears.

"What is it?" he asked, alarmed.

"I wish we were married."

"Oh God, so do I."

"I don't want a baby," she said.

"You needn't fear it. There's a way—"

Before she knew it, he had somehow unbuttoned her basque and was fumbling with the skirts. He removed all the layers of her clothes. She longed to assist him, but she knew she must not. He turned her first this way, then that, and eased her to a sitting position in order to unlace the stays. Through most of this she kept her eyes closed so that she could not see the expression on his face. As his lips pressed against her bare breasts, she fell back against the sheets, and her blush suffused her body as she yielded to feelings so warm and intense that they seemed to threaten her sanity. She could hear Greg saying, "Do you understand that I'll be very careful?" and her own voice answering, too quickly, too loudly, "Yes." Then his hands were everywhere, all at once, and her own hand was being guided under the sheets to a long hard cylinder which she guessed must be—but it couldn't be because she had seen Sean as a baby and his had been so small and soft. Perhaps it grew as men grew. But she couldn't think about that now, for he had removed her pantalettes and was touching her in that most sacred of places and she had to remember to hold her legs tightly together lest he—but her thoughts were now scrambling in her mind, now leaving her mind—and she was consumed in an indescribable spasm that caused her to moan so loudly that she was forced to muffle her voice with her hand.

She was panting and exhausted and still not certain of what had happened to her. She looked over at him, not knowing what to say, and he smiled and said, "Do you feel good?"

She nodded, breathless. He closed his eyes and shuddered and after a while he took her hand and guided it again to the remarkable object under the sheets which she, in her frenzy, had forgotten. What had come over her? What was she doing here? She moved her hand as he directed, watching his expression. He appeared to be very pained, and she wondered if she was hurting him. The answer to that question came in a few moments when he was consumed in the same sort of spasm that she had experienced and then lay back drained, his eyes closed. She guessed that he must have discharged his feelings too—experienced the same sort of peak and dénouement as her own. Aunt Louise, in her halting description of what took place, had never once mentioned—But as soon as she remembered Aunt Louise, she thought of Kate, and a feeling of shame stole over her like a sudden chill. Good God, how she had disgraced herself! If Mother ever knew. But what mattered even more than this were Greg's feelings. Would he lose respect for her? She had encouraged this! Encouraged it and liked it! Loved it, in fact. She wondered briefly if that friend of her mother's who had described sex in such negative terms was aware that certain women were able to enjoy the sensation. Linda had enjoyed it, and she, Beth, certainly had. She wondered about her mother and father and then pressed her hands against her temples as though to drive the indecent thought from her head.

Greg opened his eyes and looked at her. "At the end when you—I lowered the sheet, just a little to see you move."

"Oh!" She could feel her cheeks flame.

"You're exquisite. Opulent, like a Rubens."

Her embarrassment was tempered with indignation. "Fat?"

"Not fat, no. Earthy. Lush. Your breasts could be the subject of a long poem."

"Greg!"

"But you should know how exciting you are. I'm grateful to be the first to discover it. And also the last," he added, smiling.

She pulled the sheets up around her neck and looked at him carefully. There was in his expression no trace of the contempt she had feared, no disdain over her fall from virtue. He looked as he usually looked and certainly he sounded anything but disgusted. She breathed more easily. It had been a close call, but all in all no real harm had been done. She would still come to him as a virgin on their wedding night. Now she let her eyes travel down to his waist. Only the lower part of him was covered with a sheet and she stared, fascinated at his bare chest and his sinewy arms. Because he was lean, the strength of his body was concealed under his clothes. She wondered at just what point he had discarded his uniform, then shivered as she realized that she had been so impassioned that she had failed to notice his disrobing. In a thin voice, she asked him to hand her her chemise.

"Not so soon."

"Yes."

"Why?"

"Give it to me, Greg."

"On one condition." He grinned. "That you permit me to look at your breasts one more time."

"Greg, I really—"

He yanked down the sheet. "Oh, Lord, they're beautiful," he murmured, bending to kiss them.

"Please fetch my chemise."

"Very well." He stood up and walked halfway across the room to where the chemise had landed, and she viewed the back of the adult male body for the first time in her life. Only when she had adjusted to this startling picture did she notice the large jagged gash under his left shoulder where he had been wounded. When he turned and walked toward her she tried to concentrate on his face, but her eyes quickly scanned the lower part of him. She was confused when she saw that the organ seemed rather small and not at all what she imagined it to look like when she had held it. How could that be? He handed her the chemise and grinned lecherously as she lowered it over her head.

"Beth, you're so modest!"

"What did you expect? I've never—I—"

"Forgive me for teasing. It will take some time to overcome that sense of shame, but I'll devote my life to teaching you."

"Greg, let's get dressed." She said suddenly, wanting things to be as proper as they had been when they first entered the room. Somehow the removal of clothes symbolized the removal of identity. Naked, they were any two people in the world. Clothed, they were Gregory and Elizabeth. This was the reason she gave herself for wanting to get dressed at once. But hiding behind that reason was another that she couldn't acknowledge just now: She wanted his body as men were said to want women's bodies, and she would not be content until she had it.

When she began to dress, he helped her tighten the stays but thankfully didn't laugh as she had once feared he would. All he said was, "They mustn't be done up too tightly. You need room to breathe." Later they stood at the window for a moment, drawing back the drapes and looking down on Broadway. She had never seen Broadway from this height before. Stretched out on both sides of the avenue were square buildings with square lettering on them, a regular army of squares—big ones, little ones—solid and full of business, a line of fat soldiers with dollars in their pockets. In the distance she could see the spires of Trinity Church. Its vertical line against the endless horizontal was pleasing to the eye. Saint Patrick's Cathedral was too far north of New York's prime residential section to effectively impose the Gothic flavor that the "empire city" so badly needed. And the tall triangular sails out in the harbor, which would also relieve the rectangular monotony, were too far away for balance. In the street below, the carriages, omnibuses, horsecars, hackney coaches, and hansom cabs, in a spectrum of rushing colors, clattered north and south, while helpless pedestrians, taking their lives in their hands, attempted to cross the wide street. Beth didn't always like this swashbuckling city of commerce, but it was her home. She loved it as a mother loves her too-precocious child.

Greg put an arm around her and Beth basked in the warmth she felt. This man and this city were somehow bound together in her mind. She could see them in a small brownstone—little rooms with great fireplaces and Greg in an armchair reading poetry. But perhaps they would live in a boarding house. Especially if he renounced his family's money. That didn't matter. The room they shared would be far from the world, yet the world would be there if they needed it. She thought about the contrast of the harsh clang of traffic and the sweetness of two people caressing under soft blankets. Somehow the contrast was right.

He kissed her again, a gentle kiss. In it was the promise of years ahead after the war.

After lunch on Sunday, she went to sit by the window in her room. From here she could see the front walk at the Kendalls', where Greg would be coming to call in a few minutes. She saw him from a long way off—tall and slightly awkward, but still commanding in the blue uniform with the caped overcoat. As he entered the Kendall home, she noticed that he looked nervous. She sat waiting for a long time. She planned to follow him when he left the house and overtake him before he hailed a cab. He did leave, finally, at about four thirty, walking with his head down. It must have been grueling.

She already had her jacket on, and she flew down the stairs shouting to the group in the parlor that she was going out for a walk. She walked slowly, casually, past the Kendall house. He was rounding the corner far ahead of her and she stifled the impulse to shout for him to wait. When she reached Fifth Avenue he was getting into a hansom cab. Now she screamed like a fishwife:

"Greg!"

He looked around, surprised, then saw her and waved the cab on. As he approached her she noticed that his face looked ravaged.

"Beth, what are you doing here?"

"I saw you leave the Kendalls'. You look ghastly. What happened?"

He didn't answer.

"What's wrong? Did you tell her?"

"I started to." He took her arm and led her out of the wind. They stood under a street light.

"You started to? What do you mean?"

"I don't want to discuss it here. Let's go somewhere for tea."

"No. I want you to tell me." Her heart was racing. Something was very wrong.

"I don't know how to—it seems—oh, what's the use. Diane is going to have a baby."

"A baby?"

"The child is mine," he said quickly, lowering his head to avoid her eyes.

She felt a sudden nausea and a roaring in her ears. He looked up and quickly grasped her. She held him for support until she was able to breathe again.

"Greg how could you have lied to me? You told me you loved me." Her voice broke and she began to sob. He held her gently, but she pulled free of him and leaned against the lamp post for support. "How could you have done such a thing? How?"

"Please calm down and listen. It happened before I met you. And it happened only once, just before Thanksgiving. She—" he broke off.

"She—yes?" Beth's eyes narrowed. "Well, go on."

"Her parents were away. One maid was gone and the other—the other maid's mother died suddenly—"

"And you seized the opportunity to seduce Diane."

"Not exactly."

"No? What was it then, an immaculate conception?"

"For God's sake, Beth."

"You didn't take precautions?"

"I didn't think."

"What would have happened if I hadn't done your 'thinking' for you? You'd have two babies on the way and at least one of them would be a—a bastard."

"Please don't talk this way."

"How shall I talk? What would you like me to say? Congratulations? You do intend to marry her."

"Yes, I'll marry her. The child must have a name. And then I shall divorce her. Or she'll divorce me."

"You know that's impossible."

"The marriage will be dissolved. I hope you will marry me then."

He was insane. He didn't really mean it. Even if he did, the blow to Diane would be shattering. People rarely divorced, and when they did the scandal was sometimes enough to drive them out of town.

"And how soon after you marry her do you intend to divorce her?" Her voice was mocking.

"I don't know. I'll have to marry her at once. We're to say we've been secretly married since November. I'm so confused that I can't think straight."

"Do you know what I think? I think you intended to marry her all along. You seduced her and she was furious. And so you came chasing after me."

"That's not true. You know it's not."

"I'll never know anything for certain, Greg. Why, I don't even know if she's really going to have a baby."

"Do you think I would lie to you?"

"Why not? What would prevent it?" She started to walk away from him.

"Beth, don't go."

"Goodbye, Greg."

"Let me explain—"

But she walked quickly away from him, down the windy avenue. She didn't look back.

It had lasted only a week, Beth told herself. There must be some way to wipe all memory of it from her mind. She was lying in bed, fully dressed and covered with a quilt. Every tear had been shed, every memory of him gone over in her mind, and now she was determined to forget Gregory Allister had ever existed. That would be difficult, for he would surely be spending all his time at the Kendalls' until he returned to Washington. And after the war he would be back for good, though hopefully they would live elsewhere.

Beth had come back to the house that afternoon in a near-hysterical state. She had told her mother that she had had a ferocious headache and had thought the air might do her good. It hadn't, and now she wanted to lie down. Kate had not believed a word of this, but she had allowed Beth to go off and sulk in the hope that later on they could have a talk. Beth had been acting very strangely lately, distracted all the time and clumsier than ever. If there were a young man, Kate would have sworn that Beth was in love. But there hadn't been a real beau in months. She discussed the problem with John, who dismissed it as a phase.

" 'The thoughts of youth are long, long thoughts,' " concluded John, who rarely completed an idea without some relevant quotation.

Toward eight o'clock, Beth came downstairs. She refused any dinner but said she was behind in her marking of papers and wanted to work at the dining room table.

"Beth, sit down a moment." Kate pulled up a chair for her daughter, then sat down herself. She called for Sheilah to bring some tea. "What's wrong with you, dear?"

Beth had been prepared for this. "There's a man at school. I like him very much and I found out that he's going to marry."

Kate sighed, smoothing back her gray-blond hair. "Poor Beth. I'm sorry you have to be out there teaching with all those men obviously not of our class."

"I like teaching, Mother. And his class is certainly on a par with ours. And even if it were not, that's not the issue." Beth was dismayed. In addition to her other problems, she now had to reassure her mother. What would have happened if her romance with Greg had produced a baby? "I've just got to accept it, Mother. Get through it."

"That's a very mature attitude, Beth. I'm proud of you."

Beth was surprised. "You are?"

"Yes. There were times when I was young and my heart was broken. I used to disintegrate completely. Never could I have taught school after such a blow."

"Don't exaggerate, Mother. It was you who survived all the

deaths in the family and went on to produce a family of your own."

"But Beth, death is final and decisive. With romance there is always the lurking thought that things might have been different. Rejection in love is a personal affront."

Beth was impressed. She hadn't expected this level of understanding. Kate had actually eased the agony a tiny bit.

"Thank you for trying to help, Mother. I appreciate it."

"I wish I could do more."

"You have an interesting mind, too. You usually hide it."

"I don't hide it."

"Yes you do. All women do. We're designed for men's pleasure, not for thinking."

"Goodness, you are bitter! What sort of man was this? Have you seen him privately?" She looked alarmed.

"No. Only from afar," she intoned. (Lord, if Mother knew!) "I'd rather not discuss it."

"Very well, dear. I shan't pry. Now I must see to my guests. We'll talk later." She gave her daughter a kiss on the cheek and left the room frowning.

Beth picked up a stack of spelling papers and spread five of them before her. She began correcting them automatically, but she couldn't concentrate. In her mind she saw Greg in bed with Diane, whispering things to her, telling her she was beautiful. Diane really was beautiful. Good grief, but the situation was tawdry! Here was a man who had intimately known the bodies of two friends and neighbors, and without a thought as to what effect this could have on either one. All his noble speeches and pretensions to selflessness had been lies. Deliberate lies calculated to set her up for seduction. It had been so obvious, now that she looked back on it, and she had never guessed.

Oh, and those words he had used! "Somehow I feel I've always known you." On how many women had he used that line? Beth felt a bond with the faceless women—New York ladies, Parisian belles, how many others?—who had been victims of his charms. This comradeship made her feel better, less alone. And some of them had probably lost their virginity like Diane. At least Diane had been smart enough to trap him, thereby interfering with his philandering future—unless he intended to continue after marriage. For Diane's sake, she hoped not. She hoped he became fat and dull and so utterly undesirable that Diane refused to lie with him.

She looked at the papers spread on the table. Only five had been corrected. Three piles loomed like mountains before her. In the past week she hadn't accomplished a thing.

She could hear the sure notes of Phil Weatherly playing Mozart upstairs in the parlor. Involuntarily her mind strayed to the afternoon she had spent in Greg's arms. Angrily she swept the piles of papers from the table and watched them sail all over the room. The slow notes continued. She sat there looking at the mess, wondering where she would get the strength to pick everything up. And the music went on, a mocking reminder of what she had lost—or had never had. She vowed never to become involved with another man again. At least not for a year. Then she picked up the papers, threw them half-crumpled onto the table, and started to cry.

News of Diane's secret marriage was first brought over by Annie, a Kendall maid and a close friend of Sheilah. Sheilah, who seldom refrained from telling Annie exactly what was on her mind, questioned her closely as she stirred the stew on the large black stove. Beth hid behind the dining room door, like a spy, listening.

"You can't be telling me that the wedding was any secret," said Sheilah. "There's only one secret in that girl, and you know what I mean."

"You're a dirty-minded old woman, I'm thinking."

"Oh? And didn't I come over two days before Thanksgiving to borrow some molasses and find none of you there? Yes, and a light on in Golden Girl's room, but nobody answering."

"You keep a civil tongue in your head, Sheilah Murphy. She's my baby. I raised her myself."

"Babies grow up. I'm wondering why Mrs. Kendall didn't chaperone better. Mind, it's not Golden Girl I'm blaming. A man like that—so quiet, you know—you can't trust them."

So that part of Greg's story was true, Beth thought. It was unthinkable that the Kendalls would leave Diane at home unchaperoned, but it had happened.

"And in spite of all your wicked thoughts," Annie said, "my Diane is married now, and a richer man I couldn't imagine."

"But none too cheerful, I'm thinking."

"He's a quiet sort, I'll grant. But before I forget, there's going to be a party for them next week. Mrs. Kendall wants to know if you can help."

This news hit Beth like a sharp slap. She'd have to get out of it somehow. She'd pretend to be sick. But Mother would know she was lying. No, she'd say that she was depressed by Diane's happiness in the face of Beth's own lost love. Then mother would tell the Kendalls that she was ill. She stepped quietly from behind the door, cleared her throat, and walked into the kitchen.

"Shhh," Sheilah hissed. "This is no proper subject for Beth's virgin ears." Despite her gloom, Beth fought to keep from laughing.

When the family returned from the Kendall party, Beth was sitting in the dining room in a dressing gown and drinking tea. Her father believed she had a cold, and she had to make it look authentic.

"It was like a wake," Kate sighed, removing her bonnet and gloves.

"As you know," John said, "Allister is a rather strange chap. No one could elicit much conversation from him. Even I tried, and heaven knows I didn't feel like it."

"Beth, you didn't miss a thing." Kate paused while John walked into the family room and then said in a low voice, "This party would never have made you envious. It would have cheered you, in fact. It was obvious that some marriages are never meant to be."

"What happened?"

"Well, Greg sat immobile all evening. I swear he looked as though he were about to cry. Even his parents couldn't make him move from the couch. And poor Diane was embarrassed to death."

"I wonder that he was so rude."

"Not exactly rude, dear. No, he looked more like a man in shock. The army must have done something to him. Poor Diane, to be tied for life to a morose character like that! I wonder why she married him."

"I don't know," Beth said, looking away.

"I have my suspicions. I think the marriage was necessary."

"Oh?"

"Yes. A very unhappy mistake. Be careful with men, dear."

"Yes, Mother." Beth sighed.

"I'm very serious. Now you see what can happen."

Perhaps he had told the truth, Beth thought, but it was too late now. In the instant that it took to conceive a baby, three lives had been radically altered. One brief moment of bliss, and the future took off like an utterly misguided homing pigeon. There couldn't be a God.

"What is it, Beth? You look unhappy."

"I'm sad for Diane."

"We all are, dear. But I imagine they will work matters out satisfactorily. Most couples do. Now cheer up, and remember that Bill's coming tomorrow."

Beth wondered if all couples did "work matters out satisfactorily." John and Kate had been able to because each complemented the other and each could tolerate the other's faults. Moreover, they had both been in love when they married, and while initial love didn't always last, a marriage that began without mutual love seemed even less likely to be successful. She couldn't even venture to guess how the Allister marriage would be, and she promised herself that she would not think about it.

*   *   *

When Louise's son Bill came to town, the effect was like that of a strong, swift wind. He was a big, exuberant man, full of stories, anecdotes, and homespun philosophies, and he could usually ventilate rooms stuffy with the stagnant air of boredom. An expert investor and a fairly wealthy man, at thirty-seven Bill Shepherd was also a farmer and inventor. He had been married at twenty-five to a Pennsylvania farm girl whom he had met in his many travels through the country. They built a farm in the town of Carlisle, near Harrisburg, and then had five children in quick succession. In his spare time— which he had because his wife insisted on running the farm herself—Bill invested in real estate, the stock market, and any promising company that took his fancy. He had heavy investments in the coal industry. The farm was financially superfluous, though he loved the wide cornfields, the serene and fragrant orchards, and the plump, lazy animals. But Sally was devoted to the farm and efficient at managing it while Hannah, their Negro housekeeper, supervised their big home on the hill.

Bill also liked to experiment with equipment. He tried to improve the reaper when he wasn't fiddling with electricity or working on a carriage that would run with steam. He had cameras and developing equipment, and he considered himself a fair match for Mathew Brady, the famous photographer, who was now following the army and photographing the battles. Bill was a very happy man. His whole family seemed to be that way. The New York Shepherds sometimes spent summers in Carlisle, marveling at "Pioneer Sally" and her husband, the big businessman farmer.

Bill was in New York to attend his own interests and to handle the investments of his mother, his Uncle John, and John's former partner, Nate Klein—three financial dimwits who could quote whole passages from *Leaves of Grass,* but didn't know a stock from a bond. He rather enjoyed playing God to these distinguished people who admired him even though they did not consider him an intellectual. Sometimes he would arrive with the whole family and stay two or three weeks. This winter, however, he had come alone and was planning to remain only a few days.

He spent most of the first day closeted with John and Louise upstairs in the library. That evening they had all gone off to the Academy of Music, where even Beth enjoyed herself. Now, on the second night of his visit, they were having a dinner for him with Louise and the Kleins present. Mercifully, the Kendalls (who barely knew Bill) had not been invited. Bill was telling them about the education problem in his area.

"Sally and I had the children in a one-room school. They didn't want tutors, and they seemed to enjoy the children from neighboring farms. But the schoolmaster left to join the army right after Christmas. The children miss the place."

Beth, who had been only half-listening, now turned to him with full attention.

"Does Carlisle need a teacher, Bill?"

"Our district does, but I'm sure the town will find someone soon."

"Would they consider me?"

"You?"

Six heads turned in her direction.

"Why, Beth?" asked her mother.

John said, "I don't understand. You have a position here—"

"I want to leave New York. I'm tired of the city. I want to live in a different environment for a few months."

"Well Sally would certainly love to have you," said Bill. "And the children!"

"Please say Yes." Beth turned to her parents.

"I don't know," John said. "I don't understand. Oh, I suppose I do in a sense. But to go so far—"

Bill interrupted, "If you're worried about a proper chaperone Sally and I will certainly—"

"It's not that," John said. "It's the location that worries me. Carlisle is too close to the Mason-Dixon Line."

"Uncle John, Lee has already tried to reach Pennsylvania.

We stopped him at Antietam. I doubt that he'll try it again. Lee's no fool."

"I think he might try, Bill. They've won so many battles."

"He wants Washington. He'll concentrate his efforts there. I know what I'm talking about. I was in the army, remember?" Bill had fought at Bull Run and suffered a chest wound. When he recovered he had wanted to reenlist, but Sally had insisted that he could make a better contribution as a civilian.

John said, "Well, Beth, if you really want to go—Kate, what do you think?"

"I must admit I don't like the idea, but Beth is twenty-two and old enough to make her own decisions, I should think."

Beth wanted to hug her mother. Kate was really making an effort to help.

Beth had never made so abrupt a decision. As she approached the school principal the next day, she was tempted to change her mind and stay. She was fond of her students, anxious to teach them as much as possible before the demands of poverty wrenched them from what little schooling they would ever know. But she herself was so wretched, so anxious for change, that before she could stop herself she was telling the principal that a family emergency of uncertain duration would prevent her from completing her term. The emergency, she thought grimly, was the saving of her own sanity. As she said goodbye to the children, she tried to convince herself that in the circumstances her absence would be to their advantage.

Two mornings later, a trunk and several carpetbags were piled outside the house. The family was gathered on the walk saying goodbye when the door of the Kendall home opened and Greg and Diane appeared.

"Where are you going?" Diane asked, walking quickly toward her. Greg came up alongside, looking from Beth to Bill with questioning eyes.

"To Pennsylvania. I'm going to teach there." She spoke to Diane, not to Greg, whom she hadn't seen since that terrible Sunday.

"Who is that man?" Beth heard Greg ask Diane.

"Her cousin Bill."

Out of the corner of her eye, Beth could see him breathe more easily.

After Beth had introduced Greg and Diane to Bill, Diane said, "What a coincidence. Greg is leaving in two more days. There'll be no one left. Why didn't you tell me, Beth?"

"It was decided suddenly."

"Where in Pennsylvania will you be staying?"

"In a small town near Harrisburg."

"How long will you be gone?"

"Until June."

"Oh, Beth, I'll miss you."

She could see desperation in Diane's eyes. She looked utterly miserable, as did her husband, and Beth guessed that the marriage so far had been an ordeal for both. Yet Greg must bear the full blame for it. He had done the seducing.

The coach Bill had hired to take them to the ferry appeared, and there was a scrambling for bags. Greg picked up two, and as he passed her he whispered, "What's the name of the town?"

"You can't—"

"I want to write to you."

"Don't—"

"Please! I won't move unless you tell me."

She sighed. "Carlisle, Pennsylvania."

"I still love you." He moved on with the bags and she watched him blankly, too numb to react.

They boarded the train in Jersey City. Despite the fact that it would be a long, tiring ride, Beth was more cheerful than she had been in days. She believed Greg now. Even though their romance was certainly over, she was convinced of the fact that he had truly loved her. Her pride reinstated, she could now chat easily with Bill, who had been concerned earlier about his younger cousin's remoteness.

"You'll like it there in winter," he said. "There's not much work, aside from the milking, and the parlor is always lively. Sometimes the hands come up and we have a big songfest."

"Do you keep all the hands in winter?"

"Two of them. They've been with us many summers and I can't turn them away. They live in a cottage near the peach orchard."

"How is Sally?"

"Busy as ever. She'll be tickled to see you. There's not much woman talk about the place."

"Why do you stay there? Why not move to Harrisburg or Philadelphia? Goodness knows you're rich enough."

"Sally loves the land. I do too, of course, but she grew up on a farm and loves to work. She's the equal of any man, and proud of it."

"Are you?"

"Darn right I am. She's more of a woman than any I've met before or since our marriage."

"And you're quite a man to accept competence in women with such good grace."

"Well, thank you. But why shouldn't I accept it?"

She shrugged. "Most men don't."

"Yes—well—everybody is different, I guess. Say, what's been troubling you?"

"Me?"

"You seemed miserable when I first arrived."

"Oh that. A broken romance. I'd just as soon not discuss it." She looked at the floor of the train. Then, seeing it was covered with pools of tobacco juice (Lord, men were nauseating, the way they spat the stuff everywhere), she looked out the window.

"Are you running away?"

"Don't tell Father. He doesn't know about it."

"Of course not." He paused, thinking. "There's a cavalry barracks in town."

"I don't want to meet men, Bill."

"There's also a widower up the road. About thirty-five. He's a farmer too. Very gentlemanly and bright."

"I'm not interested. Really, Bill."

"But you're so pretty and clever. It's a darn shame."

"I don't want to think about men at all," she said impatiently.

"All right." He looked down and said, "I won't mention it again."

Oh Lord, now she had hurt his feelings and she hadn't meant to do that. Another good reason to forget about men: They turned sensitive women into impossible shrews who treated their dearest cousins badly. "Bill, I'm sorry. I'm in a frightful mood and I didn't mean—"

"You don't have to apologize."

"Yes I do. You're the most thoughtful person I know. If *he* had been more like you, I wouldn't be acting this way."

"Well—"

"And while we're on the subject of your virtues, there's something I've been meaning to talk to you about."

"What's that?"

"Bill, I know what you've done for our family and I want you to know how much we appreciate it."

"It was your father's money. All I did was help him invest it."

"You know he could never have done it himself."

"I wouldn't say that."

"Bill, you know I love my father, but you also know that he can't add a column of figures. If it weren't for you, we'd all be in the almshouse."

"You don't need the investments for survival, Beth. Your father earns a living. And you certainly contribute substantially."

"Yes, but you know what I mean. Without you, Pat wouldn't be a doctor and Joe could never have finished two years at Columbia. You never went to college and here you are educating everyone else."

"I could have gone. My parents urged me to go. I didn't care to, that's all. Why must everyone to go college?" He leaned back in his seat, stretched his long legs, and lit a cigar. "Let me explain something, honey. I'm a happy man. I like my work. And if I didn't have someone to help, I'd be lost. I mean that. Investing happens to be my skill. Your father is a scholar, your brother's a doctor, and you're a teacher. I'm an investor. I don't especially care about the money or the things it will buy—only about the challenge of it."

"Really?"

"Sure. I've invested for everybody in the county. I take my housekeeper's money and invest it. I do the same for the hands, the neighbors, everybody."

"Don't they pay you?"

"Sure, but not much. I don't need the money."

"You're too generous, Bill."

"No, that's not it. It's not generosity. It's fun. It's using my ability, like you do when you spend extra time with a student. You don't get paid for that, but it makes you feel good, doesn't it?"

"I see what you mean. But I still wish our family could support itself."

"But you do. Your father earned the principal that I invested and he insists on paying me for my services."

"But you don't take it, do you?"

"I don't need the money. Why can't you understand that? You know, Beth, we all should try to do what makes us feel good. I explain this to Uncle John every time I'm in New York. Take Sally, for instance. She could move to Philadelphia and fit in very easily. She was educated in a fine academy there. But what would she do in the city? Worry about furs, diamonds, and the Social Register? She's not interested. If she were, we'd move up there. Sally likes to watch things grow. She loves to taste morning air or see a mare foal. Your father wants to live inside books. Why shouldn't he? Does everybody in the world have to break their backs in order to achieve a life that other people consider ideal? Beth, we could have that life tomorrow, and we don't want it."

"All right, Bill. I'll try to accept your help graciously. It will be difficult, but I'll try."

"Good. And try finding your own way, Beth. Don't listen to other people. In the long run, you'll be a good deal happier. You know, our family has always done that. Consider Ma and Pa. How many couples in their position would up and leave for California in a wagon? Pa wasn't even looking for gold. They just decided to have themselves an adventure. You four children certainly have a variety of interests. Even your mother—though she's the most conventional—doesn't worry about entertaining on a modest scale."

"She's not pleased about that, Bill."

"I think she is. In a way. Or would be if she realized how much easier it is for her to be informal." He stretched again and grinned. "Yep, the lot of us are a passel of misfits."

"You're proud of that, aren't you?"

"Sure am. We'll find new roads in life that some will never travel."

"I never thought about it that way."

"Well, think about it, cousin. You'll see what I mean."

Sally Shepherd was a plump, pink-cheeked, light blond woman who looked considerably younger than her thirty-four years. She greeted Beth with cries of delight. "Beth! What a surprise! Bill, you didn't tell me Beth was coming. Quick, get the children! Hannah, please warm some stew. Come here, Beth, and let me look at you."

"I feel I ought to tell you at the outset that I'll be here until June."

Sally threw her arms around her. "That's bully! A long vacation?"

"No. I'm going to teach in the school."

Sally looked disappointed. "Well, at least you'll be here evenings to talk. Tell me all the news. Every last bit."

The days following were much like the first. The family was warm and the children exuberant with questions about life in the big city—especially the girls.

"Have you been to Madison Square?"

80

"What plays have you seen?"

"What are people wearing?"

"Tell us about your beaux."

"Tell us about the balls."

In the morning everyone gathered around the huge round kitchen table while Hannah dished out bacon and eggs, steaming oatmeal topped with cream, and fragrant coffee. Sally would come in from the barns, where she both supervised and helped the hands. Sometimes Bill would get up early enough to see Beth and the three oldest children off to school. Usually, though, he slept late and worked on his investments and inventions far into the night when the house was quiet.

The walks in the snow to the schoolhouse were invigorating. Beth taught with enthusiasm, and because of her attitude, the children were receptive. After walking home with her young cousins, she had tea with Sally before correcting papers. Later she came down to dinner, always a tasty affair that left her satisfied and deliciously sleepy.

On Saturday nights and Sundays they often had visitors from neighboring farms. Later, when the roads were passable, business acquaintances of Bill's came down from Harrisburg and stayed overnight. Though the Shepherd farm was far from neighbors, life for Beth was livelier than it had been in New York. Sally and Bill teased her about the widower down the road, who was obviously taken with her. But Beth pointedly ignored their remarks. The chief value of being here was the freedom from the pressure to marry that was ever-present in competitive New York.

In March she received a letter postmarked Washington, D.C. There was no return address, as if the writer feared that someone might open it. Unfamiliar with the handwriting, she knew the writer's identity from his salutation:

"To the woman who stopped the singing:

"I probably have no right to send you this. I've debated the wisdom of it since the day you left. I want you to know how much I love you. What happened was a mistake. I never wanted this, and no words can express my shame and sorrow.

"You made me happy. I have never been a happy man, but I was happy with you. I can't explain why. Your beauty, your mind (yes, I remember how highly you value your mind) were all part of it. But love is an inexplicable emotion, transcending all individual attributes, and how I love you!

"I won't ask you to wait or to forego marriage on my account. I have no right to do that. But should you remain single, I will ask you again to marry me when I come home and I hope you will say Yes. No matter what you do, though, I will understand."

There was, of course, no signature.

Beth was touched by the letter, and she reread it many times. The next week she received another. But both failed to cheer her. She was still much opposed to the idea of divorce. Diane could never stand the scandal. No woman should be treated that way after being seduced by a man and made to bear his baby. She loved Greg still but was disappointed in him. He had turned out to be less than a man. Often she would think of their moments together, but she placed the old Greg in a separate compartment from the one who had fathered Diane's child. She thought lovingly of the old Greg and imagined him to have died a noble death. Of the new Greg she tried to think little.

With April came a flurry of parties and square dances which were attended by the soldiers in town. The whole area of Carlisle, York, and Gettysburg had a martial flavor. The fact of the war was apparent here as it had not been in New York since the first patriotic parades of 1861. Beth was urged by her cousins to attend these dances. Bill allowed her to ride in with Dan Winters, the widower, whom everyone considered above reproach. He was a good man and attractive in his own way, with pale blue eyes and a full red beard. Beth appreciated his kindness, but she was not interested in any man just now, much less a widower with five small children. The dances were fun, but Dan's excessive attentions irritated her, and the rides to and from Carlisle became difficult. One night, coming home in his wagon, he asked if he might kiss her. A sense of obligation to him for his chauffeuring prompted her to agree to a peck on the cheek, but she regretted that decision immediately.

"I—I'm very fond of you," he stammered, grasping her around the waist and kissing her fully and passionately on the lips.

"Really, Dan, you mustn't! I'm sorry, but I'm not ready to care for any man just now."

"Why, Beth?"

"You see, I—" she thought fast—"I lost my fiancé. In the war." She hoped Dan wouldn't check this story with Bill or Sally.

"I'm very sorry, Beth. But why do you attend the dances if you feel—"

"My cousins insist that I try to forget." She cast her eyes downward. "It is, of course, impossible to forget."

He said gently, "Will you forgive me for being so bold?"

"Of course I will." His kiss, however unwelcome, had stirred up old desires. She needed to be kissed by someone, she now realized, but she wished it could be someone who just happened to look and sound and think like Greg.

They drove on through the moonlit night, he blushing in the darkness and she breathing deeply the fresh spring scents and wishing Greg were driving the wagon.

"Do you think that some day you might consider me?" he asked. She had been thinking of lying in bed with Greg and was quite aroused.

"Why, certainly." Because of her reverie her voice was caressing and she turned toward him with a look of desire. He halted the horses again and took her in his arms.

She was ashamed of the purely carnal desire she felt for this man. But once he had aroused her, she could not help responding. She wanted him to part his lips as Greg had done, but Dan was much too proper to take such liberties. After a long while he released her and they drove on while Beth shivered with frustration. Later, in her room, she tossed in bed until it occurred to her that perhaps it was possible to achieve a climax by doing to herself what Greg had done for her. When Beth had been a child Kate had warned her never to touch herself "there" but had given no reason. Later, at normal school, she had heard that some mysterious act known as "self-stimulation" could result in madness. She wondered about this now but concluded that she might easily find herself with child if she didn't try something. Later, after she was satisfied, she was pleased to discover that her faculties seemed intact.

After trying this forbidden method of release several times, she decided that it helped but was not enough. Even Greg's method had not been quite enough, Beth now thought. She felt a longing for completion that surely could be satisfied only by the sexual act itself. And that could only come with marriage. Whom could she marry when the only man she wanted was already taken? If there were only a way to prevent conception, she could lie with any man she pleased. What would her mother say if she knew of these shocking thoughts?

Yet her new-found skill enabled her to repel any further advances from Dan Winters. This infuriated him, and one night in May he blurted out his rage.

"If you don't like me, why the deuce did you act that way that night? Jesus, a man would think you were dying for it. What kind of a girl are you?"

She slapped his face swiftly and scrambled out of the wagon. Then she began running down the dark dirt road. He shouted his apologies, but she would not get back into the wagon even when it pulled up alongside her.

"You shouldn't be walking alone at night. It could be dangerous."

"Get away from here, or I'll tell Bill you tried to attack me."

"Beth, I'm sorry."

Tears of rage and humiliation sprang to her eyes. "I said get away!"

He drove on slowly, never too far ahead of her. It took her

half an hour to reach the farm and all the while she could hear Dan's horse up ahead. Once home, she said a hasty good night to Bill, who had been waiting up for her and was reading the local *Sentinel*. He handed her a letter from home and asked her how the evening had gone. She answered, "Oh, fine." Pleading fatigue, she fled to her room. She lit the lamp and studied herself in the mirror. What kind of a girl was she? he had asked. She herself did not know. Perhaps something was wrong with her. Other girls never seemed to have such longings except for Linda, whom some considered a tart.

It took a long time for her to calm down and open the letter. Kate had included, as she often did, a letter from Joe to his parents, and she read this first. It would probably describe the Battle of Chancellorsville, which had had heavy casualties, though thankfully her brothers had been spared or she would have heard by now. On the second page, the words *Diane's husband* caught her eye, and she skipped to this paragraph, her heart racing.

"As you probably know, Diane's husband has been captured. Please tender my regrets to Diane and tell her that the officers' prisoner-of-war camps aren't nearly so bad as the enlisted men's, though Pat says that typhoid and dysentery fell a great many officers. (Don't tell her that!)

"Allister had come over to our camp one night especially to meet us. I gathered that Diane wanted her neighbors to meet her distinguished, altruistic husband. Pat was duly impressed, but I found Allister awfully cynical and unpatriotic. Personally I am unable to fathom the attraction between Diane and the good captain, but who can explain the vagaries of love? I suppose I'm jealous.

"The food here gets worse every day. Oh, how I miss Sheilah's—"

Beth skipped over this part to look for further mention of Greg. There was none. Her hand trembling, she picked up her mother's letter and read about the reaction to Greg's capture.

"Diane is taking it all very well. She doesn't seem greatly

upset. I've always said they were a peculiar couple. She is great with child now and keeps to the house. Mrs. Allister visits frequently, bringing little gifts and chocolates. She is worried but says she prays frequently. Did you know that the Allisters were Catholics? You could have knocked me over with a feather! English Catholics, no less. But Joan—we're on a first-name basis—says that her son rarely attends Mass. That doesn't surprise me.

"Your brother Sean has threatened to become a drummer boy or a messenger, but your father made his objections known in the strongest possible terms and Sean abandoned the notion. With two boys at war already, I couldn't bear—"

Once again Beth searched for Greg's name and found no further reference to him. Horror tales of Southern prison camps had filtered north, and it was assumed that those unfortunate enough to be taken would never come out alive. Beth paced up and down the small room, regretting the fact that she had been so angry with him. Her imagination took her to the battlefield at Chancellorsville. It was nighttime and Greg, smoke-blackened from battle, had walked a long distance to find her brothers' regiment. She could see his solemn face in the light of a campfire, searching her brothers' eyes for some sign of her.

Joe had said that Greg seemed very cynical. He had probably been unhappy and distracted and not paying attention when the rebels surrounded him. It was her fault. And now he was going to die . . . She told herself to calm down. He'd probably emerge from prison thin but healthy and live to have five more children with Diane. But she didn't really believe it. Greg was as good as dead, and she would never have the chance to tell him how much she had loved him.

Downstairs Bill heard Beth's pacing and wondered what was wrong, but he dared not ask. Beth was so jealous of her secrets.

A week later, when school ended, Beth made plans to leave for home. The protests from the family were long and loud. Ten-year-old Jean had insisted on teaching her to ride "like a

86

proper horsewoman." Sally pleaded that Beth needed a vacation and what better place was there than this verdant land? Beth finally agreed to stay for a while. She walked alone in the tall grasses and through the orchards thinking of Greg. She picked strawberries and helped Hannah create succulent shortcakes heaped with fresh heavy cream. She finally learned to ride properly and could keep pace on her favorite sleek bay with her younger cousins. The days were long and lazy in this time before corn harvest. It was mid-June, 1863.

TWO

So we're springing to the call from the East and from the West,
Shouting the battle cry of freedom!
And we'll hurl the Rebel curse from the land we love the best,
Shouting the battle cry of freedom!
The Union forever, hurrah, boys, hurrah!
Down with the traitor, up with the stars,
While we rally round the flag, boys, rally once again,
Shouting the battle cry of freedom!

Lee's army was marching north. The rumor had been relayed from farmer to farmer and telegraphed from towns in Maryland and Virginia to cities all over the Union. A Yankee balloon had spotted them and scouts had confirmed the movements. But the main body of the Army of the Potomac was still in Virginia, reluctant to abandon the Washington area in case Lee suddenly changed his mind and bore down on the capital. Thus the Confederates were actually to the north of the Yankees. There was some protection—a file of Union soldiers had been sent ahead to defend Harrisburg, and militia units were being called down from most of the states in the area—but these could not withstand the force of Lee's entire army, should it actually reach Pennsylvania.

Beth's parents sent a panicky letter urging Beth to come home at once and bring Bill's family with her, but neither Bill

88

nor Sally would think of abandoning the farm to Confederates. Beth tried for days to persuade them, wasting precious time, and they refused to be budged. They insisted that she leave, however, Bill feeling guilty about his assurance to John that the rebels would never reach Pennsylvania. Lee was now approaching Chambersburg and moving quickly. By the time Beth gave up the fight and was ready to leave, Ewell's unit was on its way to Carlisle.

"Now you can't leave," Bill said. "They're cutting railroads. Even if I drove you up to Harrisburg, there's no guessing where they might be. Someone said Jeb Stuart's cavalry is nearby, and if they ever attacked your train—no, I won't let you leave."

Even as he spoke, the children were digging trenches in the woody area behind the house. They were lined with stones, like a well. Valuable silver, money, and antiques were to be buried there.

"How will you conceal the trenches?" Beth asked Bill later as she stumbled through the door with two statues.

"Boards, outhouse doors. We'll cover that with dirt and with squares of turf."

"Will there be time?"

"We'll have to hurry."

"The cows—" Sally moaned.

"There's no way to hide the cows."

"And the chickens and the pigs. And the corn! All the corn. Oh, and the horses. Bill!" Sally's face was white.

Bill put an arm around her. "We'll buy more animals after the war is over. We won't starve if they burn the whole place. You know that." But his face betrayed him.

Hannah was waiting for the weary group with pitchers of lemonade when they straggled into the house at nine thirty that night. The three youngest children were in bed. Everyone else sat around the great maple table drinking thirstily but talking little. Hannah served sandwiches, salad, and ice cream. They picked at the food but could work up no appetite. The rebels were now occupying Carlisle. Beth wondered if the town was now officially a part of the Confederate States of America and if they would now be required to salute the Bonnie Blue Flag. Was she now a Southern belle, a resident of Dixie? Was Jefferson Davis her president, Richmond her capital?

She looked across the table at Sally, who seemed about to cry. Even jolly Bill could not summon a smile. As she studied his grim face, her heart began to pound. If Bill was frightened, the situation must be very serious.

Bill well knew how serious it was. The last battle, Chancellorsville, had been another rout for the Union Army. That meant how many routs now if one didn'tcount Antietam, which had been a standoff? Too many. Too damn many. And now Lee had become puffed with triumph. A man on a winning streak could sometimes win on bravado alone. A perennial loser, on the other hand, might give up even if he were physically the stronger. Certainly the Army of the Potomac had been whipped and weathered into shape since the disastrous Bull Run, the first major battle of the war. But they had won no important victories. He remembered Bull Run with a shudder. They had all been so cocky in their proud new uniforms and gleaming rifles, aching for the chance to shoot a rebel. They had marched jauntily out from Washington, confident that the battle would result in the immediate capitulation of Jefferson Davis and the end of the war. On that Sunday in July, 1861, the ladies and gentlemen of Washington had followed the army over the Potomac into Virginia, picnic baskets in their carriages, patriotic songs on their lips. They watched the battle from a safe distance shouting, "On to Richmond!" eating their sandwiches, and cheering the distant, dying figures like spectators at a jolly sports event. Presently the cheers had died. The soldiers were beaten and running for their lives, realizing too late that they were, for the most part, green small-town troopers who knew little of horses and rifles confronting a rural enemy well trained as riders and hunters. The Army of the Potomac met a crushing defeat that day, and the phrase "Did you run at Bull Run?"

90

became a joke not only among the rebels but among rugged Western Yankee soldiers who taunted the Eastern dandies mercilessly whenever they met. The Western boys could point to many victories; the Easterners to few.

Bill had been wounded at Bull Run, had heard the word "disgraceful" applied to his army, and could well imagine how the men must feel now after a series of defeats and blunders that read like a memorial plaque: Second Bull Run, The Peninsula, Antietam, Fredericksburg, Chancellorsville. Lincoln had replaced one general after another and the situation had not improved. The latest rumor was that Hooker, too, would be replaced.

With all that, though, Bill had never believed that the rebels would reach Pennsylvania. The North had more men, more factories, a better communications system, and a stream of mercenaries from Europe who were anxious to settle in the new land and ready to fight any enemy for the privilege. If the North's army tactics were inferior to the South's, they had every other advantage in their favor, and when Lee touched Northern soil, the army would rise up and strike with the ferocity of a mother animal whose young family is threatened. Bill had never expected the rebels to get this far. Never.

What a seer he had proved to be! Lee had coolly bypassed Washington and was now bearing down on the Northern cities. And the army was far to the south. Where were they? Why hadn't they moved sooner? The rebs were everywhere; in Chambersburg, Gettysburg, Cashtown, York—in Harrisburg too for all he knew. Did Hooker plan to wait until they had taken Philadelphia and New York? He had heard rumors—he hoped to God they were true—that the Army of the Potomac was now on the move.

He looked at Beth, who wore the expression of a European queen awaiting execution. He should have made her leave days ago. If only his uncle would forgive him, he would do anything. He'd make him rich, a millionaire, a Vanderbilt. But John was a minor problem. There were other, more important ones. What would happen to their finances, to the value of the United States dollar? And what about the farm, the children's education? What about—and the questions kept coming, pounding at a brain that had no answers, in rhythm with the clink of spoons against the ice cream dishes.

Hannah was tense and silent, fearing that the rebels would send her south and sell her into slavery. She had planned to leave for New York with Beth, but now she too was trapped here. The family suggested that she hide in the attic, but Hannah knew that no attic, no cellar, nothing could hide her, and she continued to manage the household with the resignation of one who has already lost the battle.

The atmosphere was gloomy indeed, and no one made any effort to cheer the others. They all slunk off to bed, weary and miserable, but too panicky to sleep soundly. Beth woke up frequently during the night, half-expecting to see a rebel standing by her bed ready to tear off her nightgown. She had never in her life known such dumb terror.

While Bill and the children were in the woods the next day, doing their best to conceal the animals, Sally, Beth, and Hannah prepared lunch. Suddenly they heard voices in the yard. Looking through the window, they saw a party of five ragged men in patched uniforms that had once been butternut. Two of the men wore rags on their feet. One, looking ill, leaned against another.

"Well," Sally sighed. "I might as well face it."

"I'm going with you," Beth said stridently, her legs turning rubbery and her heart thudding. They walked through the door and stood defiantly on the porch.

"Greetings, ladies," said a sergeant. "We've come to requisition some of your provisions. And mighty tasty they look too." He stared lustfully at the women, wondering if they appreciated his double meaning, but Sally was looking past him to a man they had laid on the ground. He was obviously sick.

"That man is ill," she said. "Beth, please fetch some water for him."

As Beth hurried inside, the sergeant said, "Yes, ma'am, I was hoping you had a potion or something." The leer was gone from his face.

"What's wrong with him?" asked Sally.

"I don't rightly know, ma'am. Typhoid, I expect."

Beth returned with the water as two men carried the sick man up to the shade of the porch. He drank in gulps, some of the water spilling down into his beard, then thanked them weakly. Beth noticed that he didn't seem much older than she was.

"You must leave him here," Sally whispered to the sergeant. "He'll die if you take him with you."

"I don't reckon we can get back here to pick him up."

"Do you want him to die?" Sally demanded.

"No."

"Then leave him. You can pick him up later." Her voice hardened. "I imagine you'll be in the neighborhood for a while."

He shrugged. "Okay, ma'am. I'm really grateful to you. And ma'am?"

"Yes?"

"If you'll just give us some vittles, I'll make the men swear they never seen this place."

"Oh, would you?" Sally's round face broke into a pleased smile.

"You're a lady who's kind to the enemy. We 'preciate your generosity."

"Well, I don't care to think of that poor young man as the enemy. He's a pawn for his government."

"I wouldn't say that, ma'am. But I do thank you."

Sally turned to Beth. "Please tell Hannah to give these men some pork, beef, and vegetables." She looked at the sergeant. "Oh, and you needn't pay us with Confederate money. It's worthless here, as you must know."

"Maybe it'll be valuable some day."

"Hush!" She bent to feel the forehead of the sick man.

"Would you mind carrying him into the house for me?"

They carried him through the hall and up the stairs, noting white spaces on the walls were pictures had hung.

"You did a mighty good job of hiding things, I'll wager," said the sergeant.

"You promised me!" Sally exclaimed, trembling.

"And I mean to keep it. So do my men." He looked at them sharply, and they nodded.

They were gone by the time Bill returned. He found Sally and Beth dashing about with basins and linens, and he nodded as they related their experiences.

Sally said, "Of course, another party might discover our farm but this group made a promise."

"A rebel promise," her daughter Jean said scornfully.

"All the same, I believe that sergeant."

That afternoon they did their best to care for the soldier. Beth and Sally worked in relays while Hannah prepared soups and tea. "I'll take the broth up this time," Sally said. "He has to be bathed afterward, and you certainly can't do that."

"I'm not sure Bill would want *you* to bathe him," Beth teased.

"But I've nursed before," said Sally. "And I'm a matron. It would be most improper for you to see a man."

Beth could not suppress a grin.

"Why are you smiling?"

"I'm smiling at you, my surrogate mother." She almost wanted to tell them. She would have enjoyed seeing Sally's shocked face and hearing Hannah's Baptist epithets.

"Let me get back to him," said Sally.

"Will he live, do you think?"

"I doubt it. I don't think he'll live to see morning."

"Oh Sally!"

"We can make him comfortable."

Later that afternoon, Beth sat by his bedside cooling his head with wet cloths.

"Much obliged to you, miss." He was straining to talk.

"Thank you," she whispered.

"I have a girl at home looks like you."

"Where is home, Roger?"

"Savannah." His eyes closed and in a short time he was asleep. He did not wake up for several hours, and then it was only long enough to sip some water. During supper one or another of them went upstairs to check on his condition. Usually he was asleep and tossing restlessly. When Beth stopped in the room at nine that night, Sally was at his side looking exhausted.

"Go to sleep," Beth hissed. "I'll watch over him."

"Shhh." She waved Beth to be quiet. The man was twisting on the bed in delirium.

"Mama? Mama?" His voice was barely audible.

"Hush, child. Mama's here." Sally was affecting a Southern accent and doing a good job of it. She placed an arm under his head. "Sleep now. Mama's here."

"It's so hot, Mama."

"Don't worry, honey. I've got cool ice for your head."

In another moment he had stopped writhing. Beth sat down in a chair near the window, brushing away tears.

"He's unconscious," Sally said. "I'll stay with him until he dies. Will you ask Bill to bring a cot here? Oh, and tell him to supervise the morning chores, will you please, Beth?"

"You're very special, Sally. Do you know that?"

"Thank you."

"He believed you were his mother. I think you should write to her and tell her about this. She'd be happy to know he died believing he was with her."

"Yes, I believe she would." Sally was crying. Beth cried too. They hadn't known him twelve hours, and he was the enemy besides. But he had a name. He was young and gentle and he missed his girl and needed his mother. Like the Northern boys or the Russians or Napoleon's troops or the soldiers under Caesar. They were doomed from the day they were born.

For several days Ewell's troops occupied the town, camping on the college grounds and nearby farmyards but behaving in quite gentlemanly fashion, considering what they might have done. Lee had issued directives to his army that all provisions acquired in enemy territory must be properly requisitioned and paid for. But the soldiers quickly exhausted the townspeople's stock, and Confederate money was, as Sally had said, worthless. Nevertheless, there were few incidents in town, and early on the morning of June 30, Ewell's troops marched away. No one could understand why they were heading south. Later that day another group of rebels arrived—cavalrymen—but they too left shortly afterwards. Reports on these events filtered through to the Shepherd farm, but the family saw little of the activity.

Then, on July 1, Union troops headed by General "Baldy" Smith moved down into Carlisle. The sigh of relief was cut short, however, at 6:30 P.M. that same day, when Confederate cavalrymen under the command of Jeb Stuart moved in. Brigadier General Fitzhugh Lee, a nephew of Robert E. Lee, demanded that Smith surrender the town. When he refused to do so, the town was shelled. One bombardment, begun at 7:00 P.M., was stopped as another opportunity was extended to Smith and refused; and the firing commenced again. Hysterical townspeople clogged the streets. Bill took a wagon to the outskirts of town and picked up several refugees. Beth, Liza, and Jean prepared food and soothed the children while Sally and the hands tried in vain to calm the animals. The sounds were frightening. Each boom brought a stab of nausea to Beth. Rarely in the past had she wondered about her own death. Other people would die; not she. But now, though the shelling was far from the farm, she began to imagine herself lying helpless in a pool of blood, the family dead all round her, watching her life ebb slowly away, unable to do a thing to save herself. For the first time in her life she could see war for what it was. Not the musical abstraction depicted in New York parades, war was loud. Shatteringly loud. Just listening to it was torment. What must it feel like to fight in it? To be there in the open with no place to hide?

The youngest children were crying, and Beth tried to

soothe them with a strained smile and a quavering rendition of a lullaby. She was certain that Smith would have to surrender the town in order to protect the civilians.

At last the bombardment stopped. Shortly afterward Bill arrived with a wagonload of frightened people. Beth helped dole out soup and bread and assured the refugees that their homes were probably intact. At 2:00 A.M. sleeping arrangements were completed and the visitors bedded down on feather mattresses and quilts. At 3:00 A.M. another shelling commenced. Beth bounded out of bed and into the hall, where Sally was comforting the children, who were huddled, shaking, in a circle on the rug. Eventually the third bombardment ceased, but Beth remained awake, expecting more of it, until the sun came up.

It was a weary family who staggered around tending to the animals the next day. A neighbor came galloping over on horseback shouting that Stuart and company had gone south shortly before dawn. They had burned the army barracks and fired the gasworks, but all the family could think about was that at least for the moment they were safe—and part of the Union again. Feeling a temporary security, they all staggered back to their beds. Bill wondered why the rebels were all turning south. He had expected them to push ahead to Philadelphia.

At five that afternoon Bill drove the refugees back to town and helped to clean up the debris. Hours later, he returned to report that the firing had been high over the town, that there had been few casualties, and that the refugees had found their homes intact, except for one family whose front porch had been destroyed. He also informed them that a full-scale battle had been raging for the past two days in Gettysburg, some twenty-eight miles to the south. Apparently some Northern units had finally reached Pennsylvania, met a few Confederates, and begun fighting. Lee had then called his men back from all points, including Carlisle, as the rest of the Army of the Potomac streamed into Gettysburg. From what Bill understood, Lee's Army of Northern Virginia was also there in full strength, and the casualty list was beyond comprehension.

"My brothers!" Beth wailed.

Bill looked at her guiltily. He had forgotten about Pat and Joe. "Oh, the reports are probably exaggerated. We've never had a battle up this way. You know how rumors are."

But the next morning a neighbor told them that the battle had indeed been wicked. He speculated in the most gory terms about what the battlefield must look like and the beautiful college town that Gettysburg had once been. To distract everyone's attention, Bill related the tale of how Sally had nursed the rebel soldier. The neighbor smiled. "I hope some Southern lady does the same for our boys." He paused only briefly. "They say. there's going to be more fighting today. Sure hope we blow 'em to bits."

Beth was struck by the absurdity of this situation. Here Sally had struggled the long day to comfort her "enemy," a sweet young boy. Meanwhile, a few miles away the brothers of that boy were eagerly pumping bullets into other boys. If Roger had survived, he too would be among them, shooting and being shot at, counting the dropping bodies as points towards some "victory."

In the early afternoon they could hear a faint rumbling in the distance. It went on for about an hour, ending at about 2:30.

"Thunderation!" exclaimed a hand. "What are they throwing at each other, for us to hear it all the way up here?"

Looking off toward Gettysburg, they could see a gray cloud of smoke drifting upward into the innocent sky.

Beth worried about her brothers. Which of those distant booms had killed Joe? Which had shattered Pat's arm? Bill, before leaving to help clear the débris in Carlisle, consoled her with the thought that surely Pat, at least, had escaped injury. Surgeons were usually well behind the lines, and armies tended to spare hospitals. How chivalrous of them!

At least Greg was out of it now, though if he had to die she would have preferred a quick bullet to the heart rather than the delirious agony Roger had suffered. She remembered the wound on Greg's shoulder. What did it feel like, a bullet piercing flesh? How could anyone bear to have a leg sawed off? And why did men keep returning to the battles, knowing what awaited them? Greg himself had suffered and nearly died from blood poisoning after he had been wounded, yet he had never seemed afraid to go back. Disgusted with war, yes, but not afraid. Perhaps he had been, though, and not told her. That in itself took a courage she would never possess.

How could they do it? There must be some hidden force in men that closed off their minds to all sensible thoughts and directed that their bodies be impelled forward. She couldn't imagine any woman marching down to Gettysburg, gun at the ready. How would it feel to kill a man or woman—to see twenty or more years of life canceled in a single explosion of blood? Could a woman kill an innocent person and retain her sanity afterward? No. A woman would shrink from the thought of her own mutilation and that of others. Women would invent some civilized game like chess to determine which side must win. No woman with Lincoln's power or Davis's would stand by philosophically while children she had raised for twenty years marched off to be killed and maimed. Perhaps there was a tumor in men's brains that cut off the channels of logic.

All that afternoon, as wagons passed up the road, Sally, Beth, and the others asked for news. Most of the people lived in the area and were still recounting the shelling of Carlisle. But at three o'clock a family in a wagon heaped with household goods said that they were fleeing Gettysburg. They could tell that the father was tired of narrating the same story over and over again like a Greek bard. He had probably talked to dozens of people along his escape route. When Sally asked him about the fighting, he sighed wearily and said, "Worst bloodbath of the war. Dead all over the place. Now if you'll excuse me, I got to get on."

On the Fourth of July, a day of relentless rains, the Shepherds uncovered the trenches and tried to get out everything that might be ruined by the coursing water. It was exhausting work, and Bill was unavailable most of the time, for he was still aiding the people in Carlisle. Not a soul recalled that this day marked the eighty-seventh year of the nation's independence nor would any of them recall it until Lincoln, months later, began a brief speech with the words, "Four score and seven years ago," and then they would remember the terror and the driving rain.

But there was some cause for jubilation at the end of the long gloomy day. Bill came home with the news that there had been no more fighting in Gettysburg. It was rumored that Lee had been defeated and was now beginning to retreat. It was the first time in days that Bill looked happy.

Later, they would learn that while Jeb Stuart's men were busily shelling Carlisle, Lee had been waiting anxiously for them in Gettysburg. It would also be claimed that if Stuart had been where he was supposed to be, the South would have won the battle and possibly the war as well. Years later, Bill would say only half-jokingly, "Carlisle saved the Union."

Upon hearing that Lee had gone, Beth announced that she planned to ride down to Gettysburg.

"No you're not," said Bill."

"My brothers might be dying!"

"We don't know where Lee is."

"You said they retreated."

"That's only a rumor. It may be totally in error. Give us a day. Day after tomorrow we'll start out early for town. If the rumor is true, we can ride down there."

The rumor did seem to be true. At 7:00 A.M. on Monday, July 6, they questioned some soldiers in Carlisle. One of them said to Bill that he thought the Confederates had gone.

"Thank God. Is it safe to ride down there?"

"I wouldn't take the young lady."

"I'm going," Beth said flatly.

"You'll proceed at your own risk," warned the soldier.

Bill said, "Beth, let me go alone. I'll find out if the boys are safe."

100

"And what if they're dying and I'm not at their deathbeds?" She was almost in tears imagining it.

"I give up. Come along if you want to. Your father will kill me for sure."

"Kill his sole support?"

"Stop that, Beth. Let's go, for heaven's sake. It's a very long ride."

They started off at a good clip, Beth straddling her horse—very unladylike—and trying to get him to move faster. It was a tiring ride, made worse by the glut of other people intent on reaching Gettysburg. They detoured through side roads for a while but eventually returned to the main road, stopping on the way to eat the lunches they carried in their saddlebags. Two miles north of Gettysburg, they halted to speak to a man Bill knew. He related tales of wounded men nearly drowning in a church basement; horses and men decaying in the fields; men shot through the head but still alive, lying in yesterday's rain and twitching convulsively. At least she was prepared, she told herself, shaking, as they rode the last mile into town. In her mind she could hear the soldiers screaming. It was so vivid to her—the steady high pitch—that her head began to hurt.

Before they reached town they began to see mementos of the armies: a canteen, a forage hat or a musket, an occasional broken wagon. As they rode on, the density of the litter increased. Soldiers milled about picking up objects and placing them in carts, ramming bayoneted rifles into the ground so that they stood upright. The place seemed eerily quiet, haunted. But the silence was more frightening than the cacophony of battle. Scattered effects and inert weapons only called to mind dead men.

They reached Gettysburg, once a quiet town of two thousand, now a teeming city of walking-wounded soldiers, agitated visitors, reporters, and curiosity-seekers. The streets were glutted with ambulances, supply wagons, and stray mules and horses. In some sections, barricades indicated that there had been fighting in the village itself. These defenses were made of heaps of rocks, old wagons, lumber, and household furnishings of every variety. The wooden sidewalks were crowded with soldiers and civilians—some discussing flanking actions and charges, others assisting orderlies in removing the moaning wounded from ambulances and carrying them into the buildings. One of the men helping to carry the stretchers was a town blacksmith. Bill shouted to the man, who came over to the edge of the sidewalk exclaiming, "Bill Shepherd! We haven't seen you for six months!" Then he stopped short and his face became grave. "Looking for Carlisle boys, Bill?"

"Carlisle and New York." His gesture introduced Beth. "Is the Second Corps here in town? My cousin is looking for her brothers."

"The army is chasing Bobby Lee to the Potomac. Everyone's gone but the Third Corps. And the wounded, they're out the Baltimore Pike near the creek. Twenty thousand men at least, counting all the corps and the prisoners. The front was three miles long, and the hospitals were set up behind it."

"Twenty thousand," Beth repeated dully.

Bill said, "Then the fighting was south of the town too?"

"Mostly. On the first day the fighting was to the north and west. Only two Union corps were up then, and the rebs drove them south to the hills yonder." The man gestured. "Right through the town they came. Ewell's and Hill's men. Took everything in my shop and paid me with Confederate money. Good thing I've got money in a Harrisburg bank." He sighed. "Well, our army finally arrived to reinforce these two corps, and the next two days the fighting was south of the town." He shook his head. "I'll tell you the truth, Bill, I never thought we'd whip 'em. But we did."

Beth asked, "Were there many losses in the Second Corps?"

"Well, miss—" He looked away. "There was lots that survived, too. We're picking them up from the field hospitals and bringing them into town just as fast as we can. We couldn't get to them while the rebs were in town, but ever since they left—"

Beth was impatient. "How bad was it? Tell me!"

"For the Second Corps? Pretty bad, miss, but they gave the johnnies hell on that last day. That they did, beg pardon."

"Let's go, Bill," Beth said, agitated. "I've got to find my brothers!"

Passes to the southern part of the battlefield were being issued at a brick house, temporary quarters for the provost marshal. These were difficult to obtain because the army did not want civilians swarming over the field until the wounded had been tended to and the cleanup details had done their work. Disappointed people, many of them obviously mothers, fathers or wives of soldiers, were pleading with the guards. Some were stumbling from the house crying or clenching their fists in futile anger. But Bill had anticipated these road-blocks. Along with such standard identification as his army discharge papers, he carried two letters from financial luminaries describing stock transfers to Bill and one from the governor asking for his opinion about certain state expenditures. These missives established Bill as a gentleman farmer of considerable wealth and influence on whom Governor Curtin himself was obliged to rely. The passes were issued promptly. As Beth walked past the furious people who had been turned away she shook her head guiltily: If only they all had rich cousins.

They rode south out of town and turned left onto the Baltimore Pike. Lines of box-like ambulances with crosses on their canvas rolled in the other direction into Gettysburg. Occasionally Beth could hear hoarse cries from within them. She bit her lip, wondering if any of these soldiers was Pat or Joe. The trampling armies and the driving rains of the past two days had churned the area to mud. Mired in it or rusting in pools of rain water was the same sort of battle debris she had seen to the north of town—only much more of it. Her eyes fell on two dead horses who were swathed in flies and cawing crows. Gagging, she turned her head quickly only to see a decaying mule on the other side of the road. The stench hung over the field like a putrid fog. She began to ride with her right hand on the reins and her left hand covering her nose. A sentry, examining their passes, advised them to stay away from a hill called Round Top. Burial details weren't yet finished there and the hill was strewn with the bloated corpses of soldiers. Beth, struggling to keep from vomiting, began to wish that she had stayed with her cousins in Carlisle.

After traveling about two miles they left the pike and turned right at a dirt road that led into a wood. There was a good deal of traffic entering and exiting here, so Bill, sighting a guard, offered a goldpiece and asked him to watch the horses. They dismounted and walked the brief distance to the Second Corps hospitals. They were approaching the clearing when a cart lurched past them. In it were piled amputated arms and legs. As this grotesque image registered on Beth's brain, she sank to her knees and, grasping the branches of a bush for support, lost her hastily eaten lunch. When she looked up and was able to focus her eyes, she saw Bill, ashen faced, staggering toward her.

"My God," he groaned, assisting her to her feet "but this is beyond belief." He shook his head. "Are you all right?"

"Not really," she said miserably.

Bill led her to a rock and made her sit down. Then he asked a sergeant where he might locate Captain Shepherd.

"He's an assistant surgeon. Caldwell's division." Bill named Pat's regiment.

"You're in the right place, sir, but I don't know if he's still on the field. Most of the medical officers, they've left. I'll ask, though."

"Please. Tell him his sister is here."

"His sister. Yes sir." The sergeant looked sympathetically at Beth, who was very pale. "Pretty shocking sight for a young lady." Then he walked quickly away.

She looked around her. The whole area, as far as the eye could see, was blanketed with hospital tents. Some wounded men lay inside, some outside, and some half-crawled along-side the tents. Medical people, swimming in perspiration, rushed about with buckets of water, bandages and litters. In

104

the distance she could see men lying on tables and other men working over them with implements (were they saws?) Oh God! How could Pat saw legs and not faint dead away? From everywhere came the sounds of pain—screaming, moaning, sobbing—and of orderlies shouting directions at each other ("Set him down easy, Mitchell. Easy!") and even the sound of laughter. How could anyone laugh? Several orderlies walked by and looked at her curiously, as at a Greek statue in a refuse heap. Clouds of flies buzzed about as though excited by the activity and anxious to participate.

At last she could see her older brother in the distance. He spotted her too and waved, smiling. At the sight of his bloody smock she shuddered, quickly shifting her eyes to his face. He looked drained and exhausted even from so many yards away. The light brown hair was longer than usual and there was the shadow of a beard. Pat was too thin and gangling to be considered handsome, but he had always been appealing in a Lincolnesque way—very tall, his hair always tousled, and his smile rather shy. He was the darling of some of Beth's school friends, who found his awkwardness his best attribute. He looked as though he needed mothering. In nature, Pat, like Lincoln, was anything but a clumsy bumbler. He was practical, efficient, and quite sure of himself.

She ran toward him and he toward her, holding out his arms. Then, remembering the bloody smock, he drew back and grasped her hands.

"Beth! God but it's good to see you!"

"Yes, and I'm so glad you're alive," she said. "Is Joe—"

"Joe's unhurt. He's moved out with the army."

She sighed with relief, closing her eyes. "We've been so worried."

Pat squeezed her hand and turned to Bill. "Good to see you, Bill."

As they walked down a long row of tents, Bill asked where the field hospital for his home regiment might be located. Pat pointed south. "I think it's in that general area, Bill. Keep asking directions. The field is a sea of hospitals. Many wounded are in private homes, barns—well, just about everywhere."

"May I meet you here later? About half an hour? I would like to inquire after some of my friends."

"Sure, Bill. My tent is over there." He pointed. "Third from the end."

"Do you ever sleep during these breaks?" Beth asked her brother as Bill walked away.

"Usually. We can also sleep standing up for the three minutes we have between patients. We can sleep anywhere, as a matter of fact."

He led Beth into a tent and told her to sit down on a cot.

"Is this home?" she asked.

"This is home. Cozy, isn't it? And I have to share this vast edifice with two other doctors. But doctors at least have shelter. Many of the wounded don't. We wanted to donate these tents, but the colonel wouldn't hear of it. He said we'd be of no use to anyone if we had to sleep in the woods."

"Pat, I've never been so appalled in my life. You weren't in any danger, were you?"

"No, but Joe was. Half the company was killed."

"Half! My God, who?" Many men in that company were her brothers' friends.

"If I talk about that now, I'll cry," said Pat. "Joe, though, came through without a scratch."

"Did you see him?"

"Briefly."

"How was he?"

"Shaken. Not very talkative. But physically he was in good shape."

"I don't know how any of you stood it."

"This is the worst battle I've seen, and I've seen Antietam." He paused. "We've been working day and night since Thursday. And there's no end in sight, Beth. After we take care of our own men, we have the prisoners. And everyone needs immediate attention."

"Do you do many amputations?"

"A great many. Very rarely, we can save a man wounded in the body cavity. Usually, though, he dies of blood poisoning. And the men shot through the head aren't touched at all. There's nothing we can do for them."

She shook her head. "Pat, what happened here? Do you think we've won the war?"

"I'm afraid we're far from having won the war."

Pat told her that though the battle had raged for three days, Hancock's Second Corps (including their regiment) had not arrived on the field until the second day. A division had been sent into action that day, and most of the regiment had been killed or wounded. On the third day there had been a fearsome cannonade that felled many medical attendants behind the lines, followed by a suicidal rebel charge that ended the battle at last, but not before killing or wounding some of their best officers, including General Hancock, who would be out of the war for months. Pat didn't know many details, for he had been far too busy. He knew that Lee had been badly battered—but then so had Meade—and that he had escaped. Meade was now chasing Lee, but he had delayed the pursuit so that his army might rest.

"The army took most of their doctors with them. Kent—that's my superior officer—and I stayed behind because most of our regiment is here—dead or wounded. But the civilian doctors and the Sanitary Commission nurses are only now beginning to reach the field to help us. It's been hell, Beth. We can't even organize ourselves properly. Until Saturday Kent and I worked mostly with our own regiment and beyond that on other regiments in the brigade. But now there are at least twenty thousand wounded and only a handful of surgeons. We're working with other brigades, divisions, even other corps. Someone estimated one surgeon for every nine hundred patients."

"Good grief!"

"We're sorting bodies out like cards. Kent and I specialize in amputations, Marshall and McMahon in chest wounds. Occasionally I get a stomach wound for variety, but mostly—"

"Oh, Pat!"

"There are so few doctors. I feel guilty sitting here with you, but I've been working since five."

"Since five this morning without rest?"

"To bed at two A.M., up at five. Kent had no sleep at all."

"You'll take sick, Pat."

"It's a madhouse. If you hadn't come just now, I would have started throwing scalpels around. One brigade is using orderlies to operate. Another is using an ex-butcher to saw and an ex-tailor to suture."

Beth's mouth fell open. "Really?"

"That's what Kent says. But he may be joking. I haven't had time to check the story."

"Joking about something like that?"

"You'd understand if you'd been a doctor for the past two years." He paused. "But today is a picnic compared to Friday, when both sides fired their cannon for two solid hours. The noise was indescribable." He shook his head.

"Yes, we heard that up at the farm."

"All the way up in Carlisle?"

"Only for about an hour."

"That must have been the high point of the fireworks. Can you imagine what it was like trying to suture amid blasts that shattered the eardrums, trying to direct orderlies who couldn't hear a word? We were sweating rivers. What with the heat and the blasting, well, I thought my head would explode." He pulled a cigar out of his pocket and lit it.

"I can't drink or I couldn't operate. But God, do I need a drink."

She had never seen Pat in such an agitated state.

"And then came the rains," he said. "There's a theory that heavy battle causes cloudbursts. I don't know how true it is, but that was one hell of a downpour! It started Friday night, right after the battle, and continued all day Saturday.

"The creek overflowed, and the wounded were drowning in the fields. Some died before they were carried to higher

108

land. Kent and I were trying to operate in a small tent. One of the orderlies who was holding a lantern fainted over Kent's patient, dropping the lantern, which broke. The flames started lapping at the legs of the operating table. I ran around stamping them out while my orderly held *my* patient down. Kent, in the meantime, could not find his patient's sciatic nerve in the dark, and he bellowed at the top of his lungs for another lantern, frightening my orderly, who let my patient slip and—" He sighed. "I don't know why I'm running on like this. I must be depressing you."

"Don't be absurd. If you could live through it, the least I can do is listen, Pat."

She touched his cheek gently, and his eyes filled. "I miss home so much. All of you."

"Isn't there anything I can do? Perhaps I could nurse—"

He didn't have a chance to answer, for someone outside the tent was calling his name. She stared open-mouthed as a surgeon strode into the tent. He looked as though he were in his thirties. He was of medium height, rugged, lean, and very blond, with a thin, weathered, clean-shaved face. Never before had Beth heard the curses of a street hoodlum delivered in a cultivated Boston accent.

"Damn it to hell, Pat. I'm finished with the army! I haven't received one goddam sheet that looks clean. Do they wash them? The sons of bitches—"

"Kent!" Pat broke in sharply as he swept one arm toward Beth, who hadn't been able to suppress a gasp at the shocking language. She was sitting in a corner, and the surgeon hadn't noticed her. Now he peered at her, and his eyes widened.

"What's a woman doing here? You know we're not permitted to have—"

"My sister Beth," Pat said. "Beth, Major Kent Wilson."

The major came into the tent and sat down. He nodded at her but did not apologize. Beth noticed that his eyes moved from her face to her breasts, where they remained fixed for an instant too long.

So this maniac with the lean and hungry look was the

regimental surgeon. She had expected someone much older and one whose speech was closer to the queen's English.

He said, "You never told me your sister was a nurse."

"I'm not," said Beth.

"Oh. I was hoping you had some sheets for us."

"Sheets?"

"I'll explain later," Pat said. "No, Beth is staying with relatives in Carlisle. She only came down here to see if we were alive."

"Christ, Pat, we've got to get sheets. There's enough chlorinated lime to last awhile and possibly enough chloroform. But until two days ago there was barely enough opium, and now there are no clean sheets. The whole damn—" He broke off and turned to Beth. "Miss Shepherd, you're prettier than we are. Do you suppose you could employ your charms to beg sheets from your neighbors?"

Pat said, "Now see here, Kent, Beth's not a—"

"How many do you need?" Beth interrupted.

"As many as possible. Can you get us at least two score of them, Miss Shepherd? Do you have a horse?"

"Yes."

"A wagon?"

"I can get a wagon. But I don't understand why the army doesn't help you."

"The army insists on lopping off legs on boards soaked with other men's blood. The army thinks I'm demented."

"I see," said Beth. But she didn't.

"Will you get us the sheets?" He looked exasperated.

"I'll try. There are many families in Carlisle who'll help, I think."

"Good. And if you would, I'd like you to find a competent laundress among the townspeople. They must be clean. The army idiots don't give a sh—don't care."

He turned to leave the tent. "You'll have them soon? Cotton, silk, or satin. It doesn't matter so long as they've a tight weave." He turned to Pat. "Some civilian doctors have arrived.

110

I think they came on the back of a turtle, but at least they're here. I'm going to take a nap and you will do likewise, Pat."

"All right."

Kent left with a brief nod at Beth and another glance at her breasts.

Beth said to Pat, "A gentle soul, isn't he?"

"The uninitiated find him hard to take. But he's a capital surgeon. Harvard Medical School plus an extraordinary record in the field.

"Sis, I hate to put you through this. You could have said No."

"I want to help."

"Very well. Let me explain the reason for the clean sheets. I don't suppose you've ever hard of a Viennese doctor named Semmelweis."

"No."

"Neither have most doctors. He discovered a method of preventing the spread of childbed fever and was laughed out of Vienna. When Kent was in New York, he met a doctor who had known Semmelweis in Europe. He explained how it was done."

"How the infection was checked?"

"Yes."

"How?"

"By having the doctors wash their hands between patients. It was so simple it was absurd. They washed the contagion off at first with soap and later with chlorinated lime solution. And the incidence of disease dropped to almost zero."

"Then why did they laugh at him?"

"I have no idea. Not enough concrete proof or something. Anyhow, Kent was impressed. The war had just broken out, and he tried the method on the first amputation cases. It worked, but not enough to suit him. Then he decided that everything in contact with the patient should be cleaned before operating on the next patient. Now he's a fanatic about cleanliness."

"Oh, so that's the reason for the clean sheets."

"Yes. He doesn't want the man's limb to come in contact with the amputation tables, so he uses clean sheets."

"I take it you work the same way?"

"Of course. Kent managed to convince a surgeon in a Pennsylvania regiment to try his method, but no one else. Most doctors think he's dotty."

"Why?"

"Doctors are like any group. They're skeptical about new methods. Yet our cure rate is very high."

"Don't the others wash their hands?"

"Some do and others don't. Most don't wear fresh aprons between patients and they just throw water over the tables."

"Where did you get your supply of aprons?"

"A girl I courted in Washington made us about seventy. I think he would like you to see to their washing too."

"Can I find people to help me in this—this chaotic—"

"Ask Bill. He probably knows people in Gettysburg to help with the laundry, and folks all over the countryside will give him sheets."

"That's true. He does investments for everyone. I never guessed when I arrived today that I'd end the day as directress of laundry. Major Wilson is quite a character, isn't he?"

"He's tired, Beth."

"But so are you. And you don't behave like him. Oh, that language, Pat. Does he talk that way all the time?"

Pat laughed. "Everyone in the army talks that way."

"Everyone?" It was hard to believe. In her presence men never used foul words except for an occasional *damn* or *hell* uttered only under extreme duress.

"I must admit, though, that Kent's language is worse than that of most officers. He's almost always in a rage. But he didn't expect to see a lady here, or he would have spoken more carefully."

"All the same, he has a foul disposition."

"Kent has always been tense. He hasn't had a happy life.

112

Five or six years ago he lost his wife in childbirth and his daughter two days later."

"That *is* sad."

"And he spends most of his time arguing with the army."

"How old is he?"

"Thirty-three."

"That's what I guessed. If he's from Boston, why is he in a New York regiment?"

"He lives in New York now. Or did when he joined the army. He was a surgeon at Bellevue when war broke out."

"You know, I'm surprised that neither of you has a full beard. Or a mustache. I thought they were *de rigueur* for doctors."

"Beards are too hot in the summertime. I had one last winter. Kent hates them, winter and summer. He doesn't feel like sitting long enough for a barber to trim it."

"Oh. I suppose I shouldn't waste time talking about silly things like beards, should I?"

"I wish I could spend a month discussing silly things."

She looked around her at the dreary tent. "Pat, I promise to do all I can."

On the ride home with Bill she explained the situation, telling him about Semmelweis and the necessity for cleanliness.

"Why won't the army give him sheets?" he asked.

"There aren't enough. I suppose they think he's wasteful. From what I saw, half the soldiers don't even have sheets on which to lie."

"Well, we can get them, all right. We'll send out Jean and Danny and the hands. God, what a day it's been!"

Bill had been over to visit wounded men from his home regiment. What he had seen had crushed him. Many young men from the county lay screaming in agony, awaiting amputation. Opium and whisky were being used to anesthetize them, but nothing helped very much. When they were five miles north of Gettysburg, Bill suddenly stopped and dismounted. At his feet was a clump of grass where wild flowers were growing.

"Flowers," he said softly, lifting one to his nose. "So sweet and innocent, growing here—here, Beth, so close to that place." Before mounting his horse he gave one to her.

As soon as they reached home, Beth went to fetch the children and the hands. Then, sipping tea and eating cake, she explained to the solemn group around the table that sheets were urgently needed at Gettysburg. While Beth and Bill took naps, Sally and the children set out on horseback with saddlebags empty. Bill had sent a hand up to Harrisburg to telegraph the New York Shepherds that everyone was still alive and that neither of the boys had been wounded. It would be a while before the Gettysburg casualty lists were completed by the army. At that, many men already dead would be listed as missing or wounded.

By ten that evening the family wolfed down a late supper. All errands were successful and there were seventy sheets folded neatly in the wagon. Hannah and Jean worked far into the night making cakes, candies, and cookies for the doctors, nurses, and patients in "Cousin Pat's hospital." Some of the neighbors sent cooked hams, bacon, eggs, and vegetables. All this, along with fruits, preserves, applesauce, books, magazines, and tobacco was loaded into the wagon the next morning. Bill and Beth were off by seven-thirty.

They were stopped in Gettysburg by hungry patients and guards and ended up giving away most of the food. But the precious cargo got through to the hospital. Kent smiled and shook hands with them, and Pat removed his bloody smock and hugged them.

"Major Wilson," Beth said, "you told me silk and satin sheets would be useful, but I don't know if they would hold up under the repeated laundering of bloodstains. I brought only a few of each. The rest are cotton."

He smiled. "I hadn't thought of that. Neither silk nor satin would absorb much moisture, either. Good thinking, Miss Shepherd."

For some reason his approval meant a great deal to her. She guessed that he didn't give it often.

After handing over the sheets, she and Bill climbed back into the wagon and drove to an area a few miles out of town where Bill knew some German families. In halting German, he explained the laundry situation to the first family. Soon they had contacted two housewives from nearby farms. One woman, who spoke some English, offered Beth accommodation in her home. They all volunteered their buggies for her use and emphasized that they would do all they could to get the sheets white. Beth moved in with the Shaefers that day, sharing a room with one of the older girls. That afternoon she began the journeys back and forth to the hospital to pick up dirty sheets and deliver clean ones.

The job itself was simple. She was to wait until Pat and Kent had used up a pile of sheets and aprons and then she would take these back to the German farmhouses. Mrs. Shaefer and the two other housewives would each take a third of the pile and, with the aid of their children, wash everything as quickly as possible. If it was raining, the sheets and aprons would be hung in parlors, kitchens, sheds, or any place that would serve. With luck they would be dry by the time Beth made her next trip. If it was sunny, the sheets would probably dry very quickly.

The job was simple, but adjusting to her surroundings was not. While waiting for Pat and Kent to use up the laundry, she did not have anything official to do. Nevertheless, she couldn't just stand gaping in horror at the wretched harvest of these fields. In a short time she found herself walking among the wounded with one of Kent's orderlies.

Many of the wounded soldiers still had no shelter at all. They lay under the trees or outside the hospital tents sweating profusely, groaning and tossing, their hastily bandaged wounds festering as they awaited the ministrations of a surgeon. As though this torture were not appalling enough, it now began to rain. The trees afforded only minimal protection, so nurses—mostly middle-aged women—covered the men with oilcloth while orderlies hastily tried to assemble a few pup tents that had just been delivered. Beth knelt down, holding canteens to lips, trying to replace the oilcloth which kept slipping from the writhing bodies. A few men spoke to her, asking when they would be given shelter, but most said nothing. They either stared at her dully or they moaned.

After vainly trying to soothe one soldier who was screaming in pain, she stood up and looked around helplessly. There were so many suffering men, and no possible way to care for them all. For a dizzy instant she could see these men still lying here, days hence, motionless, their moans frozen in dead throats. She shuddered, blinking back tears, and then knelt again beside the writhing soldier.

But even as she knelt, lines of wagons were rolling up to the area. Drivers were removing large hospital tents and medical supplies. Soon soldiers seemed to materialize from everywhere to help. As she made her way among the wounded, she saw tents being erected and became somewhat more optimistic.

Eventually she was obliged to go back to Kent and her brother and collect the sheets. She had never actually been in this area before. Thus far she had been able to avoid it by contacting Pat through an orderly. She knew that Kent and Pat each had a small table near the place she had seen yesterday. She stood at the edge of the crowded operating area—a clearing in the woods—and tried to signal an orderly working with Pat. The boy did not see her, and everyone else was tearing around madly, so she decided to go in herself.

Under squares of canvas supported by poles, the surgeons and their orderlies worked over the terrified patients. Gingerly she picked her way among the shaking men who lay waiting their turn and walked past several amputation tables, looking down. There, at her feet, loomed a pile of shorn limbs. Shivering and gagging, she reminded herself that she must learn to anticipate horrors jumping suddenly from the placid green of these woods and fields. When she heard Pat's voice, she slowly focused her eyes, being careful to look at his face and not at whatever he was holding. But she would have to fight this squeamishness, for certainly she would be coming here many times, and it would be best to try to adjust at once. She had seen a good deal of blood today. Amputations, she told herself, were nothing more than life-saving procedures involving blood. If she tried to think of it that way, she would be all right. Gritting her teeth, she looked at Pat's patient. She turned away quickly and then tried again. Something in her began forming a protective cement around her emotions. After a while she was able to look at the patient for more than ten seconds before turning away. She knew then that she would be able to cope.

When the patient was carried off, she asked Pat if there were now enough sheets to take back for laundering.

"Don't know. You can count them in a minute." He sounded rushed and agitated. "Could use your help now, though." He thrust some implements, including a saw, into her hands and indicated a tottering table on which rested three large pans. "Can you wash them, Beth? My orderlies are off getting supplies. Wash in the soapy water, rinse in the clear, and then scrub with chloride of lime solution."

"Of course, Pat." She began to scrub. The chemical burned her hands. This, she suspected, was the chief reason Semmelweis' theories were scorned. Later she draped Pat's table for his next patient and stayed to watch the operation. The patient, a young boy with a smooth face, was held down by an orderly while another held a chloroform cone to his face. He tossed about for a moment, and then was still. When Pat picked up his scalpel, she walked away, but she returned soon afterward, trying not to look at the boy's face. She feared that she would burst into tears.

By the time she was ready to take the laundry back to the

Shaefers', an hour had passed and she was also helping Kent, who was working a few feet away. After returning from the Shaefers', sodden from the light rain, she was able to take the pressure off the exhausted orderlies by doing many of their jobs.

Four o'clock, five o'clock, six o'clock passed, and there was no abatement. She would scrub the instruments, take them to Pat or Kent, pick up their discarded aprons, hand them fresh ones, drape the sheets, give the doctors chloride of lime for their hands. Then, when both men were set, she would either observe the operation or rush off to fill canteens for the staff. The drizzle made the area so humid that she felt as though she were standing in water. Perspiration coursed down her face, ran into her mouth. The smell of gangrene and of unwashed bodies fairly gagged her and she found a new use for the chloride of lime: soaking a handkerchief with it and then holding it to her nose. The thrashing of the patients going under chloroform would have caused an unprepared civilian to swoon on the spot if he hadn't already done so upon seeing the rivers of blood. But Beth, drawing strength from she knew not where, managed to keep standing. She watched, wincing, as Kent Wilson cursed and bellowed his way through a shoulder-high amputation, his orderlies cowering as they handed him instruments. He worked very fast, for chloroform was scarce and there were too many patients who needed it. He cut, tied, clamped, sawed, and sutured so rapidly that Beth had trouble following the movements.

The patients were brought over, sometimes quiet and brave but often crying or screaming in pain and terror. Kent's deep voice lost its harsh edge when he spoke to them.

"Try not to be afraid, soldier. You won't feel it."

Beth watched him perform several operations, incredulous at his speed and dexterity. He looked neither left nor right while he worked, but jerked his head occasionally to shake off flies that landed continually on everyone in camp like black snowflakes. He merely extended a hand for the instruments. His orderlies had obviously been trained to anticipate what he

118

would need, and when they failed to produce the correct instrument, he would roar his disapproval.

After one difficult operation he looked up at her. His eyes were bloodshot, and the dark circles under them were apparent even on the deeply tanned skin.

"Major, you must rest."

"There isn't time, Miss Shepherd."

"But you've already done more than your share. The men are fortunate, but you may become a patient in your own hospital."

"I appreciate your help, Miss Shepherd, but not the lectures. I can't leave now."

Beth hadn't liked him when she first met him, but this curt reaction to her sympathetic advice completely alienated her. She longed to put this man in his place.

He turned to an orderly. "All right. Let's clean up. And dry the sh—the table thoroughly this time, will you?"

It was really an effort for him to talk without using that unspeakable four-letter word. Should she feel flattered that he made the effort on her behalf?

"Lieutenant Carson next, sir?" asked one of the orderlies.

"No. Bring me Corporal What's-His-Name with the shattered femur."

"But Carson is in terrible pain, sir."

"I know that, Tim. Everyone is. Christ, will you just bring me the corporal? And get someone to patch this canvas, will you? Damn thing's full of holes, and I can't operate in the rain."

As the orderly hurried off, Beth said, "A noncommissioned man over an officer, major? How very democratic."

He didn't miss the sarcasm but chose to ignore it. "Miss Shepherd, I hate to disillusion you, but the corporal is the more serious case. I'm not trying to reform the class structure. I haven't the time."

"But I thought that was your objective, sir."

"No, Miss Shepherd. Horace Greeley is in New York."

"Is he? Goodness, I thought he lived on Pitcairn Island."

He sighed. "And I thought I had suffered quite enough in enduring your brother's wit."

"I should think my brother might have the same opinion of you."

He looked at her, frowning. "What seems to be troubling you?"

"I don't like your attitude, sir."

"Excuse me?"

"When I advised you to rest, you snapped at me."

"Did I? I didn't mean to. What did I say?"

"Never mind, major."

"By way of explanation, let me point out that I've been standing here for twelve hours. I can't remember what remarks I made to whom, and I am unaccustomed to the fine sensibilities of young ladies."

She was about to retort, but she decided that he did look tired and that further conversation on this subject would only exhaust him. She took one look at the frightened corporal being borne to the operating table by two orderlies and regretted that she had sparred with the major at all.

"Let's forget it, major. It's not that important." She smiled stiffly at him, almost ashamed. Here a man was about to lose a limb and she was having foolish arguments with his tired surgeon.

Kent's temper grew worse and worse. After one argument with an orderly, he threw down his instruments and roared, "All I ever wanted out of life was peace and quiet!" Beth almost laughed aloud. If anyone added to the general noise level around here, it was Kent himself with his cursing and criticizing. But he and Pat worked desperately hard and had very little sleep. She had seen one bearded surgeon in another part of the clearing weeping from exhaustion and saying, "I can't hold my hand steady any more. We'll have to get someone else." Kent might rage and Pat might mumble to himself, but both men labored on and on.

As the sun set, lanterns were lit on lines strung above the clearing, and orderlies held other lanterns for the surgeons.

Beth was numb with fatigue, almost asleep on her feet, and Kent suggested that she return to her quarters before it became too dark.

Though she had stood up well to what she had seen and was proud of herself, her apparent calm did not last long. Halfway to the Shaefers' she began to shake uncontrollably. The trembling did not cease until she had arrived at the farm and halted the horse. Then she sat motionless in the buggy and stared into the darkness, wanting to cry but unable to do so. It was all too monstrous for tears.

On her third morning at Gettysburg, she accompanied Kent and Pat on what they called "rounds." Not at all like the formal hospital rounds of which Pat had spoken during intern days, a round here was a mad dash from tent to tent to try to check on the condition of the seemingly infinite number of men the surgeons had treated in the past few days. Staffing the tents were orderlies, Sanitary and Christian Commission volunteers, and regular army nurses. The army nurses, trained by Dorothea Dix, were highly respected by Kent and Pat. Though Miss Dix's requirements were unfair—she would accept no applicants who were young or attractive, fearing that such women would marry soldiers and forget nursing— her training was excellent. Many doctors, who had heretofore scorned the work of women in the army, had to concede that they couldn't have managed without these nurses.

The first patients they saw were coming along well. Kent quickly examined one, Pat another, and then they moved on. Beth's task was to carry bandages and medical bags and to calm patients if necessary, but she also helped Kent lift bodies and held basins for Pat's patients. And all the while she tried not to think about the probable futures of some of these boys.

Thus they moved from one tent to another. Every so often Kent would rage at an orderly who had been derelict. "How did this dressing get so filthy? The man hasn't been *marching* on his leg, for Christ's sake. Henderson, have you been washing your hands? Let me see your hands." Kent examined them, his pupils constricted and the tent seemed to rise an inch from the ground as he roared, "God damn it! How many times do I have to tell you! Wash your hands. Is that clear? *Wash your goddamned hands!*"

One nurse whispered to Beth that she was certain the doctor had grown up in the Five Points, though she couldn't account for the accent. But Kent found little fault with the nurses. "At least they're *clean!*" he thundered.

In one large tent there were several who felt well enough to flirt with Beth. She was delighted to see cheerful soldiers, but Kent did not like their remarks.

"Say, doc," said one, "she's sweet. Why don't you introduce us?"

"This is a hospital, not a ballroom."

"Major," said another, "Why can't we have more nurses pretty as this one?"

"You'll have to ask Miss Dix. Let me see that arm."

Beth held the hand of one lieutenant while Kent examined a simple fracture. When the examination was over, the lieutenant said, "Don't take this lovely lady away."

Kent stared at Beth's fingers, intertwined with the lieutenant's, and said, "Let's go, Miss Shepherd."

"Aw, leave her here, doc. I need her more than you do."

"Let's *go,* Miss Shepherd."

His medical skill, she decided, was limited to surgery and diagnosis.

Many of the men were in various stages of undress, and they blushed when they saw her. But Beth scarcely noticed their embarrassment. She was, by this time, far beyond considerations of propriety. Some of these were simple, sweet boys who tried valiantly to be brave.

As she watched an orderly sponge-bathing a patient, she asked her brother, "Where do the medical people bathe?"

"Some wander over to the streams, and the rest of us take showers using buckets with holes punched in the bottom that are suspended from tree branches. Roman decadence, what?"

She laughed. "Just thank your stars that you *can* bathe."

"Yes. Though usually I'm grimy again five minutes later."

While they were making rounds, Bill rode down for a few hours and brought Sally with him. She tended the soldiers with the same love she had shown Roger. Once Beth called her over to a delirious man and asked her to be "mother." Soldiers lying nearby listened to her and cried.

Many of the patients were dying. It was important that medical people be stoic no matter how badly wounded a soldier was, but when Beth saw blind men clawing at the air or men with incurable abdominal wounds praying aloud for death, she trembled from the effort of having to present an impassive face to the other patients. It was worse for Pat. He knew these men—had drunk whisky, played cards, exchanged jokes with them—and he could not hide his anguish. After examining one comatose soldier, he fled from the tent in tears and did not return for five minutes. Kent rarely betrayed any emotion. His face remained set in its usual tense expression during one examination after another. She had no clue as to what he was feeling.

When rounds were over, there was more surgery, more sheet deliveries, and yet more surgery. By this time most of the amputations on Union men had been completed, but there were prisoners of war who had been waiting for days. Kent and Pat worked on them for most of the afternoon.

By five o'clock, the members of the staff were stuporous from heat and exhaustion. Beth and the two doctors walked over to a small table where surgeons sometimes rested. Pat stretched out on the ground and gazed dully up at the dark clouds. Beth sat down, folded her arms on the table, and rested her chin on her arms. Kent sat opposite Beth, propping his head on one elbow. They looked, she thought, like three broken wagons abandoned on a trail.

Kent said to Pat in a flat, defeated tone, "Tim tells me that Sergeant McNulty is running a fever. I don't understand it, Pat. Every precaution was taken. He couldn't have been infected by anyone else."

"He must have been, Kent."

Beth said, "Disease is so hard to understand. Is there a miasma for every disease or are some caused by body dysfunction alone?"

Pat answered, "We don't know, really. When epidemics occur it seems that miasma is the likely explanation, because weak and strong alike are affected. The doctors in Washington assume that epidemics of gangrene and septicemia are caused by miasma. So they clean and ventilate the wards."

"All well and good," Kent said. "But by some perverse illogic they fail to scrub their instruments. If the air is bad, that air is circulating over their scalpels. Wouldn't it make sense to scrub the scalpel before introducing it into a wound? If scrubbing can clean a floor of miasma, wouldn't it also clean a knife? But there are some doctors who wipe their bloody knives on their aprons and go right on to the next patient."

Beth had seen surgeons do this in the field. She had also seen them hold knives between their teeth while awaiting the next case. She said, "But Major, if there's miasma around, it will make a man sick whether you clean your instruments or not, won't it?"

"It may. But I believe there are greater concentrations of miasma on instruments that have been used on other patients. That's why chloride of lime works so well. It lowers the incidence of disease even though miasma continues to circulate." He paused, frowning. "It lowers it. But that's all. It doesn't eliminate disease."

"Perhaps a stronger chemical—" she began.

"I've tried other chemicals. They're more expensive, but they don't work any better. Damn it, I know that what we're doing works, but I don't know why. Jenner knew that people infected with cowpox didn't get smallpox, but he didn't know why. Likewise with scurvy. The English observed that scurvy was cured with fresh fruit. Why?" He turned to look down at Pat again. "That reminds me, Pat, I've discovered two cases of scurvy among the wounded. Scurvy in the summertime! I'll tell Letterman, and I hope he tells Lincoln that this army is killing its own soldiers. All they've had in their haversacks is hardtack and salt pork, despite the fact that every doctor here has had a standing request for dried fruits and desiccated vegetables."

"Don't get apoplectic, Kent. The men can't bear to eat the things anyway. They called them *desecrated* vegetables."

"Well, I can't say I blame them, but they ought to swallow the mess like medicine. We've also asked for fresh antiscorbutics and received nothing. For Christ's sake, the land this time of year is *dense* with vegetables." Kent yanked a pipe from his waistcoat pocket, pulled a pouch of tobacco from another pocket, and went through the ritual of filling his pipe.

Pat, who was still lying down, stretched his arms above his head and began caressing the grass with his fingertips. "Beth, who wrote the line 'summer's lease hath all too short a date'?"

"What?" Beth was still thinking about scurvy. "Oh—uh— Shakespeare. What does that have to do with—"

"That's right," Pat said. "It was one of the sonnets. Don't tell me. It was about a woman. I recited it to a girl once and she—" he broke off and swallowed. "What time is it, Kent?"

"Five ten. We ought to be getting back."

Pat sighed. "Hell, I can't remember which poem it was. I used to know. So many things I don't have time for any more. Poetry. Music. I wish I could hear some good music." He sighed and pulled himself to a sitting position. "No time for any of it. Damn war."

Beth frowned. The depressing nature of his work was taking its toll on Pat. She had never known him to be very much interested in the arts. He had told her once that his only passions were women and medicine.

Kent puffed his pipe and listened to Pat's lamentations. He looked across the table at Beth, but she was watching Pat— puzzling over him—and did not notice Kent's wistful expression. She heard Kent sigh and say, "I know what you mean, Pat." Then he slowly stood up and walked back to the tents. She looked at him, thinking: Even *he* misses poetry and music.

That night the doctors urged her to leave at dusk, not wanting her alone in the buggy after dark. She was almost too tired to direct the horse. It was cool and quiet on the meandering tree-lined dirt road that led to the Shaefer farm. The screaming heat did not penetrate here, and the moaning soldiers could not be heard. She gazed west toward the mountains, now silhouetted in the remaining sunlight: the South Mountain range of the Great Appalachian Chain. Gettysburg, she realized, was just a small town tucked into the foothills. She thought of those tall timbered mountains, serene against the sky, casually embracing all the states between rebel Alabama and federal Maine. How indifferent were the mountains to the passions that had swirled on the low land beyond them, as lines of men bent and wavered and wound together and broke. The battle of Gettysburg was, to these mountains, a barely discernible puff of smoke and a bit of tangled thread.

Going from the field hospitals to the Shaefer farm was like stepping into another country. Here the pace was slow and the atmosphere gentle. Three towheaded children trailed after Beth as she entered the large kitchen. They were chattering in German and laughing. The family had finished supper some time before and Mr. Shaefer had gone out to the barns. Mrs. Shaefer said gently, "You very tired. Must eat," and she went to the stove. Although Beth and the Shaefers engaged in little conversation, Mrs. Shaefer was able to convey warmth by gestures and smiles alone. Beth was very fond of her.

She was surprised to find that after a day like this she could still have an appetite. It was the instinct for self-preservation, Beth told herself philosophically, as thoughts of the hospital fell away from her and she ate an enormous meal—kept warm on the stove by Mrs. Shaefer—of ham, potatoes, salad, blueberry pie, and lemonade. Afterward she luxuriated in her bath. A bath at the Shaefers' meant filling up a round tin tub, closing the kitchen doors, and drawing the shades. An oil lamp on the table gave dim illumination. Beth relished these twenty minutes of soap, water, and solitude in a circle of amber light. But she felt guilty that the wounded in the sweltering tents could not enjoy this luxury.

That night she dreamed that she and Greg were in a forest. He was gathering wood, and she was making bacon and eggs on an open fire. He walked over to her, laughing, but she didn't know why he was laughing, because that was when ten-year-old Hilda Shaefer woke her. She groaned, dressed, gulped down the bacon and eggs she had smelled in the dream, said goodbye to the family, and ran out to the clotheslines, where fluttering white sheets brightened the dim dawn. She drove to two adjacent farms, gathered aprons and sheets at each, and headed toward the hospitals.

It was a crisp dewy morning and the sun was glimmering in the trees toward the east. She remembered the dream again and wondered what Greg had been laughing about. She halted the horses and closed her eyes tight trying to reach him across an abyss of time, place, and circumstance. The forest, the campfire—she could see these. But where was Greg? *Why* couldn't she see him? After a while she shrugged hopelessly and opened her eyes. Ahead of her lay reality: twenty thousand broken, suffering men. Sighing, she started the horse toward her fourth day in hell.

By now Beth had listened to many accounts of the battle. The walking wounded seemed to forget their woes temporarily as they described some moment of glory that would be recounted all their lives in barber shops and saloons or in elegant drawing rooms, their minds dulling the worst of the memories while preserving and embellishing the heroism.

The men relived the specific incidents in which each played his valorous part: the wheatfield slaughter, the rebel charge, the struggle at the Round Top. After a time Beth came to know where each battle had taken place, but she was still puzzled about the sequence in which fights had occurred. It was a friend of her brothers who first gave her a coherent account of the battle. He was Rick Vaccaro, an artillerist who had lost a hand in the last hour of fighting. All wounded men who could stand were pressed into service at Gettysburg, and Rick's job was to see that supplies arriving in town were delivered to the Second Corps hospitals in the amounts needed.

Beth had come to know Rick quite well and was fond of him. He reminded her of Greg: tall and quite thin with dark brown hair and eyes. Here the resemblance ended, however. Rick was patriotic with the fervor of many naturalized citizens. He was one of the few Americans in his small New York Italian community, and he was fiercely proud of this distinction. The loss of the hand—and of the opportunity to fight for the Union—had greatly upset him. When he grew too gloomy, Beth tried to cheer him by reminding him of his wife and children waiting in New York. This usually helped his state of mind, for he loved to talk about his family.

Pat had amputated his hand, and the entire left arm was in a sling to lessen the pain. Every so often Rick would touch the bandaged wrist and say, "I can still feel those fingers. I would swear they're still there."

This morning, when Beth was hauling sheets back to the German farmhouses, Rick asked if he could ride with her as far as Gettysburg.

"I am forgetting how to walk," he said, getting into the buggy. "And when I remember the forced marches that I endured, I am appalled at my laziness." He spoke with a trace of accent, but his English, which he articulated slowly, was almost self-consciously correct. "Did your brother elaborate on the details of the march from Virginia to Pennsylvania?"

"Heavens, no. We haven't had time to discuss anything but laundry."

Rick gave her a description of the events leading up to Gettysburg. Both armies had been in Virginia when Lee began moving north. But General Hooker, then in command of Union forces, had hesitated to give chase. He'd been told by officials in Washington that the army ought to stay near the

128

capital. It finally became apparent that Lee was not going to attack Washington, for he was moving swiftly toward Pennsylvania. At last the Yankees also turned north, Hooker being replaced en route by Meade. The army had to hurry, and to many soldiers the march proved worse than the subsequent battle. They fell and died along the way, overcome by sunstroke, dysentery, typhoid, or combinations of the three. And the hulking army rolled past them, a train of wagons, ambulances, cattle, weary horses dragging artillery, and miles of exhausted men, many half-asleep, marching steadily over long hours at a time amid dust so thick that it appeared white against the Union blue. On June 28 her brothers' regiment marched thirty-two miles in thirteen hours. Kent and Pat hauled the sick into ambulances whenever they found them. The giant machine, the army, would not pause no matter how many of its parts broke and were lost along the way. On June 30 a circular was issued by General Meade. Rick quoted it exactly from memory:

". . . corps and other commanders are authorized to order the instant death of any soldier who fails in his duty at this hour."

"Oh, how brutal that sounds!" Beth was shocked that a general could write such a dictum.

"The irony of it is that Meade himself failed in his duty."

"How, Rick? He won the battle, after all."

"Yes. But if he had acted decisively, he might have won the war."

"Well, we can talk about that later. Tell me, where were you and my brothers when the fighting began?"

"At Taneytown, Maryland. Thirteen miles south of Gettysburg. We received word of the rout of our advanced corps and we marched up here that night."

He went on describing the movements as he saw them from his position within the Second Corps.

Arriving at Gettysburg in the middle of the night, the corps was rushed into position along a ridge near a cemetery. Also on this ridge or near it were the remnants of the units that had fought on the first day and been driven out of Gettysburg, a badly demoralized group of men.

The two were now riding on the road east of Cemetery Ridge. As Rick spoke, Beth glanced up, trying to imagine the masses of blue-clad men who had been there—visualizing the campfires and hearing the grumbling of tired troopers, the wheeling of artillery into position. She asked Rick about Joe's activities and Pat's, for she knew that once she returned home John and Sean would assail her with questions.

While the infantry of the Second Corps organized itself on the ridge, the doctors searched the area and selected a site where the hospital tents might be erected if a battle ensued. This was usually a problem, because no one could anticipate where a battle, if indeed there was one, would occur. But this field was unique in that the Union army occupied one long ridge and the Confederate army another, which was roughly parallel to the Union ridge and a mile distant from it. Between these elevations lay a valley—an amphitheater—of wheat fields, peach orchards, and streams. It was here that the fightting would most likely occur. The Second Corps doctors finally selected an area east of the Union-held ridge for their hospitals.

On the afternoon of the second day of the battle, fierce fighting did break out in the amphitheater. Because the Third Corps could not drive the rebels back, a division of the Second Corps was sent in. Her brothers' regiment had been in that fated division, and in that regiment had been most of their friends.

She couldn't remember who had told her that moments before the division stormed into the wheatfield, the Irish Brigade—a famous unit of the corps—had knelt in a field while a priest pronounced absolution over them. It would hearten Kate to know that so many soldiers had died in a state of grace.

Beth could not fathom how, in all that confusion, generals

could hand down orders to colonels who translated and handed more specific orders down to captains who in turn translated and interpreted them for lieutenants who designated sergeants to direct the men into position—all this while the officers themselves were shooting and being shot at. In such a frenzied atmosphere, she would not be able to comprehend a one-syllable word, much less a complicated command. She would shoot aimlessly and run around in circles (if indeed she didn't drop her rifle and burrow furiously into the ground to escape the bullets).

The battle in the wheatfield demolished many regiments, including that of her brothers. So many men fell dead or wounded into one stream of water that the stream turned red from their blood.

There followed a long night rent by the sounds of screaming wounded, of rasping saws, of shouted surgeons' directions, and of men sobbing over the bodies of dead friends. But the army awoke the next day to the realization that neither Lee nor Meade was finished. And so there was another, final day of fighting, the most awesome of the three. Her brothers' regiment had been too badly battered to be sent into action, but another section of the Second Corps participated in the spectacular finale of the Battle of Gettysburg— the Confederate assault that would later be known as Pickett's Charge.

"I wish I had a pen and paper so that I might illustrate the positions of the armies," Rick said. "The Union line looked like a fishhook and the Confederate line like a bigger fishhook, but broken at the—oh, never mind. Let us straighten those lines out for the sake of simplicity. We have two solid parallel lines running north and south and separated by a valley. One line is manned by devils; the other, of course, by saints."

She smiled. "I understand, Saint Vaccaro."

"Let us go back to the second day for a moment. Both armies are facing each other across the valley. Then Lee

131

attacks the south end of our line with the south end of his line. This results in the battles of the peach orchard, the Round Top, and of course the wheatfield. Lee also attacks the north end of our line with the north end of his. This is the battle on Culp's Hill. In both cases Lee fails to make any headway and the day ends stalemated on both ends of the line."

She nodded. "I see, yes."

"On the third day Lee makes a fatal decision. He will take the men at the center of his line and march them straight across the valley to attack the center of our line which means, of course, the Second Corps. His idea is to form an assault column and break our line in two in a classic divide-and-conquer maneuver. It is a dangerous move, because we can shoot that advancing column obliquely from almost any point in our line. Dangerous also because we can see them from our higher elevation, spot the mounted officers, and aim at them. Lee is aware of these dangers, of course. Therefore he decides to pulverize our infantry with cannon fire before sending his men across the valley. In addition, he will order most of his officers to walk, so that the Yanks cannot distinguish them from the rest."

"How do you know what Lee was thinking? One would almost think he sent you a message."

Rick smiled. "What he was thinking is obvious from what he subsequently did. Few of us guessed he would try that maneuver. But someone—Meade, Hancock, or Gibbon—must have considered the possibility, because our battery was moved up from its position in your brother's division and placed in Gibbon's division." He paused. "I recall wondering about that for a while, but I really expected the fighting to be concentrated at the ends of our lines, not in the center. I remember how calm we were that day, believing ourselves to be relatively safe. The sun was high in the sky and we lolled around. I was writing a letter to my wife, others were whittling. One man was napping. Little did we realize that our crest was being selected through Lee's field glasses as the target of a charge.

132

"At about one P.M.," Rick continued, "the Confederates opened a shattering cannonade, firing what sounded like all of their artillery simultaneously. Everyone scrambled for cover. Everyone, that is, but our artillerists, who could not very well man cannon while lying prone." The counterfire of the Union was not as rapid as the fire of the Confederacy, since the men had been told to save ammunition. But the noise was still fearsome—so steady and deafening that Rick could not distinguish the report of his own Napoleon. It went on for almost two hours, driving everyone insane, especially the doctors trying to operate back at the hospitals. All the while, the Second Corps infantry lay flat behind their breastworks, sweating profusely in the eighty-seven-degree heat, clapping their hands over their ears, and praying for deliverance. The rebels, however, were firing too high, so that most of the infantry they thought they were killing was spared. General Hancock, the dashing commander of the Second Corps, rode back and forth in front of the men, oblivious to the cannon balls and canister sailing over his head. But behind the infantry, where the shells were landing, horses were blown apart, ambulances shattered, and gashes opened up in the earth. Artillery batteries behind the infantry also suffered. Ammunition chests exploded and men manning the cannon nearby were killed instantly. Two of Rick's artillerymen were wounded by fragments and taken to the rear, and Rick himself narrowly escaped being shelled. Infantrymen were pressed into service to help him. They did their best, though their lack of experience sorely tried Rick's patience. And the artillery duel continued.

At the first indication that rebel fire was slackening, the Union artillery commander ordered his men to cease firing. He was anxious to save ammunition for the infantry assault that he knew would follow the barrage. Finally, around two forty-five, the rebel guns also became silent. There was an ominous hush on the field. Rick and his men quickly cleaned the worn-out Napoleon, then loaded the gun with canister. The smoke was beginning to clear now, and they

133

squinted, trying to see the mile-distant Confederate ridge.

Rick waited. Other artillerists waited. The infantry waited. Hancock waited.

It happened shortly after 3:00 P.M., at first a barely discernible movement in the trees. Then, suddenly, an army: rank upon rank of infantry, lines beautifully dressed as though on parade, moving fearlessly into the amphitheater. After a few minutes, more infantry came over a rise on the left. All marched confidently toward the Union-held ridge, thousands upon thousands of them. The Second Corps—every corps that could see them—drew in its collective breath.

Rick stood as if hypnotized. Here were Confederate soldiers marching in precision—out in the open with no protection at all, trampling over fences, plowing through cornfields and wheatfields. All this they did while giving the impression that they were gliding effortlessly, irresistibly, across the field. They seemed almost tranquil until they reached the middle of the valley and converged for the assault. Then suddenly they were ferocious.

"We were told to wait until they were close before we started the guns. Just as they crossed the Emmitsburg Road we were given the order: 'Number one—fire! Number two—fire!' And soon every cannon in every battery had opened upon the rebels. The infantry was firing too. We were watching them topple like trees in a tornado. It was a triumphant feeling and yet it was terrible. Meanwhile a few rebs were running forward, picking off our men. Hancock was wounded; other officers were killed." He paused, shuddering. "I heard the rebel yell then. Do you know what it sounds like?"

"I know it's shrill and frightening."

"It is that!" He imitated the sound: "Eeeee-ah-hoo! eeeee-ah-hoo! Their yells are as deadly as their rifle fire. They began coming over the low stone wall firing and wielding their bayonets. I stood not ten feet away, still ramming the Napoleon, when the rebs came shrieking into our line." He paused, looking at his bandaged wrist. "That was when they

134

hit me, Beth. They could hardly have missed. I slumped, grasping my hand—it was utterly mangled—and the two infantrymen who had been assisting me fell at my feet. The rebs grabbed the gun. I couldn't stop them. Some infantrymen came running foward to recapture the gun and they knocked me down on the wrecked hand. I must have lost consciousness from the pain, because when I looked up, the gun had been recaptured by our men.

"After a while I managed to pull myself up to a sitting position and I watched the most desperate fighting imaginable. Rebs and Yanks were tangled among each other, some shooting at point-blank range, some fighting hand-to-hand. Bullets grazed me and men tripped on me. All the while I tried to bind my left hand with a handkerchief, using my right hand and my teeth. I do not know how much time passed. The pain was acute and I was feeling faint. I sat there choking in the smoke, listening to the bullets whining and the men groaning. It seemed that all I could see in the smoke were the flashes of fire from the rifles. That was a glimpse of hell if ever I saw one." He leaned back and sighed. "Later—it seemed like years later, but it must have been only a few minutes—I could hear men shouting, 'We whipped 'em!' At that point I did not know who had whipped whom. Then an officer spurred his horse, tossed his hat in the air, and cried, 'The Union is saved!' Up and down our lines I heard men shout, 'Hurrah!' God, I shall never forget it."

Beth had been listening so intently that her buggy had slowed to a crawl. Now she halted the horse and turned around. Several yards behind her lay the east slope of that section of the ridge where the rebels had finally been stopped. Rick told her what the site looked like: a heap of muskets, scabbards, caps, canteens, haversacks, destroyed supply wagons, shattered ambulances, fallen tree branches, wrecked caissons, and Napoleons, all piled on a bed of bullets, cannon balls, and grapeshot.

But there, amid the groans of dying men, had risen the first

135

authentic victory cry of the Army of the Potomac. There had been many premature victory cries, but this one had been justified, for on that patch of gutted ground a luckless army had finally won a battle.

She looked over at Rick and said, "Oh, it must have been a glorious feeling hearing our men cheer in victory."

He nodded. "But as it happened, I was not among my own men when the cheers resounded. I came out of my stupor to find myself within a group of wounded rebel prisoners. I do not know what I was doing there with Yankee guns trained on me, but that area was in such crazed confusion that I was lucky a Yank had not shot me. A guard, seeing that I was a Union man, advised me to walk back to the hospital. If I waited for the litter-bearers, he said, I might wait all night. But quite frankly I was afraid to go. I knew they would have to take off my hand and I did not want to lose it." He looked away and swallowed. "So I leaned against a tree talking with a wounded reb. He told me how things had looked from the other side of the wall."

Rick then told of a Virginia lieutenant who had walked straight into the line of Union guns. He had started off with some bravado, masking his fear as best he could, caught up in a spirit that lifted him out of the flesh-and-blood world and into a place where the only reality was that of movement. Forward and forward he had gone, closer and closer to the deadly ridge where the Yankees were massed, and then a minie ball through the arm brought him back to an awareness of other realities. He fell forward, his comrades fell around him, dropped on top of him, splattered blood over him—and still the men from behind came on, stumbling over the wounded, surging ahead like a wave that had been doomed from the start to break into bloody foam but rolled on out of inertia.

Rick said, "He was near the wall when he was hit, so he was taken prisoner and moved up to the ridge with the rest of them. That was when I met him." Rick paused. "Soldiers have

136

more in common with one another than they do with civilians of either side. He was my enemy—my *enemy*, Beth—and a man I might have killed. Yet we sat there—both of us family men, both of us soldiers and—and cripples. We sat there and talked together as though we had known one another from childhood. Probably I shall forget most of the people I meet in my lifetime, but I'll never forget him. Odd, is it not?"

"Yes. It makes one wonder what sort of game men have invented."

"Excuse me?"

"Nothing. How long did you sit with the prisoners?"

"Until my hand felt so bad that I was forced to go to the hospital. About half an hour. There was one johnny who said to a guard, 'Yank, if we'd known you was so good we never would've tried to come over.' The guard was very modest. He just shrugged his shoulders and looked uncomfortable. Then he said, 'I never seen such a brave thing as you johnnies tried there. Even if it *was* crazy.' And he opened his haversack and gave the rebel some hardtack."

"He shared his rations with a prisoner?"

Rick nodded. "He gave him a drink from his canteen, too. There is a good deal of chivalry in both armies."

Beth shook her head, finding the entire story of Pickett's charge very puzzling. What was the meaning of it? Did it have anything to do with a cause? Or was the charge an exercise in daring? Yes, that was what it had been. And the Yankees saluted the suicidal action, the risking of lives, the flirting with odds, sharing their rations with men they had tried to kill a few minutes earlier. Was the charge another form of the rite of manhood practiced by ancient tribes and doomed to be repeated over and over again, until men succeeded in eliminating their species?

True, they had been driven: by generals, by politicians, and ultimately by the people who had selected these leaders. But basically they had driven themselves, these seekers of glory who had not believed that men could shrink from violence

137

and still remain men. She remembered the lines of Shake-speare that she had memorized in school about each man in his life playing many parts.

> . . . Then a soldier
> Full of strange oaths and bearded like the pard
> Jealous in honor, sudden and quick in quarrel
> Seeking the bubble reputation
> Even in the cannon's mouth . . .

Was soldiering the inescapable "part" that Shakespeare had thought it to be? If so, there was no point in justifying war at all. It would appear from time to time as surely as the rain and snow. And the urge to make war would eventually arise in all men, along with their deep voices and facial hair.

Unless people deliberately wrote war out of mankind's script—and they would all have to do it simultaneously or die—there would never be an end to it. Never.

She turned back to Rick, who was now fumbling for a cigar. He put the cigar in his mouth and tried to manage the lucifer match with one hand. When she reached over to take the match, he said, "No, I can do it. I have *got* to start learning to use one hand."

They started up the Baltimore Pike. Once she turned to see Rick looking back at the ridge. His eyes were wide and flashing anger.

"What is it, Rick? What's wrong?"

"If only we had counterattacked! If we had hit back after that last charge we would have whipped the whole rebel army right here. But what did we do? We sat there. We all but waved goodbye and wished them Godspeed. That damned fool Meade! That stupid son of— Now Lincoln will replace him as he replaced McDowell, McClellan, Pope, Burnside, and Hooker."

"But why? He won the battle, Rick. And the only reason he didn't counterattack was that our men needed rest. You can't fault a man for showing consideration for his men."

138

"Consideration! Rest! I do not think that rest was the good general's concern. Would you not agree that after the march I have described, the threatening note, and the battle itself— would you not agree that consideration for his fellow man was not a factor in such a cowardly decision?"

She sighed. "I don't know. I really don't."

"The reason he hesitated was that he overestimated their strength. He was afraid, by God! The soldiers were brave, but that fool—"

"And what of the doctors?" she interrupted. "Perhaps he stayed in Gettysburg so that the wounded might have doctors for a day or two. If you ask me, the army left too soon as it was. Pat said—"

"Yes, I know. But the army would never have had to leave if they had counterattacked right away. Lee would have surrendered at Gettysburg, and the doctors—reb *and* Yank— would have been here. But we delayed. And because of that the war will last another year."

"Another year? What do you mean? We routed them. They're very weak."

"They will recover. We have given them ample time to escape to Virginia. A few months, and they will be cocky as ever. After all, they are defending their own soil. And their leaders are good fighters. The Confederacy has not had to replace Lee, but we—" he broke off. "What is the use? The rebs made one wrong move. One error that might have finished them. Their Achilles heel was in full view, and *we* did not shoot it."

"Do you think they'll win, Rick?"

"Ultimately? No. Their supplies and manpower will eventually be depleted. No, we will win. But I hate to contemplate the cost."

They were now approaching Gettysburg. Because she had to go in one direction and he in another to the supply depot, she asked him if he wanted her to drive him to his destination.

"No. It is time I exercised these legs. I'll see you later."

As she drove away, she turned and watched him walk off. He looked dispirited as he trudged, his head down, along the cluttered wooden sidewalk: His service was over. She hoped his depression wouldn't last long. Rick was more American than Lincoln himself, but to family and friends in his small Italian community, he would be the Italian boy who had been wounded in defense of freedom. Immigrant groups, forced repeatedly to justify their existence, were very proud when one of their own came home a hero; and whatever Rick's disappointment about not seeing the war through to its end, the praise he would receive back home would help to make up for it.

At a tent hospital later that day she held water to the lips of a recent immigrant—a Russian who had been hired by the United States for three hundred dollars and the promise of 160 acres in the West when the war was over. Many European refugees from poverty were able to get their start in the new land this way. Too many of them died, though, and when they did the dreams of their families waiting in Europe for the great day were dashed.

Alex was a big burly private. He was not the ordinary mercenary, for he had told Beth in broken English the day before that he had come to America because America was just. He had liked that word—*just*—and he had repeated it many times while Pat examined his wound and Beth held his hand. Pat had ferreted out the bullet that had pierced his side, but soldiers hit anywhere but in the extremities stood little chance of survival. Infection claimed most of them, and it now seemed clear that Alex was to be no exception. He was mumbling in delirium now—strange words that sounded profound and mysterious. Then he began to sing softly. Kent, who had been examining a patient nearby, walked over to look at him.

"Do you know what he's singing?" Beth asked.

"The first song sounded like a Russian Orthodox hymn. The one he's singing now is 'God Save the Czar.' "

"Do you understand Russian?"

"No, but we pick up phrases from many languages, especially if the regiment comes from New York or any of the big ports. Alex is in our regiment."

"But yours isn't a foreign regiment." Some Union regiments were composed entirely of foreign troops.

"Nevertheless, Miss Shepherd, we have French, Croatians, Germans—let me see—Italians, Polish Jews, some Spanish—only one or two of each, but enough to give the regiment an international flavor. The Irish predominate, and Anglo-Saxons make up the balance."

She looked down at the delirious man. "It's a pity he has to die so far from home."

"Many of these men do." He felt the man's forehead, took his pulse, then listened to the feeble singing. "Alex used to sing sad Russian ballads at the campfire. He had a splendid voice. One night I found so many men weeping that I thought we'd lost the war. I asked an orderly to hasten to the scene at once and teach Alex to sing something livelier, like 'Oh Susannah.' After that, morale improved. That melancholy Slavic voice applied to the lyrics of 'Oh Susannah' was in itself enough to make them laugh." He paused. "Alex will be missed."

Suddenly she burst into tears. "Why does he have to die? He sounds like such a good man. All these soldiers are so young and—why do they have to die?" She had denied her feelings for too long and had built up a heavy reserve of tears.

"Miss Shepherd, I think it would be best if you left the tent," he whispered, fumbling in his pocket for a handkerchief. "Come, Miss Shepherd."

She took the handkerchief he thrust into her hand and followed him out of the tent past three other wounded patients. When they were outside he said, "I believe you are too sheltered a young woman to cope with all this, Miss Shepherd. I think—"

"I can cope." She wiped her eyes, took deep breaths, and tried to assume an air of dignity.

"Perhaps so." He mopped his brow. "But I wonder what it will do to you."

From another tent, a nurse called to him, "Doctor, come quickly!" and she didn't have a chance to ask him what he meant, for he was off at a run to the next emergency.

She walked on, still crying, thinking of the Orthodox Church, of sad Russian songs that would never be sung by this man again, and of a family waiting somewhere in Moscow or St. Petersburg or perhaps a farm in the Urals—waiting for a man who had learned "Oh Susannah" and dreamed of a land in the West and who, in the end, became confused and thought he was fighting for the czar. It didn't matter that the man in charge was Lincoln and not the czar. Soldiers the world over were taught to fight for abstractions. The leaders were interchangeable. If only he could have lived to see the West—a land where his enemy would be the tangible elements of nature, where his small achievements would have counted for something. But here was Alex, alone and obscure, dying in a bloody hospital tent in Pennsylvania. Some day someone might say, "Yep, a handful of furriners fought for the Union too." That would be all.

That afternoon, walking through a woody area toward her buggy with a bag full of bloody sheets, she came across Kent. He was sitting on the ground leaning against a tree, his forage hat pulled forward and his eyes closed, rubbing the left side of his head with his hand. His shirt was open at the neck and he was perspiring heavily. The orderly who was helping her with the sheets said that he thought the major should go back to his tent but that he was reluctant to suggest it.

"I know what you mean," Beth said. "He thinks he's superhuman."

Tim laughed. "Thought the same thing myself, miss."

Kent's eyes opened as the voices approached. He hadn't heard what they were saying. "Hello, Miss Shepherd. Tim."

"Hello, major," Beth said. "You look ill, sir." She thought

that he might make another terse comment, but he looked at her blankly.

"Major?"

"Yes. I'll be all right." He closed his eyes against the sun.

Tim said, "Why don't you let me help you back to your tent, sir?"

"I just want to rest a moment."

Tim shrugged. "Hope you feel better, sir."

Kent nodded.

As he walked away with Beth, Tim said, "He gets terrible headaches sometimes. They make him so sick that he can't move."

"Good heavens! How can he operate?"

"He never has them while he's operating. And if he's already got one, he won't—no, he can't—operate."

"Does he have them often?"

"Sometimes once a week and sometimes not for months. He told me he sees spots in front of his eyes and then the headache hits him hard, like a bullet or something."

"Is that what's wrong with him now?"

"Sure looks like it."

"Tim, I just can't leave him there. I'll get someone to put him to bed. Can you take the sheets out to the cart yourself?"

"Sure, Miss Shepherd, but I don't think he'll go." He held out his hands while she piled her sheets on top of his.

"Why won't he go? Are there others sharing his tent?"

Tim laughed. "The chief has his own tent. No, he's just stubborn is all."

She walked back toward the trees. Tim had proved mistaken, for Kent was struggling across the field holding his head steady with one hand as though it were a fragile vase. A moment later he leaned over and was sick. She rushed over to hold his head. Presently Kent stood up straight. He mumbled his thanks and turned away, embarrassed, wiping his face with a handkerchief.

"Are you going to rest, major?"

"I'm afraid I'll have to." He nodded to her, said, "Thank

you," again, and staggered toward his tent. She was about to return to her cart when she decided that she ought to ask him if he needed anything. She walked toward the long row of tents that reminded her of troops standing at attention and tried to remember which one he had entered. It was either the fifth or sixth from the left. She peered into the fifth tent. No one was there. Then she looked into the sixth. Kent was lying on a cot that didn't have a sheet and breathing in painful gasps. He had discarded his drenched army blouse, and the sight of his bare chest brought a blush to her cheeks.

"Major?" she called in to him.

He turned heavy-lidded eyes upon her. "Yes, Miss Shepherd?"

She entered the tent. "Will you need any medication?"

"No, thank you. There's no treatment for this kind of headache. Some take opium, but opium is addictive, and these things afflict me regularly."

"What sort of headache is it? Tim says you see spots. Can you see them now?"

"No. They appear and then they vanish. At that point the headache commences. It's called a migraine."

"Oh, I see." Her eyes rested briefly on his tapering chest and muscular arms. She thought of Greg. "Shall I get Pat?" she asked, in part to distract herself from the memory of a hotel room.

"No. He's busy."

"Very well, then." She turned to leave.

"Perhaps you could dampen a towel for me?"

"Of course." She found a towel on a small table amid a mess of hastily scribbled notes in Latin, a razor, a crusty food tin, and a can of pipe tobacco. For a fastidious surgeon he was certainly careless about his personal effects. There was a tin basin of water under the table. She drenched the towel, squeezed it, and laid it on his forehead.

"Thank you," he said. Then he gasped and held her arm in a fierce grip. Quickly he let it go. "I'm sorry. Did I hurt you?"

144

He had, but she shook her head. "You must be in terrible pain. How long will this last?"

"A few hours."

"I'm awfully sorry."

"I appreciate your help." He looked at her with an expression she couldn't read.

"Well, if there's nothing more you need, I'll be leaving."

He continued to look at her, his expression inscrutable, and she left the tent with a slight, awkward wave of her hand. She had just stepped outside when she saw her brother walking toward her. She waited for him, stepping to the side of the tent.

"Tim told me you decided to be Kent's Clara Barton."

"The man is very sick, Pat."

"A migraine. He has them frequently." Pat ducked into the tent. Beth remained outside, wondering how he would handle the problem.

"What happened?" Pat asked Kent.

"I have a headache."

"Damn it, I can *see* that. What caused it?"

There was a long silence. Then Kent said, "Colin died."

"Oh, no." Another long pause.

"It was my fault," said Kent.

"Bullshit. You can't expect every patient to survive amputations."

"I'll be up in a few hours. Will you handle things?"

"Of course. But that's not the problem. You're going to kill yourself if you keep on this way. Men die, Kent. You're not God. Or hadn't you realized that?"

"I don't appreciate the goddamned sarcasm."

"All right. I'll leave you alone. Do you need anything?"

"No. Go back to work, and for Christ's sake don't worry about me."

Beth was amazed at the way they talked to each other, but even more astounded at the reasons for Kent's illness. As she and Pat walked along, she asked him who Colin was.

145

"A stretcher-bearer. Wounded in the wheatfield. A very courageous boy of about eighteen. He and another boy who died were pulling the wounded out of that place long after everyone else had said it was impossible to get to them." Pat took out a handkerchief and wiped his eyes. "But in camp Colin was a comedian. God knows, medical corpsmen need to laugh once in a while or they'd go insane. He used to do an imitation of Kent that was hilarious. And Kent laughed the loudest of everyone. Well, anyway, he was wounded and Kent amputated his leg. The boy developed septicemia. Every so often that will happen, no matter how careful we are. And Kent knows it, but—"

"He blames himself for Colin's death."

"Yes."

"Does he get this sick every time these tragedies happen?"

"No. Only if he's grieving for the soldier or if he feels he's somehow responsible for the death. In this case I'd say both reasons. He was very close to the boy." He paused. "I've never known Kent to cry, Beth, but I suspect that his headaches are tears in another guise. The things that would ordinarily make us cry—sorrow, despair—give him searing headaches. He has them after battles—when an emergency is over and he has time to think."

"But not during?"

"During an emergency he's very capable. After the battle in the wheatfield a number of wounded men from our regiment were brought over to us at the same time. He didn't seem to react at all, Beth, and the rest of us were hysterical. They were lined up under the trees—so many friends—and we had to select the ones we thought could be saved."

"How awful."

"All of us were crying: doctors, orderlies, ambulance-drivers. And Kent stood there, impossibly stoical, the Rock of Gibraltar, telling us to please try to control ourselves and work fast."

"Didn't he have wounded friends?"

"Yes. A very good one died when Kent was examining him.

But Kent kept on, and he's been going ever since. Today I guess the whole thing hit him."

Pat stopped to speak briefly with another surgeon who had a wrinkled face and a long gray beard. He could scarcely drag himself back to the hospital.

Beth said to Pat as they walked on, "He looks so tired! That poor old man."

"Bob's not old. Fifty maybe."

"Fifty? He seems so much older."

"Well, he works himself to death." He paused. "What was I saying? Oh yes. I'm concerned about Kent because his kind of migraine is excruciating. I was with him once when he had a wisdom tooth pulled and he scarcely groaned. But with migraine he's threatened to cut his head off."

"My God!"

"The war's done it, Beth. A person's senses can be assaulted just so many times and then—well, we've all got problems. When given the opportunity, I will get falling-down drunk. Colin used to talk to himself for hours on end. Kent goes flat on his back with migraine."

"What jolly lives you people lead."

He laughed. "You're really out of your element here, aren't you, sis? Sick patients, sick doctors—"

"I must say I have had more enjoyable experiences in my lifetime."

He gave her a brotherly hug and lifted her into her cart.

The next day at lunch, Kent looked much better. He smiled at her sheepishly, avoiding her eyes. "Thank you for your help, Miss Shepherd."

"Not at all." She wanted to offer her sympathy but knew instinctively that he would not wish to be reminded of the incident. She turned away abruptly and spoke to another doctor from the brigade. Beth was one of the few women who ate at the surgeons' mess, a long table set up under the trees. Pat had asked the brigade medical director to extend her this privilege because she was his sister and knew none of the

Sanitary Commission nurses well. The director had agreed—partly, Pat guessed, because Beth was pleasant to look at over the stew, hardtack, and coffee.

Captain Marshall, a charming and gallant doctor, was at the top of his form today. His lavish compliments made Beth blush and he laughed at her remarks, declaring her the wittiest lady he had ever known. At the end of the table, Pat looked disgruntled. Apparently he knew things about the man of which he did not approve. Beth's brothers rarely approved of her beaux, and Pat was the worst of them all with his constant traipsing in and out of the parlor at home whenever she had a caller. How did they expect her ever to marry if none of her beaux could pass preliminary inspection? Across the table, Kent glared at Marshall and raised his eyebrows at Beth. Had she now yet another "brother" to contend with? To annoy them both, she laughed all the harder at the doctor's witticisms and batted her eyelashes a few times—an art she had never perfected and privately found ridiculous but which seemed to delight men. At this point Pat decided to join the conversation, turning it deftly to medicine. He discussed cauterization in such detail that she was unable to finish her stew. Presently he suggested that it was time to leave, declaring in pious tones that the wounded couldn't wait. Beth did not speak to him on the walk over to the hospital.

Since the migraine incident of the day before, Kent had become an object of some curiosity. She studied him that afternoon while he worked, wondering what sort of man he was. In appearance he was rather like photographic negatives Bill had shown her. The hair and eyebrows were very light and the skin deeply tanned from so many days of operating outdoors. He was attractive in his own way, but there was little of the gentleman about him. His wiry body and thin, weathered, tense face gave him the aspect of a hungry fighter. It was obvious from his accent, use of language (when he

148

wasn't swearing), and certain mannerisms that he had been raised to be a gentleman. But he seemed to delight in eschewing good manners, and he had about as much charm as a machine. His only redeeming quality, as far as she could see, was a devotion to medicine. And even then she wasn't certain whether his concern was for the patient or for proving his various theories.

She might have dismissed him as a thoroughly inhuman creature were it not for the reaction he had had to his stretcher-bearer's death. And in those moments when his face was in repose, she was surprised to discover that he looked almost sensitive. The heavy, sloping eyebrows shadowed dark gray-blue eyes that seemed kind and a little sad. Kent's face, however, was seldom in repose. When he was operating his brows were knit in concentration, and when he wasn't operating he was almost always frowning, his eyes stormy.

Watching him intently as he completed an operation, Beth wondered what thoughts went through his head. When he looked up, impatiently waiting for Tim to hand him a wad of lint, he found her staring at him wide-eyed, her lips slightly parted. He took the lint and gritted his teeth, glaring not at the slow-moving Tim but at Beth. A few minutes later, when the patient was being carried away on a litter, he turned to her and said irritably, "Miss Shepherd, I'd like a word with you." He gestured for Tim to leave and then turned to her abruptly and said, "You musn't look at me that way, Miss Shepherd."

"What way?"

"You know what way," he snapped. "I don't like to be teased, especially when I'm trying to operate."

"No, major." Her voice rose to a shrill pitch. "I *don't* know what way. And furthermore, I think you're a nasty, hateful man who finds no greater sport in life than putting people in their place. Why don't you go to hell, major!" She had never used such language in her life, but if any man deserved it this one did.

"Now listen, Miss Shepherd, it's obvious you dislike me, and since that is the case I don't appreciate your provocative behavior, especially as you have made it abundantly clear that you have no intention of fulfilling the promise."

"What on earth are you talking about?"

"Come now, Miss Shepherd. When a woman looks that way at a man—" he stopped and studied her angry face. "Is it possible that you *aren't* aware?"

She didn't answer.

His voice softened. "Miss Shepherd, you must be very careful when you are in the company of men. I noticed your behavior with Marshall today. Not all men are gentlemen, Miss Shepherd, and if you continue to tease them in this manner, sooner or later one of them will misconstrue your motives and you will find yourself in difficult straits."

"Much as I treasure your advice," she mocked, "I do have a father plus three brothers to preach at me and I really don't need a fourth, major."

He sighed. "I'm much too busy to stand here arguing with you. Do as you please, but I'd rather you stayed out of trouble. You *are* Pat's sister."

"And I'll thank you—"

"To tend to my own affairs? Very well." He kicked at a clump of grass, clenching and unclenching his fists. She turned to leave. He said, "Unpleasantries aside, Miss Shepherd, I need your help regarding a medical matter. I'd like to discuss it with you in about an hour when I have more time. It's important."

Beth paused. "A medical matter."

"You'll help me?" he persisted.

"Yes. But only for Patrick's sake. And for the soldiers." She glared at him. "I'll be back in an hour, major. That will give me time to don my nun's habit."

As she walked swiftly across the field to her cart, her heart pounded in fury. She had never once flirted with him! Who in her right mind would flirt with the likes of that? All she had done was study him for the strange creature he was, attempting to judge him fairly, and he had placed a sexual interpretation on the whole affair. What did he think she was about? Did he think she had maliciously set out to drive him mad with desire so that she could then step on him, grind him into the ground, and walk off chuckling? For all the trials women had to face—running homes; bearing children; nursing the sick, the old, and the helpless; denying their intelligence in order to sustain the pride of their masters—were they seen by men as cruel, grasping fiends who seduced men, beat them down, and transformed them into helpless slaves? *Really!*

She stormed through the woody area, visualizing a large assembly of accusing beaux, and she nearly collided with an object that suddenly bounced into her path. Looking up angrily, she saw Pat, who grasped her hand.

"You look as though you plan to murder someone," he said with a teasing smile.

Her eyes blazed. "I'd like to." She repeated the conversation she had had with Kent.

"He's so obnoxious. If it weren't for the soldiers, I'd never lift a finger to help him."

"I think he's very fond of you."

"Like hell he is!"

"Beth, your language is beginning to sound like ours."

"Oh? Am I now to endure another lecture?"

"Sis, calm down. You're tired. We all are."

"Don't change the subject. You all think of me as some sort of tart. And all I've done is haul sheets and help everyone. Like a charwoman. And you—"

"It's just that you're too attractive to be swishing around here among the troops. It sets them on edge."

"Well, that, dear brother, is just too bad. If they can't keep their feelings under control, the problem is theirs, not mine."

"Kent knows that."

"He does not."

"Yes, he does. He likes you very much, but he knows you don't like him and he's angry about it, so he makes inappropriate remarks. He must be feeling awfully ashamed of himself by now."

"I doubt that." She sniffed, folding her arms in front of her and lifting an eyebrow in her favorite schoolmarm pose.

"I will, however, straighten him out on the subject of proper conduct with my sister."

"What will you say?"

"Quite a bit. Don't look alarmed. To his face I've called him a—well—let's just call it a choice epithet."

"And he stands for it?"

"Not always. Sometimes he asserts his rank and we don't talk for a while. Usually, though, we're straightforward with each other."

"Let him apologize on his own, Pat."

"I'll give him twenty-four hours."

"Then what?"

"Then he will hear a lecture on manners."

"Pat, you know he won't listen. Save your breath."

"He's done the same to me, honey. We take criticisms from each other that we wouldn't take from the surgeon general."

"In a way you're as close to him as you are to Joe and Sean, aren't you."

Pat nodded. "He's a little crazy, but he's a good man."

"Well if he's good to you, that's something in his favor."

She reported to Kent as promised, an hour after their encounter. He was in the middle of an operation, so she stood well away from him and tried not to look at him at all. When he was finished, he came over to her with a nervous smile. In her most silken tones, Beth asked, "Now what was that favor you needed, major?"

He cleared his throat. "Yes. Pat tells me you have a fine hand."

"It's fair. Why?"

"Mine is lousy, as is that of every damn orderly in the place, and the clerical people don't have a man to spare."

"And?"

"I'd like to dictate five case histories to you and have you deliver both the papers and the men to whom they refer to Dr. Clark in New York."

152

"You want me to go home to New York?"

"Yes. There will be other nurses somewhere on the train to chaperone, and an orderly to help care for our men. Your task would be to see that the patients remained clean, fed, and comfortable until they reach the hospital."

"Did Pat plan this as a way of getting me home?"

"No. But you do look tired. And you're irritable as well."

"Ah, but look who I have for a model."

"Touché. My remarks were out of order, and I apologize. Will you be free tonight to take down the histories? And tomorrow night if need be? I intend to go into some detail."

She was amazed at the way he had disposed of his apology in one sentence. He was certainly lavish with his criticism and stingy with his regrets. But the idea of going home appealed to her. She was exhausted.

"Could you arrange for someone to take a message to my cousins?"

"Of course. Will you need any supplies? Clothes and such? I can send a wagon."

"Major, I don't think I could handle five men and luggage too. I'll ask Bill to ship my trunk later if I decide to stay in New York, and I have two carpetbags down here with essential supplies in them."

"Fine. I'll have a man ride up with a message. And I'll arrange for you to spend the night in one of the nurses' quarters. The German houses are too far from town and we may finish quite late. Oh, I'd like you to arrange for one of those people to take over the laundry pickups. Their work has been excellent."

"I'll see if one of the men can help."

"Splendid. I can't tell you how much I appreciate this, Miss Shepherd."

My, but he was being gracious. "I was planning to go home anyway when Lee and his men arrived unexpectedly," she said airily.

He smiled. "Then it's not an imposition?"

"Not at all, major. I could use a long rest at home."

"I notice you've lost a great deal of weight in the short time you've been here. Another pound and you'll take sick." He surveyed her thoroughly. For a moment she wanted to stare back in the same way. It would serve him right. But she dreaded another lecture. He turned to Tim. "Try to find a messenger for Miss Shepherd. Oh, and fetch her some of my stationery and a pen." Then he said to Beth, "Give my best to your cousins, will you?"

Major Wilson was so thoughtful all of a sudden.

The writing-up of the case histories was to take place in the dining room of a farmhouse. Early that evening she walked with Kent across a field and through a patch of woods where branches and stones impeded her progress. Although she wasn't wearing hoops, it was difficult walking.

"Watch your step, Miss Shepherd. I shouldn't have brought you this way. There's a longer way that's easier to navigate."

Not a minute later she tripped over a stone, lost her balance, and went sprawling in a tangle of skirts. Kent had been too far away to catch her. He hurried to help her up, lifting her under the shoulders.

"Are you hurt?"

"No. Just shaken."

He pulled her erect and continued to hold her, looking intently into her eyes. She had not had that much experience, but she knew the look. It meant he wanted to kiss her. Almost against her will, she disengaged her arms and turned away from him. His expression had aroused her unexpectedly, but after this morning's harangue it would never do to permit him to kiss her. As they maneuvered this part of the woods, she did allow him to take her hand in his, and she noticed that it trembled slightly. She had to credit him with self-control here in this deserted wood where he could have kissed her or done anything else, for that matter. And her appearance today invited such behavior. She was quite disheveled now, the

154

hairpins slipping and her hair blowing about her face. Even before the fall, she had had a somewhat wanton look. Her thin calico dress clung from perspiration in all the wrong places and she was only wearing one petticoat. It couldn't be helped, especially here in Gettysburg where it was beastly hot and the work never stopped. But to him she must look like a tart, and it was probably only out of consideration for Pat that he kept his hands off her.

Why was she apologizing to herself? He was just as disheveled with what looked like a two days' growth of beard and his hair longish and unkempt. But with men, it made no difference.

As they reached the clearing, she quickly disengaged her hand. He looked awkward, but he said nothing. At one point she found him staring fixedly at her breasts as he had done the day she met him. He caught her eye, reddened slightly, and hastily looked away. They didn't speak for the remainder of the walk, and in the silence she could almost read his mind. He was thinking of how it would feel to lie with her. For a moment she wondered the same thing about him, then forced the picture out of her mind.

In the farmhouse Kent spread notes, written on scraps, all over the dining room table, organized them, and scribbled outlines. Beth, meanwhile, toured the h ouse with its owners, pausing to visit wounded men convalescing here. By the time Kent came for her, it was eight thirty.

"Don't you have to get up early tomorrow?" she asked.

"Pat will handle the hospital. I'll be there by seven. This work is very important."

He began to dictate. He was slow enough for Beth to maintain her neat script, and he spelled some of the Latin words. But she had writer's cramp and her back ached by the time they ended Case History 3 and finished for the night. Beth was to occupy a bed in this same large farmhouse, where another nurse was also quartered.

He stood up to leave. "Did you find the material interesting?"

"Yes, I did. Some of the things I saw you do were explained."

"Good. Then you understood. I thought you would. Dr. Clark may question you." He cleared his throat. "Thank you, Beth. We'll finish this tomorrow night." It was the first time he had called her by her first name. She thought of doing the same thing, but to her he could only be "Major." The title suited him better than the name, for it too was remote.

He stood in the doorway for a moment, looking as though he wanted to say something else. Then he smiled and said good night.

The next day she said goodbye to her German friends and arranged for a young man to pick up and deliver the sheets.

"You've done so much for the army," she declared to a group of wives and young people who had laundered the sheets. Mrs. Shaefer beamed and translated into German. The German immigrants, whose sons had fought as bravely as any others, suffered shame whenever native soldiers sought to raise their own self-esteem by calling the Germans cowards.

They made her eat a huge lunch of steaming knackwurst, vegetables, and mashed potatoes, and elicited a promise that she would come back in happier times. She was sent away laden with food of every description. Beth dispensed most of this among the medical personnel and the patients, but she hid several small cakes in her own carpetbag.

It was now July 11. She had first seen the battlefield on July 6. Not even a week, and she had almost adjusted to the place. One day she had nearly fainted at the very thought of amputations, and the next day she was washing instruments for the doctors. Never before had she seen dead men, except at wakes; now she was so accustomed to watching Kent or Pat pulling army blankets over soldiers' faces that the awesome fact of death scarcely registered with her. She had watched two soldiers die, and there were countless others who lay in moribund condition. All this—and she had not fainted, had

156

not faltered, could still talk rationally, enjoy a meal, and even flirt with Dr. Marshall. How was it possible?

The one thing she had never expected to see in this depressing setting was people rollicking with laughter. She was totally unprepared for what she witnessed that afternoon.

Pat and Kent were doing fewer operations now, and these were mostly higher amputations—cases where gangrene had set in—usually in the patients of private surgeons who had helped the army during the worst of the emergency and then had gone home. She came by with her sheets at about two o'clock and was amazed to see that neither Kent nor Pat was working. They were standing near Kent's operating table with four of their orderlies and Pat was holding the group spellbound with some story that he could barely relate over his own hilarity. As Beth came up to them, Pat was delivering the punchline:

". . . and then she said, 'Who do you think you are? Magellan?' "

With that, Pat laughed so hard that he literally toppled over and ended up on the ground, convulsed and holding his sides. Kent and the orderlies managed to remain standing, but they were staggering back and forth, roaring, weaving, and bumping into the operating table. It went on for quite a while, with one or another of them stopping only for a breath before dissolving again. Eventually she began to laugh too—at them; they looked so ridiculous. Pat, rolling on the ground, looked up at her, stopped laughing for a moment, and said, "*You* didn't hear this, did you, Beth?"

"I heard the part about Magellan. Tell me the entire joke."

"Oh, you *didn't* hear it," said Pat. As though it were now all right to continue laughing, he promptly began again.

Kent wiped his eyes and still laughing, said, "It's a long, very complicated story, Miss Shepherd."

"Yes, but you seem to have the time to tell it, and I'd really enjoy a good joke, major."

"Well, actually, Miss Shepherd, it's a military joke. You would have to know the details of certain maneuvers."

"Maneuvers!" Pat slapped his thigh, and the orderlies began to whoop, holding on to each other.

By this time Beth knew that the joke was bawdy and that no one would ever tell her the first thing about it, but she wanted to hear more of Kent's ridiculous explanations. "Oh, look at them laugh!" she cried. "It must be a marvelous story. Please tell me, major. I know more about military maneuvers than you think."

But Kent would no longer play the game. "Miss Shepherd, I'm sure you are aware that this story is not for young ladies."

He looked down at Pat and commenced to laugh again. She shook her head. The story must be funny indeed, if grouchy Kent Wilson could behave like this. She saw the colonel walk by and heard him mutter, "Exhaustion," as his eyes surveyed Kent's staff. Now she realized that the laughter was more than a response to a silly joke. Perhaps the surgeons and their aides were slowly going mad.

Later, when Kent and the orderlies had walked away, she said to her brother, "I do think this place has affected your brains. How long have you been here?"

"Let's see. From the second to the—nine days, I guess."

"Nine. Well, I'm leaving just in time. Pat, you and Major Wilson should have seen yourselves. I'm surprised the colonel didn't put you both in straitjackets and pack you off to an insane asylum. And all because of Magellan." She paused, thinking. "I can't imagine why a woman would ask someone if he thought he was Magellan. Did it have something to do with having a girl in every port, or was it—"

"Never mind," Pat said, and abruptly changed the subject. "You must be anxious to get home, sis. I'll bet you miss the folks."

She sighed. "Yes. I wish you could come too. It doesn't seem fair that I'm free to go home while you and Joe—"

"It was our choice. We volunteered."

"But no one expected the war to last more than a few months. Now it's eighteen sixty-three and Rick says the end is

158

nowhere in sight. So many others will die, Pat, and there will be cities full of widows and children, not to mention the girls who will never marry at all."

"You're not worried about that, are you?"

"Not as worried as my friends. If I don't marry, I at least have a career. I should hate becoming an old maid aunt installed in your house like an antique. I'd be resented by your wife, laughed at by your children, totally dependent upon you for every penny." She shook her head. "No, I shall live with dignity in a boarding house. Elizabeth: poor but proud."

He smiled. "I can't picture you that way, honey. You'll get married. Do you have any beaux?"

"Well, I might have one if you had let me finish my conversation with Captain Marshall."

"Marshall is engaged, and I know the girl."

"Why didn't you tell me?"

"I told him to stay the hell away."

"Oh." She was so disappointed at Captain Marshall's deceit that she didn't question her brother's high-handed method of handling the matter.

"Do you have anyone, Beth?"

"Not exactly."

"What does that mean."

"Let's just say No."

"You always did speak cryptically."

"Do you have any new girls?"

"There's one woman," said Pat, "but I'm not ready to marry. Unlike Joe."

"I didn't know Joe wanted to marry."

"Did want to. Can't now. He carried a torch for Diane. You know that."

"Yes, but I thought he gave up long ago."

"Not at all. He used to tell me that some day she'd come back to him. He cried when he found out she was married. And after meeting her husband, he was more wretched than ever."

"Why?"

"Allister is so intense, so serious about causes, politics, whatever. I found the fellow interesting, but Joe didn't like him. He couldn't understand why she had married him."

"Greg came to see you during the Battle of Chancellorsville, didn't he?"

"During? No, it was before we knew there'd be a battle. Soldiers don't pay social calls during a fight, Beth."

She smiled, feeling foolish. "No, of course not." She had known so little about battles a month ago when she had fantasized about Greg bravely making his way over to the boy's regiment so that he might have a moment with the family of his beloved before risking death. She recalled the second part of her fantasy: the part about his being so tormented with uncertainty about her that he couldn't fight. "How did he come to be captured, Pat?"

"I don't know the details. Joe found out what he could about it. Gibbon's division was detached from the corps and was still in Fredericksburg. Apparently Allister ventured out too far when they tried to turn the enemy's flank. The colonel over there said that Allister's action was daring and gallant, and I daresay that didn't set too well with Joe. He was the one who had hoped to be Diane's hero."

So Greg had obviously been thinking about the battle and not about her. That removed a good deal of guilt, but it caused her to wonder how much he *had* thought about her in the months since she'd last seen him.

She opened her mouth to ask Pat another question about Greg. Kent chose that moment to return to the operating table and Pat was again in the mood for banter.

"Hello, laughing gas. When you laugh, I would swear you'd inhaled nitrous oxide."

"At least I remain standing," said Kent.

"That's because you're only five feet ten and obviously envious of my height."

"Green with envy. I can't sleep for worrying about it. You know, out West they have a plant called the tumbleweed, which I understand bears a striking resemblance to you, Pat."

"With all due respect, major, I envy the tumbleweed. Should plant life ever be subjected to your tirades, that weed at least would be able to roll away."

"Did you also know that in order for it to roll, its upper parts become detached from its roots and are buffeted about in the wind? As I say, the resemblance is amazing."

They both turned to Beth, expecting a smile, but she was too preoccupied to react to this nonsense.

Later she walked with Kent to the farmhouse, responding little to his conversation. All she could think of was Greg and Joe and Diane and herself and the impossible web that had woven itself among them. She was still in shock when they sat down to work.

"You seem distracted, Miss Shepherd."

"I'm thinking about home."

"I trust you have several admirers to replace those you will be leaving."

"Not several, major. One." She was tired of his implications that she was a flirt.

He looked surprised. "I didn't know there was a young man."

"I wasn't aware that I was supposed to inform you," she snapped.

"No need to be testy, Miss Shepherd. Are you ready to begin?"

This evening his manner was back to normal. Last night's pleasantness had vanished. He was dictating much too rapidly and rattling off the Latin terminology like Virgil.

"Major, you're going much too fast. I'm getting most of the English but missing some of the Latin. Would you repeat the word for some kind of wound? *Vulnus* something?"

"Sclopeticum. S-C-L-O-P-E-T-I-C-U-M. Gunshot."

"It seems to me that you could dictate in English and let the linguists up north translate for the world into Latin."

"Why compound the problem? You're familiar with Latin, are you not?"

"Of course I am. But I'm not Julius Caesar."

"Cleopatra perhaps?" His grin was almost a leer.

"Would you like me to leave? I'm getting weary of your not-too-subtle innuendoes."

"Forgive me. It's been a bad day."

"Do you ever have a good one, major?"

His lips tightened. "The Fourth of July was very exciting. You should have been here."

She remembered Pat's description of the soldiers drowning in the rain and the doctors trying to operate inside the dark tents. She said softly, "It's getting late. Why don't we finish this?"

He nodded shortly. When he picked up his notes, his hand was shaking. She couldn't tell if it was anger, nerves, or fatigue, but she regretted her sarcastic comment even though he had provoked it.

They finished at about nine thirty. Kent gave her the name of the military hospital in New York and told her to skim over the case histories she had written down in case Dr. Clark questioned her.

"You're functioning as a surrogate doctor on this trip, Miss Shepherd. We have no physicians to spare. I doubt that there will be one anywhere on the train. I'm counting on you to make certain that the men are not exposed to contagion and to see that they are fairly comfortable. We've only been given straw for them to lie on, and the train may not have springs."

"No springs?"

"These trains have been used to transport cattle—"

"Cattle!"

"Yes. They're filthy. But you'll have plenty of sheets for the men and can keep them clean."

"Why send them home at all?"

"They'll be better off there with Ed Clark than in this pesthole. Everyone's trying to move men out of here as rapidly as possible." He closed his eyes and pressed his temples with his hands.

"Are you getting another headache?"

162

"Just an ordinary one. Not a migraine."

"You must be tired of the war. I've only been here since Monday, and I don't think I could stand much more." She rested her elbows on the table, cupping her chin in her hands, almost too tired to hold her head up. "Do you approve of the war, major? The cause?"

"I'm not sure what the cause is. They change their minds about that every month. As to freeing the slaves, that should have been done a long time ago and without war. War is murder given legal sanction."

"Why are you here, then?"

"I'm in it as a doctor."

"How would you free the slaves without war?"

"By paying their owners for their release. Without slavery the Southern economy would collapse. They won't ever release the Negroes until they have enough money to pay them some sort of wage."

"But the slaves would all move north and the plantation-owners would have no workers."

"The city slaves who work in industry might. But most plantation Negroes would stay where they are, doing work they know how to do. The situation there would be little changed, as a matter of fact. The rich would still prey upon the poor as they do in the North. Except that now the Southern poor man would be free to be exploited by the rich man of his choice. Glory glory hallelujah."

"Yes, I know. The war will never change the class structure. But paying the South, major? That's so hypocritical. We would be taxing our hard-working laborers to pay the wealthy plantation-owners for 'property' they have no right to own. How can you suggest that?"

He knit his brows and leaned forward. "Money doesn't bleed, Miss Shepherd. Money doesn't die in trenches and get eaten by vultures. Hypocritical? Isn't it hypocritical to slaughter generation after generation of young men in the name of justice and freedom and to do nothing about attaining said justice or freedom when the war is over, so that yet another generation has to die for the same collection of unfulfilled promises?"

"You're simplistic. The situation is far more complicated than that." She lifted her head from her hands.

"I grant you that. Men make it more complicated. But you asked me if the war is just. I submit that no war is ever just to the men who die in it, and I question its value to those who survive. Why must every shred of progression or even regression be attended by an outpouring of blood? I don't want war. You don't want war. Everyone I speak to claims that he deplores war. Where does the war come from, then? It comes from all of us in part, but particularly from the leaders on both sides who are too drunk with power to consider negotiating a peace. Lincoln himself considered some method of monetary recompense but no one listened. It's far easier to call up callow youths as volunteers. The poor devils think war is marching and singing and don't find out until too late that war is dirt and pain and wormy graves." He paused and lit his pipe. "I removed both the arms of a prisoner—a rebel sergeant—the other day. Two arms, Miss Shepherd, for Dixie. And the man didn't even own a slave. Most of those men don't. But they are maimed and they die for those who do."

"Where would we get the money to pay for the slaves?"

"From the same coffers that financed the war." He said this without even pausing to think about it.

"People will pay for defense, major. Only a few abolitionists would vote funds for the slaves."

"You're right. It probably couldn't be done. Only slaughter suffices in impasses of this sort. Slaughter has been used to solve problems since the beginning of time. In every nation and in every generation. At least slavery is a moral issue, but slaughter has occurred in cases where men didn't even have a reasonable issue to dispute. I used to be naïve enough to think that men would be ready for peace when they had ample food, shelter, and a long enough lifespan. But I guarantee that when food is as abundant as manna from heaven and men

164

have the option of living forever some group will find an obscure ideological reason to attack some other group or keep them in bondage. It's part of man's nature." He was speaking quickly now, almost breathlessly. "There's a drive among all of us to identify ourselves with one or more groups. It doesn't matter what the group is: Yankees, Calvinists, musicians, Catholics, Greeks, or even thin people. The main objective of the group is to assert its superiority over another group and fight them, subdue them, eliminate them, sometimes with drawing room sarcasm, sometimes with deprivation, and too often with cannon. I'm no different from other men, and so to the extent that I can I withdraw from groups." He leaned back again, puffing his pipe.

"But groups are necessary for progress."

"Yes. But they are ipso facto the cause of destruction as well."

"Still, one has to distinguish among them. Some are more just than others. Some groups deserve to lead and others ought to be disbanded."

"There's the rub, Miss Shepherd. How can one disband a group without harming innocent people?"

"I can't answer that." She shook her head in frustration. "I only know that withdrawing from groups is no solution."

"It's a solution for me."

"You don't like people, do you?"

"As a rule, no."

"They're not all evil, major. Why don't you concentrate on their good qualities and—"

"Miss Shepherd, I'm getting weary of having to justify myself to you. It's obvious you don't like me." He looked into her eyes, expecting her to either confirm or deny this statement, but she said nothing. "I must be on my way. We'll be moving the men tomorrow afternoon."

"Very well."

"Good night, Miss Shepherd."

"Good night."

He was certainly touchy. He could lecture her at length

about her behavior with men, but she was not permitted to question his misanthropic attitudes. Still, what he had said made sense of a sort. In some respects she agreed with him. Kent did not seem given to rhetoric, though, and she wondered why he had run on so long. She supposed that most people, no matter how taciturn, tended to jump at an opportunity to present a pet idea. By doing so Kent had, in fact, contradicted his own isolationist philosophy, for he obviously needed someone on whom to test his ideas. She wondered if he realized that.

Kent's patients were taken to the train in ambulances and placed five abreast in the cattle car, clean sheets covering the straw on which they lay. Their bodies were covered with several sheets, and the men were instructed to remain covered unless Beth authorized removal of the sheets. Beth and the orderly were given food, water, soap, towels, medications, bandages, and other supplies for the men. Nurses on the train, who had their own charges to attend, were envious.

"You have so much more than we do, major. It isn't fair," said one, looking dolefully at her own scant supply of provisions.

"If they were my patients," Kent growled, "they wouldn't be in that condition and they would have enough supplies. Now go tend to your own business."

"Major Wilson!" Beth hissed. "I've got to travel with that woman. Hold your tongue."

"I hope you don't give in to her wheedling. I don't want any of our things used by anyone else. Nothing. We have barely enough for our own men, and Pat and I had to move heaven and earth to procure them at that. Do you understand, Miss Shepherd?"

She was looking pityingly at the distraught nurse.

"Do you understand?"

"Oh no, major. I'm afraid I can't grasp your subtleties."

166

He sighed elaborately and walked to the door of the railroad car. "Goodbye, Miss Shepherd."

She didn't answer.

He frowned and left the car.

It was a long train ride. The men were in pain and often cried out as the springless train bumped along the tracks. She plied them with food and water, told them stories of Louise's adventures on the overland trail, and even sang "The Girl I Left behind Me" and "The Bluetail Fly," to the annoyance of the other nurses on the train.

"You gonna marry me?" asked one of the soldiers.

"Not you, you spalpeen. She'll marry me."

Beth smiled. "I guess I'll have to marry both of you."

The orderly was attentive, helping Beth hold one or another man down every time the bumps were bad and attending to the bedpans when necessary, while Beth modestly turned away. Once, while the orderly was rendering this service, she looked out the window as the state of Pennsylvania streamed backward into the setting sun. How lovely this country was! A rich farm and dairy land, a creamy-butter land that she could taste. They were passing through Pennsylvania Dutch areas. The people here were German-speaking (Dutch was an American corruption of *Deutsch*); they came from Bohemia, Moravia, Switzerland, Holland, and France, as well as Germany. She caught a glimpse of two housewives chatting in a meadow. They were wearing black bonnets and long aprons and carrying baskets on their arms. She could not see their faces, but she knew that their cheeks would be pink (with health, not rouge) and shading toward the color of the apples that would fall from bursting autumn trees. The train rolled on past rippling grain fields, ruddy barns, pastures dotted with cows, phalanxes of ripening corn—on toward the cities, where food was siphoned through sooty markets and faces were pallid under limp, graying bonnets. Still, she thought,

167

the cities had their own lushness: in the scent of books lining the walls of the Astor library, in the whistle of a ship in the harbor, in the passionate shout of a newsboy. Philadelphia and New York: the tying-in places, the centers that channeled adventure from everywhere else, distilled it, and served it up to people who had chosen to live in the city for that very reason: to share the excitement of other people.

The train lurched suddenly. She caught her balance and turned back to the suffering men, who were sweating under their restricting sheets. As she watched them, her mouth began to feel drier and drier until she could no longer taste the delicious land she was passing through.

It was past midnight when the train, which had broken down once, finally creaked into Philadelphia. Here many soldiers were to be transferred to military hospitals. As attendants boarded the train to remove the soldiers, many of the patients murmured thanks to God that the wrenching ride was over. For Kent's patients, though, there was more travel ahead. They were being transferred here to another train that would take them home to New York. She gave instructions to the litter-bearers, then stepped out ahead of them onto the crowded platform and tried to lead the procession through the mob. It was a warm, humid night. Lanterns swayed overhead, silhouetting the pained faces of the wounded. Every so often she would look back to see if her patients were still coming. What would Kent say if one of the men ended up in a Philadelphia hospital?

The second train was intended for passengers, and it boasted not only springs but a clean interior as well. In one of the cars, half the passenger seats had been removed for mattresses to be laid against a wall. They had actually allowed for the possibility that wounded men or sick people might be traveling! Beth was overjoyed to see this opulence, but the soldiers did not take kindly to the prospect of another train ride, however comfortable.

"Gee, Miss Shepherd," said one, "couldn't we go to a hospital here?"

"Dr. Clark will take better care of you. And don't you want to see your families?"

At this, several faces fell.

"They ain't gonna like what they see," said another man. "My wife won't want me. I'm only half a man."

"Nonsense," said Beth. "Why, there's a friend of mine who's married to an amputee. She's just glad her husband is alive."

"Do they have any children?"

"Not yet."

"I'll bet they won't, either."

"But Douglas, you can still—" She began to blush as she realized what she was saying. This produced the biggest laugh of the day. And though she was embarrassed, she was pleased to see them cheerful. At this point she revealed a surprise that Pat had managed to procure for the men: a bottle of whisky. By midnight the bottle was finished and the men were a good deal cheerier.

Though Kent's patients were usually sent to military hospitals in Baltimore, Philadelphia, or Washington, these five were going all the way to New York because they had been selected for a private study being conducted by Kent and Dr. Clark. They had all been wounded on the second day of the battle and by the same type of projectile: minie balls. They were all missing legs and had all been treated by Kent as soon as they were brought off the field. Kent had carefully noted every detail of each surgical procedure, beginning with the moment when the first sheet was laid on the operating table. He had followed up each case with a meticulous progress report entered each day. Only one of the men had shown suppuration after surgery and now he too was healing well. Kent had told her that he wished there had been time to do the histories of fifty or even a hundred patients. But he had been much too busy. Still, his hope was to prove that the chloride-of-lime hand-washing and instrument-cleaning procedures, and the use of clean sheets and surgical smocks, lessened infection.

The train moved on through the night. The soldiers twitched and snorted in the sleep, pain distorting their faces. Toward dawn, one of them woke up and talked to her, asking her if she thought the girl he loved would still want him.

"Of course, Willie. Of course she'll want you." Tears came into her eyes.

"Why are you crying, Miss Shepherd?"

"Because you've had to suffer so much and now you're worried about offending the sensibilities of someone who will love you all the more for what you've been through."

"Do you really think she'll want me?"

"I do indeed." And if she didn't, Beth thought, then it would serve her right if Willie shot *her* through the leg.

They arrived in Jersey City about 9:00 A.M. Monday, July 13. The men had to be transferred to a wagon that Dr. Clark had sent down. Beth wrapped the sheets tightly around them and held her breath while the orderly and an ambulance attendant clumsily carried them off. Once settled uncomfortably in the wagon, they moved to the harbor and into the hold of a ferry. Beth breathed deeply of the sea air, which she had not smelled in a long time. She was home. Home to have breakfast in bed every morning (Sheilah wouldn't mind indulging her for a while) and to sleep, sleep, sleep. She sighed, remembering Kent's words: "All I ever wanted out of life was peace and quiet."

Dr. Clark was about Kent's age—a pleasant, bespectacled, earnest man who perused the case histories and questioned her in detail.

"How is Kent?" he finally asked.

"Very busy," she answered evasively, recalling with anger her last encounter with the nasty major.

"A most unusual field surgeon, trying to do research as well."

Beth didn't comment. Dr. Clark must have noted her reticence, for he did not pursue the subject.

170

"Well, thank you, Miss Shepherd. You've helped us a great deal. Perhaps you'll consider becoming a nurse?"

"Or a doctor."

"Oh? You hope to become another Elizabeth Blackwell?"

"Why not?" She was always irritated when people characterized Dr. Blackwell as a freak worthy of P. T. Barnum.

"I admire your spirit," he said. "And let me thank you again. I'm sure your family will be glad to see you."

Beth left the hospital and walked out into the summer day. It was all over. She could now remove the agony of Gettysburg as one removes a soiled dress and slip into the familiar frock of home. She did try to make the change, thinking of home and of summer parties to come. But the frock didn't fit any more. She had changed in the past two weeks, and she doubted that she would ever look upon the world in quite the same way again.

THREE

No more shall they in bondage toil,
Let my people go!
Let them come down with Egypt's spoil,
Let my people go!
Go down, Moses,
Way down in Egypt's land,
Tell old Pharaoh,
Let my people go!

Beth walked west on Twenty-third Street between First and
Second avenues thinking of how surprised the family would
be to see her today. There hadn't been time to write that she
was coming home. John would be at work by now, so Mother,
Sean, and Sheilah would be her welcoming party. And
perhaps the Kendalls. Could she bear to see Diane, now great
with Greg's child?

For some time now she had been trying to find a hack. She
had waited at First for about ten minutes and finally, in
frustration, had begun to walk toward Second. The city was
very quiet for a Monday. Many of the stores were closed and
traffic was unusually light. Strange—none of the people at the
hospital had mentioned a special holiday. Then she

remembered that it was noontime. Perhaps everyone was home eating the midday meal. At Second Avenue she searched again for a hack. The dark clouds overhead threatened rain and she wanted to avoid being drenched. But there were no hacks here either, nor were there hansom cabs or buses. The only vehicles passing were private carriages, and these were speeding by like Roman chariots in a race. Where on earth were they going?

It was then that she became aware of all the people. The sidewalks along Second Avenue were filled with groups of men and women talking to each other in excited voices and occasionally glancing northward as though expecting something. That was it. They were having a parade and the police were clearing the streets. What could the city be celebrating on July 13? She considered asking someone about it, but the sky was growing darker. It appeared that she would have to walk all the way home, so she had better move briskly. She thought, as she hurried, that the parade was obviously a celebration of the victory at Gettysburg. But she'd rather go home than wait around to see it. She was that tired.

Between Second and Third avenues she could hear shouts from the paraders. They seemed to be coming down Third Avenue rather than Second. Now she'd be trapped here for half an hour. Odd that she could hear the marchers but not the music. Nor could she discern a drumbeat. The militia had deteriorated badly since the glorious fife-and-drum spectacles of 1861.

She was close to Third Avenue now, but she couldn't move, because spectators were blocking the way. She stood on tiptoe but could make out nothing. Then a sign loomed high over the crowd. On it was scrawled, "No Draft."

Puzzled now, she turned to a stocky, middle-aged workman. "What's going on?" she asked.

"They're protesting the 'scription, miss."

"Yes, I saw the sign. Have they actually begun drafting?"

He looked at her incredulously. "Where you been, miss? Ain't you heard?"

"I've been out of town. I just returned this morning."

"Oh. Well. They started the drafting on Saturday morning. There was no trouble then and nothing much yesterday, but this morning they all met in the Central Park and—"

"Oh, I see. This is a demonstration of protest. I thought it was a parade."

"A *parade!*" He clapped his ruddy hands and laughed ironically. "A parade! This here ain't no parade, miss. It's a riot."

She knit her brows. "I don't understand."

"They been killing and burning and looting all morning. Uptown in the forties and fifties. Now they're coming down here." He gestured toward Third Avenue. "There's a *mob* out there. Thousands of 'em with bricks and clubs. Some with knives and broken bottles. They're saying they're gonna break down the armory to get the rifles."

"Oh, my God!"

"They're burning houses and killing niggers. Killing the police too, and any rich man they can lay a hand on." He sighed. "But they'll never be catching the rich. The rich got protection."

Beth stared at him dumbly and then looked in the direction of Third Avenue. All morning long, while she had helped settle the soldiers into hospital beds and conferred with Dr. Clark, the northern part of the city had been in the grip of a mob. She still could not see them, but she could hear them. What she had thought to be a poorly organized parade was a crazed herd—murderers. This, after Gettysburg! She began to feel faint. The roaring in her ears almost drowned out the shouting of the mob, and the dark sky seemed to shimmer and recede. No, she mustn't faint. Not here. Lowering her head, she began inhaling the steamy air in great gulps. Then she shook her head to clear it and gazed idiotically at the workman as she tried to decide what to do and where to go.

There was a break in the line of spectators ahead of her and through it slipped a Negro boy of about ten. Running at breakneck speed down Twenty-third Street, he passed Beth

174

and the workman. And in pursuit, a white woman with long loose gray hair. She was grotesquely fat—the puffy sort of fat that is distinguishable from the solid corpulence of the well-nourished. She ran after the boy. The look on the wrinkled face, strained by effort, was one of crystalline hatred. The woman held up her skirts with one hand and clutched a rock with the other, screaming "A nigger! Get him! Kill the bastard!"

Beth dropped her carpetbags and ran after her. Four men came running up behind Beth, but she kept her eyes fixed only on the fat woman. The boy had tripped and fallen and the woman was bending to attack him when Beth, gasping for breath, reached the two.

Beth tugged at the blubbery arms, trying to drag the woman back. As she struggled, she saw several rescuers arrive at the scene and reach for the boy. But now the woman rose, whirled and attacked Beth with the rock, flailing at her head. Beth ducked quickly enough so that the rock only grazed the temple. Almost by reflex she seized the arm holding the rock. She was grasping for the other arm as the woman began hammering at her. The pain in Beth's cheek was excruciating, making her eyes smart, but she held tightly to the one doughy arm and continued to grapple for the other.

Suddenly Beth felt a violent tug at her waist. She was dragged back, out of reach of the woman. She turned her head and saw the workman. He was shouting, "Sweet Jesus, miss! Are you trying to get yourself killed?"

"That woman was going to murder—" she stopped and gaped in horror. There had been no rescuers after all. In the spot where the boy had fallen, there was now a group of six people, including the fat woman, who had turned away from Beth when the workman intervened. They were all bending over the boy and pounding violently at him. She could not see the child, but his cries stabbed at her until she screamed insanely, "Stop it! Stop it!"

"Miss, we've got to be hurrying!" The workman had grabbed her arm and was now dragging her across the street and back toward Second Avenue. Looking over her shoulder, she saw a man in the group stand up and shout, "This one's dead. Let's find some more."

The fat woman also stood. Then she leaned over and spat. "That's one nigger we don't have to die for."

Beth's head began to spin. She said to the workman, "Let me go. I'm going to be sick." The man dropped her arm, then held her head as she retched violently into the gutter.

Beth was still gagging when he seized her arm again and began hurrying toward Second Avenue. She managed to keep pace with him until they rounded the corner on Second, out of sight of the fat woman. Then she sank to her knees on the sidewalk and began to cry weakly.

The workman said, "You're hurt, miss. Here . . ." He pulled a handkerchief from his pocket and awkwardly dabbed the blood from her cheek. "There now, why don't you come home with me?" He gestured toward First Avenue. "My wife'll tend to you proper."

She said nothing but continued to cry while he knelt and pressed the handkerchief against her temple. After a while she managed to control the sobbing. She said, "Thank you very much, but I must get home."

He assisted her to her feet. "Where do you live?"

"Sixteenth off Fifth."

"Fifth? Mother of God, miss, you can't be going over there and passing right through the mob. They're all along Third by now, way down maybe as far as Astor Place. Come home with me."

"I can't. I'd only worry about my family."

"But miss—"

"I'm going home," she said firmly.

He sighed and handed her the carpetbags she had dropped. "I picked these up when you ran after that woman. Tough job holding onto them and you too. I dropped them once or twice. Hope I didn't break nothing."

"Oh, don't worry about that, Mr.—uh—"

"Sullivan, miss."

She took the bags. How heavily they taxed her now-limp arms and her unsteady knees. "Look here, miss," he interrupted. "Take my advice and don't interfere with them. You want to be ending up as dead as that nigger boy?"

At the mention of the boy, Beth began to cry again. She turned from the workman. Later she would wish that she had taken his address for a thank-you note. She began to stumble south on Second Avenue.

She headed downtown for a block, glancing to her right as she reached the street corner to see if the mob was still on Third. It was. She would have to continue down Second until the mob had gone so that she could cross Third Avenue and head west. But now she heard hoarse cries of "To the armory!" and saw a great mob of people surge into Second Avenue just ahead of her. Another howled from behind, and she could also hear shouting over on First Avenue. Beth, trapped on four sides, decided that there was nothing to do but cross through the mob and then run home as fast as possible. She walked west on Twenty-second Street and then began to plow through the rioters. Men drank from whisky bottles and women shouted to one another, their voices shrill and frenzied. Beth was shaking in terror, but considering her appearance they might possibly take her for one of their own and let her alone. She was bleeding from the abrasions on her right cheek and temple. Her bonnet and blue calico dress were bloodstained.

One drunk man noticed her and said, "Cop get ya, honey?"

She walked past him, trembling.

Another said, "Where's the nigger hurt you? I'll lynch him."

She continued to edge her way through the thick mob, trembling uncontrollably. Foul cursing rent the air on all sides, but chants and slogans seemed to predominate.

"Down with the rich man!"

"Kill the nigger-lovers!"

"Rich man's war and a poor man's fight!"

She looked up and saw people atop buildings. Others hung out of windows. To her left men were overturning street cars and tearing down telegraph poles. To her right were huge clouds of billowing smoke. She tried to quicken her pace, but that was impossible in this dense, deranged crowd. Where were the police? Where were the fire squads? She could hear fire bells, but she saw no wagons. Those people who were not chanting, burning, or destroying were milling about with glazed eyes that reminded her of some of the shock patients at Gettysburg. She was not sure which of the people in the crowd were rioters and which were merely enthralled spectators. She wasn't sure of anything except that she had to get away as soon as possible.

When she had passed Third Avenue and was hurrying west, she noticed that the mob was thinning. As she walked toward Fourth Avenue, she saw fewer rioters and more frightened people like herself. At least it seemed that way. She couldn't be sure. She searched in her carpetbag for her house-wife kit and from among the sewing supplies extracted a pair of scissors, which she held tightly in her right hand. If anyone so much as touched her, she would use them. She debated whether she should go for his eyes or for his stomach. And if he turned for any reason, would she plunge the blades into his neck or his lower back?

It wasn't until she was past Fifth Avenue and running toward home that she became aware of the bestiality in herself.

Sheilah peered through the window at the wild-eyed woman, thin and disheveled in a dirty cotton sunbonnet and bloody clothes, who was knocking on the door. She had caked blood on her face and a pair of scissors in her hand. Sheilah was about to run, frightened, from the window when Beth saw the maid's face peering through the curtains and shouted, "Sheilah! It's me, Beth!"

Sheilah's eyes widened. "Mother of God!" she exclaimed, hurrying to the door and shouting up the stairs for Kate to come down.

Kate, who had reached the upstairs hallway as Beth stumbled into the house, nearly lost her balance when she looked down and saw her bloodied daughter. "Oh! Oh, good heavens!" She gathered up her skirts, ran down the stairs, and enveloped her daughter in her arms. "Beth, what happened to you?"

Tears stung Beth's eyes and she couldn't speak. She was so happy to see her mother.

"How—why—when did you get here?"

"This morning. From Gettysburg."

"You were in Gettysburg? When were you there? Did you—"

"Mother, it's an awfully long story." Beth wiped her eyes.

"But—but why these bruises? Why—"

"A woman in the mob hit me. I was—"

"The mob! Oh my Lord!" She examined the bruises on Beth's face. "Goodness, why are we standing here? Sheilah, please get some bathing water and bandages and—and ice for the swelling. I'll take her up to her room."

Lying in her bed, bathed and nightgowned, with an icebag soothing her swollen cheek, Beth told the two women of her adventures since the arrival of Ewell in Carlisle. Midway through her narrative, her father and Sean appeared, carrying rifles. After explaining to them how she had gotten here and listening to more horrified exclamations, she asked what the rifles were for.

John answered, "In case the mob becomes too unruly. Our police may not be able to handle them."

"Father, how bad is the situation?"

"No one knows. But our militia regiments were at Gettysburg, and the city doesn't have much protection."

"But what will we do?"

He shrugged. "None of the neighbors has left yet, but we're planning to evacuate. In the meantime, I suppose, we'll just have to defend ourselves." He paused. "But it's Phil I'm really worried about."

"Haven't you heard from him?" asked Beth.

"No. I hope he can get here before one of those monsters finds him."

Beth closed her eyes. "I—I saw them beat a Negro boy."

The four of them gasped. "Where was this?" John asked.

"On Twenty-third Street near Third Avenue. They killed him. I tried to stop them and a woman struck me."

Kate sat down suddenly in a chair near the bed. Her face was ashen. Sheilah ran out of the room to fetch smelling salts. By the time she returned, breathless, Kate was standing again and saying calmly, "I think we all ought to leave and let Beth get some sleep. She was awake all night on the train." Kate kissed her daughter and so did John. Sean smiled and said, "Nice to have you home, sis." Then they filed out of her room.

Her head throbbed acutely. Suddenly she remembered Kent's headaches and sympathized. She doubted that she would be able to sleep if the situation were as bad as John had implied. She ought to get up and help the family prepare to evacuate. But the thought of standing up was unbearable. Crisis or no, she had to rest for at least an hour. Even the soldiers who had spent the second night at Gettysburg occupying territory that bordered on Confederate-held land had managed to sleep. She could not understand this when they had told her about it, but she could now.

It was nighttime when she woke. Her head felt a little better and she was very hungry. She lit a lamp, slipped into a dressing gown, and went downstairs. There was some sort of commotion in the family room. She entered to find Phil Weatherly and a mass of frightened Negroes standing like tense panthers and talking rapidly in low voices. Phil saw her and came over to welcome her home.

"How bad is it, Mr. Weatherly?"

There were tears in his eyes. "They burned the Colored Orphan Asylum."

"Oh! Oh, how awful."

180

He cleared his throat. "You have guests for the night. The overflow has gone to your neighbors'."

In a corner of the room, John was showing a tall young black man how to use a rifle. Two old women were praying on a couch near the fireplace. Sheilah came in from the dining room with plates of sandwiches, and Sean appeared in the doorway, his arms full of sheets and quilts. The scene reminded her of the siege of Carlisle.

Now Kate came in and rapped sharply on the wall. She spoke in as soft a voice as she could, for there was fear that they might be heard in the street.

"Please, everyone, would you give me your attention for a moment? There are ten men and boys and eighteen women and girls among you. If you would, the men will sleep down here and the women and children can sleep in the two empty bedrooms, the guest room, and the other rooms upstairs. I'll let you decide who is to sleep on the beds. We do have two cots, but most of you will have to sleep on quilts, I'm afraid."

"We're grateful for anything," said one woman.

"Well, thank you. Now enjoy your food and don't worry."

Beth wondered how anyone could enjoy eating when they were being hunted like animals, but she was proud of her mother's strength and spirit.

Out of the corner of her eye she could see John mounting a rifle in a window. "What is he doing, Mr. Weatherly?"

"Your father has the unfortunate reputation of being a nigger-lover. We're going to mount one here and one in the parlor."

"I thought I'd seen the last of war at Gettysburg," she said.

"Beth, your father told me earlier that you'd been down there. Your parents were frantic with worry. They didn't get news until the sixth. Many people still haven't heard."

"Where was your son?"

"Not at Gettysburg. I believe he's going to South Carolina."

"When he hears about this he'll be worried sick."

"He would know I would come here."

"Where have the other Negroes gone?"

"Some to Brooklyn and Jersey, some to police stations. The fortunate ones, like us, are being sheltered in private homes."

"Have the rioters killed any Negroes?"

"I don't know. Our neighborhood got word of the trouble early. Naturally I couldn't contact your father, but I gave at least fifty people his address. We dispersed and arrived here at different times. Some of the people were discovered and chased. One, I believe, was actually caught."

"Who was that?"

"I don't know the man, Beth. I know few of the people here."

Sean came walking by with three chamber pots. He casually placed one near Beth's feet, another in front of the piano, and the third near John's armchair. Though Beth understood the gravity of the situation, she could not help cringing at the sight of chamber pots decorating the family room.

Phil looked at her face and he smiled. "Comic relief," he said.

After a while she excused herself and went to the buffet in the dining room for a sandwich. Catching her reflection in the mirror, she noticed that her cheek was badly swollen and that she had a black eye as well. The fact that Sean had not teased her about it—that no one but Kate had even mentioned it— was a measure of the terror everyone was feeling.

She was in the hall munching a sandwich and talking to her father when there was a rapping on the door. John, fearing rioters, shouted "Who is it?" A voice shouted back, "Nate Klein." When John opened the door, he dissolved in laughter. "Natty Nate," as he was often called, had abandoned his impeccable attire and was dressed in baggy pantaloons and an open-collared patched shirt. It took a moment for John to realize that Nate had donned the costume in order to be unobtrusive among the rioters. Nate explained that he had taken his wife, daughter, and younger son to his married daughter's home in New Jersey and then returned to keep an eye on his bookstore, on Fourteenth Street. He had stopped by to see how the Shepherds were faring before proceeding home to Twenty-second Street.

"Good heavens," he said to John as he peeked into the family room and the dining room, noting the size of the group. "There's no reason some of those people can't come over to my house. Where's Phil, by the way?"

"Upstairs, mounting a rifle. And I don't think any of them ought to leave. *You* can disguise yourself, but how the deuce can they do it?"

"Yes, I suppose you're right. Why can't you send some over to the Kendalls'? They're only next door."

"The Kendalls left for their country home about an hour ago. And those neighbors who stayed are already sheltering many Negroes."

So the Kendalls had left. Beth wondered if they realized that a bumpy twenty-mile carriage ride might be risky for Diane in her seventh month of pregnancy. Which would be worse? A gang of rioters breaking down the door, or a premature birth by the side of the road? Beth would have advised Diane to stay in town.

John said, "Nate, there's one favor you can do for me, as long as you plan to strut about in that ridiculous outfit. Run over to my sister-in-law's and see if you can persuade her to come over here. I'm worried about her."

"Very well. Anything else?"

"Yes. Tomorrow you can help me gather food for our visitors. Kate tells me the larder needs filling."

"Yes sir." Nate winked, then saluted smartly and turned on his heel, playing loyal cavalry scout to John's General Meade. The crisis had brought out heroic traits in the two normally reserved and placid men. Beth had to smile.

Nate returned later to tell them that Louise felt quite safe in her own home. She had every intention of defending herself and her boarders with her own rifles (relics of the California trek) and she wasn't afraid of the rioters. When Nate called, she had been rallying everyone together as though she were the captain of a wagon train. No, they wouldn't have to worry about Louise.

As the hosts for this large group made plans and assembled marketing lists, the Negroes themselves sat uneasily in the family room and in the dining room on chairs, and on the floor, clutching their children to them and looking around with terrified eyes. In the corner of the room, two women— one of about forty and the other closer to twenty-five—sat together, leaning against the wall. Beth, pretending to be serving a plate of sandwiches on a tea wagon, could easily eavesdrop on their conversation. Every so often she would half-turn, looking elsewhere but sneaking glances at the women.

The older one was saying, "My man he come home in the middle of the day, he say, 'Lily, they fixing to kill us.' We grab the little ones and we run downstairs. Mist' Weath'ly down on the sidewalk shouting, telling us to go to Sixteenth Street. Got here 'bout three o'clock."

"I must've left before you. We got here early. Course we don't have no children. You got six now, don't you? And a son in the army?"

The older woman laughed shortly. "Boy in the army. He shine the officers' shoes."

"Funny. They making white men fight. Drafting 'em. And niggers they wanna fight, army makes 'em shine shoes." The younger woman pushed stray hairs into the knot at the back of her neck. "Don't understand that a-tall."

"They got a few nigger soldiers now. Mass'chusetts got a regiment, and down South they training some niggers. Some slaves they freed."

"But how come it take so long? They fighting for two years and nobody wants niggers. They say they wanna free the slaves, but don't want darkies helping 'em. Don't make no sense."

The older woman folded her plump arms. "White men don't think niggers is good enough to fight. Captain say to my son, 'Billy, we let niggers fight, white men'll desert. They don't want niggers wearing uniforms. Makes 'em think they as good as white men.' Billy say, 'Then why you wanna free the slaves?' Captain say, 'It's the cause, that's why.' Billy, he say he don't understand. Captain say, 'See, boy? Now you got your answer. We don't want niggers 'cause niggers ain't even smart enough to know what the cause is.' "

The younger woman laughed. "You joking? Captain say a thing like that?"

"That's right." She paused, shaking her head. "Can't figure white men nohow, 'cept for the ones outside. *They* say they hate niggers, I know they mean it. The rest of 'em, they call us lazy and dirty. Tell our sons they ain't smart enough to be a soldier. Then they go marching down Broadway singing 'John Brown's Body' and saying they fighting the war for the nigger. Outa their minds, you ask me."

Beth thought: the women were right. It didn't make sense. Unless, as Greg had said, the Negroes were not the real issue in the war. But if this wasn't the issue, then what was? Tariffs? Saving the Union? Envy of the Southern aristocracy? Was it all of these things? None of these things? Perhaps it was a problem no one had yet been able to articulate.

She had seen twenty thousand men lying in the fields at Gettysburg. She had seen an innocent boy murdered in the streets of New York. And the cause of it all remained a mystery.

At 1:00 A.M., with the rain coming down in sheets, everyone settled down and went to bed, Beth sharing her room with two elderly women whom Kate had provided with cots. John called the rain a deus ex machina, for it was heavy enough to extinguish the flames that had been raging unchecked in many parts of the city. But for the rain, many said later, all of lower Manhattan would have burned to the ground.

Her two roommates tossed for most of the night, but even without that distraction Beth would have found it difficult to sleep. The memories of the day kept assailing her. Whenever she closed her eyes she could see again the overhanging clouds, the sign being held aloft, the fat woman pushing her

185

way through the spectators. She touched her swollen face and felt the woman's fist pounding at her cheek. Woven among these thoughts, ever-present, was the image of the boy being clubbed to death under the dark noon sky. From the hall she could hear the chimes for two o'clock, three o'clock, four o'clock. If only she hadn't slept this afternoon, she might now be enjoying some pleasant dreams. But the night dragged on and the rain splattered endlessly against the window. When at last she did fall asleep, her own voice promptly woke her. It was shouting, "You've got to get up! Pat and Kent are waiting for the sheets!" After a moment she realized where she was and her thoughts turned to what she must face today. She sighed deeply, wondering if she'd ever again know a moment's tranquility.

By Tuesday morning everyone had faced the fact that the city was under siege. The police could not control the rioting. It continued unabated, and there was renewed fear that the city might yet burn. Nate Klein reported all this when he arrived at nine in the morning and joined the enlarged household for breakfast—a splendid meal of soup, coffee, and soda bread prepared by Sheilah and several Negro women and offered buffet-style in two shifts. Beth called this feast for thirty-four the miracle of the loaves and the soup bones.

It was decided at breakfast that John and Sean would join Nate in the quest for food. Sheilah, insisting that three men could not do a proper marketing, demanded to go along with them. John borrowed some clothes from a Negro laborer and was surprised to see that the outfit took years off his age. The younger appearance put zip into his footsteps and he gazed in wonder at the well-shaped arms that were revealed by the rolled-up sleeves of the cotton shirt. He'd forgotten, during his years of heavy frock coats, that he owned such arms. Or such a chest! Soon he was strutting back and forth in front of his wife, speaking gravely of his "mission" to "forage for food and spy on the rioters."

186

"You're a frustrated cavalryman at heart," Kate said, "But don't get any ideas about joining the army."

"No, I won't join the army. I'll stay here to protect you." He thrust out his chest. "But I daresay I'm flattered that you can picture me as a cavalryman. I'm still a young man, by God, even if I am fifty-three."

The food-purchasing party set out shortly after ten and returned about two hours later after searching the city for the few markets that were open. They were laden with bundles of flour, sugar, vegetables, meat, and milk. There were also newspapers, and candies for the children. They had seen several small gangs of troublemakers, but nothing resembling the enormous mob that Beth had encountered on the previous day. A policeman had told them that the rioting was now widespread and no longer confined to one part of the city. All were hoping that the militia arrived from Maryland before the city was altogether destroyed.

After a lunch of bread and cheese, washed down with glasses of tea, Kate urged the youngest children and the elderly to take naps. Kate herself went to her room for a rest. Beth went to sit in the library. About four o'clock her father, Nate Klein, Phil Weatherly, and a Negro couple entered the room. John began pouring drinks while Phil made the introductions.

"Jim and Susan Pierce, Beth. They're my neighbors and among the few people in this group that I know personally."

Beth whispered, "Hello, Jim and Susan. You're the first people I've been formally introduced to."

John said, "You don't have to whisper in here, my dear. The books lining the walls will absorb normal speech." He offered whisky to the men and, prompted by Beth's indignant look, poured weak vermouth for Beth and Susan. The group now formed a circle with Tim, Susan, and Nate on the couch, Beth and Phil on armchairs placed at right angles to the couch, and John on his desk chair facing them. The Pierces appeared to be in their late twenties. Both were very thin and dressed in mended cotton clothing. They seemed nervous.

John said, "What is your trade, Jim?"

"I'm a barber, sir. My wife's a laundress."

"Well, presumably the unpleasantness will be over soon and won't affect your employment."

"Yes, sir."

"Do you have any children staying with us?"

"Yes, sir. Two little girls. We all grateful to you, sir."

"Now you mustn't—"

"Taking us in and sharing your food. We sure lucky. Almost didn't get here at all."

"Phil mentioned that some had been chased, but I did not know you people were among them."

Susan's eyes were glazed. She said, "They throwing stones and screaming, 'Dumb niggers. Stupid dumb apes. No ape gonna take our jobs away.' "

"God!" Nate shuddered. "Where was this?"

"Sixth Avenue," said Phil, his voice flat. "A small group of them."

Susan said, "My little girl she only four years old. They hit her arm with a stone and she crying, 'Why they hurting me, Mama? I ain't done nothing, Mama.' Jim pick her up and we start to run, me dragging the older one."

Jim said, "The older one she just say to me before, 'Why they call us apes, Papa? Apes is like monkeys, ain't they?' I say Yes and she say, 'They sure dumb, ain't they? Don't know people from apes?' "

"Good for her!" Nate exclaimed.

John turned to Phil. "You never told me you were publicly insulted."

"John, how *can* you be so naive?" He sighed. "Let's just say that it's an incident I'd like to forget."

"But to be called apes! How in God's name did you stand it?" John was less concerned about the stone throwing than about the fact that a distinguished friend and his people had been abused with words.

Phil said, "How did I stand it? Oh, I suppose the way I stand drawing room guests talking to me in monosyllables or hostesses who first praise me as their anomalous guest—the darky who plays Mozart—and then check to see if I know how to use a dinner napkin. These people on Sixth were just a cruder variety of the same species."

The three whites in the group glanced at each other. "But surely you're not implying that Nate and I are members of this—er—species," John said.

"No, no, of course not." Phil waved impatiently. "If anything, you two are just the opposite. You see Negroes as nobler than we are—which may not be the best thing either. But all I've ever asked of you—of any of your race—is to be seen *as we are.*"

Phil sipped his drink. "There was a time, very long ago, when I was actually treated like a normal person. Can you imagine that? As you know, I was raised in a Quaker community in Rhode Island. My father was a respected blacksmith and I was a happy, innocent schoolboy. There wasn't any prejudice in that town—at least none that I noticed. But that happy state of affairs did not last long. One morning—I must have been about nine—my father and I were in town to go to the general store. Two strangers were on the street coming the other way. As they passed us, the man, not troubling to lower his voice, said, 'Odd-looking things, aren't they?' And the woman—she was looking directly at me—said, 'Yes, very peculiar.' Then in a lower voice, she said, 'Do you suppose they understand us?' And the man answered, 'No. They don't have fully developed brains, you know.' " Phil swallowed. "I saw my father stiffen and bite his lip. Then he looked down at me and he forced a smile and pointed at a carriage rolling by. He said, 'Did you hear those people talking about Mr. Schmidt's horses?' I knew my father was only trying to protect me, and I suppose I wanted to shield him from the knowledge that I was aware of what had happened. So I smiled and pretended not to notice that he was no longer striding but walking slowly and that he seemed years older." Phil clenched a fist. "That this proud, intelligent man could in one stroke be so humiliated!" His voice broke and he looked down, swallowing.

Nate began to speak, not gently but in a clear firm voice. "Phil, I don't think anything I can say will change how you feel. You've been debased, your people have been debased, and there's no denying that. But those two louts were only practicing an art that has been taught to them by rulers of men through many generations. The cleverest way for one group to successfully subjugate another is not with weapons but with the suggestion that the second group is composed of infrahuman creatures. The device has been used all through history to keep the masses down. Tell them they're ignorant. Tell them and tell them and tell them again. If it's said loud enough and often enough, most of them will come to believe it. Ridicule, mock, suggest that they are pigs, apes, clowns, or idiots, until the people, not believing themselves to be capable, obligingly remain subservient."

Nate tugged on his beard and leaned forward. His eyes were riveted on Phil, but the others were all staring at Nate. "Now the French Revolution and the uprisings of eighteen forty-eight indicate that this may be a technique that no longer works. But in this country the whites are still attempting to use it on the Negroes. Don't let them do it, Phil. Don't let them."

Beth looked at Phil, who was sitting opposite her. He was nodding politely at Nate, but he seemed utterly beaten—like a man who has fought too long and is simply very tired. Jim, however, was listening intently. He was sitting beside Nate and he turned his head to face him.

"You remember I told you what my daughter say: 'They sure is dumb, ain't they? Don't know people from apes?' Well sir, she young. Ain't been ruined yet by this—this here technique. And she won't ever be if she keep on thinking that *mean* remarks is just *dumb* remarks." He paused. "But if we call some whites dumb, we calling 'em infer-human or whatever you call it, ain't we?"

190

"In a sense—yes. But perhaps you'll have to resort to such measures." He grinned. "Except when people like John and I offend you. You're not permitted to insult intellectuals."

Jim smiled. "I figured that, sir."

"Intellectuals never *mean* to be unkind, you see."

Jim nodded. "Don't matter what they do, long as they don't mean it."

"That's correct."

"Then we'd be better off with infer-humans leading the country, right sir?"

Nate started to laugh. "I daresay you've grasped the technique quickly. Keep it up, young man. You'll go far."

John said, "Nate, this is ridiculous. Trading insults is not the way to happy race relations. Perhaps trading compliments—"

"We live in the *world,* John," Nate began dryly. But his next words were lost.

From the direction of the parlor came the loud crack of rifle fire. John threw open the sliding doors and collided with his son Sean. "What—what happened?"

Sean was panting with excitement. "I shot over their heads, Pa. You should've seen 'em run. They—"

"The rioters?"

"A gang of ten or twelve. Came up our street throwing bottles."

"Are they gone now?"

"They were gone in three seconds. Ran like jackrabbits."

"Do you think—" John stopped talking and walked back into the relatively soundproof library, motioning for Sean to follow, and closed the doors. "Do you think they knew we were harboring Negroes?"

"No. They couldn't have known, Pa. There are more than sixty colored people hiding in houses along this street. If the mob knew that, they'd've sent five thousand people up there, not ten."

"Yes, of course." John took a deep breath and mopped his brow. "Well, young man. I must say we're proud of you."

191

From the group in the library came a chorus of praise for Sean. Then everyone was crowding into the library—Kate, Sheilah, frightened children, and their nervous parents.

John tried to lighten the mood by parodying Richard II:

This happy breed of men, this little world,
This blessed plot, this earth, this realm, this . . . Manhattan.

Several people laughed, but Kate declared that if John didn't hush, she would see to it that he was shipped home to his beloved England, where he could quote those lines all by himself on London Bridge.

They discussed what had happened. One man said, "Ain't no Irishman wouldn't like to hang a nigger."

Sheilah whirled upon the man almost before he had finished speaking. "You'd better be holding your tongue, do you hear? Them people out there ain't only Irish. There's a lot of others doing the killing, and don't you be forgetting it!"

"Hush! Hush!" Kate commanded, shutting the library door so that Sheilah's loud voice wouldn't carry.

"I'm sorry, but I gotta be speaking my mind." She glared at the man. "There's Irish police out there protecting you, and Irish soldiers fighting the war for you, and I'll not be having you saying the things you been saying." She paused and took a deep breath. Then she continued in a more subdued voice, "Some Irish are wild, I'll grant. And some're as mean as the devil. But when you say *all* you're talking about me and Mrs. Shepherd here and a lotta dead boys at Gettysburg. Yes, and Sean who shot that rifle, he's half-Irish, and so's Beth. Maybe she'll be wanting to tell you how she tried to protect a poor colored boy."

Phil said, "You're quite right, Sheilah, and I'm sure this young man intends to apologize."

He glared at the youth, who said dutifully, "I apologize."

"Well," said Sheilah, "just be remembering what I said. You niggers have suffered and I ain't denying it, but us Irish have suffered too, and I won't have *nobody*, nigger *or* white, forgetting it." She turned to stare at Nate Klein and John, the only non-Irish whites in the library.

The room was dead silent for a moment. Then a little girl, not understanding the reason for the silence, hissed at her mother, "Can't we even *whisper* in here?"

Kate seized the opportunity to divert attention from Sheilah. "As a matter of fact, my dear, you can talk in this room. Not too loud, but louder than before. Why don't we all leave and let the children play and chatter? Will someone please volunteer to supervise?"

"I will, Miz Shepherd," said the girl's mother. "And I'll see the door stays shut. Thank you."

Everyone left, including Sheilah, who returned to her dusting of the parlor, in which task two women were assisting her. Kate made no mention of the maid's outburst then or afterward, and neither did anyone else. Before going to her room to freshen up, Beth peeked into the parlor, and saw Sheilah whispering amiably with a Negro woman of about the same age. It was as though nothing had happened.

Beth remembered Sheilah's description of the potato famine in Ireland: the farmers trying desperately to find life in earth that had denied them its sustenance; the slow starvation, the children crying in the night until they were too weak even to cry. And then the long weeks in the hold of the sickening sailing ship to America, where they could get help. Except that there was almost no help at all. American natives shuddered as the Irish swept ashore. There were so many thousands of them in the early forties and fifties. Dressed in thin rags, carrying bags of belongings tied with rope, to the natives they were beneath contempt. Children died by the hundreds in festering slums while the native Americans stood by, their sensibilities offended. The Irish sought food and received only muddy splashes from the wheels of carriages with liveried drivers.

How had Greg said it? The upper classes, in their infinite humanity, would take up the cause of one of the lower classes and ignore all others. And when the reckoning came, it would be the lower classes knocking each other out and leaving the aristocracy untouched. Was it happening now, as the Irish struck for living wages and the wealthy brought starving Negroes in to break the strikes? As the rich asked the Irish to volunteer for the war against slavery while seeing to it that their own sons were spared?

Now the Irish were reacting. Encouraged by Southern-sympathizing Copperheads who took advantage of their indignation, they were venting their anger on the innocent Negroes who, unlike the wealthy, were visible targets. This left the aristocracy free to deplore such crimes with impassioned rhetoric before sitting down to their dinners of seven courses. And whom would the Negroes attack if they were the ones being scorned by the wealthy? The Irish, of course, Beth concluded. They would hate the rich but strike out at the Irish, for the Irish were there.

Wednesday, the third day of the rioting, was wickedly hot. Beth, drenched in perspiration, helped prepare lunch, assisting three Negro women. For a long time the only sound to be heard above the whispering and murmuring in the family room was that of the distant firebells in the city. Occasionally they would hear the report of rifles too, and the woman would shudder.

"I hope it's the police and not the rioters," Beth whispered.

A black woman of about Beth's age nodded gravely but said nothing and continued to slice her onions. Beth had noticed her from the first night. She was strikingly beautiful, her face marked by high cheekbones and large luminous eyes. Next to her, Beth felt clumsy. But more disquieting was the woman's attitude. She was usually silent, but there was a meaningful arch to her eyebrows, grace and elegance in the length of her supple body. She was not hostile, yet she seemed to be saying, "I know who I am and I'm quite pleased with myself." In the midst of a siege, and without uttering a word, she conveyed her message.

194

Beth found herself bristling with envy. She felt uncomfortable with the woman's beauty, her poise, and her pride. But then Beth remembered. The woman was black. She could not compete, could not take away Beth's beaux or her job; Beth did not have to fear her. And yet—was that fair? Was Beth just as prejudiced as the rest of the world? She mopped her brow. Was she big enough to permit this woman to compete with her? Could she stand it? Until now, Diane and other white women had been her only competition. Could she accept Negro women, Indian women, and Chinese women as well? She was angry at the tall, silent Negro woman who was making her ask these questions of herself. It was too hot and miserable today to think about such things. She picked up a pile of sliced carrots. Throwing them into a pot, she abruptly left the room.

She strode into the garden, desperate for a breath of fresh air. There she found her brother sprawled in a chair, the noon sunlight baking his freckled face.

Sean said, "I don't know how those Negroes can stand being cooped up in there day after day. I have to get away every so often."

"Who's doing sentry duty in there?"

"Willie. The tall skinny one. There are three of us alternating five-hour shifts. I'm off until one."

"You haven't seen anyone since yesterday, have you?"

"No, and I don't think we will. They know we have guns now. Besides, Mr. Klein says that the militia will be home today or tomorrow."

"Those poor boys. First Gettysburg and now this. But I hope they get here soon. There was looting on Fourteenth Street. If Mr. Klein loses his bookstore—"

Sean laughed. "Those dreary histories and Latin translations? Who in the mob would want them? The whole city may fall, but Klein's bookstore will stand forever."

"Well, you can laugh all you want, but he's not so stodgy as you think. The riots have turned him and Father into regular cavaliers."

"Yes, that's funny to see, isn't it? Those two in workmen's outfits? But if they're cavaliers, then you're a warrior. I can't imagine you fist-fighting with anyone. I didn't think girls knew how to fight." There was admiration in the clear blue eyes.

Beth herself was proud of the courage she had shown, but she wasn't proud of what had happened minutes later. She had run through the streets with a pair of scissors almost anxious to plunge the blades into someone's back so that she could see the blood and hear the screams. This, after a lifetime of believing that women abhorred violence.

Beth squirmed in the garden chair. The past two days had been one unrelenting moment of truth and she was tired of feeling guilty. Very well, she had been violent. All it meant was that women had all the faults of men. Women were human beings.

"What are you thinking about?" Sean asked.

"Oh, nothing. I wish there were a theater open so that I could go see a comedy and laugh." She thought: One could stand only so many hours of analyzing the complexities of White and Negro, rich and poor, men and women; so many hours of considering one's own contribution to the problems of society. There had to follow the impulse to forget the whole mess and flee.

For three days the city had been held in an iron grip. Negroes were lynched and hanged, policemen killed, buildings burned to the ground, and looting widespread. Five million dollars in property damage was estimated later. Hundreds of rioters were killed, many burning in buildings they themselves had set afire. And there was no force strong enough to stop the force of destruction itself.

Finally, on Thursday, the long-awaited militia regiments were marching through the streets of New York. Among them was the "Fighting Sixty-ninth," an all-Irish regiment. Its green flags were tattered and blood-stained, and its ranks had been thinned by many battles. Yet when the sixty-ninth

196

marched by, its troops were in perfect alignment and its bands rendered spirited country airs. The amorphous mob, whose music had been drunken slogans uttered by voices both guttural and shrill, was briefly silenced, shamed.

The presence of the militia put an end to the violence. By late Thursday the Negroes could talk in normal voices. They began making plans to leave. An army private came by and told John that a military escort would arrive at five o'clock and accompany the Negroes to their homes.

People said their goodbyes over glasses of lemonade. Many speeches of gratitude were delivered to the family. As Beth looked around, she realized that many of these people had become individuals to her. They were no longer "the Negroes"—a shapeless mass of characterless people who were all presumed to possess certain traits. There was Jim, who was young and still had hopes for bettering his condition, even if that meant using white tactics. By contrast, Phil seemed defeated, too tired to continue. There were the two women who had discussed the hypocrisy of the army, both of them as puzzled as Beth herself. Beth looked at all of them, until finally her eyes rested on the beautiful woman whose name, she had learned from Sheilah, was Marie. She still felt uncomfortable in the presence of so much perfection. She might have tolerated the looks alone, but the looks, the grace, the pride—it was too much to bear. She hated herself for being so petty, but at the same time she knew that she was not prejudiced against Negroes as a group. After all, most black women fell well within average range. She would not want to deny all of them their freedom simply because she was so envious of one of them. No, she wasn't prejudiced at all. Except against paragons of beauty and grace. But she'd overcome that too. Some day when she was more secure in her own strengths.

Sean seemed rather sad to see his fellow sentries depart and suggested that they all have a "riot reunion" in the near future. But Sheilah was the saddest of them all. She and a cook named Betty had become fast friends in spite of, or perhaps because of, Sheilah's tirade in the library. Both were widows of about the same age and both had sharp tongues. Beth suspected that their comments on the behavior of various characters in this four-day drama accounted for much of the muffled giggling in the kitchen. When Betty left, Sheilah, once again the lone servant in the house, was miserable.

At five o'clock a group of mounted militiamen came riding up Fifth and turned west on Sixteenth Street. Behind them rolled three military wagons. The Negroes came out of the homes that had sheltered them, piled into wagons shouting their goodbyes, and in no time at all the cavalcade was rolling off toward Sixth Avenue flanked by the blue-coated soldiers. The Shepherds and their neighbors stood in front of their homes and watched. Beth and many other people wept. She didn't know why. Had the triumph of justice moved them to tears? Or were they crying from shame that an armed guard for Negroes should be necessary in the land of the free and the home of the brave?

The riots were the only subject of conversation for days afterward. No one—not even the press—could agree on the causes. John and Sean were convinced that the Copperheads had organized them. John also cited an editorial postulating that Lee and Davis had planned the riots to synchronize with the attacks on Pennsylvania so that New York, many of whose businessmen needed Southern trade, would be induced to support the Confederacy. The war, John reminded them, had never been popular among New York businessmen and politicians. Beth offered her theory and Greg's. She believed the riots to have been spontaneous uprisings with some encouragement given by the Copperheads. Kate was silent most of the time. When she spoke at all, it was to plead that the subject be changed.

By this time New York was heavily patrolled by the militia. There were troops bivouacked all over town and sentries on every corner. Despite all the protection, Phil remained barricaded in his house; they didn't see him for weeks. Gradually the rioters returned to their jobs, many ashamed of their conduct but no less indignant over the gross unfairness of the draft laws. (Eventually, though, the city raised money for those poor who wished to pay three hundred dollars for a substitute.) Ringleaders were rounded up and prosecuted, though many were never found at all. And slowly everything returned to normal.

Sometime during her stay at Gettysburg, Beth had heard that General Grant had taken Vicksburg and now controlled the entire Mississippi River. This, coinciding with Lee's rebuff in Pennsylvania, was very heartening news. People began to talk about an end to the war by Christmas.

Only a month had elapsed since the peace of Bill's farm had been shattered by the approach of Lee's army, but Beth felt as though years had gone by. After Carlisle, Gettysburg, the mobs, and the siege of New York, it seemed as though she had experienced everything there was to experience. She felt a good deal older. But it was over now. She was home, the rioting had ended, and her mother and her friends would expect her to resume the old pace of life.

She went out into the garden one day carrying *Godey's Lady's Book* for July and sat down in a wicker chair to leaf through it. There was the usual color print foldout of young women with demure expressions evoking Renaissance portraits of the Virgin Mary. They were clad in summer dresses with layers of ruffles, and sashes at the waist. One twirled a parasol behind her head. Another held violets to her lips. Two more merely stood there looking saintly. Beth turned the pages. This month's song for the pianoforte was "I Am Old and Gray," written by Lieutenant A. F. Lee (presumably no relation to Robert E.) and composed by Joseph M. Stewart. Now that she was feeling old herself, she paused to look at the lyrics:

I am old and gray; I am old and gray;
My strength is failing me day by day.

Yet it warms my heart when the sun is gone
And her robe of stars the night puts on.

She decided she wasn't so old after all and turned to glance at a story that began, "It was 'grand hop' night at the headquarters of Newport fashion . . ."

Didn't this magazine know that there was a war going on? Did its editors realize that there were slaves in the land and immigrants half-crazed from starvation? She riffled through the pages. Not a mention or a reflection of these facts. When she reached an article entitled "Chitchat upon New York and Philadelphia Fashions for July," she began to laugh. It was the frenzied sort of laughter that she had seen in Kent at Gettysburg, a part of her realized, but she couldn't stop. Tears streamed down her face and her sides ached. She read the title again: "Chitchat upon New York and Philadelphia Fashions for July." She remembered running through the streets—no hoops, no ruffles, no sashes, and most unfashionably bloody. When her hilarity had subsided, she recalled that she was supposed to take *Godey's* seriously. Gettysburg and the riots were not real life. *Godey's* was real life. She must either try to understand *Godey's* or deny that she was a woman of refinement and taste.

In August, Beth decided to return to Carlisle. It was hot in New York, and her thoughts turned to the cool, breezy days at the farm. But Kate was reluctant to let her go.

"We're sending Sean to Latin school in the fall. We'll be here all alone."

"But Mother, I have a position there."

"They need teachers in New York too."

"I suppose I *could* stay," Beth said without conviction.

"Is it the young doctor?"

"Excuse me?"

"Kent Wilson, is it?"

"Oh, no. He's probably left Gettysburg by now. And where did you get the idea that I wanted to see him again?"

200

"You mentioned that you worked closely with him, and I wondered if—"

"We didn't get on very well. Kent doesn't like people, and I was no exception."

"From all accounts, he likes Patrick."

"For some reason they were able to tolerate each other."

"I see." She paused, thinking that she didn't really see at all. "I wonder why Pat hasn't written?"

"I wonder too. Those ungrateful characters might have found some time to send me a note of thanks."

"Beth, you never did tell me the details of your work at Gettysburg."

Beth told her. When she was finished, Kate commented, "No wonder you're so bored at home, dear. Awful as the experience must have been, you did do important work. Perhaps you could nurse here in New York. Normally I would discourage your nursing, but—"

"I'd like to study medicine."

"A doctor? Oh, Beth, that's no decent profession for a woman. You have to doctor men, see them—"

"Mother please don't be a prude about it. And don't worry, either. They'd never admit me to medical school. If they did, I doubt I could stand the ridicule of my fellow students. I'll continue to teach."

Kate's face relaxed. "Will you stay here?"

She thought about it. Greg was far away, probably dead, and so remote in time from this bloody summer that she no longer associated him closely with New York. She might as well stay. She would miss the farm, but there seemed no compelling reason to return.

"All right. I'll have them send my trunk. They'll be disappointed."

Kate sniffed. "They have each other. I should think they'd understand my wanting my little girl."

Beth smiled. In a rare gesture, she hugged her mother.

Kate was touched by this affection. She and Beth had never been as close as most mothers and daughters of their acquaintance, but this past spring Kate had missed her more than she had believed possible.

Born during their wealthier days and sandwiched between Pat and Joe, Beth had quickly become the forgotten child. Not that her parents hadn't loved her. But she and Pat were only twenty-three months apart, and Joe had come along twelve months after Beth. At a time when Pat was doing bright things to amuse his parents and Joe was raising a colicky ruckus, little Beth had been tended by various nurses and ended up a remote child who doted on tales of gallant men who, she imagined, would love only her. Her favorite poem—one her father had read her as a child because of its simple meter—was by William Wordsworth:

> She dwelt among the untrodden ways
> Beside the springs of Dove,
> A maid whom there were none to praise
> And very few to love.
>
> A violet by a mossy stone
> Half-hidden from the eye,
> Fair as a star when only one
> Is shining in the sky.
>
> She lived unknown and few could know
> When Lucy ceased to be,
> But she is in her grave and, oh,
> The difference to me!

Beth had wept when she first heard the poem, and Kate hadn't quite known why. Beth was remote, yes; a dreamer, yes; but certainly no shy violet. If she saw herself in the "unknown" Lucy, it was probably because the poet had recognized Lucy's value as Beth wanted her own value recognized. This was the only explanation Kate could come up with for Beth's fascination with the poem.

Beth had been a constant trial for Kate, whose duty it was to prepare the girl for her adult role. Beth resisted such instruc-

202

tion with passive disinterest. Kate had always wondered why. Her first clue to Beth's behavior had come when Beth was 11 and talking with one of her friends in the garden. Kate had overhead the conversation while potting plants near the garden door.

"When I get married," Faye had said, "I want my husband to treat me like a queen."

"Like a queen?" Beth had repeated.

"I want him to worship me and give me diamonds and rubies and—"

"Yes, but what will *you* do?"

"I'll wear the diamonds and rubies."

"What kind of fun would that be?"

"Well—well it would be fun, that's all. What kind of husband do *you* want, Beth?"

"Someone who needs me."

"Oh yes, I want my husband to need me too."

"But if you're up on a pedestal he won't, Faye."

"Won't need me?"

"Do you know what I've noticed? Girls are either up on pedestals or down on the floor."

"You mean like our maids?"

"No, goodness, I don't mean *cleaning* floors. I mean—well—girls are never in the middle. Boys are in the middle, but girls are either high or low. My brothers—when they want to say a bad word they look up at me. Pat told me I shouldn't listen to rough men talk because I'm a little angel. But when I want to say *anything* they look down at me. Do you see what I mean?"

"Yes, I guess so." Faye sounded doubtful.

"We're never in the middle unless—" she paused—"unless men aren't too bossy. Like my father. Sometimes he really listens to my mother. It doesn't happen too much, but when it does—you should see how different she is."

Kate had almost blushed when she overheard this. In a sense it was true, but for Beth to see it this way was embarrassing. The child was too precocious. For Beth to try to live by such ideas would be folly—detrimental to her own happiness.

There had followed a campaign to interest Beth in feminine arts, feminine goals. But the men in the family had interfered. Not deliberately, but simply by being. They were a constant reminder to Beth that there were many paths in life that she would never travel. And the older Beth became, the more intent she was on traveling at least some of those paths. There had been open rebellions with Kate, hot words exchanged, and then, with maturity, the futile protests had become dignified assertions: "I'm eighteen, Mother. I want to teach, and we need the money. It's no disgrace. It's not immoral. Now please be reasonable about this."

That had been four years ago. Both of them had changed. Kate now recognized her daughter as an ally. Kate could not join the battle, could not fully apprehend its meaning, but she regretted the years in which she had tried to stifle her daughter. They had been wearing years for both. Beth had traveled the forbidden paths anyway and seemed none the worse for it. Indeed, she was, strangely, more womanly. Kate was glad to have her home.

In one of Pat's rare letters, Beth at last received acknowledgement of the train ride with the wounded soldiers:

Dear Beth,

I'm awfully sorry about not having written sooner, but you must know how busy we have been. Thank you for helping us with our research work. Dr. Clark wrote that he was amazed at the condition of the men. They healed freely, in no time at all, &, last heard, were all home with their families. Kent & I both appreciate what you did.

We returned to our reg't on the 12 inst. & have been working hard here in Virginia. I rec'd Ma's letter about the riots. I'd already read the full story in the papers, and the thought that you might have been hurt in the mob where people were stringing up Negroes and burning them alive made me ill. If anything, Kent was sicker still, holding himself responsible for sending you home on that of all days. For all the gore he sees, Kent does not have a strong stomach when it comes to violence. Nor do I.

Hope you are fully recovered now, little sister. Take care of yourself and please write.

Love, Pat.

There was nothing in the letter about Gettysburg. Nothing about the German families or Bill and Sally or the soldiers she had nursed whose chances had been questionable when she left. Pat's letters were always so hurried. Then she remembered his long days in the sun, seeing and smelling nothing but blood and gore. She guessed that the moment he had any time to himself he probably ran off to some harlot. She wondered if Kent also sought solace in this way. It pleased her to know that Kent had felt guilty about sending her home. After his nasty parting remarks at the train, he deserved to suffer qualms of conscience.

That same week she received a letter from Sally, telling Beth that her luggage was on the way to New York and expressing disappointment that she would not be returning to Carlisle. Sally had occasionally nursed at the Gettysburg field hospitals and at Camp Letterman, the military hospital set up there later. She had worked closely with Kent and Pat.

"I felt so proud to be assisting the most efficient team in Gettysburg," she wrote. "Kent is a genius, and it hurts me to see him ridiculed by his own colleagues. I suppose that's why he's so edgy, poor man. However, some former skeptics have tried doing things his way and with good results. Perhaps truth will triumph in the end."

Beth wondered why so few had adopted Kent's surgical procedures. She supposed that they were doubtful because his cure rate, though good, was well short of 100 percent.

On a rainy Saturday in August, Rose Kendall came over to tell them that Diane was in labor. The doctor had been notified, and the nursery was being readied for the great event. There was no need for Mrs. Kendall to voice her trepidation. There was always fear, especially with a first child. Would the passage be too narrow, the labor too long? Would there be some unexpected hemorrhage or childbed fever? Waiting for a safe birth was one of the worst ordeals families had to endure.

"She wants to see you, Beth."

"Is there anything I can bring her?"

"No. She just wants to talk."

Beth had seen Diane several times since her return from Pennsylvania, but she had confined her conversations to accounts of Gettysburg and the farm. When Greg's name was mentioned, Beth saw to it that the subject was changed.

She walked into the room as Diane was suffering a labor pain. Beth could not bear to witness the torture. Her eyes scanned the room briefly. She had not been here in many years, but it seemed unchanged. Aside from the graphic evidence of the double bed in which Diane now lay, there was no evidence that Greg had ever shared this room with her. The chamber reflected the character and tastes of Diane only: fragile mother-of-pearl inlaid chairs, delicate ivory fixtures for the dressing table, ruffled organdy curtains, candlesticks in the shape of cherubs. Greg must have felt uncomfortable here.

Diane said, "Hello, Beth. Excuse me. This pain was a little sharper than the others."

Diane was beautiful even now, damp and panting, the enormous bulge like a great pillow laid carelessly on top of her. Her angel-fine hair was matted around her forehead, but her face was exquisite even in its suffering. How could anyone manage to look so lovely at a time like this?

"It'll all be over before you know it," Beth said lamely.

"Look who is consoling whom. You haven't ever had a baby." Diane chuckled weakly. "Just wait."

"No, and watching you I don't think I'd care to."

"You will, though."

"I do want children," said Beth.

"Beth, I was thinking just now—when we were little girls we

206

were close as sisters. I know it all changed later, but we were close, weren't we?"

"Yes, we were."

"You and Joe and I. Remember the clubhouse we built in your back yard?"

"That silly lean-to?"

"I don't know why I suddenly remembered that clubhouse at this of all times. I guess I wish I were a child again. Having a baby forces one to be an adult, doesn't it?" She smiled. "Do you remember how scornful Pat used to be? He never would join the club or contribute to our little newsletter."

"He was much above it all," said Beth. "But I once saw him looking at us from behind the oak tree. I could tell by his expression that he wished he hadn't been so haughty."

Beth's mind drifted down a long tunnel of years to a time when Diane was not a rival, but a friend; not the wife of the man she had loved, but a little girl who had loved her "family" living next door. When had those years come to an end? When had the closeness of Joe and Diane taken on a sexual aspect and the friendship between the two girls turned to competitiveness?

"I miss Joe," said Diane. "How is he?"

"Judging by his letters, he seems fine."

"Do you suppose he ever thinks of me?"

Beth swallowed. "I'm sure he does. But of course he knows you're married—"

"Yes," Diane said shortly. "I'm married." Suddenly her eyes filled with tears.

"Diane, what is it?"

"I don't know how I'm going to feel about this baby."

"Don't know?"

"The baby was not planned."

Beth cleared her throat and looked away. "Indeed?"

"I *had* to get married."

"Diane, are you sure you want to tell me—"

"You must know already. The whole neighborhood knows, I'm sure of it. I think even Mrs. Allister suspects."

Beth didn't know what to say, so she nodded slowly.

Diane said, "He didn't love me. I didn't love him either by the time I learned of my condition. Then, of course, it was too late."

Silence hung in the room for a long moment. It was broken by Diane's groan as she suffered another labor pain. Then she said, "Could you pour me a glass of water, Beth?"

"Of course." Beth's hand was trembling as she poured the water into a crystal glass. "Diane, I thought you did love him. The night of the dinner party—"

"Oh, I was mad for him at first," Diane said, propping herself on her elbow and sipping the water. "We met at a ball. While we were dancing he made some remark about General McClellan and I said that I thought McClellan was too full of himself to devote all his efforts to a cause. Greg said something like 'Good observation' or 'Interesting idea.' I don't remember exactly. But I was so flattered that he had listened to one of my opinions. Most men don't, you know. I suppose he thought I was clever." She paused, sipping more water. "He ran on about all sorts of things. I didn't understand most of it. Even my comment about McClellan was borrowed from a friend of my father's. You know I have no interest in politics. But I was so pleased that he considered me bright enough to understand him. He called on me several times. I must admit I encouraged him to. Having an intellectual man as a beau was rather a novelty. I began reading the paper and listening to my father's discussions. I wanted so to impress Greg."

"Why?"

"No one has ever thought me clever, Beth. You must remember how our mothers used to regard us. I was the beauty and you were the brain."

Beth smiled. "Yes, I remember, and I used to wish you would move to California so that I wouldn't have to suffer comparison to you."

"I felt the same way at times." She paused. "But here was my chance to prove that I wasn't an empty-headed piece of fluff. I

208

fell in love with Greg and I wanted to marry him. He came to call one day when everyone in the house was gone and I—well, I was certain we would be married, so I—you see I'd always been curious about—what really *happens* in the marriage bed and I wanted him to—"

"You t—" Beth began, catching herself on the *too* and turning scarlet, wondering if Diane had noticed. But Diane continued. "I asked him to do it, Beth." She blushed and mumbled, "Birth pains must be like whisky. I never expected to tell anyone about that."

Beth was remembering how she had acted with Greg. It had never occurred to her that the same might have been true in Diane's case.

"And so we were wed," Diane said. "And we found that we didn't have a thing in common. I had begun to suspect that on the night of your dinner party, when he offended my father with some of his revolutionary talk. I remember thinking, 'I don't understand him,' and later—I thought it was so disloyal—it crossed my mind that he could be downright boring at times with his politics and all. I began thinking that perhaps we weren't meant for each other after all. But by that time I was with child. He nearly cried when I told him."

"Are—are you saying," Beth stammered, "that you fell in love with him because you wanted to prove that you were clever?"

"I guess so," Diane sighed.

"Oh God."

"I know it must sound insane."

"Were you trying to prove it to him?"

"I know this must sound foolish, but it was my parents I wanted to impress. I've thought about it during all these months that Greg has been gone and it was my parents. I don't know why."

Beth shook her head, unable to speak. Three lives wrecked, she thought. Four if you counted the baby. And all because parents had had to characterize them. Pound it in with a heavy hammer that Diane was beautiful and Beth was bright. Pound it in until Diane was driven to prove for good and all that she too was deep. So she picked the one man who had not deemed appearance to be of primary importance in a relationship and decided to marry him. It was sadder still because Diane, given a chance, could have cultivated something besides charm. But no one had ever felt she needed to.

And now came the realization that Greg had told the truth. He *had* loved her. He hadn't used Diane either; she had encouraged him.

She was grateful for the doctor's coming in at that moment. The bustle, the questions, and the pain distracted Diane. She didn't see the look on Beth's face.

Later, when the baby was born, Diane's misgivings were dispelled. Laura was an enchanting child. She looked so much like her mother that Diane could, if she tried, forget who the father was. She adored the little girl. And for the first time in months there was the color of life coming back to her cheeks.

"I want to marry again," she told Beth. "Of course I'll have to wait to be sure, but I'm certain he's dead. No one has heard from him."

And later: "If he is alive, I shall divorce him. He wanted that anyway, I think."

And if Greg was alive, Beth wondered, what would happen to *her?* She could barely remember him now, though this was due in part to her deliberate attempts to banish him from her memory whenever she thought of him. But now a new Greg emerged—a victim. He had loved her, Beth. He was everything she had once thought him to be. And if he were alive she would marry him.

The war would end soon. Gettysburg and Vicksburg had turned the tide. Perhaps Greg would be home by Christmas.

In the following months, Beth and Diane gradually grew closer. Though Beth blamed Diane for what had happened, she could easily understand how it had come about. Beth had somehow adjusted to the fact that she would never be an outstanding beauty; had, in fact, often longed for the freedom of the boys. But Diane had gone on and on, convinced inwardly of her simplemindedness but determined to catch the most brilliant of beaux. Only Joe had ever mentioned Golden Girl's brain: "Diane is analytical. She has a way of seeing through to the heart of things."

Beth had noticed this when Diane had so accurately, if belatedly, pinpointed the root cause of her own infatuation with Greg. But in a world where intelligence was synonymous with sophisticated drawing room repartee, Diane had never needed to develop this skill. Men were too busy admiring her slanted blue eyes to bother talking to her.

It was Rose Kendall and Kate who had committed the basic sin. It was they who had grouped and categorized and set the girls on preordained courses in life. But they, in turn, had probably been treated this way by their mothers. How could they have predicted a disaster like this?

Perhaps the best response was to blame no one totally and blame everyone a little. Yet when she did that, the tragedy of Gregory and Elizabeth seemed ascribable to little more than the random acts of nature. And this Beth would never accept. In fact, it annoyed her that she had so thoroughly analyzed the problem that now she could blame no one. Could it be that people invented devils just to have someone to accuse in these "blameless" crimes?

All she could do now was hope that Greg was alive and that, if he were, he still wanted to marry her.

During the months since Greg had been captured, his father had made several attempts to learn his son's condition. Others at Libby Prison in Richmond were allowed to send and receive mail, but no one had heard from Greg since just after his capture, nor was any mention made of him in letters from other Libby prisoners. In early October Mr. Allister paid a phenomenal sum to an unknown informer (Diane suspected it was a gun-runner) and received the information that Greg was alive and reasonably healthy but was being denied mail privileges owing to certain difficulties with the guards. When

Diane related this news, Beth, after her initial delight at learning that he was alive, was apprehensive. Yes, she admired Greg's honesty and outspokenness but there were times in life when it was best to keep one's mouth shut. If Greg were being punished, the cruelty of the guards would not end with a mere denial of mail privileges. They would probably deprive Greg of sufficient food, medicine, and other necessities. Well, at least he was alive. If the war ended by winter, he would have a good chance of surviving. If not—but here her mind stopped. Of course the war would be over by winter. The South was shattered already. If the Confederates wanted to preserve any remnant of their old life, they would be wise to surrender at once.

FOUR

In the beauty of the lilies Christ was born across the sea,
With a glory in his bosom that transfigures you and me.
As he died to make men holy, let us die to make men free
As God is marching on!

It was Christmas. The songs of love and peace pealed from organs in candlelit churches. An end to the war was urged by priests and by ministers, and by rabbis celebrating Hanukkah. But Pat had said it all on his first night home:

"They won't budge and we won't budge. It'll take another year at least."

And Beth sat in the garlanded, mistletoed parlor mentally erasing Greg's name from the book of her future. He'd never survive another year in prison.

Later, with the hope induced by Christmas making inroads into her pessimistic mind, she revised the "never" to a more acceptable "perhaps." This was necessary if she were to enjoy the holidays at all. And enjoy them she must. The months to follow would certainly be an extended wake.

Many young men were home on furlough, and Beth often found herself the belle of parties marked not so much by the men who were there but by those who were not and would never be again. The forced retirement from the spotlight of the beauteous Diane made Beth the object of many a young

213

man's fancy. It was a pity that she couldn't appreciate the attention. Kate, especially, seemed disappointed with Beth's indifference. To please her mother, Beth danced most of the dances and promised to write to several soldiers. "Why not?" she thought. "I might end up married to one of them."

Two days after Christmas her brother Joe, who had been given a late furlough, arrived home. Beth, who hadn't seen him in more than a year, was shocked at his appearance. Dark and attractive like his father, Joe had always had the soft, pampered look of a rich college boy. Now he was hard and thin, his features more angular. He looked tired, beaten, not at all like the fun-loving brother of the old days. Joe, as an infantry lieutenant, had been in the thick of battle several times in the course of the war.

He walked in the door smiling expectantly and he hugged Beth and the others as exuberantly as he had in the past, but Beth could see a look on his face that had never been there before. It was a strained expression—as though he had to make an effort to adjust to this soft, silly world of his youth. After a day or two he seemed more relaxed, and when Diane came to call one afternoon he brightened considerably. He spoke little about the war. The only event he would discuss in detail was the dedication of the cemetery at Gettysburg. He talked to John, Pat, and Beth about it one night after dinner.

"Everett's speech was two hours long. It seemed endless. Bombast, rhetoric, allusions to every battle in the history of mankind. I slept through most of it, and I was standing up. And then came Lincoln. It was over in about a minute. At first we were grateful because we were so tired. But later, when I thought about it, I was annoyed. It was perfunctory—as though the whole battle were being placed in a package and tied with red, white, and blue ribbons."

"That's exactly what he intended to do," said Pat. "To cover the whole mess with neat white headstones and muffle the screams with rhetoric. That's how they keep wars going. What the army should have done was choose the moment when all

214

the politicians and reporters were there in force and then disinterred some of the bodies."

Beth shuddered. "Pat!"

Joe said, "That sounds like a Kent Wilson remark. I'm not implying that the war is folly. All I said was—"

John spoke up. "Now just a minute. I read that speech and I found it powerful. Remarkable, in fact. The eloquence—"

Joe interrupted. "Eloquent? Maybe it was that, Pa, but he didn't say much about the battle."

"He stated the objectives of democracy," said John, "and most succinctly. A good leader ought to be able to communicate to the people exactly what it is that men fight for."

"Father's right," said Beth. "I read that speech. It was almost as beautiful as the Declaration of Independence. In some ways it was more beautiful."

Pat said, "Since when have you become a flag-waving patriot? Are you justifying this war because that skinny rail-splitter has a way with words?"

"I'm not justifying any war. Why do you always mis-interpret me? I'm saying that, given that the war exists, the speech clarifies its purpose."

Pat looked at her irritably, thinking that her future husband would not appreciate her casual participation in men's con-versation. "That speech was an insult to my intelligence."

"For heaven's sake!" She glared at him. "Can't you ever see beyond your scalpel, Pat?"

Pat held up his hand. "That's enough, Beth. Let's not ruin the evening squabbling about the eminently forgettable re-marks of Old Abe."

"Trying to back away, are you? Well, I won't let you. I loathe this war, Pat. I'm disgusted with the government, the military, and Lincoln too for that matter. But the speech—well let me put it this way: approving a man's ideals does not mean approving the methods used to attain them. I'm opposed to the war but I loved the speech, and that's that."

"That's that," Pat repeated. "The lady has spoken."

"And won a point too. You just won't admit it."

The argument raged for another ten minutes, until finally Pat suggested a game of poker. As the three men left the room, John winked at his daughter and murmured, "You were splendid, my dear. Pat's retreating under fire." He walked off chuckling.

Beth didn't smile at all. Among the things she had missed during the last two years were the lively debates with her brothers. She resented the fact that they had extricated themselves by proposing a game in which women could not participate. Cowards!

Joe and Diane spent most of the holidays in each other's company, to the mortification of their parents. Diane explained that her interest in Joe was based solely on the fact that he had been her childhood friend, but the two sets of parents still thought it improper for them to whisper together in corners. And the looks they exchanged across a room were positively outrageous. Diane was lovelier than ever now, motherhood having improved her figure instead of destroying it, as was the case with many women. Beth suspected that Joe now knew the truth about Diane's marriage and was standing by. This pleased her. When she married Greg, she would feel better knowing that Diane had a husband who adored her. The thought of the scandals that the four of them would face when the divorce and remarriages were effected sometimes troubled Beth. But she tried not to think about it during the holidays.

Two days before New Year's Pat announced at dinner that Kent Wilson would be dropping by on his way back from Boston, where he had spent the holidays.

John asked him, "How did both of you manage furlough at the same time?"

"The brigade medical director insisted that we get some rest. We were promised every Christmas until the war ends."

"Why?" asked John.

"Because we work hard, I suppose."

Beth said, "I can vouch for that. But considering the way he criticizes the army—"

"But he also—we also—save a heck of a lot of lives. If I may be so bold, I think we deserve a month, not a paltry week and a half."

"I agree," said Beth. "It amazes me that neither of you has taken sick."

"No, we've been healthy. Except for the headaches."

"He still has those migraines?"

Pat nodded.

Kate, who had heard much about Kent's battlefield cursing, questioned Pat about the background and character of the man.

"Let me see. His father was a lawyer in Boston. Well-born, but not very wealthy. His mother died when Kent was very young. He was raised by housekeepers. I don't know much about that part of his life. He won't talk about it. When his father died, he left Kent just enough for a Harvard education. After graduation, Kent went on to Harvard Medical School. I believe he worked some of the time for his tuition. What else? He was married. His wife and daughter died in childbirth. He moved to New York and was a resident at Bellevue. He has a younger sister and two nephews. I can't think of anything more. Does he pass inspection, folks?"

"That hardly sounds like a description of a Plug-Ugly," said John, alluding to a notorious New York gang, so named because of the plug hats they wore.

"Oh, Beth exaggerates," said Pat. "He uses a few hells and damns once in a while. We all do. Excuse me, Ma."

"It wasn't really the swearing I objected to," Beth said. "It was his attitude toward people."

Pat looked at his sister and frowned. "Beth, sweetness and light do not increase efficiency. Not when so many men need immediate care and the medical equipment is in short supply. You know that."

"Oh it's more than that, Pat. He has a grudge against the world."

"Perhaps he has good reason," said Pat.

Kate said, "If he upsets Beth, I'm afraid we cannot extend him our hospitality."

"He doesn't upset me, Mother. There were times when we actually got on well. Have him here, by all means."

"Do you like him?" Kate asked Joe.

"He's a type. Arrogant and short-tempered."

Beth said, "He's Leif Ericsson with Boston Brahmin overtones. And a dab of the Bowery B'hoys."

"Isn't there anything positive to say about him?" asked Kate.

"He's intelligent," shrugged Beth.

"A bloody genius," Pat asserted. "Honest, folks, you'll like him."

On New Year's Eve, Beth wore the delicate coral velvet dress her mother had made her for Christmas. It was low-cut and narrow through the bodice, necessitating the tightest lacings which pushed her breasts up and out and diminished her waistline. Though she hated the confinement, she had to admit that she looked stunning and was anticipating the compliments she would receive from the officers Mother had invited to tonight's party.

She and Diane, with the enthusiasm of schoolgirls, had spent the afternoon experimenting with new hairstyles. Beth, who was usually indifferent to fashion, felt a need to be glamorous tonight, New Year's Eve being the last jolly evening they'd be likely to see for some time. And so Diane had piled Beth's thick brown hair on top of her head, Grecian style, and lent her a pair of long golden earrings to complete the regal effect. Even Sean complimented Beth when she sailed downstairs and into the parlor.

The guests that night were greeted as they arrived by whichever member of the family happened to be standing nearest the door. At one point the task fell to Beth. She opened the door to a man who nodded at her. He wore a caped overcoat and an officer's hat. She smiled and said, "Won't you come in?"

218

He stepped into the dim, gaslit hallway, removing his hat. "Good evening, Miss Shepherd."

She recognized the voice before the face. "Major Wilson! I didn't realize it was you. Here, let me take your coat."

She placed his coat in the closet and then stared at him curiously. Her last memory of Kent had been of a thin man with a deeply tanned face and longish straw-colored hair. His attire had been trousers and an army blouse, the sleeves of which were always rolled up. Over this he had worn a rumpled waistcoat. Most of the time he had been covered with a surgical smock. She had never seen him in uniform. He looked very correct and distinguished with the maple leaf shoulder straps and the gleaming brass buttons. His hair had been cut and his face seemed less leathery, but he was still thin. Nevertheless, she preferred the battlefield Kent. The officer-and-gentleman attire did not suit him.

His eyes quickly scanned her. He said haltingly, "You look very well."

"Thank you, major." She was determined to be civil to him for Pat's sake. "May I return the compliment?"

"Thank you." His face was very serious. She was about to direct him into the parlor when she heard another guest at the front door. She opened it and greeted an old friend of Joe's.

"Beth!" he cried, clasping her hand. "You look like a queen. No, not a queen. A goddess!"

"Thank you, Jim." She blushed, then said to Kent, "Jim is a college friend of Joe's. Major Kent Wilson, Lieutenant James Powers."

Kent nodded toward the man. "Lieutenant?"

"Major?"

The two men stared idiotically at each other. Neither had a thing to say. Finally Jim turned to Beth again. "You do look beautiful."

Kent cleared his throat and Beth said to him, "Oh, major, Pat is in the parlor." She gestured toward her brother. "Can you see him? Near the window to the left of the fireplace?"

Kent peered into the parlor. "Yes, I see him," he said

crisply. Then he pointed at a bag he had placed on the floor. "I was asked to stay the night. I have a bag—"

"Oh, of course. Pat will take it up for you. Leave it here for the moment."

Kent nodded shortly and left. He seemed annoyed about something. And just a moment before he had been so pleasant.

As Beth entered the parlor, Pat was introducing Kent to his mother. Kate, expecting a maniac, was pleasantly surprised at this man whose only problem seemed to be an uneasiness with strangers. He was quite attractive and most polite and his language was impeccable. Surely Beth had exaggerated his faults. Diane came over to meet him, magnificently dressed in yellow satin and looking ethereally lovely. Kent commented on her to Beth later when she was serving him punch.

"A beautiful woman. I'm told she is married."

"And with a baby. Her husband is at Libby Prison. Gregory Allister," Beth heard herself say.

"Yes, I heard about that. I knew him."

"I believe he once spoke of you."

"He was at Harvard when I lived in Boston. A friend of a friend. I'd seen him around camp, too. One night he came over to meet your brothers. Pat left me with him for a while. An awfully idealistic fellow."

"Yes."

"But intelligent enough. I normally can't abide these conscientious aristocrats."

No, Kent Wilson hadn't changed a bit. "What did you talk about?"

"Politics. Allister is very political, as I am not." He lit his pipe. "And social ideas. He said he favored racial intermarriage and I agreed with him. I believe these social taboos are a plot perpetrated by lunatics to keep people so busy fighting about nonsense that no progress is ever made."

"Yes, you're right," she said hastily. She didn't want to get bogged down in a philosophical discussion. "Did you talk about anything else?"

220

"You're very curious."

"I'd like to tell Diane."

"I don't recall. That he missed home, I suppose. His wife. So many men talk to me about these matters. Me of all people. I'm not adept at handling that sort of thing."

"No, you're not," she agreed. "You were never very sympathetic and understanding with me."

He smiled. "I always felt you were strong enough not to need people's solicitude."

"Not always, major. In any case, Diane will be pleased to know that you spoke to her husband."

"It's heartening to know that I will be responsible for tidings of comfort and joy."

"You are, without a doubt, the most sarcastic—"

He held up his pipe. "Spare me, Miss Shepherd. It's just that an account of my political discussion with Allister will not cheer his wife. The way to do that would be to effect his release from prison."

"His father is wealthy. He's already paid for information about Greg. Do you suppose he *could* buy his release?"

"Allister would never stand for it."

"No, I suppose not," she said sadly.

"He's got integrity. I'll say that for him. And I can't say that about most people."

Beth glowed with pride. Even cynical Kent Wilson admired Greg.

Among the guests at the party that evening was Peter Weatherly, Phil's son, now a sergeant with a Massachusetts Negro regiment. Pete, like his father, was intelligent and well-educated. He would have made a fine officer, but Negroes were almost never given commissions. He had fought in the assault wave on Fort Wagner in Charleston the previous July and had suffered a chest wound from which he had since recovered. It was fortunate for him that he had been hurt and so could be sent to the rear at once. His regiment had held the fort and been almost totally annihilated. The fort had not been taken by the mostly white invaders but the heroism of the one black regiment had impressed the country. Pete was a full head taller than his father and very slim. His hair was close-cropped, and he was clean-shaven.

Beth spotted Pete standing alone and walked over to chat with him. Pete was very fond of her. She had amused them all one night last fall by declaring that women too were slaves in society—all of them from Mary Todd Lincoln on down—and when the war was over she expected all men, black and white, to address themselves to the sexual inequities. Pete had never known any woman as political as Beth and was looking forward to more of her lively rhetoric. But tonight Beth was the gracious hostess.

"Pete, you look marvelous!"

"War does wonders for one's appearance."

"You know what I mean. Besides, I've seen what war does to men's appearances."

"Yes. Pop told me you were at the massacres last summer."

"When do you think it will end, Pete?"

"Another year. Possibly longer." He saw her face fall. "I'm sorry, Beth. Do you have someone?"

"Yes. If I tell you a secret, will you promise—"

"Of course."

"He's someone my family doesn't know about. He's in Libby and he's been there for about eight months. What are his chances of ever coming out?"

"Have you heard from him?"

"He's not permitted mail privileges."

"I'd say he's alive now or you would have heard from a chaplain."

"Even if he's alive now, what chance does he have of surviving another year?"

"I don't know, but I'm sure there's a good chance, Beth."

Pete didn't remind her that the South had very little medicine, that the North wouldn't allow any to pass through the blockade, and that her beau was probably exposed constantly to typhoid, pneumonia, scurvy, dysentery, smallpox, and consumption. He also refrained from discussing the diet

222

on which prisoners were forced to live. Perhaps some officers' prisons were better than the enlisted men's, but Libby was rumored to be a living hell.

"Don't worry," he said. "A great many men survive prison. And many manage to escape, you know."

"I know, but—"

"Try not to worry, Beth."

"Very well. At least you've given me a wisp of hope."

He smiled at her wanly.

Beth was serving refreshments when she noticed Kent speaking to a group. John had asked him if he thought scientific progress could affect social progress. As Kent answered him, using mathematical concepts, Beth noticed that the eyes of his listeners were beginning to glaze over. Kent was concentrating so seriously on what he was saying that he did not seem to notice. She wondered what would happen when he realized that no one in the room cared a fig for mathematics and his listeners would be unable to comment on his ideas.

"The curve of scientific progress," he was saying "is exponential." He did not gesture to illustrate what he meant. Did he really believe that they understood him? "And that of social progress is linear with a slope of—well, in my opinion, never higher than point two. And when these curves are placed side by side, I think the dichotomy is, or will be in the near future, alarming." Before continuing, he looked up at a sea of blank faces. Then, embarrassed, he lapsed into silence.

"That's very interesting," said John, who had trouble calculating percentages and called upon his children when required to do so. But Kent was apparently relieved that someone in the group seemed intrigued and he continued to talk about the two types of curves.

Beth groaned inwardly and walked over to where Jason Winchell, a New Yorker who had moved with his wife to Illinois, was debating with Joe the merits of the Western army versus the Eastern.

"You're slobs, the lot of you," Joe said to Jason. "No discipline at all. Your uniforms are a joke—" He was half-teasing and half-serious.

"Joke or no, we took Vicksburg, didn't we? The war won't be won with Eastern dandies. I saw a group of New York militia in Washington last week. It was raining, and one of the men asked why they hadn't been issued umbrellas. Umbrellas!" Jason began to laugh.

At this point Pete walked over to them. "We've heard enough of East versus West. I'd like to introduce another variable in the forces of the, ah, Union: black versus white."

"The ex-slaves make bully soldiers," Jason said enthusiastically, without a trace of the patronization Pete had been expecting. "Hell, why wouldn't they? They're fighting for their freedom."

It wasn't long before Pete and Jason were discussing the great number of slaves who had been liberated along the Mississippi and were now being mustered into the Union army.

In the noncombatant corner, Kent, whose mathematical observations had failed to move his listeners, was now standing apart with Aunt Louise, discussing the proposed suspension bridge to Brooklyn and explaining the engineering principles governing the design of this unusual structure. He did not seem especially interested in meeting any of the charming young ladies that had been invited tonight, though he glanced at them occasionally. Pat was pursuing the well-proportioned daughter of one of Kate's friends, to the chagrin of Beth's schoolmate Mary, who adored Patrick.

"He doesn't care for me at all, Beth!" she wailed. "He's been chasing that girl in the blue dress all evening."

"Mary, there are other men in the world besides Pat."

"I know there are, but—"

"Go talk to Major Wilson, the one speaking to Aunt Louise."

"Him?" she sniffed. "He's like a stuffy professor."

"Talk to Edgar, then. Joe's friend."

"Edgar's awfully dull."

"What can I do, Mary?"

"You can't do anything, Beth. No one can. May I go up to your room and fix my hair?"

"It looks fine. But go right ahead."

Mary walked off with her head down. Beth sighed. She hoped that Pat would hurry up and get married so that she wouldn't have to listen to the laments of her heartsick friends. Why hadn't they fallen for Joe? Joe was twice as handsome. It was just as well, though. Diane had fallen for Joe. Yet even in the old days it had been Pat that everyone wanted. He had a shy charm that was totally disarming. And his tall awkwardness and tousled brown hair made him seem boyish and vulnerable—traits that appealed to many of Beth's friends as they appealed to Beth herself. Pat, however, preferred lively, high-spirited women who, because they were unpredictable, had the ability to hurt *him.* Beth had had to listen to his laments, too. It was annoying to be in this position. Didn't anyone care how *she* felt? She was returning from the kitchen with a tray of refreshments and met Kent standing by himself near the door to the hallway. She offered him a sandwich from her tray.

"Are you enjoying yourself, major?"

"The guests are congenial."

It was an evasive answer, but she didn't press him for a clarification. He asked her if her own young man were present among the gallants here this evening. Where had he heard about a young man? Then she remembered mentioning one last summer so that he wouldn't think her a flirt. She was not about to deny it now. Besides, it would be a relief to talk to someone about Greg, even if she must keep his identity a secret, as she had done in talking with Pete.

"He couldn't come home this Christmas," she said.

"Do you keep secrets from your brother? Pat told me there was no one special."

She colored. "That's my business, is it not?"

"Undoubtedly. And I can see I'm making you uncomfortable. If you will excuse me—"

He moved away from her and Beth followed him with her

eyes. It seemed that being a doctor and a lay mathematician was not enough for him. He now fancied himself a district attorney as well. How dare he cross-examine her about whether there was or was not a beau!

A young officer came over to talk to her, but Beth only nodded absently at his comments. She noticed that Kent was now talking to the flustered Mary and that their conversation lasted only a few minutes before Mary went to sit alone, looking more and more desperate as Pat continued to lavish his attentions elsewhere. Kent, in the next hour, spoke with several of Beth's school friends but periodically he glared across the room at Beth, who was being pursued by two men who stalked and outstared one another in an effort to eliminate the competition.

When the party was over and the guests had departed, Kent said to Beth, "I can see you haven't changed since Gettysburg days."

"Meaning?"

"Meaning you enjoy being the center of attention. I fear that your young man has been forgotten." As he talked, she noticed that his eyes strayed to the lowest point of her deep neckline.

"Not that it's any of your business, but I'm not generally considered a belle."

"Indeed?"

"I enjoy the attentions, but I'm interested in only one man."

"Then he *is* real."

"Now see here, major, I've had just about enough—"

"For a while I believed you were using a mythical figure." She set her teeth. "And why would I do that?"

"I've no idea. But if he's real, why do you keep his identity a secret from your family?"

"There are complications."

"He's of an inferior class? I'd always thought you very democratic."

"It's not his class. I cannot discuss my reason, major."

226

"What intrigue! I rather thought you spent your time in more enterprising ventures."

"You're totally obnoxious! I don't see why you're pursuing this matter. Unless Pat—did Pat enlist you as a spy?"

Kent sighed. "No, Pat didn't enlist me as a spy."

"Then why—oh, never mind! I have things to do."

She left the parlor and stormed down to the kitchen. She had promised Sheilah earlier that she would put away the stacked dishes. Finding herself alone, she began heaving the silver into drawers and came close to breaking one of her mother's crystal glasses. To have this churl insinuate that she was a liar! He either disliked her thoroughly or—or possibly he was jealous. Could he actually be jealous? No, not likely. If he cared at all for her, he wouldn't mock her in such a cruel fashion. But then Kent's behavior had always been strange. Well, it didn't matter what his motives were. She was not in the least interested in him.

She did not speak to Kent again that evening nor at breakfast the next morning, except once when she asked him to pass the maple syrup. After breakfast she sat in the parlor with her father, Joe, and Sean, while Pat and Kent packed their bags upstairs for the return to the front. Joe had been given a late furlough and would not be returning for another week.

For the first time since his arrival, Joe was talking about Gettysburg. Sean had repeatedly broached the subject, but Joe had avoided discussing it. His account of the battle now sounded to Beth like a summary of a newspaper article. He spoke very quickly, his face plainly showing that he was doing it only for Sean's sake.

"Sickles moved his corps out into the valley without any orders from Meade, exposing the left flank of our corps and abandoning a strategic hill called Little Round Top. The johnnies tried to storm up there, but an engineer reached the scene in the nick of time and ordered a brigade to defend the hill. If we had lost Little Round Top, we would have lost the entire ridge."

"Were you up there, Joe?" asked Sean.

"No," he said shortly, and continued his account. "Reb sharpshooters were in Devil's Den, trying to hit the men on Round Top, but they couldn't—"

Sean interrupted. "Then you were only in the Wheatfield?"

"Yes," he answered dully.

"How long were you in there?"

"What?"

"In the Wheatfield?"

Joe didn't answer. He was staring fixedly ahead and he was trembling slightly. In a few moments he was shaking badly and beads of perspiration appeared on his brow. His fists were clenched and he was breathing hard. John and Sean stared open-mouthed at him and Beth, who had seen reactions like this in soldiers at Gettysburg, gripped the arms of her chair, trying to decide what to do. She heard footsteps to her right and looked up to see that Kent had entered the parlor. He stood there, his bag in his hand, and looked at Joe for a moment. Then he set down his bag and walked swiftly over to him.

John said, "He was telling us about Gettysburg. The Wheat—"

"Yes," Kent nodded. "May I talk to him, sir?"

"Uh—please. Do you wish us to leave?"

"If you would. Just for a few minutes."

Beth started to rise too, but Kent motioned her to remain seated. Neither John nor Sean noticed this gesture, and they were puzzled when they saw that Beth was not following them. They lingered for a moment, then walked from the room.

Joe was panting now and perspiring heavily. Kent, standing in front of him, said, "Joe? Joseph?"

Joe looked up at him blinking.

"Joe, it's over."

Joe spoke in gasps. "We were trying to get off as many rounds as—but it was hopeless—it—Linc and Charlie and Allen were down. They—the johnnies were all around us. We had to push forward—we—" He paused, gulping for air. "When we were pulled out, Allen was—he'd survived Antietam and he used to brag that no reb could ever—and his head was gone. His head was—" Joe took a deep breath and closed his eyes.

Kent said, "Few men have the experience of losing most of their platoon. It will take some time for you to recover from this."

"They were on all sides—all sides. I saw a hand land at my foot. Just a hand. No body with it. And—and I couldn't tell if it was ours or theirs. A hand." He broke off, clenching his fists.

Beth felt sick. She had heard other accounts of the Wheatfield when she had nursed its survivors at Gettysburg, but at the time she had been inured to the most gory descriptions of slaughter. Now, after so many months away from the carnage, she experienced the same revulsion she had felt when she first saw the gruesome field hospitals.

Kent turned to Beth, gesturing awkwardly toward her and then toward her brother, indicating that he wanted her to sit next to Joe. Her knees nearly gave way as she took the few steps to the couch. She sat down heavily and placed an arm across Joe's trembling shoulders—an act that calmed her as much as it did him. Kent sat down in a chair facing the couch, and for a long time no one spoke. Then Kent asked, "Are you feeling better, Joe?"

Joe held up his shaking hand and studied it. "Look at me. No stronger than some of my troopers. I had a corporal who acted like this after an engagement. He—"

"Acted like what?" said Kent. "Good God, man. you'd be insane *not* to react this way. The men who departed Gettysburg singing 'Glory hallelujah' are the ones who need their heads examined. Not you." He sighed. "Joe, I think you ought to leave."

"Leave the army?"

"I'd discharge you with a visual problem or a lung condition. You choose the affliction."

"You'd lie to get me out?" said Joe.

"You deserve to be out. You've seen the worst of the war,

and your term won't be up until—what is it, June, July?"

"June. But I intend to reenlist, Kent. I have a platoon to command. I'm no coward. I can't just—"

"Of course you're not a coward. You've been risking your neck for years."

"I can't do it, Kent. But it was bully of you—kind of you—to offer to help. Thank you."

"Not at all. If you change your mind when we're back in Virginia, come and see me." Kent stood up and walked over to the fireplace. He said to Beth, "Isn't there a liquor cabinet somewhere near here? It seems to me I saw one last night—"

"To your left. Under the portrait of the man—"

"Yes, this is it here." Kent opened the cabinet, asked, "Miss Shepherd, would you care for a brandy?"

"I? Oh goodness no." Didn't he realize that ladies only drank sherry except at weddings, when they were permitted small amounts of champagne?

Kent handed the brandy to Joe and said, "What you need now is distraction, not reminiscences of Gettysburg. Try to enjoy your furlough."

Beth was amazed. This was the same man whose words last night had implied that he was not sympathetic or understanding. But Joe was a patient in this situation, and she supposed that made a difference to a doctor.

"Do you want your family to come back in?" Kent asked Joe.

"All right."

Beth rose. "I'll get them, major." She went to the hallway door where all of the family was now assembled. "He's fine," she whispered. "But please, folks, don't bring up the subject again. If he wants to talk about Gettysburg, let him approach the matter himself."

"It was my fault," said Sean.

"You didn't know," said Beth gently. "But I've nursed men like Joe, and remembering a battle is sometimes as bad as actually fighting in it. And the Wheatfield was the bloodiest—well in any case, try not to mention it."

230

She stood aside, and the family—they were there en masse, including Sheilah—sauntered into the parlor as casually as possible. Pat, ever in command of a situation, walked toward Joe talking animatedly to Sean about a new game called baseball. John, in an overly hearty voice, asked questions about the game. And finally Joe described a baseball game that he had played in camp. The men began to relax. Kate, never adept at concealing her feelings, sneaked alarmed looks at Joe while informing Sheilah in a quavering voice that since it was New Year's Day, John would be making calls this afternoon and she would be receiving guests. Sheilah, in turn, pretended that this yearly ritual was a fascinating surprise to her and nodded gravely between furtive glances at Joe.

Beth, forgetting how angry she had been with Kent the night before, stood with him near the hallway door and asked, "Will he be all right?"

"I think so, yes."

"I wish he would leave the army."

"I don't think he will, Miss Shepherd."

"I've often wondered what men mean by cowardice," she said. "Is the refusal to murder and maim really cowardice? I can understand that the refusal to stand up for one's rights might be cowardly. But when standing up for them means murdering, I'm not so sure."

She was thinking out loud, not really talking to him, but as he looked directly at her, she continued. "I should think *not* fighting would be the heroic thing, if a man considers himself civilized. I realize it's not so simple as that, but that's how I feel."

She noticed that his eyes had widened with what seemed to be understanding, then glazed over as though he were thinking of something else. She was about to turn away when he looked at her in an odd way. It seemed to her a look of discovery, but she wasn't sure.

"That's right," he said finally.

"Excuse me, major?"

"I wish I had said it that way."

She could tell that he wasn't referring to Joe but to some event in his own experience. His face seemed troubled. She didn't question him, for she sensed that to do so would distress him. A few minutes later, when he and Pat were leaving, she could see that he was still distracted with some memory.

Joe wouldn't discuss the incident with the family, but several days later he commented, "I take back what I said about Kent. I like him." Beth wasn't certain that she did, but Kent's manner with Joe had impressed her.

Only one year had passed since she had met Greg, and as the holiday high slid into the abyss of January, Beth dwelt on those memories. She recalled the day they had stood looking at New York from the hotel window, she seeing only warmth in their future; small rooms with great fireplaces and cozy, quilt-heaped beds. But now, as she walked through streets that tunneled the icy wind, she could see him freezing under thin blankets near drafty prison walls. From what Joe wrote, Virginia was beastly cold this winter. Greg might be ill even now. And who would care? Certainly not the Confederates. For all the chivalry the opposing armies often showed one another, she could not imagine them going out of their way to keep the prisoners warm. More likely they would expose their enemy to every manner of suffering and then applaud the "gallantry" of those who survived all odds. Such was the thinking of men, those illogical fools who shot at their enemy and then shared their rations with those who, against all probability, made it through the bombardment. Beth would never forget the lesson of Pickett's Charge.

Even at winter camp at Brandy Station in Virginia, fatal diseases were commonplace. And the doctors were not immune: They found out in February that Pat had had pneumonia and nearly died.

Joe wrote:

He had decided to take a walk in the winter snow, being weary of the hospital atmosphere. A rainstorm came up, soaking him to the skin and the disease set in almost at once.

For a day or so his chances were doubtful. But Kent sat with him for two days and nights, forcing soups into him and keeping kettles boiling, driving the orderlies mad with incessant commands for steaming towels, medications, and what-nots, and telling me all the while that it was the grippe and nothing for me to worry about. Like a fool, I believed him and discovered the truth later.

Pat is fine now, so don't worry about him. Kent still has him on bed rest, though he's healthier than the lot of us by this time. A lot healthier, I imagine, than his taciturn superior officer, who wouldn't accept Pat's thanks or mine and wouldn't admit that staying awake and alert for forty hours was anything out of the ordinary.

Kate and John sent Kent Wilson a warm note of thanks and received a brief reply:

> Dear Mr. and Mrs. Shepherd,
> Thank you for your note. Patrick is fully recovered now and there is no cause for alarm. Nor should you be concerned that this disease is apt to afflict him again. Basically he is a healthy man and I shall personally see to it that he remains so.
> My regards to your family,
> Kent Wilson

"I see what Joe means," John remarked. "The man finds it difficult to accept thanks."

"He's a dear, sweet man," gushed Kate, "and I don't care a whit that he's not effusive on paper. He'd obviously risk his own health to help Patrick."

"He very well might," Beth agreed, studying Kent's handwriting. She had seen it before on notes in Gettysburg. It was unusual, angular, and left-slanted, with no embellishments at all. Though legible, it was hardly in keeping with the fine artistic script that most people attempted in correspondence. The handwriting was like Kent himself. But this latest deed of his had elevated him several notches in her esteem.

*   *   *

In April, 1864, the war entered its fourth year. Ulysses S. Grant, the hero of Vicksburg, was now in command of all the armies, but his job would be difficult. The Western army controlled the Mississsippi, but the Army of the Potomac was still hammering its way toward Richmond in endless Virginia battles that had long since ravaged much of the state. The worst of these was fought in May in a place called the Wilderness; a dense, gloomy wood with foliage so thick that the armies broke into platoons and fought one another with little visibility, eye-watering battle smoke adding to the confusion. Eventually some of these woods caught fire and wounded men were trapped in the flames. Among them was Nate Klein's son Josh.

When Kate heard that Josh was dead she immediately took over, since the Kleins had no close relatives in New York. According to Jewish custom, food could not be prepared in the home during the seven-day mourning period. Kate therefore made arrangements with friends of the Kleins to have meals taken to the family three times a day. Kate herself was responsible for dinner. Each evening at seven, she, Beth and John walked to the Klein home carrying warm plates of food.

The Kleins had two grown daughters and another son, fifteen. The Shepherds and others tried to distract the family by talking about the news, the weather, the price of potatoes— everything but the deceased, for it was thought that to mention him would be cruel. But one night Kate shocked everyone by introducing the subject of Josh and encouraging the family to talk about him. To Beth's amazement, they seemed eager to talk and soon they were reminiscing about incidents from Josh's boyhood: the pranks he had played on his sisters or the declaration he had made to his parents at the age of ten—that he was a man now and entitled to some respect. Even Ruth, who had been inconsolable, seemed grateful for the opportunity to speak of her son. There were tears as they told these stories but there was laughter too—and the realization that Josh would always be with them.

Though Kate had been able to ease the pain of the Klein family, she herself was very despondent. One day she went up to her room, sat down at her small oak desk, and began to write:

My son. Soft and mewing as a kitten. Nestling contentedly at the breast, testing the power of the little lungs and tiny fists and stubby legs. My son. Smiling proud little smiles because he has taken a step; hiding his face in my skirt because he has said the word correctly and I have cheered so loudly that he is shy: falling over a stool and hurting his knee and coming to me for comfort; but leaving soon thereafter for bigger stools and bigger falls and not needing comfort quite so much. My son. Older now, needing more and more food. Will he ever get enough to eat? He has stature, and stature brings the bravado. "Look, Ma, I can stand on my head. Look, Ma, I can fight with the boy next door. Look, Ma, I can fight with the rebel in Virginia." And suddenly it is the child's voice that is screaming, "Mama! Mama! I'm wounded and the flames are getting close. Save me, Mama!"

Kate folded the paper and placed it in a drawer amid her scented handkerchiefs. She knew that what she had written was morbid and that if she ever read it again she would cry. But Kate believed that crying as much as one pleased was a good thing. She sat on the bed, thinking about her own sons and crying. After that she felt better.

Though many of their acquaintances had lost sons in the war, the Kleins were the first among the Shepherds' close friends to suffer such a tragedy. In Josh's death the war was brought home sharply to everyone. After Joe had survived Gettysburg, they had begun thinking him invincible. And of the war itself, they had made such comments as, "Lee's licked. It can't last much longer." But the Wilderness was followed by another battle, that of Spotsylvania. And by another, Cold Harbor. Casualty lists filled the papers day after day and Beth was often chosen to read them first.

Beth's hands always trembled when she checked the lists. Then, seeing that her brothers' names were not on it, she would drop the paper, exhale loudly, and say, "They're safe." At that moment Kate would leave the room for a few minutes and go up to her room and kneel in thanks to God. John would wipe his forehead with a handkerchief. All through May and June, Beth and her father took turns perusing the dreaded lists. Often they came across the names of acquaintances but only after the words "They're safe" were uttered, did they mention others who had been killed or wounded.

In late June Joe wrote them at last, saying only that the fighting had been "hard." The family, who remembered Joe's waking nightmare, wondered what he wasn't telling them. In another letter he said that the doctors had been working round the clock tending to the wounded of the two-month-long battles and skirmishes. Never in the war had the fighting been so continuous. In the past there had always been respites between engagements. But now, though individual fighting units could rest from time to time, the army as a whole was engaged constantly, and that meant no rest for the medical people. Joe wrote:

> Kent nearly ordered Pat discharged for not taking proper care of himself. Now, though Pat is tired, he's hale and hearty. Both of them, however, are as demented as ever. When they aren't shouting curses at each other, they're laughing themselves into oblivion—a sure sign of fatigue. One day I found them conjugating Latin verbs. The idea was that if they kept their mouths going they could keep their minds alert (though Kent was the first to admit that the example of politicians contradicted this theory).
>
> Lee is now on the defensive. He couldn't possibly try another stunt like Gettysburg. The war will certainly be over by Christmas.

At about this time it was learned that eight hundred prisoners confined in Libby Prison had been sent south to Macon, Georgia. This occurred after an attempted cavalry raid on Richmond. The raid had failed, but Confederate authorities, nervous about having eight hundred Yankee officers in their capital when their liberators were so close, decided to send them south. Beth gathered that Greg was among them, and Mr. Allister's informer soon confirmed this. She shuddered. Libby Prison was bad enough, but Georgia in the summertime would be wicked.

Nor was there any hope of exchange. The Union refused to release Southern prisoners, claiming that the war would drag on interminably if these able-bodied men—and that was questionable, the Union prisons also being deathtraps—were sent home only to bear arms again. So there were no exchanges and no paroles, and the families of those in captivity had to carry on in limbo.

In July, Pete Weatherly was captured, and Phil feared that Pete had been sent to Andersonville, another Georgia prison, this one for enlisted men. It had been in existence only since February and was already said to be a charnel house of filth and disease where men had scarcely any shelter from the elements and were given only maggoty meat and ground corncob to eat. The death toll there was the highest of all the prisons and Phil was certain that Pete was already dead. John tried to cheer him by insisting that Sherman's army, now in Georgia, would be liberating the prison any day now. No one believed this. Sherman was far to the north, trying to seize Atlanta, and the Confederates were holding him back. In Andersonville, every day was a crucial one, and it would take weeks or months for Sherman to get there—if he marched in that direction and if the prisoners were not, in the meantime, transferred. Everyone assumed that Pete was lost though they never hinted as much to Phil.

The months dragged by like a creaking wagon. Diane, who now admitted to Beth that she and Joe hoped to marry, found the visits from Greg's mother more and more tedious as the summer lumbered on. Beth couldn't summon the courage to tell Diane about her relationship with Greg. She was not certain how Diane would react, and she thought it better to wait.

237

During the summer Beth became acquainted with Joan Allister, a tall, thin, bright-eyed woman who doted on her granddaughter and called on the Kendalls often. Beth, who spent a great deal of time playing with the baby in the Kendalls' garden, listened eagerly when Joan spoke of her son. Beth gathered that he had lived much the same sort of life as she, even though Greg had been very wealthy. As the only boy and the middle child, Greg too had retreated into books and fantasy at an early age. His father was much too busy to notice him and Joan too was always serving on philanthropic committees. Thus Greg had always been somewhat detached from his family. The detachment had somehow resulted in a passionate idealism that Joan felt was adolescent in a man of twenty-eight. She asserted that men could not singlehandedly save the world and she hoped Greg would come to realize this. He was much too serious, and for this reason she approved of his marriage to Diane.

"He needed someone lively and cheerful," Joan said, "like my daughter-in-law."

After one of Joan's visits, Diane was far from cheerful. "I hate myself! Do you realize what a mess I've made of things because I was so impulsive? Look at me. A wife, a mother, and in love with another man. Oh Beth, I should have married Joe years ago."

"You can still marry him."

"I intend to. But think of the scandal. And imagine what the Allisters will say."

"Does Joe know the whole story?"

"Yes, but I told him I was carried away by the moment; not that I deliberately, uh . . . encouraged . . ." She trailed off.

"Why did you tell him?"

"Joe has always been a brother to me. I often confided in him."

"*Do* you love him, Diane?"

"Oh, yes. I feel secure with him. He accepts everything about me and I feel the same way about him. I suppose it was because we grew up together. I always let other men turn my head, but in the back of my mind Joe was always there."

238

"Like an old shoe?" Beth regretted the remark as soon as she made it.

"I do love him, Beth. You must never doubt that."

"Do you feel romantic toward him?" Beth persisted.

"Of course I do. But a husband should be one-tenth romance and nine-tenths friend. A woman has to *live* with a husband."

"You've grown up."

"I wish I had grown up a year and a half ago."

"Don't worry, Diane. Everything will work out." Now was the time to tell her, but Beth couldn't do it.

In the last months of 1864, the Eastern generals were at last fighting the war in earnest, while civilians, ever contrary, were demanding an end to hostilities even if the Confederacy *did* remain a separate nation. Beth, who felt bored and ineffectual, isolated as she was in New York, began making plans to join the Sanitary Commission as a nurse. It was almost September now. The year had gone by quickly and she had scarcely noticed its passage, so monotonous were the days. Why should she stay in New York doing nothing when she could be nursing the soldiers in Washington or Baltimore, or perhaps even nearer to the front lines, if the surgeons permitted it?

Before relating these plans to her parents (she was determined to override their certain vetoes) she sent off a note to the school principal notifying him that she would not be returning in September and stating her reasons. The principal, a paunchy middle-aged man who perspired profusely even in wintertime, came puffing over to Beth's house as soon as he received the letter. He told Kate that he wished to speak to her daughter alone. Kate, quite perplexed, nervously showed him into the parlor, then fetched Beth, who explained to her mother that he had come to discuss the following year's curriculum.

"Miss Shepherd," the principal began, mopping at his brow, "I don't imagine your family has been apprised of this preposterous notion?"

"Not yet, sir, but I intend to tell them. And I am offended by the word *preposterous*. Is it preposterous to render a service to our brave—"

"And what of the immigrant children? Are you going to abandon those poor souls to the scourge of illiteracy? With the men in the army and only a few qualified female teachers left—good grief, things were bad enough the winter you left us so abruptly with—what was it?—'a family emergency'? It's downright irresponsible, your going off again!"

"Irresponsible! I'm not planning a holiday, sir. I'll be nursing sick and wounded men. How can you call such work irresponsible? Education can wait until the war is over, but the men in the field—"

His face was florid. "Education wait? Wait indeed! Do the wealthy dismiss their children's tutors, Miss Shepherd? No more should you abandon your impoverished students. You must stay on until the men come home."

"Until the men come home. Of course. Until the true teaching talent returns."

He ignored the sarcasm. "So you're determined to forget these children. By doing so, Miss Shepherd, you're insuring their futures as unskilled and illiterate laborers. You're abetting in a monstrous crime against the poor."

In the end, she was persuaded to stay. The principal had hinted that desertion now would guarantee her unemployment after the war. If she didn't marry Greg, she would need this job.

So Beth stayed in New York, and soon she was back in her crowded classroom for another season of times-tables, penmanship, and monotony. The curriculum was dull, but the school board wanted it and therefore Beth had to teach it. Only rarely was there the opportunity to inject some spirit into the proceedings, and the principal usually objected to her innovations.

She was teaching eight- and nine-year-olds this year. Most of them came from abysmally deprived homes. Antiwar

240

feeling was strong among the adults in this district, but Beth's charges, especially the boys, were as intrigued with the war as was her brother Sean. She was, of course, obliged to read them simple tales of their countrymen who were invariably "fearless, gallant lads"; who "soaked the ground with their blood" as they "routed the cursèd foe"; and who never expired without expressing some noble hope for their country. As she read these tales, she could hardly suppress laughter at the thought of Joe or Greg using the term "cursèd foe" or Kent calling his orderlies "gallant lads." And she remembered one soldier saying, "Please, miss. A brandy and a cigar before I die." But the children, perhaps because they saw little nobility around them, ate up these fairy tales; and Beth's attempts at pointing out the truth—that all men are afraid at some time in their lives or that nobility is not necessarily best measured by the number of rebels slaughtered—fell upon deaf ears.

The children who had relatives in the army had the highest status in the class. There was always some argument about whose father or uncle or brother was the bravest. She walked into the class one morning to find that a boy whose brother was an infantryman in the Irish Brigade was sneering at one whose father was an ambulance attendant.

"My brother killed six johnnies. What did your father ever do?"

She gave no indication of having overheard the boys, but at the end of the day she announced that she was going to tell a story about the heroes of the Wheatfield. The story, which she made up as she went along, was part truth, part exaggeration, and part fiction but she hoped it would have the desired effect:

"I met a major at Gettysburg," Beth began. "This man wanted the war to end as soon as possible, but he didn't want to see the gallant heroes die. One day he heard that there was terrible fighting on a small patch of land called the Wheatfield. He was very sad and he said, 'What can we do? All my noble comrades are dying!' He shouted for men to run and save the valiant soldiers, but everyone was afraid to go. Everyone was afraid to save the heroes." She paused for effect.

"And then he saw two men carrying a stretcher. Tall and proud and fearless they were. They came to the major and they said, 'We'll go, sir! We'll save them!' Their names were Colin and—" she tried to think of another name— "Hippocrates."

" 'Ah, gallant lads,' shouted the major. 'It is, I fear, a dangerous mission and yet it must be undertaken. You must find every wounded soldier you can and bring them at once to the hospital or the Union will be lost!'

"Well, those boys ran in and out of that awful field under the heaviest fire imaginable and they took every soldier they could find and brought them to the hospitals. Yes, they kept on and on, running back and forth, until they could scarcely breathe. And at the very end when almost everyone was safe in the hospitals, a shell exploded near them and they were badly wounded.

"The major knelt beside the two dying boys and said, 'Do you have any last words, my lads?'

"Hippocrates said, 'I saved these soldiers for the Union, sir,' and Colin said, 'May the stars and stripes fly forever over the land of the free.'

"And they died." Beth lowered her head.

"The major was inconsolable. He went to his tent and that is where I found him, boys and girls, lying on his cot, utterly prostrated with grief. He told me that when the war was over he would tell the world the story of the heroes of the Wheatfield, those heroes but for whom we would have lost our finest soldiers. And he told me that he had never in this tragic war seen such gallantry and bravery as that exhibited by these fearless lads from the noble ambulance corps who saved many many men, who died gladly for their country, and who never—" she looked meaningfully at the worst of the class braggarts—"who never killed another human being."

One of the little girls cried. The others were solemn. The

boy whose father was an ambulance driver sat up straighter in his chair. Beth tried to suppress a grin as she imagined Kent turning purple with rage over the cloying description of him. But she hadn't meant the tale to be mocking or unkind. The story of Colin, Kent's stretcher-bearer (who doubtless would have laughed if he could have heard it) was every bit as moving as were those of front-line soldiers. And Kent had indeed grieved for Colin. Grieved for him and exhausted himself trying to save the others. Kent had more nobility than he'd ever admit.

She hadn't thought of Kent in months, but she was glad that when she did think of him she could quickly recall his finer attributes. She wasn't one to make sweeping negative judgments and she was quite pleased with this generous quality in herself.

In early September they received word that Sherman had taken Atlanta. It was a great victory indeed but it wasn't quite enough to destroy the Confederacy and it didn't change the situation of the Army of the Potomac. The boys were still in Virginia, stalemated at Petersburg, and their hard-driving General Grant ("I propose to fight it out on this line if it takes all summer") was, by midautumn, more than a little frustrated. There seemed no way for the army to get into Petersburg and break the Confederate railway center.

The war dragged on, and civilians at home dragged on too—through streets emptied of their young men but jammed with the grand carriages of stock-speculators who were making fortunes from the war in railroads, iron, and other military necessities. It was a crisp colorful autumn, but for Beth it was a boring season of much busyness and little challenge. What with correcting the heaps of papers, appearing at her mother's lint-scraping parties, and continually mending her cotton clothing and underwear (cotton was scarce and they had to make do with what they had), there was never a moment's idleness. But there was never any excitement either.

A facsimile of excitement came from the presidential campaign, which lasted from August until November. But campaigns depressed Beth: She couldn't vote. Nevertheless, she had opinions and she voiced them to eligible voters (mostly her father and Nate Klein) at every opportunity. McClellan, the Democrat, was supported by men who sought "negotiations" with the South. On the face of it, this sounded reasonable but everyone knew that "negotiations" might mean recognizing the sovereignty of the Confederacy. She wouldn't have minded that, except that it would probably mean the continuation of slavery. She knew that McClellan's men would never consider Kent's idea of paying the South for the release of the slaves.

Lincoln's insistence on fighting the war to the bitter end was not to Beth's liking either, but his motives at least were pure. There was no doubt that he meant to see the slaves freed. Technically the Emancipation Proclamation had already freed them in the belligerent states. Therefore his wish to fight to the finish meant that the states would no longer be belligerent and the slaves, free in theory already, would be free in actuality. So, despite her reservations about the faults of the administration, Beth was a Lincoln supporter and was pleased when he won the election.

In November a plot by Confederates to burn New York was foiled by authorities who had advance word of the plan and were able to seize the men as they simultaneously set fire to several hotels. The event made John Shepherd wonder if perhaps they shouldn't consider moving to some peaceful little town where they wouldn't have to worry about riots and conflagrations. Living in New York, he raged one night, was like living on top of a bomb and he'd be damned if he'd spend another day in this hellish place. But he didn't budge; nor had anyone expected him to. John was very much the city man.

The war news was all about Sherman. Taking off from Atlanta in mid-November and burning the city behind him, he severed his cumbrous supply and communication lines and led an army of sixty thousand men into the heart of Georgia,

244

directing them to live off the land. For several weeks there was not a word to be heard of Sherman other than propaganda pieces gleaned from Southern newspapers describing the army as hopelessly surrounded by Confederates. But at last, in December, the army emerged at Savannah, fat as hogs after looting and burning all but a few farms and plantations along a path sixty miles wide and three hundred miles long. Later, conscientious Northerners would question Sherman's tactics, but in 1864 all anyone could think of was ending the war. Few had tears to shed for the destitute Georgia families.

Amid the cheers for Sherman, there were still unhappy voices. John and other fathers of boys serving in the Army of the Potomac were a bit put off that the triumphs kept coming from Sherman's men and not from their own boys, still mired in Virginia. Their boys were as brave as Sherman's, and they'd have to win a victory before the end of the war; they'd just have to. Phil was upset because no mention had been made of the liberation of Andersonville. Had Sherman sent troops to Andersonville, or didn't anyone care?

For the most part, however, people were happy enough with what had been gained and Beth shared in their cheers. The South was now cut into three parts. The war would have to end soon.

Four days before Christmas, Beth was in the family room with a group of twelve-year-olds trying to teach them to sing the Hallelujah Chorus from Handel's *Messiah*. Rose Kendall, a pillar of her church, had fallen ill with the grippe the day before and had pleaded with Beth to help her. The Christmas pageant was two days away and now Beth was the only one who could ready the performance. Rose wouldn't hear any excuses. Hadn't Beth bragged just last October about teaching her class to sing the "Battle Hymn of the Republic" in four parts and with no mistakes? But the "Battle Hymn" was far simpler than the Hallelujah Chorus." The latter was a complicated oratorio piece with voices sometimes following other voices and sometimes singing together in intricate harmony and with different words. The music was difficult enough for adults, but for twelve-year-olds it was almost impossible.

Despite this frustration, Beth was content. Pat and Joe were expected home tomorrow, and Sean would be returning from his Connecticut school the day after. The family was overjoyed at the prospect of having Pat and Joe home again for the second Christmas in a row. Most families were not so fortunate. At the beginning of the war the boys had missed the holidays, but this year Joe had reenlisted and managed to secure this furlough as part of the bargain. Pat was still holding his superior officer to the promise he had once made of giving Pat and Kent every Christmas until the war was over.

The scent of gingerbread wafted through the house, mingling with that of the evergreen. The tree was still untrimmed, but they hoped to finish it tonight to surprise the boys. Kate and Sheilah had been busy for weeks, knitting indestructible socks and scarves enough to stretch, end to end, from New York to California, and baking cookies, fruitcakes, and breads. It promised to be a pleasant holiday.

She was standing facing the children, who were clustered in four groups singing from sheet music while Beth indicated their parts like a conductor.

> King of kings
> Forever and ever!
> And Lord of Lords
> Hallelujah! Hallelujah!

At this point they all began to smile. Beth wondered why. But they sang on (not very well) to the end. Suddenly a male chorus behind Beth joined in for the finale. She turned and found her two brothers and Kent Wilson forming a blue line across the room. The singing had been so loud that she hadn't heard them come in. Joe had grown a mustache and Pat now sported a modest beard. Kent was clean-shaven as usual, which was quite unfashionable, especially in a doctor of his rank. All three were very thin.

"You're home a day early!" she exclaimed as she ran to greet them.

"We were able to make good connections," said Joe.

She hugged her brothers and then turned awkwardly to Kent, not knowing quite how to greet him. Finally she extended her hand. "Welcome, major. Will you be staying with us?"

"I'm here between trains." He took her hand in a way that reminded her of the day she had fallen in the woods at Gettysburg.

Kate, entering the room, said. "He's scheduled to leave at eight o'clock this evening, but I won't hear of it. Do stay the night, Kent."

He looked at Beth as though for approval.

"Of course, major. You just arrived. It's a long way to Boston."

He smiled. "Very well."

Sheilah shouted from the dining room, "Fruitcake and eggnog, everyone!"

"Is there brandy in the eggnog?" Joe shouted back.

"No. You'll have to be getting it from the bar."

Beth looked at the children, still standing at attention with their music open. "Oh, children, can you wait a few minutes? I must have a short chat with my brothers, but we do have to finish this rehearsal. I won't be long."

Kent said, "Go ahead, Miss Shepherd, I'll rehearse them."
"You?"

"I sang this as a boy in Latin school. I know it well."

Beth was taken aback. She could not conceive of him as a child. Somehow she imagined him to have sprung fully grown from the head of a craggy surgeon. But no, Kent had once been a child doing all the foolish things her brothers had done and singing in school choruses. She could not picture him with a high voice and a smooth angelic face singing praises to God.

He turned to the group. "All right, first sopranos, you stand here. Where are the seconds? Seconds over here. (Miss Shepherd, will you go drink your eggnog?) First altos move to the left a little bit. Fine. Second altos stand up straighter. That's fine." He picked up some sheet music, walked over to a second piano that they kept in the family room, and struck a chord.

Beth grinned as she closed the dining room doors behind her. It was obvious that Kent had volunteered his services in order to escape the emotional homecoming scene. A few minutes later she could hear him in his battlefield voice shouting "Forte! Loud! Good. Now, first altos—"

"He's a man of many talents," she remarked to Pat as she ladled eggnog into a cup.

"He knows a great deal about music. But just listen to him. He's handling them like a regiment."

They could hear his voice as though he were in the same room. "No! No! First altos wait for a moment and then—" He sang the part for them twice in a deep voice that was anything but lyrical. The best that could be said for it was that it was on key.

Beth smiled. "I don't care how rough he is with them, so long as they learn the chorus."

Eventually the music was forgotten as everyone dipped into the eggnog, which Joe had insisted on spiking heavily. The conversation was a hodgepodge of army stories, scandals, dances, politics, and food. Kate told the boys that they looked like cadavers and saw to it that their mouths were never empty, while Sheilah whined that they'd all ruin their appetites for supper. John came home, and there was another round of affectionate hugs. And everyone kept drinking eggnog.

By the time Kent appeared in the dining room to announce to Beth that the chorus was ready, everybody but Kate (a temperance advocate) was tipsy with Christmas cheer. Beth walked unsteadily into the family room to hear Kent lead the chorus through two downright coherent performances.

248

"That's splendid, children! Major, how on earth did you do it?"

"With charm," he said.

"Was he charming, boys and girls?"

The children grinned nervously, not quite daring to answer the question. Beth smiled and said to Kent, "No matter, major. In this case the end justifies the means. Rose Kendall will be delighted." She turned to the children. "Very well. You're dismissed."

They breathed a collective sigh of relief, looking uneasily at the terrible Major Wilson, but he surprised them by saying cheerfully, "Good luck, everybody."

After they had gone, Beth thanked him and insisted that he join the family. He followed her into the dining room, though he appeared to be reluctant. She guessed that Kent felt as if he were drowning whenever sentimental currents ran too strongly. And this family reunion grew increasingly more cloying as the eggnog, and later the whisky, flowed. Sheilah started serving dinner, expecting no one to eat. To her surprise, the three soldiers cleaned their plates, Pat actually asking for more.

The conversation was by this time loud and jocular, with frequent allusions to family anecdotes and the old days. Attempts to draw Kent into the conversation failed.

"Kent looks ill at ease," Beth remarked to her mother as they were cleaning up.

"He reminds me of myself when I was a little girl without any family," said Kate.

"But he has his sister's family in Boston."

"It isn't enough, obviously, or he'd be a different sort of person. For all Kent's cool exterior, I think he's rather afraid of people."

"Afraid! If you could have heard him issuing orders in the field—"

"I mean afraid to get close to them."

"I doubt that, Mother. I don't think he'd be afraid of the devil himself."

"Some day you'll understand what I mean, dear."

After dinner the family trimmed the tree while Kent sat in a corner playing the piano. Kate asked him if he knew the "Coventry Carol," which her adoptive parents had sung to her as a child. When he played it, Kate wept. Kent turned away embarrassed.

Diane, to Joe's delight, stopped in that evening, and Louise arrived with her arms full of gifts. All the while Kent continued to play—sometimes from music and sometimes by ear—Bach, Handel, Brahms, Mozart, and occasionally a ballad like "Greensleeves" or a carol. In this way he was able to fit into the effusive group without having to be effusive himself. The family was impressed. He was a creditable pianist.

The next morning they saw him off. Kate urged him to come back in time for New Year's. This time he didn't seem to need persuading. He and Pat exchanged mysterious smiles. Beth wondered what the secret was. Probably a bordello— "parlor house" as they were called—that Pat had heard about. Kent had made a much better impression on her this year than last and she wished him the merriest of Christmases. Wherever he spent it, she thought wickedly.

Beth had her share of admirers at the parties that week, and she enjoyed the light flirtations. Nevertheless, she was not seriously interested in any of these men, and too often their gallant remarks only served to make her intensely desirous of Greg. At one party there was a lieutenant who was tall, thin, and dark, and she eagerly accepted a dance with him, pretending he was Greg. Her fantasy was shattered when the man opened his mouth. She had expected a deep voice, and what greeted her ears were several little squeaks. It was no use at all! She'd been pretending and fantasizing for almost two years, and nothing made her feel better. How much longer could she stand it? She envied Joe and Diane. They had been together for the past two Christmases while she had had to wait alone, not even able to share her frustrations with anyone.

Occasionally she had doubts about how Greg would feel

when he did come home. Prison was said to do things to men's minds. Perhaps he wouldn't care for her at all, and the two-year wait would have been in vain. Would she then regret not having married one of these young men? She did want to marry, and at twenty-three she ought to marry soon or there would be no one left. War had already carried off the best of the men. But more serious than the prospect of spinsterhood was the thought that she would never know what it was like to lie with a man, really lie with him and have him enter her. She must marry, if only for that. And for children. Her daughter would have a fuller life than she. She hoped to have love in her marriage, too, but she could not imagine loving anyone but Greg.

One morning Beth overslept. As she passed through the hall she could hear Pat and Joe talking in Joe's room. Beth stood still, listening. The voices were clear, for the door was slightly ajar. In the past she had often picked up interesting tidbits by eavesdropping on her brothers' conversations. Since women were denied information about the outside world, she felt no compunctions about acquiring it surreptitiously. They were talking about various officers and soldiers she had never heard of. She was about to walk on, bored, when Pat mentioned Captain Marshall, the doctor who had flirted with her at Gettysburg.

"Did I tell you about Marshall's latest escapade?"

"No," said Joe. "What did that character do this time?"

Pat started to laugh. "While we were all at mess, he smuggled a girl into the cabin. I returned early and watched them finish things."

"Did they see you?"

"No. I stood there clearing my throat waiting for someone to acknowledge me."

"I don't believe you cleared your throat," said Joe. "I think you're a sneaky voyeur. Was she worth watching?"

"What do you think?"

"Where did he find her?"

"I don't know. Where does he find any of them? When they

were finished, the girl saw me. She shrieked and ran for her clothes."

"And Marshall?"

"He begged me not to report him. I told him I wouldn't, if he'd find me one like her." He paused. "You know, Marshall was after Beth at Gettysburg and she was attracted to him."

"Good God. I hope you told her about the illegitimate children all over Washington."

"I told her he was engaged. It was simpler."

What did he mean "simpler"? Of all the condescending attitudes, Pat's took the prize.

Pat said, "She was quite a belle down there. The whole camp was salivating."

"I'll bet they were."

"She was mad as blazes at Kent for telling her to behave herself."

"Didn't she behave herself?" There was an edge to Joe's voice. He was her younger brother, but he was talking like her father.

"Of course she did, but you know how men look at her. And Kent was very upset about it."

"Jealous, was he?"

"I rather think so."

"And frustrated as hell, I'll wager. Gettysburg was a long stint for you people, and he was never able to survive two weeks without a woman."

"He's been more restrained lately," said Pat.

"Oh?"

"He's interested in a young lady."

"Good. I think Kent needs someone. A Washington belle?"

"No. And I'm not at liberty to discuss it."

A young lady? Kent had a young lady? She was astounded. During his recent visit he had seemed quite taken with her, Beth. She listened to more of the conversation but they were now discussing maneuvers in the siege of Petersburg. They continued in this vein until Joe announced that he was going down to breakfast. She walked on. So Kent had a young lady.

Why should she care? She was waiting for Greg. It was her pride, she decided. For a time during the homecoming dinner she had thought herself to be the only woman capable of making an impression on Kent. But there was another. Who was she?

Kent returned two days before New Year's bearing a house gift of a silver-framed engraving of a New England landscape for John and Kate. They thanked him warmly and complimented him on his taste.

"Actually I have no taste for art. My sister had to explain what was considered good."

"That doesn't matter." Kate laughed. "You approved it. Was your Christmas pleasant?"

He nodded.

"How is your sister's family?"

"My nephews enjoy the holiday."

"Don't you?"

"Yes."

"I think adults enjoy watching children, don't you?"

"Yes. That's right."

John said, sotto voce, to Beth, "I daresay he's not one for pointless pleasantries. But the engraving is a fine one."

The evening was quiet. There were no parties to attend, and all members of the family were home but Sean, who had a call to make. After dinner they all retired to the parlor. The arrangement of chairs and couches was such that there were two conversation areas in the room. As John and Joe headed for one of them, Pat moved toward the other. Kent, as Pat's guest, followed him, and when Beth and Kate walked into the room Pat motioned Beth over to his area with a loud "We were just talking about amputations." This was all Kate needed to hear. She immediately opted for John's corner of the room while Beth sat down next to Kent.

They chatted for thirty seconds about Semmelweis's theories. Then Pat drifted over toward the liquor cabinet and took his time examining the contents therein. Having finally settled on Scotch, he poured some into a glass—no water, no ice—and brought the bottle and another glass over to Kent, setting it down on an end table beside him. Then he sauntered over toward his parents and sat down with them. Beth thought his behavior especially rude. Why had he asked Kent here if he didn't intend to talk to him? Kent, however, did not seem in the least upset about it. He poured himself some Scotch and, after a few remarks about the train ride from Boston and the hazards of the railroads in general, he abruptly changed the subject.

"Is your young man home this season, Miss Shepherd?"

"No, he's still missing," she said, praying that he would not pursue the subject.

His face was serious. "I'm sorry. I was hoping something would be resolved by this time." He sipped his drink.

"What do you mean?"

Without looking at her he said, "I had hoped to court you, Beth."

Her mouth fell open. Then she was the woman Pat had been talking about in his conversation with Joe the other morning! "Why, I—"

"I suppose it sounds incredible—" He swallowed some more whisky.

"Why no, Kent." Their new intimacy prompted her use of his first name. "No, it's not. But you've never before spoken of courtship."

"Let me phrase it this way, Beth: If the situation changes, remember that I'm here."

"Kent!" she said with concern, thinking as she said it that she would never have thought it possible to feel compassion for this man.

He shifted uncomfortably. "Spare me your solicitude."

"Kent, I like you, but there is someone else. I swear it."

"I see."

"But I do like you."

"That's heartening, isn't it?"

Under the circumstances she could forgive his sarcasm. "Have you felt this way long?"

"Since Gettysburg."

"Why, I had no idea!" she lied. She had felt the physical attraction herself. No doubt that was all it was.

"I'm not one for elaborate speeches."

"Elaborate speeches! You *did* make elaborate speeches, though. About what a flirt I was and—"

"Only because you were so appealing that you were distracting."

She blushed. "Oh but last year—last Christmas—"

"Last Christmas I was jealous—as I am now. My hopes had been raised by Pat's assertion that there was no man. And then you told me—" He stopped abruptly. He had probably intended another sarcastic comment and thought better of it. "Well then, nothing is changed."

"I'm sorry, Kent."

He tapped nervously on the end table, then poured himself another drink. Beth, absently smoothing her skirts, kept stealing sidelong glances at him. Two memories came vividly to mind: the day she had walked into his tent and blushed at the sight of his chest, and the day in the woods when he had held her. On both occasions, she now realized, she had been strongly attracted to him—as she was this very moment.

He was looking blankly before him, sipping his drink. She decided that she must say something. Anything. He must not walk away now.

"Are you still very busy? In the army? I mean—"

"Not as we were at Gettysburg. Busy enough, though."

"Still searching for sheets?"

"Now we have a supply of several hundred. And the wife of one of my orderlies has consented to supervise our laundry."

He turned to face her and she noticed his eyes. They were a deep gray-blue, nicely enhanced by the darker blue of his uniform. He was looking at her expectantly. Was he waiting for the answer to a question? She could not remember a word he'd said. Well she'd have to say something. "Have you made any progress in accounting for the blood poisoning cases you do have?"

"No. The contagion still spreads occasionally."

"It must be frustrating."

"Frustrating," he repeated, looking at her as though in a trance. Then he blinked. "Oh. Yes it is. After the war I'd like to study tissues under the miscroscope—to see which chemicals destroy tissues and which don't. Perhaps I can find a substance that will stop the contagion without harming the tissues."

At Gettysburg this conversation would have fascinated her but now she could not concentrate; and all she had gleaned from what he had just said were the words "after the war."

"Will you practice in New York?" she asked.

"I think so, yes. I was a surgical resident at Bellevue but now I intend to have a private practice." He was looking at her in a way that excited her: eyes penetrating, lips slightly parted. Now she wondered how she must look to him. If only she had a mirror to see if, in this light, her dark eyes looked luminous enough and if her lips were glossy. She was wearing a muted green dress with black piping and a high collar that covered her neck. The dress itself was nothing special but green was a good color on her, bringing out the red highlights in her upswept hair. She wondered if he thought she was pretty.

But why was she thinking this way? She had all but told him that courtship was out of the question.

In the other corner of the room Pat was holding the floor with some tale about the Irish Brigade. Everyone, including Kate, was feigning absorption with the story; but Beth knew that they must be wondering what was going on over here, and she wished she could conduct her light flirtations in private. Kent seemed oblivious to the other people in the room and continued to scrutinize Beth's face until she was blushing. Both of them had abandoned attempts at conversation. The breathless silence was broken suddenly by the loud clatter of the door knocker. Kent sighed and sat back, reaching for his pipe. "Your family is expecting callers?" he asked, trying to keep his voice even.

Now she remembered that Nate and his wife had been invited. She said, "The Kleins. I don't believe you've met them."

"No."

"Their son was killed in the Wilderness."

"He wasn't in our regiment, was he? I don't recall the name."

"No. And he was in another corps. The Sixth, I believe."

"Was he an only son?"

"They have a younger son. And two daughters. If the daughters count." she added.

"Excuse me?"

"Sons are the ones that really matter."

"Are you describing your own situation?"

"Partly. But it's a universal truth."

He turned to her irritably. "I had a daughter. It never occurred to me to care that she wasn't a son. She was perfect. She—" He broke off and took a sip from his whisky glass.

She remembered that his child had lived only a few days. "I'm sorry, Kent."

He acknowledged this with a nod. "Beth, you can be anything you want to be. Don't blame your fate on everybody else. Self-pity doesn't become you."

"It's not self-pity. It's a fact that women are considered inferior to men, and if you're too blind to see it—"

"I suppose you're right, but as I've told you before, I'm not an espouser of causes. With the exception of medicine, and even there the political aspects of it annoy me to distraction. But for what it's worth, I draw no distinction between the sexes so long as the individual is mentally capable. For example, I'd hire you to do research in my laboratory."

"Why?"

"Because you're observant and you ask the right questions. Oh, admittedly you're much too sentimental. But in a laboratory there are no men to dote upon. Only mice. Although, knowing you, you might favor a mouse." He

257

drained his glass and set it down. His eyes looked glazed. He could not be a drinker if two drinks could affect him this much. But then again, it had been straight Scotch.

She said, "Kent, you haven't changed in all the time I've known you."

"Ah," he said. "Now the truth comes out. You were expecting me to change."

"I didn't say—"

"What specific changes did you have in mind?"

"I never said I had changes in mind. I simply remarked—"

"But my immutability is obviously a problem."

"There *is* no problem with you. There's another man."

He raised an eyebrow. "Yes, of course. The elusive other man. Let's pretend for a moment that he doesn't exist, shall we? What exactly is it that troubles you about me?"

She hadn't liked that "elusive man" remark. Did he still think she was lying to him? "What troubles me about you is the sort of comment you just made. You're awfully sarcastic and sometimes you're very—cold."

He puffed his pipe thoughtfully and said, "I see. You were expecting a reincarnation of Lord Byron?"

She laughed.

"Yes, sometimes I'm cold, Beth. I've told you that before. But if I can accept you and your profusion of emotion, it would seem that you could make the same effort. And as for sarcasm, Miss Shepherd, I think you rank me."

"That's a hard record to beat."

He smiled uncertainly and she smiled back, thinking that he really was very appealing in spite of his barbed remarks.

At that point John brought the Kleins over to meet Kent, and Beth had no chance to speak to Kent alone until much later that evening when the family finally retired, leaving Pat to chaperone.

Pat looked from one to the other and said, "Can I trust you two alone while I go to bed?"

Pat had never done this before so late at night. He obviously

258

was promoting the romance. Perhaps he had even coached Kent on how to approach her. Things were happening so fast that Beth didn't know what to think.

Pat left the room. She and Kent sat silently on the couch staring at the Christmas tree. Her heart pounded. In a matter of minutes he would probably attempt to kiss her and she wanted very much to be kissed. But Greg was waiting for her and she must not be unfaithful to him. Yet Kent had seemed so hurt earlier this evening when she told him once again that there was another man. She owed him one friendly kiss if only to assure him that she was still fond of him. One kiss and that would be all. The more she thought about it, the more she wondered how it would be. It was difficult to imagine him in the role of a lover. Kent, the cursing despot of the field hospitals who, amid the lovely young women at last year's New Year's party, could think of nothing better to discuss than mathematics and suspension bridges? Yet he had been married and he had had women since—.

"You look most attractive tonight," he said.

"Thank you, Kent." She turned to him. He was looking at her intently and leaning slightly toward her. The moment had come. She could see now that a "friendly" kiss was impossible, for the expression on his face was not precisely friendly. She must either turn her head away now or—but his lips were on hers before she could make the decision. Her curiosity about him, which had been building since Gettysburg days, suddenly exploded in unbearable excitement. He must have felt this, for he parted his lips and probed at hers until she was responding in the same erotic manner. Eyes closed, she lost herself in the sense of feeling. There was the hardness of his arms and the softness of his lips and the slightly scratchy texture of his face, and all of it generated longings in her body that demanded a resolution. He kissed her neck and her cheek and her lips again until she could bear the excitement no longer and had to pull away from him.

Neither of them spoke at first, but the episode had quickly

changed the nature of their relationship. She now felt very close indeed to the terrible Major Wilson who was, in fact, a human being and a very passionate lover.

Impulsively, she touched his cheek, then let her hand run over his nose and lips, thinking of the mystery of men and the strange thoughts that lay concealed behind their faces. She was envious of their self-proclaimed superiority, but she marveled at their apartness—she would never completely understand them.

"Why are you doing this, Beth?"

"Does it annoy you?" She drew her hand into her lap.

"No, it excites me."

"Do you remember the time I studied you when you were operating? Was that exciting?"

"God, yes. But I didn't understand your reason."

"Men fascinate me sometimes."

"Men?"

"You. I remember how intent you were when you worked. You thought I was teasing you, but I wasn't. I was watching you, trying to guess what you were thinking and admiring your ability."

"I would never have guessed that. I thought you realized how beautiful you were and enjoyed my agitation. I wasn't thinking rationally at the time, but I am now. I want to marry you."

"Oh!" Her eyes widened.

"You needn't decide at once."

"I've explained the problem, Kent."

"Yes, you have."

"And you still—"

"You will decide."

She could not imagine what reason he would have for wanting to marry her. He scarcely knew her. For a moment she was tempted to ask him that question, but she knew it would sound odd. A woman ought to assume that her charms alone were reason enough. There had been reasons for Greg's proposal; they shared similar dreams, thought alike. But there was no experience in her relationship with Kent that she could point to and say, "Yes, this is the reason we were meant for each other."

"You look puzzled," he said.

"Your proposal was unexpected. I'm stunned."

"Well, I've been thinking about it for some time. You would have preferred a longer courtship, I suppose, but the war makes that impossible. I'm not a good correspondent, Beth, and in any case I wanted to ask you in person, not in writing."

Again she was tempted to ask for a reason, but she refrained. "Well I can't say Yes, Kent. You understand why."

"I understand." His voice shook slightly, and he reached for her again and kissed her deeply and gently, his eyes closed. Some far-off bell in her mind was ringing a guilty thought of Greg shivering in the dingy prison, but even this could not check the intensity of her response to Kent. The feel of his lips on her neck and shoulder was a wildly erotic sensation that made her want to reach out and merge with him completely. The thought that this merging was impossible made her feel physically ill. And as she pulled away, panting, she asked herself why it had to be this way. Why did she have to withhold herself when what she wanted to do was to take him and be taken by him?

"Kent, we have to stop."

"Yes."

"It's after one. We ought to be going to bed."

"You mean to sleep?" he said, trying to smile.

"I mean to sleep."

He walked ahead of her up the stairs and did not notice that in her frustration she stumbled on one of the steps. He kissed her quickly at her landing and then turned away. As he started up another flight to the guest room he mumbled a hoarse "Good night." Even his deep voice excited her.

Beth lay awake for hours trying to appraise the situation realistically. There was no question that she wanted to lie with him—wanted desperately to lie with him—but no self-respecting woman married only for that reason, especially if

261

she was waiting for a man she truly loved. She was fond of him, but she knew that he would be difficult to live with. Men like Kent should never marry at all. She could see his wincing at the baby's cries and her having to apologize as though it were somehow her fault. That had happened with her parents when Sean was little. Yet how different would it be with Greg? He too seemed too brilliant and sensitive for the banality of domestic routine. If it came to that, though, she herself dreaded some aspects of marriage. Men weren't the only ones who drooped when transplanted to the soil of repetitious routine. She wanted marriage, but she also hoped to escape the boredom of it. Like a syllogism with two contradictory premises, there was no conclusion, no solution. She knew that Kent was a poor risk. About Greg she was more optimistic. He was more open. He would understand her problems and perhaps even help her manage the household. Or would he?

Beth closed her eyes and tried to drive this dilemma from her mind. Presently she thought about Kent and how much she had enjoyed being kissed by him. She looked forward to another such encounter tomorrow.

At breakfast the next morning they avoided one another's eyes. But her heart raced all the while, for he would be here another night and she wondered how much kissing they would do by the time New Year's Eve was over. After breakfast he suggested that they go for a walk. Elaborately he asked other members of the family to join them, but all declined with various excuses. Catching Kate's eye, Beth could see approval. John tugged at his beard, looking uncertain. Kent puzzled him. The man was certainly well-informed, but he seemed indifferent to literature, politics and other subjects that John held dear. They had finally managed a discussion on philosophy but Kent had focused on Descartes's mathematical theories and John had lost him. Good grief, he'd as soon discuss an accountant's ledger. Still, he didn't have any special objections to the man. If this was Beth's idea of a beau, that was fine with him. Perhaps opposite types attracted her. John didn't really know his daughter, much as he loved her.

In the hallway Kent paused to look at a portrait of a dark-haired little girl in a ruffled blue dress sitting on a love seat, her hands folded demurely, her eyes dark, wide, and distant.

"That's you, isn't it?" He looked at it with a wistful half-smile that was almost paternal.

"Do you like it?"

"Very much. You were a dreamer even then, weren't you?"

"Why do you say that?"

"You look as though you were thinking of something else. Not the painter."

"I probably was."

She wondered what sort of childhood he had had, and as they walked up Fifth Avenue she asked him about those years. He grumbled that he didn't like to give long-winded personal narratives. To specific questions he answered her shortly, not wishing to elaborate.

"How old were you when your mother died?"

"Five."

"Did you and your father get on?"

"No."

"And your sister?"

"We get on well enough."

"Did you love your wife?"

He nodded but said nothing. Then he suggested that they walk toward the Croton Reservoir. She asked him no more personal questions, realizing that she could never marry a man without knowing something more about him. Who was he? What had he felt toward people—his family, his wife? How could he expect her to marry him if he was unwilling to tell her about himself?

Not knowing what else to talk about, she asked him if he liked New York as well as Boston.

"In some ways. Actually I prefer the country, but I need to work near the big hospitals."

"I'm a city person, I think. Though I did live on a farm for a while just before Gettysburg."

"Yes, I remember. Your cousins used to drop by the hospital every so often. The wife—I believe her name was Sally—helped us."

"You were there a long time. You must have been exhausted."

"Gettysburg was the worst battle of the war; the worst, I believe, that was ever fought on the North American continent. Pat always called it the Second Battle of Borodino."

"You must be glad that the war is almost over."

"God, yes! It's hard enough for a doctor to deal with the day-to-day accidents and illnesses. But when he's involved in a situation where murder and mutilation are planned, it's demoralizing. Rather like the punishments sergeants mete out to privates: digging holes and filling them up again. We patch up an arm, send them off, and get them back again and patch up another part. On the third day at Gettysburg, during the cannonade, a stretcher-bearer told me that he felt the same frustration. He was lying on his stomach while shells landed all around him and he watched several men get hit. He couldn't stand up and walk over to them to see if any could be saved because shells were raining down all over the place. And in the midst of that cacophony a fife-and-drum corps began playing " 'The Star Spangled Banner.' "

"They were playing music?"

"That's right. 'The rockets' red glare, the bombs bursting in air—' Like a goddam Greek chorus describing the scene. He swears this is true and I believe it. A rebel prisoner told me that one of their bands played polkas during battle. Polkas, mind you." He shook his head. "But the stretcher-bearer told me that *he* felt like the demented one, for finding the situation so ludicrous. He wondered what the point was in saving lives if they turned around and did the same thing all over again—to the accompaniment of music, no less."

As they walked past the mansions on tranquil Fifth Avenue, the war seemed like a distant memory. It was difficult to believe that she had been involved in what the people in these splendid homes would call "the unpleasantness."

264

"You know, Kent, I became inured to all the suffering. After a while I didn't hear the screams any more."

"I know. But I hope you've reverted to normal. No one should be like we were. Like Pat and I still are. That in itself is a form of madness."

She remembered his telling Joe something similar. Then she recalled the conversation with him right afterward, when she had mentioned heroism and cowardice. She wondered again what he had been thinking but did not ask him.

He said, "Beth, I won't forget your train ride with the soldiers. I never did thank you for that. When I heard about the riots and you being trapped in them, I—" he broke off.

"When you heard?" she prompted.

"I was sick."

"It wasn't your fault, Kent."

"That doesn't matter. It happened. It always does."

"What do you mean? What always does?"

"Nothing."

"Tell me."

"It's not important, Beth." He paused. "You look cold. Do you want to turn back?"

Why had he suddenly become so moody? Last night he had seemed quite gregarious and affectionate, and she had half-expected the change to be permanent—at least with respect to her. Perhaps he was irritated because she had not eagerly accepted his proposal. Or possibly her questions about his personal history had brought forth memories that were intruding on a happier present. As they turned back toward home, she decided that she definitely could not marry a man so cryptic and evasive. She would have to tell him that tonight, and she was not looking forward to it. But she would rather wait for Greg, rather suffer the agony of a divorce and a remarriage—a process that might take years and subject her to the cruelest gossip—than marry a man who would not share himself with her.

Despite these feelings, she wanted to spend with him what time they had left. She felt a certain obligation to Kent. After

265

all, he had selected her from all the women in the world, and the least she owed him was the favor of her company. But she must not encourage him too much. She must merely be pleasant and gracious.

This New Year's Eve party was livelier than any they had known since the war began. It was held at the Winchells'—two houses away—and it featured a small orchestra. There was a good-sized group, and everywhere there seemed to be optimism about an end to the war. The music was spirited and the drinking heavy, and everyone but Kent enjoyed himself. Beth did not dance with the men. She remained with Kent, not minding his jealousy but wishing that he danced. She wanted to waltz—to swirl deliriously under the great chandelier until the spinning sensation made her head feel as light as it did when she drank champagne.

Kent was the object of a good deal of gossip by the women (Did Beth intend to marry this man?) and several disgruntled looks from would-be suitors of Beth's. One outspoken enlisted man took her aside and accused her of succumbing to Kent's profession and rank rather than his charms. Another implied that she was chasing Kent only because he was a doctor and doctors were rich. To these accusations she only smiled and nodded agreeably as she turned down requests for dances. At last Joe, who for obvious reasons could not dance with Diane, took his sister out onto the floor. But waltzing with a brother could not generate the same excitement as waltzing with a beau. After two dances she returned to Kent's side near a long buffet set up along one wall of the Winchells' drawing room, which tonight had been converted into a small ballroom.

"You dance well," said Kent.

"I wish it had been with you."

"I'm sorry."

"Do you know how to dance, Kent?"

"No."

"Have you ever tried?"

266

"I would feel foolish."

"But you like music so well. You have an excellent sense of timing. The other night when you were playing the piano—"

"Nevertheless I cannot dance. If you wish to accept the invitations of the other men—"

"You wouldn't mind?"

He said nothing.

"Well, Kent?"

"Yes, I would mind," he admitted.

She gestured toward a small couch in a corner of the room. He followed her there and they both sat down. She said, "You're not enjoying this party, are you?"

"Are you?"

"Yes, I am."

"I'm not used to parties," he said.

"What you mean is that you hate them."

He grinned. "Well—"

In a corner of the room several young officers were becoming drunk. They were now singing in voices loud enough to be heard over the orchestra.

We'll hang Jeff Davis to a sour apple tree,
We'll hang Jeff Davis to a sour apple tree,
We'll hang Jeff Davis to a sour apple tree,
And send him straight to hell!

Kent said, "Someone ought to quiet them before they begin the more colorful songs on the fate of Mr. Davis."

"What are they?"

He smiled. "I never make indelicate remarks in front of ladies."

"Oh, come now. You never apologized once for the four-letter gems you used in Gettysburg."

"But you will allow that I made every attempt to avoid usage of the cruder expletives."

"There are cruder ones in the English language?"

"Yes indeed." He paused. "And if apologies are in order,

why did you never apologize for telling me to go to hell?"

"At the time I meant it."

"I thought you were teasing me."

"You know that I wasn't."

"Yes. I can see now that the way you walk is natural to you. You walk that way in front of your own mother."

"How do I walk?"

"In a way that makes men want to—uh—take you by force."

"Good grief! And you felt that way that day?"

He nodded. She looked at his face and blushed. Pat, standing a few feet away from them, noticed their expressions and gave Beth a disapproving look before turning to stare Kent down. After leaving them alone last night, what had he expected? Suddenly he was playing the role of defender of her honor.

It was after one when they returned home. Everyone was tired, especially Kate and John, who had danced together many times this evening, looking as young as their children. Sean retired at once and so did Joe. Once again Pat, Kent, and Beth sat alone in the parlor.

"I thought I'd get some sleep on this furlough," sighed Pat.

"By all means go to bed. You need the rest badly," said Kent, elaborately sympathetic.

"Oh no. Tonight I shall wait you out."

"I've asked your sister to marry me."

"Indeed?" Pat looked from one to the other and smiled. He did not ask if Beth had accepted the proposal but his expression indicated that he thought she might have. "Well, this puts matters in a new perspective, doesn't it?" Pat rose. "Suddenly I feel very tired. I trust you'll both remain as well-dressed as you are now."

"Pat!" Beth exclaimed. "How can you—"

"My statement stands," he interrupted. But the haste of his departure belied his sinister tones.

"What do you think of that?" Beth demanded as Pat rounded the doorway.

268

"I'll take my revenge when we're back in camp."

"What will you do?"

"I'll make him snap his heels and salute me and call me 'sir.' " He quickly rose from the chair he had occupied while Pat was in the room, and he sat down on the couch next to Beth. Without any preamble, he embraced her and began to kiss her hungrily. His abrupt and passionate manner so excited her that her response was almost uncontrollable. In moments her body was sensitized to the point of agony. The kisses and caresses became more and more frenzied until they broke apart, looking helplessly at each other, both of them trembling, breathing hard, and silently asking the question, "What now?"

He said, "You do want—more, don't you?"

She nodded, looking away from him. "But I can't."

"Your morality forbids it?"

"No."

"No?" His eyes widened.

"I mean Yes. Morality." But her only concern was being unfaithful to Greg.

"I stand ready to marry you at any time."

"I know that, Kent."

"And you still wish to wait for—him?"

"You told me that you would understand."

"I know I did. But I hoped you would change your mind. Your ardor led me to believe that you might be interested."

"You're very attractive, Kent."

"Then it's only my body you want? What an unexpected reversal of the classic situation." He sat back and studied her.

"Kent, please don't think—"

Suddenly he embraced her so violently that she fell back against the arm rest of the couch. He held her in a strong grip with one hand and let the other run over her basque. He reached below her waist but could feel nothing but satin material fortified with petticoats. Her dress was low-cut, and now he pressed his lips against the flesh that bulged above the tight stays. Beth was aroused but at the same time indignant. She knew he was angry and was offended by the manner in which he chose to display it.

"Stop that this instant!"

He drew back slowly and looked at her as though in shock. "I'm sorry." He moved to a corner of the couch, his head down. She sat up, smoothing her skirts and pushing at her hairpins. Finally he stood up and walked towards the door.

"Good night, Beth."

"Kent—"

"Try to forget that this happened."

"But—"

"Good night." He walked quickly away and into the hall.

The three men were scheduled to leave at 9:00 A.M. the next morning. Breakfast was a solemn affair. Pat and Joe, wretched at the thought of returning to freezing Petersburg, were suffering hangovers from the night before and sat glumly staring into their cups of black coffee. Kate's eyes were red and brimminng, and John, affecting a terrible cold, was also fighting tears. Beth ate her meal mechanically, tasting nothing. Looking across the table at Kent's plate, she could see that his fork too was moving very slowly. She would not look up at his face. Only Sean seemed to appreciate the sausages, eggs, heaps of fresh biscuits, and strawberry preserves that Sheilah pressed upon them.

At length the men were standing in the hall; hats on, coats buttoned. Kate kissed each one, including Kent who, to Beth's surprise, seemed touched by the motherly affection. Then Kate, seeking to delay the final goodbyes, looked at the badges on their hats and said, "Why are your shamrocks red instead of green? I've always wondered."

"They're not shamrocks," said Joe. "They're trefoils."

"They look like shamrocks."

"We Irish call them shamrocks," Joe said. "But the army doesn't. Ours are red because we're in the first division."

Beth remembered that Greg's trefoil badge had been white.

270

He had been in the second division of the Second Corps.

"I maintain that they're shamrocks," Kate said. "They'll bring you Irish luck. You too, Kent. Do you have any Irish blood?"

"To my knowledge it's all English."

"No matter. The shamrock will protect you."

"We have to be going," said Pat, his voice shaking.

In the confusion of tearful farewells that followed, Beth found herself face-to-face with Kent.

"Goodbye, Kent."

"Goodbye," he said, avoiding her eyes.

She ought to say something else. As her brothers walked toward the door, she tried to think of how, precisely, to let him know that she still liked him. But Joe was shouting, "Kent, we'll be late," and he had gone.

There were no letters from Kent when he was back in camp, and since Pat never wrote, she hadn't a clue as to how he was. Joe made a passing reference to him in one of his letters—something to the effect that Kent was quieter than usual. But other than that, she learned nothing. Finally she decided that he had been taken aback upon discovering her strong sexual drives. In a man, of course, lust was expected. In a woman, it was unthinkable. For the first time she felt a deep shame for her cravings and wrapped herself in the isolation of winter as if it were a cocoon.

In February both sides agreed to exchange prisoners. But Mr. Allister's informer had more bad news. Greg, along with other officers, had been transferred again. When Sherman's army threatened Macon, he had been sent to Savannah. There he had attempted escape to Sherman's lines. He was caught, but mercifully not killed, and was imprisoned in a camp in South Carolina. Finally he had been sent back to the starting point: Libby Prison in Richmond. He had been confined there since December. Because of his conduct, he was not being considered for release.

As Diane related this news, Beth tried to conceal the intensity of her disappointment. Later, though, her spirits began to brighten. After all, he was alive and the war would be over soon. On this point everyone agreed. Union armies had practically surrounded Richmond and Petersburg. Surely the spring campaigns would end the war. By March or April he would be liberated.

She began following the war news carefully, perusing the papers for indications that the final battles might begin soon. But it was very cold in Virginia, and when the thaws finally came the mud was knee-deep. There followed heavy rains, which soaked the armies who were facing each other in the trenches. Nobody moved before late March.

Once the battles commenced, however, Richmond was evacuated by the frantic Confederate army. The war had a few more days to go as, on April 3, 1865, Yankee troops were streaming into Richmond.

Shortly after the fiery fall of that city, Greg turned up in a hospital, very ill. Pat, who had been transferred from Kent's unit in March and had gone up to Richmond, had seen Greg's name on a prisoner list and had gone to see him. He managed to get a telegram through to Diane:

"Greg alive. Too ill to move now. Home in two, three weeks. Letter follows. Pat Shepherd."

Diane came over to see Beth that day, crying in confusion. Beth cried too, but for another reason. He was coming home. Memories long ago put away on dusty shelves were taken down and polished. Beth's joy had to be kept secret, however, and so, in the days after the news came she ran up to her room after school and looked in the mirror holding dresses up against her, trying to decide which one to wear on the day she finally saw him. She practiced facial expressions—love, joy, concern—that she would signal to Greg at every opportunity. She rehearsed speeches of greeting and made mental notes of several anecdotes she must be sure to tell him. When she was with the family she couldn't conceal her excitement. Kate questioned her about her frequent, secret smiles and she said airily, "Oh, I'm just so glad the war is almost over and all the men will be coming home." Kate was pleased. Obviously Beth was waiting for Kent Wilson but was too proud to admit it. The fact that Kent had proposed was common knowledge by this time but no one dared question Beth about the mysterious argument that had so distressed the two of them last New Year's. Whatever it had been, Beth had apparently chosen to forget it, for Kate had never seen her daughter so happy.

John had discreetly checked into Kent Wilson's background through friends in Boston who were thorough enough to provide a genealogy as well. Both branches of the family were Connecticut-based (New Haven, New London, and Colchester) and had arrived long before the Revolutionary War. The list revealed a number of barristers, lawyers, and businessmen, but no doctors except Kent. Satisfied with Kent's background, John nevertheless had doubts about the man's stiffly elusive character. But if Beth wanted him, John would give his full blessing. Kent had treated Joseph kindly and had probably saved Pat's life. No doubt he would be good to his daughter. Kate, who was fond of the taciturn young doctor, thought ahead to a splendid postwar wedding. She knew from Beth's behavior that things would be patched up as soon as Kent came home.

The surrender of Robert E. Lee to Ulysses S. Grant at Appomattox Court House in Virginia was effected on April 9, 1865. The next day New York went wild. Church bells rang out, laborers clanged ropes of tin cans, businessmen sang, boats in the harbor whistled, pipe organs pealed, and people hugged strangers in the streets. The Allisters informed Diane that they were leaving for Richmond at once to see their son. Diane, explaining that her daughter might be distressed by her mother's absence, told the Allisters that it would be best if she remained in New York. While the city spun wildly, Diane sat in Beth's room moaning, "What am I going to do? What am I going to tell them?"

"Wait until he's better."

"Yes. Yes, that's what I'll do."

"Come, Diane. Let's go dance in the streets."

"I don't feel like dancing, Beth."

"But consider the bright side. Joe will be coming home too."

"It's raining, Beth."

"We'll take our umbrellas."

"Oh, all right. It would be better than sitting here hating myself."

And so they joined the throngs, John chaperoning them every step of the way. They listened to choirs singing "Te Deum," they talked to neighbors and strangers alike; and they returned home early that evening, Beth drunk with excitement, Diane nearly swooning with mixed feelings, and John reciting Poe's "The Bells."

That evening people dropped by to share the news with one another. Some of the neighbors went from house to house, but others remained in the Shepherds' parlor until it was overflowing. Phil, the Kleins, the Kendalls, half the neighbors on the block, everyone was there but the men who had fought and won the war. Beth missed the men in uniform. They were the ones who should be here tonight, singing the songs and getting drunk on John's best whisky. On the day of victory Beth could feel the war more keenly than when it had raged. Suddenly she wanted to be with Bill, Sally, and Hannah; with Pat and Kent and the wounded soldiers; with the German housewives and the medical orderlies and all the people with whom she had shared Carlisle and Gettysburg.

She had been a soldier for a short time and tonight she wanted to share the victory with other soldiers. She imagined all her comrades sitting together now at the surgeons' table in Gettysburg, lifting beer steins and singing "Auld Lang Syne." She found herself crying because she missed them all and they would never work together again and because women could not drink beer anyway. On this glorious night, while hilarity flowed around her, she sat in a corner and cried.

Gettysburg had been the crucial battle of the war. At Gettysburg the tide had turned, the Southern cause had been lost for good and all. It had symbolized, in Lincoln's words, "a new birth of freedom." But for Beth it had symbolized something else. For the first time in her life she had been desperately needed and she had come through. She had hauled sheets, lifted bodies, washed instruments, soothed fevered men, and assisted in a research project. For one week she had done the work of a man and done it well. It was a terribly irony that men could achieve importance in peacetime but women had to wait until calamity struck.

She dried her eyes and looked around her, trying to smile. The war was over. Greg was coming home. Yet Greg had not lived through that week with her. Kent had. And it was he that she wanted to see tonight.

She was glad she had waited for Greg, who was warm and affectionate, who understood her as Kent never would. But on this night—just this one night—she wanted to be with Kent; wanted to hear him joke with Pat, to see him get drunk, to laugh, to feel his kiss.

She recognized her feeling as being akin to the emotion she had felt long ago when she had finished normal school. The girls had been happy that the long ordeal of study was over, but they had cried when they said goodbye. So it must be with soldiers in the army. They had loathed the war, but they had fought it together and won it together, and they would miss each other.

Tonight she wanted Kent, if only to say, "We did a capital job, didn't we?"

On Saturday morning, the day before Easter, while Beth and her mother were standing in front of the hall mirror putting on their bonnets for a last-minute shopping trip, John came home unexpectedly and stood in the hall staring like a man in a trance. His eyes were red.

"Not Joe!" Kate screamed. "Oh, tell me it's not Joe." And Beth thought: The war is over; how could Joe be dead?

"No," said John. "It's the President. He was assassinated last night."

Beth's immediate feeling was one of relief. Her brothers

were safe. But then the weight of the event crashed down on her like a building in flames. Lincoln, the symbol of everything the Union had stood for, was dead. As John gave a sketchy account of the news that had come in over the wire—in a theater box, the night before, a man had shot Lincoln in the head and escaped by way of the stage—Beth was filled with a sense of foreboding. If Lincoln could die by the hand of one man even as the bells of victory pealed across the nation, then anything was possible, any cruel improbable event. The world was so untidy. It had no structure, no logic at all. She listened to Kate's and Sheilah's crying, then closed her eyes, trying to take it all in, visualizing the world in fragments. She had never loved Lincoln as others had. She had criticized the war itself, the unfairness of the draft laws, the trampling on a Bill of Rights and other offenses. Yet he had freed the slaves, had won the war, had advocated compassion for the battered South and was, on balance, one of the most effective Presidents the nation had ever seen.

Who was Andrew Johnson? What did he stand for? How on earth could a nation so recently divided function with an unknown at the helm? Standing there, fingering the bonnet in her hand, she tried to look ahead to the future. All she could see was a shattered glass ball.

She could hear church bells tolling. They had been hearing them for a while, but ever since the victory, bells had sounded occasionally and no one had paid any attention. John hung crêpe, Kate and Sheilah hurried to church, and Beth went for a walk and watched the people drape the city in mourning clothes. By noon New York was shrouded in black from one end to the other.

It took two more weeks for the body of Abraham Lincoln to reach New York. It was to lie in state overnight in City Hall. John and Kate went to pay their respects along with a silent, thin Phil Weatherly, who still didn't know if his son was dead or alive, and now had seen the emancipator of his people slain. Beth could not bring herself to go with them. She waited

276

instead until the next day when the procession moved north toward the railroad depot. From there it would proceed to other cities and ultimately to the gravesite in Springfield, Illinois.

Sixteen black horses drew the giant hearse from Broad to Fourteenth, then up Fifth Avenue, and a hundred thousand participated in the procession, twenty thousand of them Union soldiers and two thousand Negroes. Beth, crushed against Mr. Kendall and Diane in the thick, weeping crowds, still could not believe that it had happened. Just a short time ago they had celebrated the victory. The world seemed un-real—had seemed that way since the day John had come home with the announcement. Beth could not shake off the thought that anything might happen now, to any of them and at any moment. Even during the shelling of Carlisle she had not felt this uncertainty.

They had a letter from Joe that day. Beth read it aloud during dinner:

Dear folks,
It's over at last! I only wish I were home to share the victory with you. When we reached Appomattox Station yesterday (the ninth inst.) we had no idea it would end so quickly. Suddenly Lee and Grant were meeting, and before I knew it our side was firing victory salutes. Grant put an end to that soon enough and sent down an order that the johnnies, being no longer our enemies but our fellow countrymen, ought not to be taunted in this manner. He asked us to cease firing salutes and start sharing rations with them. I must confess that after four years of despising the d——n rebels, I was ill disposed to order my men to exercise Christian charity. However, after some reflection, I recalled that those ragged creatures would not be returning to Broadway parades but to ravaged farms and hungry families. I pity the Georgia and Carolina boys. They say Sherman didn't leave so much as a yam for those people to eat.
Some, like Kent, had no trouble accommodating to the new order of things. In no time at all he was assisting Confederate

surgeons with the staggering load of casualties they had collected en route to this site of victory. (The march from Petersburg to Appomattox is a story in itself, and I'll describe it at some future date.)

Having parted with a goodly portion of our not-too-delectable rations, we Yanks made a feast of what was left. An abundance of whisky sent down by Major O'Hare made the feast a grand one indeed. I wish Pat were here with us. I think I told you the last time I wrote that he had gone up to Richmond.

At this point in the letter the ink changed from blue to black and the writing was scribbled.

It's now more than a week since I wrote the above and we've just heard about the tragedy. I'm sitting here outside my tent with Andy, Kent, and Jimmy and we've been talking about it. I worshiped Father Abraham, as you know, and even Kent admitted that though he had not liked Lincoln or any politician, his passing made him feel uneasy about the future. Andy said—

Beth's mind wandered as she read. She was amazed that Kent should have had the same reaction to Lincoln's death as she. One could disagree with a leader, one could accuse him of many misdeeds, but unless he had acted for purely selfish motives (and Lincoln certainly had not) his citizens would look upon him as a father and fear for their security when that father died.

At the end of April Phil received a note from an army nurse. He read it many times, pinching his cheek to assure himself that he was not dreaming. Then, laughing and crying, he hurried over to the Shepherds', shouting the news even as Sheilah was opening the door. Pete was alive! Very ill, yes; too weak to write. But alive and coming home. After spending five months in Andersonville he had been sent to prisons farther removed from Sherman's line of march and at the war's end had been confined in North Carolina. A hospital steamer would be bringing him to New York within the week.

278

For the first time in months they gathered around the piano. Louise and Phil sang "When Johnny Comes Marching Home" and Beth sat listening, wondering about the future. With Greg home and her brothers safe, she knew she would be happy. But just three weeks ago she had seen a glass ball shatter. She could not banish that memory.

FIVE

So within the prison wall
We are waiting for the day
That shall come to open wide the iron door
And the hollow eye grows bright
And the poor heart almost gay
As we think of seeing homes and friends once more.

Tramp, tramp tramp the boys are marching
Cheer up comrades they will come,
And beneath the starry flag
We shall breathe the air again
Of the free land in our own beloved home.

April passed—and the first week of May. Beth waited. At school she lived for the moment she arrived home, and at home she lived for news of Greg. Where would it come from? Would Pat write? Would she hear it from Diane? He *must* be better by now.

Pete Weatherly's ship had already arrived, and he was now convalescing at home. Phil came by one night to tell them of Pete's condition. In a choked voice, he said that Pete was emaciated, wretchedly depressed, and did not want visitors. Army doctors had said that Pete's prospects for recovery were good, but they were referring only to physical improvement.

No one could predict how Pete would behave. None would guarantee that he would ever regain his spirit.

Beth heard Phil speak, but she would not listen. She closed her eyes, remembering Greg as he had been on the last day she saw him. She would not think beyond that.

On a Saturday afternoon in the middle of May, Beth met Diane as she was following Rose Kendall into their house. "Beth, I had a letter from Mrs. Allister this morning," Diane said breathlessly. "Honestly! A letter! It took a week to get here. If she'd only sent a telegram, I'd have had more time!"

Beth's heart began to race. "Do you mean Greg is—"

"The ship docks at noon tomorrow. And he's coming here, not to his parents' home. My mother is in a tizzy! We've ordered the sickroom supplies and the flowers, but there's so much more to do." She walked toward the stairs to her house. "Please try to come over tomorrow, Beth. I'll need you."

For a long time Beth stood immobile on the sidewalk, trembling. Only one more day—and then she'd know if his feelings had changed, if *he* had changed. The moment she had longed for was drawing close, and now doubts began to assail her. Perhaps he was as withdrawn and despairing as Pete. Perhaps he no longer loved her. What would she do?

One day. She hoped it would pass quickly. But a part of her wanted it to last forever.

The next afternoon Beth took up a stand at her bedroom window and waited for Greg to come home. It was after two o'clock in the afternoon when an army ambulance stopped before the Kendall home and Beth saw the nurse lead Laura out onto the sidewalk. Diane emerged from the ambulance first, followed by Mrs. Allister. The attendants then lowered a stretcher, but Beth's view of Greg was blocked by a tree. The men moved a few steps and then lowered the stretcher almost to the sidewalk so that Greg could see his daughter. Now Laura obstructed her view of Greg's face. As the stretcher was raised again, she caught a glimpse of him. His face was white and gaunt. Huge black hollows circled his eyes. He was carried toward the stairs and out of her view before she could study him more closely.

She turned from the window and sat heavily on the bed. She did not know him. What had they done to him? Was this the same man who had sat beside her—healthy, strong, and smiling—talking of the future, of plans to change the world? He didn't look as though he could sit up. Kate and Beth were expected at the Kendalls' early that evening. When she first spoke to him, it would be in the midst of a group of people. She hoped she wouldn't faint or burst into tears in front of them. In front of him. She took a pale green silk dress out of the closet. It had taken her two weeks to select this dress. Now she could work up no enthusiasm to wear it. She was afraid. There were no guarantees of anything any more. The assassination had taught her that and the sight of Greg had reinforced the lesson. She was in a thick wood with wolves all around her. Though she knew the path leading to town and safety, there was no certainty that she would get there before the wolves attacked.

Pat, who had tended the soldiers on Greg's ship, came home later that afternoon. Between mouthfuls of the best food he had eaten in months, he told them about his recent adventures and informed them that Joe would probably be home in June after the review of troops in Washington. After a while Kate asked him how Kent was.

"Well enough. I haven't seen him since before the surrender. He sent me a letter, though. He's going to remain with the occupation forces in Virginia for several months. He wants to compare notes with Confederate doctors."

"Isn't he anxious to set up his own practice?"

"There's time. Don't forget, Kent has no family and no prospect for one." He looked meaningfully at Beth, but she chose to ignore him. Kate, seeing that Beth did not look especially concerned, was puzzled. She had been waiting for him, hadn't she?

"Is he still such a terror?" John asked.

"He's the same," Pat said quickly with a slight change of expression that Beth noticed and wondered about.

"So you left his unit and went to the prison camps," Kate said hastily. "Gregory arrived earlier today. How was his trip home?"

Pat did not have a chance to answer. There was a knock at the front door and Sheilah showed Diane into the dining room. She looked extremely agitated.

"I must speak with Beth," she said. "Please excuse me, Mr. and Mrs. Shepherd. Pat."

Beth stood up and walked toward the door. She glanced back to see if Diane was coming and noticed that Pat was looking at Diane with what seemed an expression of pity.

In Beth's room, Diane sat on a chair and Beth, careless of her silk coverlet, sat on the bed. Diane said, "You should have told me, Beth."

Beth looked directly at her. "How did you find out?"

"It was a long ride across town in that ambulance. From the time we took him from the steamship until he was settled in the sickroom, we exchanged only a few words. Mrs. Allister did most of the talking. When she and my mother finally left me alone with him he said to me, 'I gather there is someone else?' I don't know how he knew, but he did. I said Yes. He looked relieved. I expected him to look relieved, but I didn't expect—" she broke off, looking down.

Beth gulped. "What did he tell you?"

"About that winter. He said he had seen you several times and had proposed." Suddenly she burst into tears, "Beth, I'm so sorry. You've had to keep that secret for so long. If only you had told me."

"I was afraid you might be angry."

"No. He told me how concerned you were for my feelings. No, I would not have been angry. You forget, Beth, I no longer loved him when I learned of my condition." She was crying hard now. "If only you could have married him then."

"Don't cry, Diane. We can be married. After the divorce, you and Joe and Greg and I can—Diane, please."

Diane continued to cry. At length she blew her nose, smoothed back her chignon, and said, "Pat didn't tell you, did he?"

"Tell me what?"

Diane stared at her.

"Tell me what, Diane?"

"Greg is very ill."

"I know that."

Diane's voice was a whisper. "He's dying, Beth."

When what Beth had been fearing was finally stated as a fact, Beth thought to herself, "So it's decided at last." Then her being seemed to split into two pieces so that one half stood off to the side saying, "It's outrageous! It's not to be borne!" And the other half of her, the cynical portion which had dominated her thinking of late, said, "But of course it would have to end this way. Greg has never been real and you've known all along that you would never have him." She did not cry. She listened to the two voices screaming in her head and pressed a hand against her forehead.

She felt an arm around her shoulders and realized that Diane had sat down on the bed and was trying to comfort her. She looked at the green dress hanging on the door of the closet and decided that she would not wear the dress. She would wear the blue muslin she had on now and burn the green silk.

"Beth, I'm so sorry," Diane whispered.

"Does Greg know he's dying?"

"No, he hasn't been told." She paused. "I've arranged for you to be his nurse."

"His nurse," Beth repeated dully.

"If Mrs. Allister learned the truth at this time, I think it would kill her."

"Yes."

"So you're to be his nurse. I've explained that even though you're not a matron, you did nurse the sick at Gettysburg. And since Pat's to be his doctor—well, the point is that you will be able to spend as much time as possible with him."

Beth nodded.

"It was the only thing I could think of to do."

There was a rapping on the door and Pat walked in. He stood before Diane and said gravely, "The weeks ahead will be difficult. I'll try to make your husband as comfortable as possible."

"What's wrong with him?" asked Beth.

"Consumption. Generalized infection. He was weakened by malaria last summer in Georgia. We tried to build him up, but he was too weak to fight, and we thought it better to send him on home so that he could—uh—be with his family."

"And no one has told him he's dying?"

"No one, Beth."

"Do you think he suspects?" asked Beth.

"I doubt it." Pat looked pityingly at the swollen-eyed Diane. Then he turned to Beth. "Diane will need your support, Beth. I'm glad you're here to give it." He said to Diane, "If there's anything any one of us can do . . ."

"Thank you, Pat."

Pat nodded, then backed toward the door. "I'll be there tonight," he said. And he left.

Beth said to Diane, "I'm so tired of pretending."

"You don't have to Beth. I won't mind if you—"

"But I like Joan Allister too. There's no point in scandalizing the community if he's going to die, is there?" Her voice was bitter.

Diane twined her fingers helplessly. "Beth, I wish you'd cry. You'll feel better."

"I mustn't. I want to see him and I can't appear there with swollen eyes. I have to go now."

Diane walked her to the door of his room—one of the Kendall guest rooms. Beth opened the door quietly, walked in, and found him dozing. Yes, he was dying. She had seen many like him at Gettysburg, the faces almost devoid of flesh, the body too tired to long sustain the effort of breathing. His brown hair was lusterless, yet it contrasted too sharply with the very white skin. He was clean-shaven. How nice of the army to tidy him up for death.

She couldn't wake him. He needed all the rest he could get. She stood there, motionless, feeling a faint chill even though the room was very warm. The vases of flowers everywhere reminded her less of spring than of burials. Unable to stand the sweet, overpowering scent, she took a step toward the window for some fresh air. When she turned back to Greg, he was stirring. His eyes opened slowly and they searched her face for a moment before registering recognition.

"You came to see me," he said.

She nodded, swallowing, looking at his eyes. The same eyes: large and deep. She had almost expected someone different. A dying man, a stranger. But this was Greg.

He said, "You haven't changed. Not at all."

She still could not speak. Greg's face, Greg's voice. The long-remembered voice that had stayed with her when the rest of him became shadowy: deep and unaffected, no accent, Greg's voice. No. Pat was wrong. He wasn't dying. Greg wasn't—

"How have you been, Beth?"

"I? Oh, very well, The same. . . ." They had once talked so easily together. Now she could find no words.

He cleared his throat. "Diane told me you were not betrothed to anyone."

"No." She smiled. "Still a spinster."

"Well." He did not smile. He looked away and said, "Did you receive the letters I sent to Carlisle?"

"Yes. Both of them."

There was a long pause. He stared fixedly at his night stand. She wondered who would be the first to speak again. Did he still care for her? He must care for her if he had told Diane about that winter. But why wasn't he saying so? She would ask him outright. "Do you still feel the same way as when you wrote—I mean—"

"Yes," he said hoarsely, still looking away from her.

286

"Then you still love me?"

"I love you. But I think the proper question is, Do you still hate me?"

"Hate you? No! How could you—oh, you're thinking of the last time we saw one another."

"Loading your baggage into the coach, yes."

"Oh, everything's changed now, Greg. I understand what happened."

"Do you forgive me?"

"There's nothing to forgive. I love you."

He laughed shortly. "It's very kind of you to say that to a man just out of prison. But do you mean it? Will you marry me?"

"Yes! Why do you think I'm here, Greg? To accept a proposal."

Only then did he turn to look at her. His face had come alive. "You'll marry me?"

"Right away. That is, as soon as you and Diane divorce. Not being a Mormon, I don't find bigamy appealing."

"You're not afraid of scandal?"

"Not any more. I'd enjoy seeing the biddies on the block swoon." She sat down in a chair next to the bed. The pretense she had to maintain—facile jokes about bigamy, divorce, and scandal—was physically draining. "So we'll be married. Thank God that's settled. Now let's talk about you. How are you feeling?"

"Fine, now that you're here." He smiled for the first time.

"Was it—was prison—very awful?"

"I don't want to talk about it. I want to talk about us."

He began to say something else; then he started to cough. Consumption. But he had more than consumption. A generalized infection, Pat had said. In case one disease did not fell him, the other would.

She said, "Until you're better, we have to pretend that I'm here in the capacity of a nurse."

"Why?"

"Because you can't upset your parents right now by revealing that you're in love with another woman. Wait until you're strong again."

"Oh, I suppose you're right. But as soon as I'm well I intend to tell them."

She thought for a moment that she might cry, but she did not. Instead, she bent down and kissed him on the lips.

He said, "Oh, God, that feels good. Kiss me again and come closer this time so that I can hold you."

But at that moment they could hear footsteps in the hall. Joan Allister briskly entered the room and Beth quickly lifted a vase of flowers, pretending to be moving them.

"Hello, Beth," Joan said warmly. "Are you making Greg comfortable?"

"I hope so," Beth's voice squeaked on the word *hope*. Out of the corner of her eye she could see Greg's grin.

"I want to thank you for offering your services," Joan said. "You've no idea how much we admire you and Patrick."

"Thank you, Mrs. Allister."

Joan sat down, distractedly arranging her skirts. Then she launched into a monologue about the doings in New York during Greg's absence. Beth could hear the strain in her voice and she sympathized. Greg, who was not listening, merely nodded vacantly every few minutes and stole surreptitious glances at Beth. Finally Joan suggested that they leave and allow Greg to rest.

"Yes, Greg," said Beth, in a clipped professional tone. "Pat gave me strict instructions to see that you sleep, and I'm afraid I've been too lenient."

When Joan was at the door, Greg winked and murmured to Beth, "I hope to have some interesting dreams."

"Yes," she said, glancing toward Joan. "It must feel good to be home again."

"Very interesting dreams," he whispered just as she turned to leave.

When Beth left the room, she found Joan Allister clutching

the upstairs banister and trying desperately not to cry. There was another guest room across the hall, and Beth whispered, "I think you need a moment to yourself, Mrs. Allister." Beth opened the door to a room that was dark and musty. The drapes were drawn and the window closed. A dead room in a dead world. Beth led Joan in and gestured for her to sit down. Joan, who had always been attractively tall and lean, now looked gaunt. Seated, she looked like a bent reed wrapped in acres of brown silk. The bright amber eyes had become dull and her gestures, always animated, were now simply nervous. She alternately clasped and unclasped her hands as she spoke. "Pat didn't tell us the truth until this morning. I'd guessed it, of course, when I was with Greg in Richmond."

"I'm so sorry, Mrs. Allister."

"I know you are, my dear. Thank you for your kindness." She paused. "Poor Diane isn't able to cope at all. When she saw how he'd changed and later when Pat told her—why, she's utterly unable to face it, and Gregory needs her so desperately."

"He needs you too, Mrs. Allister."

"Yes, but do you think I alone can give him the strength—" She covered her face and sobbed, "Why him? He's always been so kind, so gentle. Even as a child he—oh, my poor son."

Beth touched Joan's shoulder awkwardly. "Let me get you a cup of tea, or perhaps some sherry."

"No thank you, my dear. But if you don't mind, I would like to be alone for a moment."

"Yes, I understand." Beth quietly left the room, then hurried down the stairs, stopping in the front hall briefly to say to a maid, "Tell Diane I'll be back later."

Her family was in the garden when she came home. She walked quietly up to her room and closed the door, hoping that no one would bother her. She wanted to throw things, to take an ax and smash everything in the room. In lieu of that, of course, she was obliged to sit meekly on the bed and cry as silently as she could.

When she had gone over to the Kendalls' earlier, she had

felt only resignation. He had been a dream and he would fade like a dream. She had been ready to accept that. But now that she had seen him and heard the long-forgotten voice she realized that he was no dream. He was very much alive—to himself and to her. He had plans for a future; he demanded a future; but he would have no future.

She could have borne it much better if he had simply lain there smiling resignedly at her. She might have been able to shut the vibrant Greg of the past out of her mind and accept the passive one. But he had talked of wanting to hold her, had smiled and even winked at her, probably remembering that day in the hotel room, had spoken of the exciting dreams he hoped to have. For a moment she had half-believed that they might indeed recapture the past some day.

Crying, she told herself that she would not go back there. They would have to find another nurse, or Diane could tend to her own husband. It disturbed her that this doomed man had come home to her so desirous of life. If he had died in prison or if he had come home broken, she could have stood it. But this? Never.

The shame she felt for having such thoughts stabbed at her. It was he who was dying, not she. It was not his fault that he had to leave her now. He had not taunted her with unreal dreams. They were real to Greg. She loved him, and she could not run away. She would have to witness his slow deterioration and allow him to pretend, if he so chose, that he did have a future.

The years without Greg stood before her like a line of yawning faces stretching off over the rim of the horizon. She could not bear the thought of them. If she were to get through the weeks ahead, she too would have to pretend that he was going to live. Perhaps he would live after all. Greg had too much spirit to permit himself to die. But his aliveness was illusory. A thin piece of paper thrown into a flame might flare brightly for a moment, but unless the fire were fed with material of substance, it would die.

She heard footsteps in the hall and her mother's voice

290

calling, "Beth, are you home? I thought I heard you come in."

Beth opened the door to Kate. Her mother gasped when she saw that Beth had been crying.

"What is it, dear?"

Beth told her. All of it, except the hotel room. Kate tried to maintain her composure, but it required great effort. "Oh my! Oh, my Lord! Does anyone else know of this?"

"Diane does."

"Diane knows about you and Gregory?"

"You guessed correctly about the reason for their marriage, Mother. She did not love him when she found herself with child, but they had to marry. Had Diane not been in that condition, it would have been I who married Greg."

"My goodness! You never once intimated—"

"I was about to when the bad news was given me." She paused. "Diane intends eventually to marry Joe."

"Joe!"

"I knew you would be shocked. I expected you to swoon."

"I'm most concerned about you, dear," Kate said simply. "Is Diane the only one who has shared this tragedy with you?"

"Yes. Don't tell anyone else. Not even Joe. He doesn't know about my part in this."

"I won't say a word."

"I'm going to marry Greg."

"I understand, dear."

"You don't believe me, do you? He might still get well."

"Perhaps he will."

"And you won't mind if I marry him?"

"After all that waiting, I'd mind if you didn't."

It must have taken a great deal of love for Kate to say that, Beth realized. She burst into tears again. "He's going to die, Mother."

For the first time since Beth had been a child, she needed her mother. Kate stayed with her until Beth, drawing strength from the fact that someone close to her understood, gathered her wits about her and prepared for the evening visit to Greg.

*　　*　　*

Because Beth was still teaching, she could not be with Greg until after three. Even if she had been free during school hours, there would have been little opportunity to be alone with him. Mrs. Allister was in constant attendance, and there was an unending stream of visitors. Greg's father was a very tall, commanding man whose feelings about his son were either well-hidden or nonexistent. Beth did not like him. Greg's two married sisters, who had come to New York to see their brother, were more affectionate, though the younger one cried easily and left the room abruptly while the family offered Greg lame excuses for her sudden departures. But a young lieutenant, who had served under Greg at Chancellorsville, was lively and cheerful. Beth was pleased that someone, at least, was able to keep Greg laughing.

Though Beth was considered his nurse, there was no plausible reason for her to demand being alone with her patient. Propriety decreed that bathing and other indelicate services be relegated to the Kendall maids. Since Pat was responsible for all strictly medical matters, this left Beth with few official duties beyond rubbing medication on his chest or taking his pulse. And even these services were never rendered in private. There was always someone else in the room: Mrs. Allister, Mrs. Kendall, Pat, Greg's friends. As Beth bustled about efficiently, Greg would wink at her, smile, or murmur remarks with double meanings.

Her worst moment came after she had fed him some bitter medicine. He swallowed it, made a face, and then, looking longingly at her face and breasts, said in a caressing voice, "Delicious . . . ambrosia." She blushed furiously, dropping the spoon which fell and clanked on the seat of a chair. As she retrieved it, several visitors—friends of Greg's parents—who had been talking to each other, exchanged amused looks over the nurse's clumsiness. When they resumed their conversation, she hissed at Greg, "You mustn't do that!"

He whispered, "But I want to tell you how lovely you are, and this seems to be the only way."

That evening she and Diane managed to work out a plan that would remedy this impossible situation. Diane would always visit him after three, usually with little Laura in tow. As soon as Beth arrived—between three thirty and four—Diane would send Laura down to the nurse and she herself would go to her room. Mrs. Kendall, under the impression that Diane and her friend Beth were still with Greg, would be unlikely to come upstairs and with luck would spend the time shopping or doing errands. Diane would in some roundabout way indicate to the Allisters that she wished the late afternoon hours to be her time alone with Greg. Thus the Allisters would remain at home. If, despite these precautions, anyone were to come up and find Beth alone with Greg, she could offer the excuse that Diane had left to fetch something from her room and Beth was checking on her patient. Aside from these few hours, she would have no time alone with Greg except for those stray minutes she might be able to grab in the late evening after Pat had examined him.

On Tuesday afternoon—the day Diane's plan went into effect—Beth walked in to find Diane arranging flowers and Greg smiling delightedly at the antics of his daughter, who would soon be two years old. Laura was chattering and strutting around very importantly while her father praised every smile, every one-syllable word, every last ribbon in her hair. Witnessing this scene of intense fatherly pride, she resolved to try to be close to Laura after Greg was gone.

"Well," Diane said as Beth entered. "Here's the nurse, Laura. Aunt Beth needs a moment alone with Papa. Do you know how long a moment is, sweetheart?"

"See Papa?" said Laura, giggling.

"A moment is two hours," murmured Diane, hustling Laura to the door and winking at Beth. "Take good care of him, nurse." She pulled Laura into the hall and closed the door against the little girl's howls of protest.

Beth said, "Greg, there's no reason Laura can't stay here. You're so happy when you're with her."

He smiled. "I see her often during the day. And how could we enjoy a kiss with those bright eyes boring into us?" He was resting against propped-up pillows. A sheet covered his waist, and he was wearing a white nightshirt which he had opened so that most of his chest was exposed.

"Greg," she said in her nurse's tone, "Pat said that if you insist on having the window open, you must remain fully covered to guard against drafts."

"Drafts! This room is like a sealed jar."

"But you mustn't expose your chest."

"Oh, 'mustn't' I?" He reached out for her and she sat on the bed and kissed him. It was the first uninterrupted kiss they had had since his return, and it felt good. Weak he might be, but his lips were passionate and insistent. And when at last she sat up, smoothing her hair in case unwanted visitors called, he wistfully began reminiscing about their brief winter courtship. His recollections were far more vivid than her own, and she realized that in prison he had had little else to think about.

Later that afternoon she noticed a yellowing, dog-eared portion of a print on the night stand beside his bed. She picked it up and examined it. It was a single scrawny evergreen tree standing in the snow.

"Is this yours, Greg?"

"Yes." He reached for it and held it fast. "A friend of mine in the army owned it. Somehow it was ripped and he threw the main portion away. I found this on the ground and decided to keep it. It was in my pocket when I was captured. They stripped me of all my other belongings but they never found this." He leaned back, still clutching the picture. "It had a special meaning for me. I recall another prisoner hiding the spoon he ate with. I guess he felt the same way."

"Was this all you had?"

"No. They gave us books, cards, other things. But it was all I had of my own. Actually—this may sound foolish to you—I loved this tree. Do you understand?"

"I think so," she said doubtfully.

"It was my friend, Beth." He covered his eyes and turned away.

For a moment she just looked at him, trying to put herself in his place. But it was impossible. She knew nothing of the conditions that would drive a man to call a piece of paper his friend. She touched his hand and said, "Tell me about prison, Greg."

He removed his hand from his eyes. "Which one? There were several."

"Tell me about Libby."

"It was a converted warehouse on the James River. We were confined in six large rooms. At one point—just after my capture—there must have been close to a thousand prisoners there."

"In six rooms?"

"In the daytime we had some space in which to move because we were upright. But at night, lying down, it was bad. We were packed into long rows. One couldn't turn over in his sleep without rolling on top of someone else."

She shook her head slowly.

"Were the guards brutal?"

He didn't answer.

"Can't you tell me, Greg? I want to know what you've been through. To understand—"

"We weren't permitted to approach within three feet of the windows or we would be whipped or shot, depending upon the whim of the guard."

"Did you ever—"

"Yes. I wasn't shot, though. I was sent to the dungeon."

"The dungeon! Good grief, what was it like?"

"Beth, I really can't talk about it. Of my prison years, the only thing I can recall looking forward to was food. Civilized people would never recognize those rebel concoctions as food, but we lived for every vile mouthful." He looked at her. "Beth, remind me to tell the Kendall cook not to fix me large portions. I feel compelled to eat every morsel even if I'm sick afterward. I can't bear to see food wasted and if I ever see anyone throw it away—"

"I'll tell the cook and I'll ask Diane to tell the family."

"Thank you."

"Greg, I know you attempted to escape when you were in Georgia."

"Yes," he said solemnly. "It's a soldier's duty to escape."

"And that's why you risked your life?"

He grinned. "I thought you realized I was being sarcastic. No, I didn't give a damn about a soldier's duty. All I could think of was my stomach."

"Well I don't blame you for being indifferent to the army regulations, but I admire the reasons that made you fight."

"Do you? I've almost forgotten what those reasons were."

"You said the poor were being sacrificed for the rich and you felt you had to be there. I think that was the moment I fell in love with you. Your ideals—"

"Beth—please—could you try loving me for other reasons?"

"Other reasons? What do you mean?"

"I can scarcely remember my 'ideals.' In prison I dreamed of food day and night. And when I was driven by other hungers I thought about you. I forgot my 'ideals' entirely. And I also discovered that the appeal of my causes varied with the actual distance between me and my fellow man."

She knit her brows, unable to believe that this was Greg talking. "Greg, you must have held onto *something*. After all, you would not allow your father to buy your way out of prison."

Greg's eyes widened. "How did you know he made the offer?"

"I didn't know. But it seemed likely that he would."

"Yes, he tried. But I couldn't permit that. How could I have lived with myself, knowing that half my comrades were rotting away in that place while I escaped only through the mediation of a rich father?"

"There, you see?" she exclaimed triumphantly. "All that talk about loss of ideals. Why, even Kent said you were one of the few men he knew with genuine integrity."

"Kent?"

"Kent Wilson. The surgeon."

296

"Oh yes. My fellow alumnus. I didn't know you knew him."

"I worked with him at Gettysburg. I think I told you yesterday that I was at Gettysburg."

"Yes you did. I'd hoped you'd never have to be exposed to war. I heard the rebs had reached Pennsylvania, but I was certain that you would escape in time."

"I wasn't really in any danger."

"Many men who fought at Gettysburg ended the war at Libby. And if I hadn't been captured, I would have been up on the crest with Gibbon."

"Trying to stop Pickett?"

He nodded. "And I doubt I would have lived to tell the tale." He paused. "They told us in prison that Gettysburg had been a Confederate victory. We were resigned to rebel victories, of course, but not in Pennsylvania. I had visions of them racing north and seizing New York. Then the Negro who brought us our food came by and whispered the truth. Some of the officers began singing the Battle Hymn of the Republic. I suppose that was the most poignant moment I can remember in Libby Prison." He shook his head. "I'm sorry. What were you saying about Kent?"

"He came home one Christmas with Pat. I talked to him about you, using my concern for Diane as an excuse. He told me that you would be unlikely to consider any intervention by your father."

Greg smiled. "Kent said that? I vaguely recall a conversation with him during the war. But if memory serves me, he didn't seem much impressed with my integrity. I believe he called me naïve."

"Well, he may be cynical but he still recognizes quality when he sees it."

"You seem to know him very well." There was a hint of suspicion in Greg's eyes.

"He was Pat's commander," she said hastily. "I could hardly avoid knowing him."

"Don't mind me, Beth. I'm jealous of everybody. I used to have nightmares about your not being here when I returned. And now—" he studied the print he was holding—"Now I wonder if you're disappointed that I'm not the same man you knew."

"Oh, but you are! You're just a bit disenchanted, but that's all. After a few weeks—" She trailed off as he began coughing, red patches appearing on his cheeks.

When the spasm had passed he said, "Beth I intend to work for my father until we're settled. Then perhaps—"

"In the bank? But I thought—"

"The way I make a living is of secondary importance. All that matters is you. And Laura."

"But politics. You were going to—" She was talking as though she expected him to recover, and at this instant she did.

He smiled. "Politics. Some day perhaps but not immediately, all right? I'm too tired to make the simplest decisions, let alone decisions affecting thousands of people."

"Yes, I see." He hadn't altogether abandoned his dreams. He'd just set them aside temporarily. Greg was becoming more practical and this made her love him even more. She hated to admit it, but she rather liked the idea of her being placed above mankind in his list of priorities. They'd get back to the revolution later when he was—and then, driving the thought away, she held a playfully clenched fist at his chin and told him he'd better button his shirt against the draft.

As the days went by, she discovered that many of his old passions no longer interested him. His main concern was her: kissing her, holding her hand, listening to her accounts of the days in school. When they did talk of some of his old social observations, he seemed very bored.

"I used to run on about a great many things. How did you stand me?"

"I loved listening to you talk."

"Well, I'm glad of that, anyway."

What had happened to him? The ideas he had once had—ideas she quoted proudly while never revealing the source—

were no longer of interest to him. She felt like someone holding another person's coat, ready to assist him on with it while he walked away, oblivious.

But in many ways Greg hadn't changed at all. He still loved poetry and wanted her to read it to him. They talked about literature, music, and the theater for hours on end, and he frequently reminded her of how much they would have to catch up on after he got well. The fact that he might not get well never seemed to occur to him. Pat told her one night that this was quite common in young men:

"He's only twenty-nine. Many men of that age will not accept it. Mrs. Allister told me that his wills and such were put in order just before his return to Virginia, so there's no compelling reason to make him face up to the inevitable. Perhaps he should die with his dreams."

Kate often went into Beth's room shortly before bedtime and talked to her daughter. Beth was eating little and getting thin. The double strain of watching the man she loved die and having to keep her feelings a secret was taking its toll and Beth badly needed support. Kate would sit near the bed with her crocheting while her daughter propped pillows behind her and talked about Greg, sometimes crying, sometimes angry, and often resigned: "He's dying. I'll just have to face it."

Kate wondered what it was about the man that had kept her daughter so infatuated with him for two years. A week's acquaintance did not seem enough time for Beth to fall so totally in love. Was it possible that they had been intimate? No, of course not. Beth was every inch a lady, despite some of her modern ideas. And yet Beth did things that made Kate doubt her own self-assurances. It was not anything she could pinpoint; just a way Beth had of half-closing her eyes or hugging a pillow when she spoke of him. Often she would stop abruptly in the middle of a sentence and look away as though afraid to meet Kate's eyes.

Perhaps it was true, but Kate decided that this was the time not for questioning but for support. She tried to help her daughter as best she knew how and prayed that Greg's death would not permanently cripple her. More and more, Beth came to depend on her mother's strength and understanding. She had always loved Kate abstractly as her mother, but now she loved her as a human being and did not know how she could ever have stood it all without her.

Kate herself had changed, and she was aware of it. There were times, though, when she asked herself if she had really changed or if she had been the same person all along, one who had merely affected the cloak of Victorian respectability in order to maintain her position and that of her children. That heavy cloak was as much a part of the dress of most women as were the hoops. If one belonged to a class or a society, one abided by the rules or was cast adrift forthwith. It was easy enough for Sally to write her own rules. She lived far from the cities. It was easy too for John and for the boys. Unusual behavior was tolerated in men—up to a point. But for most women there was no escape. One followed the rules to the letter and the rules grew more elaborate every year, many women having nothing better to do with their time but write etiquette books.

With the war, though, there had been a change. Respectable women suddenly found themselves widows and sought employment as teachers or nurses. Women from the finest families were nursing in military hospitals. Though most men did not like this state of affairs, they were forced to suffer the ladies' good offices. And something quite unexpected had happened. Despite the tragedy, despite the hard labor of working and raising families at the same time, women were beginning to feel freer and (yes, Kate had to admit it) happier. The rules had been cast aside when the emergency so demanded; and Kate, though she herself was little affected by the war, began discarding some rules of her own.

To be sure, she was still fervently religious. But in her mind God had never been a harsh judge but a benevolent father who would understand human transgressions and make

300

allowances for them. John had once said that sin was a relative thing depending upon circumstances. Kate had resisted this idea for years, but lately she had come to see the merit of it. Indeed, she had probably always seen it. Her beloved immigrant family had none of them been saints. Yet she was certain that they had all gone to heaven; certain too that she would see them there. A priest might have said that, no, her father had missed church the week before he died and would therefore be condemned to hell. But the priest was not God. The priest would not care that her father had worked himself so hard on the docks in order to give his family food to eat that he was just too tired for church. No, and the pope wasn't God either. Christ had probably meant something else when he vested Peter with the power to judge these offenses. And Scripture had misinterpreted Him. God understood that some "sins" were not sins at all.

Beth had loved Greg. Greg had been about to go away, and she had wanted him as a woman wants a man she might never see again. What was sinful about that? God would understand, even if some among his flock would not.

Though Greg was getting sicker, he didn't seem to know it. Beth continued to talk of the future. Someone had once told her that it was better not to lie to a dying man but to share the truth. Yet what could she say to a man who had no future? Could she say, "Heaven is near, Greg, and isn't that exciting?" Could she simply accept the fact and talk of other things? What could she talk about? Any story she began would have an ending somewhere in a future he would never know. If he chose to believe that he was going to live then she would pretend so too.

The long afternoons began to take on an unreal quality. The sun, slanting in through the west window, would illuminate his face in an almost supernatural way, as thought he were already dead and had appeared here so that she might have one last look at him. She would stare at him, thinking that this was not Greg but some caricature with sunken cheeks and

301

a ghastly pallor that took on color only when he coughed. When the sun was low enough that shadows rather than harsh light played upon his face, she would see in him a glimpse of the vibrant man she had known years ago.

The best time was just before dinner. His face was in shadows and the nightly fever had not yet begun, and she could pretend that they were married and in their room together, talking about their day.

She had made a vow to herself never to cry in his presence, and so she tried to pass the days in amusing chatter. Once when he told her how much he loved her, she did cry. But he had not been suspicious of that. He had been touched by her response. Sometimes he asked her to read poetry; she took care never to read a sonnet but to concentrate on poems of adventure such as "The Rime of the Ancient Mariner." One day she came across Bryant's "Thanatopsis" and she scanned it silently before turning to a poem she could read aloud. Certain lines from songs or literature often echoed in her head over and over, taunting her like an annoying parrot, and there were lines from "Thanatopsis" that bedeviled her for days after she read them:

> . . . yet a few days and thee
> The all-beholding sun shall see no more
> In all his course.

The words accompanied her as she tidied his room and held his head when he coughed violently into handkerchiefs, and stroked his hand when he lay back against the pillows. The sound racketed around in her brain until she thought she would scream aloud: "Yet a few days. . . . Yet a few days . . ." and she would look at him and try to remember every feature of his face, every nuance of his voice, and then close her eyes to determine whether a clear memory of him was imprinted in her mind. "Yet a few days . . ." The words urged her to cry, but she would not cry, and in time the words lost all meaning.

302

Pat saw Greg every night and Greg was not pleased with the endless care.

"Oh, my God, it's the medicine man again," Greg groaned one evening. "I can't endure another examination. Please, Pat."

"That's enough out of you. Breathe deeply."

Pat listened; then he fixed his eyes on Beth's.

"Well, doc?" asked Greg.

"Your heart just stopped beating," said Pat.

"Cogito; ergo sum," said Greg.

"Not necessarily," said Pat.

And so they bantered back and forth as they usually did, but Beth noticed that Greg never once asked, "Am I getting better?" or "What's wrong with me?" Greg never asked and Pat never volunteered.

The company Greg had commanded during the war had not yet been disbanded and was still in Washington. Thus Greg had seen only one army friend since his return home two weeks earlier. But on this Saturday evening another soldier stopped by to visit. Beth was downstairs in the parlor with Diane, waiting for Greg to awaken from his nap, when a tall, powerfully built man with unruly black hair was shown into the room. He appeared to be about thirty years old. In a booming voice he introduced himself as Jack White, Greg's platoon sergeant in the days when Greg had been a lieutenant. Home on leave, following the birth of his son, the sergeant had seen the announcement of Greg's return to New York in a week-old newspaper and had come right over. Inquiring as to the nature of Greg's illness, he was given evasive replies by Diane and did not know what to expect when Beth finally showed him into Greg's room.

Greg was awake and reading a book when he heard heavy footsteps. He looked up, and his eyes widened with amazement and delight. "Jack! I can't believe it!"

"Hello, captain." The sergeant strode into the room and

clasped Greg's hand. Beth perceived that the man was shocked at Greg's condition and was struggling not to let it show.

Almost before the man sat down, they were talking about the army. As Beth walked in and out of the room with handkerchiefs and basins, they never paused except when she had to poke a thermometer into Greg's mouth or dole out his medicine. Greg seemed starved for news: "How's McMahon? . . . Did Polanski ever get his promotion? . . . Did Jones marry that girl?" There were questions about the leaders: "How can you stand Humphreys after Hancock, Hays after Gibbon? . . . Is Grant as tough as they say?" And there was the inevitable, "Jack, do you remember the time. . . ." followed by laughter and more laughter. She didn't hear any mention of battles, nor was reference made to prison or to Greg's condition. Listening to them, one might have thought that service in the army had been an utter lark. The conversation and all the laughing quite exhausted Greg, and after about three hours she was obliged to ask the sergeant to leave, though she cushioned this blow by eliciting a promise that he would return on Monday.

She and the sergeant walked downstairs together, and at the door he said, "I'd like to talk to you, nurse. Miss Shepherd, is it?"

"Yes." She peeked into the Kendall dining room and, finding no one there, motioned him in. They sat at the table.

The sergeant minced no words. "He's dying, isn't he?"

"Yes, he is."

The man swallowed. "He don't know, does he?"

"I don't think so, sergeant. He must know he has consumption, but he never talks about it."

She answered a few more questions about Greg's condition and then, noticing that the sergeant was on the verge of tears, tried to steer the subject to Greg as he had been in his healthier days. "Was he a good officer, sergeant?"

"It depends how you look at it. He was great in battles and good with the training too, but he didn't take camp orders serious." The man smiled. "He used to try to shout like the rest of 'em, but if the order was real stupid, he used to start laughing right in the middle of delivering it. Officers ain't supposed to do that."

"The men must have liked him."

"Well, some did but a lot of 'em didn't. He used to criticize the army and the government, and most of the men they didn't like that. Me, I thought he was right."

"I'm surprised he spoke out, sergeant. Didn't the higher officers object?"

"They did, but they didn't say nothing because he was too good in battles. He was tough as General Barlow and he didn't lose many men neither. Always knew what he was doing. Even when he was captured, they say he was out there alone. Didn't think it was safe to bring anyone with him and he was right." The sergeant shook his head and grinned. "But good as he was, he never took it serious. Used to tell me the war was a sham and he'd talk about—say, miss, I don't know if I should be telling you these things—"

"It's all right, sergeant. Gregory and his wife are personal friends of mine. I'm well aware of his unorthodox political views. Do go on."

"Well, he used to talk about how some people were always losers in this world. And he'd even get mad at dead people. Some French queen who ate cake and a man who played a fiddle in a fire. Lord, how he could run on. He drove me crazy."

Beth smiled. This was the Greg she remembered. What had happened to him? "Did he get on with any of the men?"

"He wasn't one of the boys, if that's what you mean, miss. He could drink pretty good, but he didn't like to play poker or gamble, and in the army officers don't have much else to do. Most of the officers they thought he was a snob, but that wasn't true because he did like a few. Liked enlisted men too. The ones with senses of humor. Wry, he used to call it."

"Were those the men you were talking about upstairs?"

"Mostly."

"He must miss them. I've never known him to laugh so hard."

The sergeant smiled. "War and all, I guess we had some good times." He stared ahead for a while and his face grew wistful. "He used to be so strong, miss. So alive. And now he—Lord, I've seen too many of 'em go. *Too many*, miss." There were tears in his eyes, and he leaned on the table covering his face with his hands.

She sat looking down, wishing that she knew how to comfort people when they cried. Then she began to think about what the man had just said. Greg liked his fellow man—but abstractly. He couldn't get close to most of them. In prison, he had been troubled enough by it to question his ability ever to effect reforms. She thought to herself: He shouldn't feel that way. Many leaders were aloof from the men they led and still were good leaders.

But how on earth had he tolerated prison? Not only had he been forced to live on top of people, but Libby's mindless discipline must have driven him mad.

In a way this explained his attachment to the torn print. Thrown together with other officers in a large room, and all but indistinguishable from them, he had clung to the print. The evergreen was his—exclusively. Exactly what it represented to him she did not know, but it was the only tangible symbol of his uniqueness, and he must have needed that badly.

The sergeant was clearing his throat and standing up. Earlier he had seemed somewhat intimidating, but now he looked like a gentle bear. As he said good night to her, she had a strong impulse to run to him as she would to a father and be comforted in his arms. No man but this one could have soothed her, for she wanted someone who cared enough about Greg to weep for him. But she could not run to him. They were in the Kendall home, and the man was married, and she'd have to explain to him why she was so upset, and if anyone saw them and told Greg. . . . She clenched her teeth.

The thing might be more bearable if she could grieve normally. But she couldn't even do that.

A flood of people came to visit Greg on Sunday. This, following the strain of Saturday night, left him exhausted. At six o'clock even his family went home and Beth ordered him to take a nap. Two hours later, when she walked into his room again, she found him awake.

"I didn't think you'd be up so soon," she said.

" 'Up?' I can hardly raise my head from the pillow."

She smiled. "I mean awake. I told Pat not to come over until you had rested. Ten o'clock I told him."

She sat on the bed, his arm in her lap, and stroked his hand. A breeze stirred, bringing the fresh, heady scent of early June into the room. Summer was coming awake after a confused spring of victory roses and lilacs for the President. Even from this warm room she could sense the quickening in the world outside, the restlessness, the need for people to get outdoors and breathe and laugh again. Greg, almost as though he were sensing this too, lifted his arm—it required great effort—and he caressed her basque. It felt good—so good that she wanted to cry out in pleasure.

But he was too weak to continue. After a moment his arm fell heavily against the sheet. She embraced him, laying her head lightly on his chest, trying somehow to press her health against him so that he could absorb it and be strong. But he began to cough. It was a bad attack, and she had to support him, holding a handkerchief. After it was over, he lay back and looked at her, his eyes painfully sad.

"I wanted to caress you," he said. "Wanted that so much, but I just couldn't do it." He sighed and said bitterly, "Beth, it's no damned use."

Her throat ached as she struggled against tears. She must not cry. He must not see her cry. She took his hand and tried to think of something else. Swallowing, she began counting mentally to a hundred.

Greg saw that she was near tears, and he wondered what she must think of him. Of course he was sick and she understood that. But how much longer would he have to wait before he could be a man again? Beth needed a man, not a chronically ill neuter who hadn't the strength to caress her. He turned his eyes away, embarrassed to look at her. He didn't want her pity. He closed his eyes and pretended to sleep. After a while she extinguished the lamp, kissed him softly, and left.

Dim city light shone through the window, outlining the hulks of furniture. Often on these long nights he would look at the dark shapes and see death in them. Like Poe's raven, they never moved. Sometimes he reached for the print of the evergreen tree that he kept on the night stand, and he held onto it as though to ward off evil spirits. He was not superstitious—or never had been before. But now he looked for ways to keep death away. During the day it was easier. Beth would come in, her muslin dress billowing, her face like sunshine, and in her he would find life. It became a game. As long as she was alive, he would remain alive. They were so alike, so attached. As long as one lived, the other must live.

But there were moments when he wanted to give himself over to the fearful night shapes. He suspected that they were waiting for him, and sometimes he felt too tired to fight. How much easier it would be to let them claim him. Then he could sleep forever and not have to struggle with a body that no longer worked. He closed his eyes and waited for daylight. Things always looked better in daylight.

But daylight was a long time off. At nine forty-five Beth came into his room and found his fever so bad that he was tossing and kicking off sheets. As she pressed cold cloths against him, he muttered, "Beth?"

"I'm here, Greg."

For a long time he just looked at her face. It faded for a moment and then it came back sharply. Then it began to waver like a reflection in water and her voice sounded far off and he was calling to her through water but he couldn't see her and then she was there again, her brown hair gleaming red in the light, but he couldn't touch her because the campfire was between them and the colonel was saying, "We'll have to take those heights," and Beth was talking about his head . . . a rebel had pressed the muzzle of a rifle against his head and all around him voices were shouting, "Keep your hands up, Yank" and all around him in the dungeon rats scampered and then Laura was crawling down the dank slimy stairs saying, "See, Papa?"

"Laura! Don't come down here! No!"

Beth pressed another cloth against his forehead. She had not known he was delirious until the moment he had cried out, and now her heart sank. He would not last long. Time was running out, and there were so many things she had wanted to tell him: private thoughts that could not be shared with anyone but him. He continued to toss restlessly, murmuring barely audible words she did not understand. Then she realized that for Greg time had already stopped. His mind was gone. They would never talk again. She shook her head, crying brokenly and telling him she loved him. He heard her and he said, "Beth?" He had recognized her voice. Perhaps he was still rational. She spoke his name several times. Then he said, "O'Connor, you're to hold this position until Hartley's men get here."

She numbly listened to him, wondering why, even while he was dying, he had to be plagued with war memories. Wasn't it enough that he had fought the war once?

"The guard Clayton . . . I'll kill him . . . smash his head to a bloody pulp."

Who was Clayton? A prison guard? Now, in his last moments, she saw a violence in Greg that was astonishing enough to make her stop crying.

The door opened and Pat walked in. He looked down at Greg, frowning, and said, "He's Catholic, isn't he?"

"Yes."

"Honey, will you tell the family to get a priest? I'm a coward."

"How long will it be, Pat?"

"I don't know." Pat listened to Greg's rasping words and said, "He must have seen a great deal of violence."

She nodded.

"When they're awake, they can forget it. But when they're asleep or consumed with fever—" He broke off. "You'd better tell the family, Beth."

She couldn't move. She continued to stare at him helplessly. Would he have wanted her to watch him die? Her wish was to stay with him as long as he breathed, but would *he* have wanted her to be there? She tried to put herself in his place.

She looked down at Greg for the last time, trying to remember what his last conscious words had been. It took a moment for her to recall them and then she caught her breath.

"Beth, it's no damned use."

Pat turned to open his medical bag. She quickly picked up the evergreen print from Greg's nightstand before Pat could see her. Then she left the room.

Later, as his family arrived, Beth sat in the parlor pretending to comfort Diane but actually being comforted by her. At last Diane gained the strength to go up to his room, where she and the Allisters would wait. Beth walked up with her but did not go inside. As she turned to leave, the priest came out of his room.

"Is he dead, Father?"

"No, my child. In extremis."

He had called her child, and this word seemed to bring back her childhood so sharply that she found herself sobbing like a child with all the rage and hurt she had expressed so freely in those long-ago days.

"He will soon be with the angels," said the priest soothingly. "Are you his sister?"

"No, Father. I am no one." She turned and ran down the stairs, wanting to scream like a child too, but the parlor was full of people. She walked out the door and into the night.

310

She remained awake all night, sitting on her bed, listening to the sounds of the city. Her parents had been asleep when she came home. She had wanted to wake her mother but decided against it. Her father would wonder what was wrong with her. Pat was still at the Kendalls'. Why was it taking so long? Greg's prison years had been long. His illness had been long. Must his death be an endless agony too? How had that gentle man become like a caught fish wriggling on the end of a hook in one last violent convulsion? She picked up the book of poems she had read to him and hurled it across the room.

She held up the print of the evergreen tree and studied it, remembering him saying, "All that matters is you. And Laura." Greg had become an empty vessel waiting for someone to fill it. Whatever had once been inside was gone. The violence he had met had boiled off his life fluids and prison had cracked his structure. In prison he could only cling desperately to a picture. Once home, he held onto her in the same way.

Kate, awakened by the noise of the book Beth had thrown, walked into the room.

"Whatever is wrong, dear?"

Beth handed the print to her mother. "See this, Mother? It's Greg's friend. I must take care of it for him."

He died shortly after the sun came up. It was a magnificent June morning of winking flowers and trilling birds. The sky remained clear throughout the day, as skies tend to do when those rare situations come up for which dismal gray drizzles are far more appropriate. There was a two-day wake, which was attended by New York society and covered by all the important newspapers. The casket was closed. Diane and the Allisters agreed that Greg would not have wanted people gawking at him. The Kendall drawing room was shrouded in black crêpe and drapes were drawn against air and light. Dozens of candles flickered as mourners shuffled slowly from the door to the flower-strewn casket to the grieving family. Potentates, who were present only because James Allister was an important man, delivered unctuous platitudes while their wives flourished lacy handkerchiefs and sniffled.

Beth's grief was reflected in bizarre behavior. As people who had scarcely known Greg performed this macabre ballet, she covered her mouth, laughing. Greg would have thought them grotesquely comical. People turned to stare at Beth, raised their eyebrows, wondered how young Allister's sensible nurse could laugh at a time like this. Kate bit her lip and worried continually.

By the morning of the funeral, the pain had penetrated to Beth's nerves. There was no anesthetic laughter now; only a stabbing bitterness. She stood with her family in a newly dyed black silk dress outside the Kendall home and watched the handsome soldiers carry the flag-draped coffin down the stairs. They handled it easily, for they were probably accustomed to this sort of thing. What could be more natural for them in view of their recent occupations?

The Shepherd family was silent in the big black carriage that crept along behind the others toward the small stone church his mother had selected. And Beth, looking out, noticed that the people on the sidewalks were dressed gaily for summer, their steps livelier than they had been these four long years. They looked at the somber cortège and turned away. Such scenes, which had been so common during the war, irritated them so soon after the trumpets of victory had promised them their long-awaited revelry. Now was the time to rejoice; how dare anyone offend them with yet another black procession winding through the narrow cobblestone streets?

Beth thought that the funeral itself would be the worst part, but she was surprised to find that the ancient Latin words were more comfort to her than she had expected. The solemn high Mass, so familiar to her from childhood, was soothing, like a gentle mother's voice crooning to an infant. Though she did not believe most of it—God, heaven, the promise of recompense somewhere for the agonies endured with pa-

312

tience here on earth—she was impressed by one truth: Everybody died. It wasn't so terrible or unique. Everybody died, and Greg would not be alone.

> Agnus Dei, qui tollis peccata mundi,
> Dona eis requiem.
> Agnus Dei, qui tollis peccata mundi,
> Dona eis requiem.
> Agnus Dei, qui tollis peccata mundi,
> Dona eis requiem sempeternam.

The repetition of the words that had been spoken over the dead for hundreds of years lulled her into an acceptance of the event: Everybody died.

Only later, when the sun pierced through the opening doors of the church, was she cruelly confronted with the reality: she would never see him again.

She would never see him again, she thought again later, while the slow notes of taps sounded through the still cemetery and the flag was folded quickly and neatly over the long narrow box and handed to Diane. Greg had always been just beyond her grasp. And now even the mirage was gone.

That night she took out the print of the tree and looked at it. This had been with him when they stripped him of everything, when they tried to deny him his identity. This picture had told him who he was. She turned it over and wrote "Gregory James Allister." And at the bottom of the print she wrote a single Latin word:

Sum.

I am.

SIX

We're tenting tonight on the old camp ground;
Give us a song to cheer
Our weary hearts, a song of home
And friends we loved so dear.

Many are the hearts that are weary tonight,
Wishing for the war to cease.
Many are the hearts looking for the right
To see the dawn of peace.

Tenting tonight,
Tenting tonight,
Tenting on the old camp ground.

Pat Shepherd was feeling very much alone these days. His mother and sister, preoccupied with Diane's tragedy, were sad and distant. His father was helping Nate Klein set up his book store at a new location on Broadway. Sean was spending June visiting a classmate in Connecticut, and Joe was still in Washington awaiting discharge. So Pat was lonely most evenings and disappointed that his first weeks at home had proved so dreary.

He was working at a veteran's hospital, awaiting official discharge from the army, and on free evenings lately he preferred visiting bordellos or drinking to passing the time at home. One night he went alone to an unfamiliar saloon near the barracks at City Hall Park. The place was crowded with veterans. He sat down at the bar and listened to two middle-aged officers at a table singing "Tenting Tonight," the song that, more than any other, caught the mood of the Union soldier. He remembered a night last year in Virginia when all of them—even Kent—had stopped at a campfire to sing.

"Bathos," Joe had said of the song as he sang it.

"Māwkish, cloying," agreed Kent, singing harmony.

And Pat had said, "Will you both shut your mouths and let me cry in peace?"

The war had made of them a fraternity, the like of which they would never see again. He wondered, as he watched a soldier limp over to the bar on a wooden leg, why fraternity exacted such a price. They had been forced to be kind to each other, and that mandate had come from the threat of annihilation. He remembered Bowery hoodlums—tired, dirty, and hungry—carrying wounded men to safety through the flaming Wilderness. It had taken a war for them to save men they would have fought and perhaps killed in the gang fights of New York. But the war was over now. The men who had made up the armies would gradually drift apart, until finally each was alone. Most of them, because men had to have enemies by which to define themselves, would select their adversaries from among their former comrades. If they were ever to be close again, they would have to find another common enemy.

The officers had stopped singing and were now settling in for some hard drinking. Pat knew no one here. He wished Joe were with him. Or Kent. He frowned, remembering those two wretched months following their last Christmas furlough. To this day he couldn't understand what had happened to Kent. One thing he did know, though: he must never tell Beth about it.

The last months of the war had had the quality of all jobs

that require finishing touches. No one felt like facing it any more. The main work had been done. All that remained were the final battles—and few of the men Pat knew were enthusiastic about risking their lives that one last time, knowing that the end was so near.

There was a gloomy atmosphere in the train as Pat, Joe, and Kent boarded it in Jersey City on New Year's Day, 1865. When Joe sighted a friend and went to talk to him, Pat decided to ask Kent what had happened between him and Beth.

"She's still using the mythical-man excuse," Kent said shortly.

"Maybe he's real. Do you want me to ask her?"

"Don't bother."

"There are other women, Kent."

"Other women be damned."

"There were several at the party who seemed taken with you."

"Only my late wife has ever been 'taken' with me."

Pat had never heard Kent speak of his personal life in this way. "Your parents cared about you," he said.

"Shit."

"They didn't care?"

"They couldn't abide me." Anticipating a question from Pat, he turned abruptly away. "I'm going to take a nap." And he slept slumped in his seat, his wide-brimmed hat pulled down over his eyes.

The ride was monotonous. Soon Pat found himself chatting with a private across the aisle, an Irishman from New Haven who had a lyrical brogue. Thomas Smith seemed intelligent and well-read. Pat talked with him about the progress of the war and plans for reconstruction. Eventually they found themselves discussing the wounded.

"A man in my platoon was so damaged that he took his own life," Smith said.

"In his place I might do the same thing," said Pat.

" 'Tis a sin just the same, sir. You're Catholic, are you not?"

"A lapsed Catholic. But there are physical sufferings that

are impossible to endure. I think God, if there is such a Being, would understand suicide under those conditions."

Smith shrugged. "And what of the man with no physical afflictions? Would he be committing a sin, sir?"

"It would depend upon his reasons." Pat turned to search for a cigar and noticed that Kent was attempting to tug his hat still lower over his face. He was not asleep after all. "What do you think, Kent?" Pat asked.

"I don't recognize religious sin. I'm an agnostic," Kent said, pushing his hat back.

"You have a set of personal ethics, don't you?"

"Obviously I obey the law or I'd be in jail."

"Ethics and the law are only remotely connected, Kent."

"Indeed?"

Pat turned to Smith. "Major Wilson won't admit that he has a conscience." He said to Kent, "How do you feel about suicide?"

"It's the only civilized way to die."

"Civilized?"

"A man makes his own choice."

Smith looked at him oddly. "Would you take your life, Major?"

"Of course."

"Under what circumstances, sir?"

"Any of a number. The thousand natural shocks, et cetera." Kent pulled his hat back down over his eyes. "Wake me when we get to Philadelphia. I have to buy tobacco."

When they arrived in Philadelphia and left the train to stretch their legs, Smith said to Pat, "Something's bothering him, sir."

"A girl," Pat said.

"Do you think he'll be taking his life?"

Pat laughed. "No. Kent is given to many variations of temper. You're witnessing only one of them."

"But he said—"

"I've said the same thing myself, Smith, in bad moments."

Smith shook his head. "I'm thinking, sir, that there's too

many dying as it is. When healthy men like you start wishing for it—well, sir, it's immoral, that's what it is."

"But we're not serious."

" 'Tis no subject to be joking about, sir. And you a doctor."

"There's an ironic fact about doctors," Pat said. "They're dedicated to saving lives and will work mightily for that end. But doctors are also able to see better than anyone else the futility of it."

"Of life?"

"That's right. The pointlessness of it. That men would live, work, struggle for twenty years or more and have their heads blown off in one second."

"Yes, I see."

"So it isn't at all strange that doctors would question the meaning of life. The army has turned many a sober and dedicated surgeon into a hard-drinking and morose philosopher."

"Would you be including yourself, sir?"

"I've despaired many times, Smith, but I'm not going to kill myself. The war's almost over, and there are a great many things I hope to do when peace comes."

Pat's talk with Tom Smith made him more aware than usual of the depressing atmosphere back in camp, especially among the medical people. There were pneumonia, dysentery, consumption, and scurvy cases filling the cots. Many boys died without ever seeing battle. It was a hard winter, bitter cold and blustery, and the young soldiers were taking sick by the score. Back home they would have had enough warmth and food to resist disease. But the army didn't care—didn't trouble itself to feed them properly or shelter them properly. These men who had been directed to save the Union were treated worse than animals, and there wasn't much the doctors could do about it.

Kent, who before Christmas had thundered around demanding medication, bandages, and antiscorbutics, now seemed to have given up the fight. He still worked long hours, but automatically, like a machine. When he was finished, he

318

went to his quarters and lay on his cot, but he didn't sleep much. Pat sometimes went to fetch him late at night when an emergency case came in and found him wide awake, either reading by candlelight or staring into space. This was unusual, for Kent had been known to sleep through bombardments. There were other changes too. He didn't talk very much or eat very much or react to others. Officers who counted on him for his wit or for the bawdy jokes he had picked up in Washington brothels were disappointed.

"What's the matter with Kent?" they would ask. "He's lost his sense of humor."

"He's worse than I was that Christmas," said Joe. "I wish I knew what to say to him."

Pat tried to talk to him, but Kent shrugged it off. "No, it's not Beth. I was crazy long before I met Beth."

"You're not crazy. You're unhappy."

"I'm tired of the war."

"That's all it is?"

"That's all."

Tim told Pat that he had gone over to City Point with Kent and Kent had visited a brothel, then stopped at a saloon with Tim afterward.

"I'm not sure that I should tell you, sir, but I think he's become—well—unhinged, sir, and I don't want him to make a bad mistake. I thought you might be able to talk to him."

"What is it, Tim?"

"Well, we had some drinks and he told me he was in love with one of the whores—uh, girls, sir."

"In love?"

"Yes, sir. I asked him how in love, and he said, 'Very much, Tim.' Gosh, captain, what if he decides to marry her?"

Pat smiled. "He won't marry her."

"I don't know. The way he's been acting lately, I think he needs to hold onto something—even a prostitute—to keep from going under. He told me—" Tim stopped and blushed.

"What did he tell you?"

"How he—how they—no, captain, I can't repeat that."

"It's not like Kent to run on about his sexual performances."
Pat frowned, thinking of his sister.

"Well, he was drunk as a lord, sir. Major Wilson's not a
drinker, and he had five in a row before he passed out."

"He passed out?" Even Pat had never disgraced himself to
that degree and he drank a good deal more than Kent.

"Out cold, sir. He fell across the bar. But I took him to his
quarters and sobered him up."

This was serious. To pass out in front of Tim! Kent no
longer seemed to care whether or not he had his orderly's
respect. And all that talk about loving prostitutes. It was bad
enough that he gave the women twice as much as they asked
for and never had enough money to do much else. But loving
them? What was wrong with him?

"Don't upset yourself," Pat said crisply. "Everyone has his
bad days. Kent will be fine. I do appreciate your concern,
though."

Pat was worried. In army medical language Kent's depression fell into the category of "nostalgia." If he kept on as he
was, he would soon approach "insanity." There was nothing in
between and no way of treating these problems except with
kindness and advice. Pat had tried that already. All he could
hope for now was that the war would end soon.

As the Army of the Potomac prepared for the final battles,
Pat's regiment, indeed most of the army, occupied territory in
the Petersburg, Virginia, area. There was an old deserted
house here, the dining room of which was used as an officers'
mess and the other rooms as quarters and recreation areas for
the officers, who sometimes spent evenings after supper playing cards or chess or twanging banjoes. Kent rarely joined
them but went back to his own quarters at "the hospital"—a
farmhouse—right after supper. One evening, however, he
joined Pat and another friend in the library of the house but
sat in a corner reading one of the books in the former owner's
small collection—a chemistry text. An infantry captain

320

approached him. The man had been drinking and was spoiling for a fight.

From across the room, Pat saw Gilbey's swarthy face as he spoke and gestured at Kent, who sat motionless, his face devoid of expression. Kent mumbled something that caused Gilbey to gesture more emphatically. Pat could not hear the words but he could guess at the topic of this one-sided discussion. The autumn before, Kent had asked Gilbey's commanding officer to discharge a man under Gilbey's command while Gilbey himself was away on furlough. He had been a veteran of Antietam and Gettysburg, wounded twice, who had gone berserk one night, cursing Gilbey and the generals, denouncing Lincoln, and throwing stones in all directions. One of the sentries, a sympathetic man, had awakened Joe, the lieutenant in charge, rather than summon the provost guard. Joe mentioned the incident to no one but calmed the man, staying with him until he slept. The next day he brought the private to the hospital—then located in a barn—and asked Kent to talk to him.

"I'm not crazy, doctor," said the soldier. He was a gangling redheaded youth who seemed no older than eighteen. "Please don't write that on my records."

"I see no evidence of insanity," Kent said to Joe.

"Perhaps he has some other affliction," Joe said.

"Shall I find one, Joe?"

"Please."

Kent said to the soldier, "You've just contracted consumption. I can tell by looking at your hair. I'll recommend discharge. When you return to New York, I want you to cough for a while. By February you may commence your miraculous recovery."

The boy was near tears. "Why are you doing this for me, sir?"

"Because the army had no goddamned right to classify a man like you as a lunatic. Anyone who runs howling in protest in the manner just described is, in my opinion, completely sane."

"I'm sorry to hear you're so sick," said Joe, "but I must recommend that you stay sick when you get home. When your comrades come home on Christmas furlough they will want to see you in bed, soldier. Understood?"

"Understood, sir."

"Good. Now stagger back to your quarters and pack your things. And don't forget to cough."

Pat looked at his brother. Joe, during the first years in the army, had been a demanding officer. He had, for the most part, been unsympathetic when a man broke under pressure. But since his own ordeal at Gettysburg he had softened a good deal. And now, Pat thought, it seemed that he had gone to the other extreme. But it was Kent who would really be in trouble if anyone discovered what he had done.

When the soldier had gone, Pat said to Kent, "I hope you know what you're doing. If Gilbey finds out—no, I mean *when* Gilbey finds out—you'll have a lot of explaining to do."

Kent shrugged. "Don't worry about it."

Tim Kelly, who had stood by quietly, nodding his approval of Kent's action, suddenly burst into song. It was a snappy tune written about men rejected by the army for physical reasons. It had a lilting melody, and Tim, Irish to the bone, did a lively jig as he sang.

> O, I wanted much to go to war
> And went to be examined.
> The surgeon looked me o'er and o'er,
> My back and chest he hammered.
> Said he, "You're not the man for me
> Your lungs are much affected,
> And likewise both your eyes are cocked
> And otherwise defected."
>
> So now I'm with the invalids
> And cannot go and fight, sir.
> The doctor told me so, you know.
> Of course he must be right, sir.

The song became more hilarious with every verse and by

the end of his performance a group of laughing soldiers had crowded into the barn to listen. Though no one knew for certain what had prompted the singing, there were doubtless some men around who knew of the corporal's outburst. It would only be a matter of time, Pat thought, before some shrewd soldier, wanting to make points with Gilbey, pieced together the facts and presented them as a gift to his captain.

The informer did his job very quickly and capably. Within half an hour of Gilbey's return to camp, he was blustering into the hospital demanding the truth from Kent.

"Why did you discharge him, doc?"

"Haven't you seen the record, captain?"

"He was crazy as a loon, isn't that correct?"

"Speak to the colonel, Gilbey. He has the record."

"Tell me the truth, doc."

Kent's voice rose. "The truth is in the *record.* As I recall, he had consumption. And if you persist in—"

"I gather you approve of lunatics' running loose in the streets."

Kent set his teeth. "Wholeheartedly. I'm a very tolerant man, captain. I've tolerated you for the last five minutes."

"I'll see that you're prohibited from practicing medicine, Wilson."

"Gilbey, you will remove yourself from this hospital or I shall be forced to summon the provost guard. Is that clear?"

"I'm going to report you."

"Damn you to hell, you slimy bastard!" Kent's voice rose to a shattering roar, civilized speech abandoning him. "I ordered you to leave. If your ass is not out that door at the count of three, I'll have you arrested."

Gilbey went, but he took his time about it. Several patients had been awakened from opium-induced sleep by Kent's outburst, and one was shouting. "Get the rebel sons of bitches! Charge! Charge, men!"

Pat and the orderlies began to laugh. Kent, who was still shaking with rage, shouted, "Quiet, damn you!" The patient now echoed, "Quiet! Quiet! All quiet along the Potomac."

In the following months Captain Gilbey took frequent occasion to remind Kent of the incident by glaring at him across the mess hall or making pointed remarks in his presence about subversive elements in the army and the harm they would do to their country. They had not, in all this time, exchanged a single word.

Tonight, however, Gilbey was drinking, and he was livid. Finally Kent closed his book and stood up. Putting on his overcoat, he began to walk toward the door. Gilbey grabbed his arm and now Pat could hear them.

"You're not going anywhere until you tell me the truth. Why did you recommend discharge, doc?"

"He had consumption." Kent's voice was almost toneless. Pat wished that he would roar as he had in the old days.

"You're lying, by God!" shouted Gilbey.

"Let go of my arm."

"I could have you court-martialed."

"Splendid. I could use the rest in jail. Let go of my arm," Kent said for the second time.

"Are you ordering me?"

"I am." Kent wrenched his arm free and walked toward the door, but Gilbey ran ahead of him and blocked the exit.

"I won't be ordered around by a coward,"Gilbey said.

Kent raised an eyebrow and studied the man's clenched fists. "Are those supposed to pass for balls, Gilbey?"

Pat thought, Kent's asking for it. A second later Gilbey's fist was in Kent's eye. Pat was on his feet immediately, but before he could intervene, Kent had spun Gilbey around, grabbed one of his arms, twisted it into a hammerlock, and sent him sprawling toward the center of the room. Then Kent opened the door and walked out. As another man helped Gilbey to his feet, Pat stood with his hands on his hips, glaring down at the officer. "You're one stupid son of a bitch, Gilbey. When you provoke a surgeon to fight you're taking the chance that when your leg is blown off his hand will be so badly infected from the teeth he was forced to knock down your throat that he might not be able to operate. Kent should have pulverized you. I would have." Pat turned and instructed another officer,

"If his arm pains him, send him to Marshall. He's damned lucky Kent didn't knock *his* eye out. Why do infantrymen underestimate the strength of surgeons? Hell, we lift bodies, we handle saws all the time. And our reflexes are well-developed too, as this jackass just learned."

Pat left abruptly and raced down the stairs. He caught Kent at the door. "Let me look at that eye."

"Just let me go to bed."

"Go ahead. I'll be over in a few minutes with some ice. Kent, why didn't you do a proper job on that bastard?"

"Because one of us would have had to patch him up afterward."

"It's strange. There was no anger or passion in what you did. You acted like a man slapping off a mosquito."

"An apt simile."

They could hear men in the parlor singing, "The Girl I Left Behind Me." Kent stood for a moment before opening the door. He shook his head and said, "All I ever wanted out of life was peace and quiet. Why won't they let me have it?"

When Pat reached the farmhouse, a quarter of a mile away, Kent was on his cot, lying flat on his back and fully dressed, an arm flung over his eyes. How thin he looked, Pat thought. Wasted almost. Kent heard Pat come in and stirred.

"Ice for your eye," said Pat. "And a glass of whisky."

"Thank you." Kent's left eye was swollen shut.

"Stay in bed tomorrow, Kent. I'll handle things. Oh, and Harrison is on his way to report Gilbey." (Pat did not know it yet, but Gilbey would be replaced by Joe Shepherd.) He handed the icebag to Kent, who held it against his eye as he sat up and reached for the glass of whisky. Pat said, "Be careful, Kent. Some day one of these stunts is going to cost you your profession. It nearly cost you your eye. You have more heart than sense. So does my brother. But *he* didn't sign that record."

"Thanks for the ice pack. It feels good."

"Did you hear what I just said?"

"I don't care."

"About your eye or your profession?"

"If you're going to run the hospital tomorrow, you'd better get some sleep, Pat."

Pat had the sensation of talking to a ghost. He and Kent had once had close rapport, based on mutual interests, humor, and a shared affection for Beth. But now his friend had gone away, leaving only a shape without a third dimension. Pat missed him.

About a week later, when they were eating the midday meal in the mess hall, Pat was relieved to witness a return of Kent's old sarcastic spirit. He maintained a running commentary on the quality of the food from the leathery beef through the gas-inducing beans to the teeth-demolishing hardtack. When the coffee was served, Kent—who had swallowed a mouthful of grounds—sighed, looked up and down the length of the table, and said, "Dregs: A Memoir of the Union Army by Kent Matthew Wilson."

"The master dreg of the pack," observed Marshall.

"I didn't know your middle name was Matthew," said Pat. "That's awfully biblical for an agnostic."

"The truth is that I've been chosen to write the Final Testament," said Kent. "On the day of judgment, the Devil will appear among the anxious Christians, Jews, and Mohammedans and say, Terribly sorry, folks, but you've been wasting your time. The true religion is, and always has been, the worship of Zeus. All ye who have not hearkened to the Truth of Mount Olympus shall be doomed to an eternity of beans and hardtack."

"Praise be to Zeus!" shouted a captain at the end of the table, scrambling up and bowing toward the north.

"Greece is that way, McGuinness," said Kent, pointing east.

"Kent, have you been at the whisky or at the opium?" Marshall demanded.

"Neither. I saw a vision last night hovering over a slops bucket in Ward B. (Ward B, for those of you who have never visited our modern facilities, is the closed-in back porch of the

326

farm house.) The vision was Zeus himself disguised as a patient. He told me to go forth and spread the word."

"And what you spread was the contents of the slops bucket," said Pat.

"That was supposed to be my line, Pat." Kent looked at him and smiled—almost sadly, Pat thought. Then he stood. "I leave you gentlemen to contemplate your sins. That should keep you occupied for the better part of what remains of the war."

As Pat left the mess hall a few minutes later, he caught a glimpse of Kent walking into the woods behind the farmhouse. It was a nice day for February and he probably wanted to sit under a tree and enjoy the fresh air. Between the sick smell of the hospital and the greasy smell of the mess hall, they'd had hardly a breath of clean air all winter. Deciding to join Kent, who seemed jollier than he had been since Christmas, Pat slogged cheerily through the mud, kicking at melting lumps of snow, looking at the trees, and imagining them full of leaves. He thought of a redheaded girl back home and began to sing softly:

> Maxwelton's braes are bonnie
> Where early falls the dew,
> And it's there that Annie Laurie
> Gave me her answer true . . .

He stopped singing when he spotted Kent in the distance sitting on a rock, his back to Pat. As Pat approached Kent he noticed that he was examining something. He moved closer and saw that it was a pistol. For a second Pat was immobilized. What was Kent doing all alone in the woods with a pistol? Then, abandoning the path, he ran swiftly in a straight line toward his friend. Hearing the noise, Kent turned and then sat as though hypnotized at the sight of Pat Shepherd hurtling at him like a cannon ball. Crashing into Kent, Pat knocked the pistol out of his hand.

"What the hell do you think you're doing?" Kent shouted.

327

"What are *you* doing?" Pat stood shaking, trying to catch his breath.

"What? Oh, do you mean you thought—I was examining it, that's all. Before he died, Lieutenant McCarthy asked me to give it to his brother in New York. He said it was a rare model."

Pat began to stammer. "In—in the woods, Kent? You're examining revolvers in the woods?"

"I've had it here in my belt, and when I sat down there was nothing else to look at."

"Oh Christ, you're a bad liar."

"I'm not going to kill myself, Pat. Stop following me and go fiddle with your stethoscopes."

Pat clenched his fist and took a step toward Kent as though to strike him. His face went red with fury. "You supercilious lying son of a bitch! What do you expect me to do? Walk away? Did you do that when I had pneumonia? Would you walk away if I were behaving like you are now? Like it or not, Kent, I care about you and I won't let you blow your brains out." Pat took a deep breath and stood there limply, his rage spent.

"I am a son of a bitch," Kent said almost in a whisper. "I'm sorry."

"Just tell me the truth, will you?"

Kent stood up slowly, walked over, and picked up the pistol and tossed it to Pat. "Look at it. It's not even loaded. I was examining it, that's all. I have no intentions of committing suicide."

"That day on the train you talked about suicide. You said—"

"Well, I've heard you speak of slashing your wrists. If I panicked every time you picked up a scalpel, I'd never have time to practice medicine. I admit this looks suspicious, but I'm telling the truth, Pat."

"But something's wrong with you. For God's sake, tell me what it is."

He didn't answer for a moment. Then he said, "I feel empty. Except for the years with Nancy, I've felt that way most of my life."

"Empty? What do you mean?"

328

"Ennui, I suppose."

"Loneliness?"

"No. Just an indifference to everything but medicine. And sometimes music."

"What can I do, Kent?"

"Nothing. It's been a bad winter. I'll get over it."

"You won't. You just said you always feel this way."

"Some times are worse than others."

"Do you still want Beth?"

"Very much, but this isn't her fault."

"Why do you feel this way?"

"I'm not sure I know. But thank you for caring."

"Jesus, of course I care. Don't be so damned grateful. A lot of people care, Kent. My brother and Tim. And Beth. I think you ought to remember that."

There was a gradual change in Kent in the ensuing weeks. He talked more often, gained some weight, and sometimes played chess in the evening with other officers. But the truest sign of his improving frame of mind came when Tim said. "The chief is swearing again, captain. I think he'll be all right."

Pat was pleased by Kent's improving spirits—happy to have his friend to talk to again. In those muddy, ragged days of February and March they discussed subjects they had never before broached. Kent showed Pat a daguerrotype of his wife Nancy, a very fair, thin young woman with kind eyes and a mischievous smile. Pat, in turn, told of his intention to find a girl when he returned home: "Someone gentle and giving. I don't give a damn any more how big her tits are." They talked about violence, about marriage, about home.

One day Pat stood at the parlor window of the farmhouse watching the rain whip the winter-solid ground into mud and listening to an orderly singing a song that the young soldiers, who missed home desperately, sang often:

Just before the battle, Mother,
I am thinking most of you
While upon the field we're lying

329

With the enemy in view.
Comrades brave are 'round me lying
Filled with thoughts of home and God,
For well they know that on the morrow
Some will sleep beneath the sod.

The city of Petersburg had been under siege since the summer before, the armies sniping at each other and occasionally engaging in battle. The men had been pressed close together in long trenches that transmitted diseases up and down the line as if they were messages crackling over telegraph wires. Disease killed more soldiers than did wounds, and on this drizzly day, the parlor and dining room of the farmhouse and two of the rooms upstairs were filled with sick men. Most of them had pneumonia, many would be dead by tomorrow. Seventeen- and eighteen-year-old boys would be dead. As the orderly next to him softly began another verse of the maudlin song, Pat's throat began to hurt and he swallowed several times. Tears rolled down his cheeks. He couldn't stand it any more.

He hoped that Kent, making rounds among the pneumonia patients, had not noticed. But Kent's practiced eye scanned patients and staff the way a sharpshooter scans likely targets. He walked over to where Pat was leaning against the window and said, "Pat, you need a drink."

"They're boys, Kent. Young boys. . . . It's the rain," he continued distractedly, his words tumbling over one another. "It's warm in here, and when men are warm and dry and see the rain, it's worse than when they're out in it."

"You mean we're alive and those men are dying and don't know it."

"Yes."

"Try not to see these boys as people. When I work I make their features and their expressions disappear. They're bones and flesh. Anatomy and physiology. I see them as machines and I don't think of their human qualities."

"What would happen if you did, Kent?"

330

"If I were to see them as they are? I don't know. I try to look at the world obliquely. I think that if I ever faced this—or any of life—squarely . . ."

"What would happen?"

"I think I'd fall apart."

"Lose your mind?"

"I don't know."

"I think the migraines are a way of losing your mind for a while."

Kent said nothing. The orderly continued to sing. The rain slapped against the windows, and somewhere in the parlor a man groaned in pain. Pat could feel himself reeling.

Kent said, "Go upstairs and lie down."

"I can't. There's too much to do."

"Christ, Pat, you know damned well there's not much we can do. In surgery we've made progress. But pneumonia? Consumption? What the hell can we we do that a six-year-old child couldn't do?"

"I recovered from pneumonia."

"Only because you were basically healthy. These boys aren't."

"Your skill saved my life."

"I wish I could believe that, but it's not true. We've used those same methods on others and you know they rarely work. I'm an ignorant jackass. So are you. So are all medical people here and abroad. We don't know very much, Pat—about the cause, about the cure, about anything. Most medicines we have are useless. Jesus, go up to your cot and rest, will you? The orderlies and I can care for the men."

"Are you sure?"

"I'm in charge here, Pat, and you will take orders from me. Go upstairs and get drunk. There's a bottle of whisky in the kitchen cabinet near the stove."

Pat did as he was told, thinking that things were really bad when even the doctors were propping each other up. What they needed to see this thing through were women—women to spoon-feed them love and sanity. Pat staggered up the stairs

331

inventing the perfect woman. He sat down on his cot drinking out of the bottle, imagining that she was with him. Then he fell woozily back on the bed and, after checking to see that none of the other cots was occupied, he made love to her.

One Sunday morning in March when the promise of spring was in the air, Joe, who strutted around with some pomp having been issued his captain's bars, stopped at the hospital and suggested that Pat and Kent take a ride with him to a town nearby. There were only two patients that day, and another doctor from the brigade was at hand, so the doctors went along with Joe. They arrived in the town in time to see some people filing into a tiny Catholic church. Joe decided to attend Mass and Pat went along "for sentimental reasons," dragging Kent in with him: "If nothing else, you can look at a few Virginia belles." But Kent drummed his fingers all through Mass, to the annoyance of nearby worshipers. As they were filing out, Kent sighted the pipe organ in the balcony of the church—a magnificent one for such a small town.

"I've got to play that thing. Joe, will you inform the priest that I'm going up there?"

"You can't play the organ during Lent."

"If bands can play military music during Lent, I can play something decent, for Christ's sake."

"Kent!" Pat hissed. "Watch your language. We're in church."

But Kent was bounding up the stairs to the balcony.

People were still coming out of church when Kent began playing a secular piece by Bach. The harmonics of the fugue expanded in ever-widening circles until they exploded off the walls of the church and were deflected, reverberating—a portrait in sound that spoke of nameless things. Many of the people who had risen but not yet left their pews sat again and were transported to places they had known once, long ago before the war—places that they could no longer remember but that they were certain had once existed, for the sound was taking them closer and cloer to the essence of those places.

"Who is it?" asked one plump, dignified lady of her neighbor.

"A Yankee."

She sniffed. "Well if all Yankees played music like that I wouldn't care if they did win the war."

Later he played some solemn music: Gregorian chant and a Mendelssohn psalm. But much of the music was loud, fast, and almost frenzied. Pat, recalling Kent's frequently-voiced wish for peace and quiet, had to smile. Perhaps he meant it in another sense.

People had come in from the street, and now the church was nearly full. Pat went up to the balcony to watch Kent play. Most of the time his eyes were half-closed and Pat, hearing much that was unfamiliar, wondered if he weren't sometimes composing as he played. Between pieces, he asked Kent where he had learned to play so well.

"I was once going to be Mozart," he returned tersely, and resumed playing.

Eventually Pat left him and went out into the street where the townspeople stood listening. It was Lent, but the priest said that in view of the fact that the organist was an officer of the occupying army they didn't have much say in the matter anyway and might as well enjoy it.

Pat would learn that Kent had been an organist in a Boston Episcopalian church while still in his teens and later while trying to earn the money for the last year's tuition at medical school. And he did make up half the pieces as he played. "I temper the tempered clavier," he told Pat, and muttered that in any case surely they didn't expect him to remember all of Bach's notes.

As the music pealed out through the open doors of the church and into the street, the sharp lines between North and South became fuzzy. It wasn't long before Pat was chatting with a raven-haired blue-eyed Virginia belle, of whom he quickly became enamored. By the time the music ended, he had discovered to his dismay that she was promised to a Confederate cavalryman. Yet for an hour the world had been dizzy and delightful, as in the days before the war, and it had all happened because a troubled man had looked for solace in a church organ.

They rode from church to the hospital joking about Kent. Several young belles had fluttered around him after his performance, and he had blushed and tried to escape.

"What's the matter with you, Kent?" Joe asked as the horses clopped down the muddy road. "You could have had your choice of any one of those girls."

"I gallantly restrained myself so that you two might have a chance."

Pat was puzzled. Obviously Kent didn't bother to respond even when he was being pursued.

"Didn't you like them, Kent?" he asked.

"I don't like 'belles.' They remind me of hummingbirds. Feathers and noise. If they have substance they hide the fact well." He smiled to himself.

"What's so funny?" asked Pat.

"Do you remember Beth at Gettysburg trying to act the belle? Batting her eyelashes at Marshall?"

"Yes, I remember." Pat smiled.

"Looked like a nervous tic," Kent said, laughing.

Seized by the memory, he laughed harder, and the two brothers looked at each other and shook their heads. Both hoped that Kent would find another girl like their sister after the war.

At the hospital a doctor whom Kent knew slightly was waiting for them. His name was Colonel Adam Patterson of the regular army. He extended his hand. "How are you, major?"

"Functioning, sir."

The colonel smiled. "That's quite remarkable under the circumstances. But I won't waste your time with chatter. I'm here to spirit away your assistant surgeon."

"You're what?" Kent was stunned.

"The Army of the James needs a few more doctors. Weitzel's corps is outside Richmond. We'll need medical people not only for the fighting but for the prisoners confined at Libby and Belle Isle. Also for Confederate wounded in the hospitals there, and civilians too. The Richmond citizenry is close to starving. Weitzel says that Confederate deserters file into camp every day, ready to take the oath of allegiance in exchange for a bite of salt pork and a bean or two."

"They've been crossing into our lines too," Kent said.

"Yes." The colonel cleared his throat. "But we will still need doctors up at Richmond."

"Do I have the option of objecting, sir?"

"No. But what are your objections, major?"

"Captain Shepherd is a fine surgeon. His cure rate is high." Kent looked at Pat. "If there's any way of keeping him here . . . There *are* other doctors in the corps, colonel."

"Who are inferior?"

"I didn't say that, sir. But you know as well as I that the heavy fighting will be in this area. Now there are plenty of doctors who can handle problems like nutrition, convalescence, and so on, but there aren't as many good surgeons."

"We have chosen other doctors," said the colonel. "We have also chosen Captain Shepherd."

"But he has a brother in this regiment," Kent protested.

"We'll send him back, then, after the Richmond problem is over. But I rather think that hostilities will have ended by that time, don't you?"

"I don't know," Kent snapped. "Will that be all? I have work to do."

"Do you indeed?" The colonel's lips tightened. "I don't like your tone, major."

For a moment Pat thought that he would demand that Kent salute him and Pat dreaded that prospect. Kent, to Pat's knowledge, had never saluted anyone. But Patterson addressed Pat. A wagon would be by in an hour to carry him north. With that the colonel left.

After emitting a stream of oaths, Kent said, "There's not

much time, Pat. You'll have to pack in a hurry and then brief me. The damned son of a bitch—hitting me with an announcement like that!"

Joe walked over to his brother, laying an arm over his shoulder. "Do you have time for a chorus of 'Auld Lang Syne'?"

No one looked at Pat when he said goodbye. Three of their orderlies gazed out the window, Tim looked at the ceiling, Kent at the floor, and Joe played with his forage hat. Pat tried to smile. He told them he'd see them after the war. They were all New Yorkers, weren't they? They'd have reunions every week. Pat smiled and no one looked at him. He shook their hands and no one looked at him. Finally he hurried out to the wagon. He turned around. Everyone was waving. He tried to see the faces but they were too far away.

He was gone only a few days when the news filtered through that all the fighting was in the Petersburg area. Pat sat idle in front of Richmond, twiddling his thumbs and feeling guilty. At last, at two o'clock in the morning on April 3, they saw flames in the distance and realized that the Confederate government was fleeing Richmond and burning its arsenals behind it. The next morning Pat marched in with the Twenty-Fifth Corps. No army was there to oppose them. After four years of plotting the Battle of Richmond, they did not have to fight for the city at all. The task of the victorious army would be to extinguish the fires and rescue their civilian enemies.

Weitzel's Corps had a large Negro infantry—50 percent of the corps. Since the beginning of 1864 the army had been accepting increasing numbers of black men into its ranks. There was, Pat thought, justice in the fact that many of the victors marching into the once-glorious Confederate capital were former slaves. Pat had been assigned to a Negro regiment and he climbed out of an ambulance so that he might march into the city with the troops.

The units ahead of Pat's were now fighting fires and controlling civilian mobs that were raiding Confederate commissaries. Pat's regiment, well behind in the long line of rescuers, could take a moment to reap the glory.

For as long as he lived, Pat would never forget it. The Richmond Negroes came pouring out of homes and buildings, marching alongside the smart black platoons, weeping or laughing with hysteria born of amazement that an event like this would ever come to pass. They were seeing "niggers" dressed in blue uniforms, carrying rifles and all the other accouterments of the white soldier. Not for any of these black gods the disgrace of a master's whip, the helplessness of knowing that he was doomed to a lifetime of subservience. The men, women, and children who had been slaves this morning and were now emancipated looked at these soldiers and saw what it meant to be free. Perhaps in time they would find that what they had seen was an illusion. But now they were drunk with the miracle of it. They fell on the ebony columns, kissing and hugging the men in gratitude, the white officers included. Every so often another building containing explosives would go up, and each time the noise sounded to the slaves and their rescuers like a victory salute. The mood was delirious. Pat found it difficult to tear himself away, for it was heartening to see that the war had indeed accomplished something. But there was work to be done in Richmond. In the hospitals thousands of Confederate soldiers lay sick and dying. Civilians, (white and Negro), long deprived of adequate food, were also ill. Somewhere in this sea of flames were the Union soldiers who had been imprisoned.

Thus for Pat the war ended in a makeshift hospital in Richmond. For Joe and Kent, it ended a week later in a town named Appomattox after a chase westward in pursuit of Lee's dying army. And for Gregory the war had ended two years ago in a dingy, overcrowded, vermin-infested room facing the James River. Pat had seen the twin prisons: Libby for the officers: Belle Isle, across the way, for the enlisted men. He had wanted to burn them, but too much of Richmond was already in flames and the population was in jeopardy.

Gregory Allister and several other sick prisoners had been sent to a civilian hospital by the fleeing Confederates. They were dangerously ill when Pat found them. Greg smiled when he recognized Pat. His weak hand grasped Pat's firm one and he said, "Thank God." Pat tried to talk to him about prison life, but Greg would not discuss it. All he could think of was his freedom. All he had wanted was the chance to live.

These were the thoughts that went through Pat's mind as he drank whisky after whisky among the weary veterans of the Army of the Potomac. He looked around at these glassy-eyed drunks and decided that all—including Pat himself—were as sorely wounded as his patients. The war was a bullet that had driven itself through each of them. The task of healing now fell to the women. It would be their responsibility to nurse an entire generation of men back to sanity. He raised his glass slightly and murmured into it, "Women of this grand and glorious republic, it's your battle now."

SEVEN

Get ready for the jubilee,
Hurrah! Hurrah!
We'll give our hero three times three,
Hurrah! Hurrah!
The laurel wreath is ready now
To place upon his loyal brow,
And we'll all feel gay when Johnny comes marching home.

After a final review of troops in Washington, the boys began coming home. All summer long the regiments paraded up Broadway to the accompaniment of cheering, singing, and flag-waving. They were a weathered, tough group of men who bore little resemblance to those soft, starry-eyed youths who had marched out four years earlier. The ranks had been filled and emptied and filled again and emptied, but some, like Joe, had been there from the beginning, had managed not to get themselves killed, and were now coming home for good. There were no official statistics yet, but the losses, would be told soon enough. Taking into account both North and South, over half a million men had died of wounds and disease. Half a million in a nation of 32 million. One in sixty-four, and most of them young. Beth had once tried to count to a million and become tired at twelve thousand. Yet fourteen thousand had died at Andersonville alone.

The summer went by in sickening waves of heat. Without

school to occupy her, Beth spent much of her time in a stupor. It was doubly bad because Greg had not died quickly but had disintegrated slowly in body and spirit. A fast death in the zenith of life would have been easier for her to accept. Her memory of him could have been whole.

The times between meals, when she dusted or cut up onions for Sheilah or made beds, her mind, having nothing else to fill it, turned to Greg. The family wondered what was wrong with her. Kate told them that Beth was depressed because so many of her beaux would not be coming home. Kate was distressed over her daughter's condition and tried to interest her in parties and other young men. None of her suggestions appealed to Beth. Eventually Kate, realizing that grief must be allowed to run its course, let her daughter alone. When school started, things would be better.

Beth herself doubted that she would ever feel alive again. Greg's death had been hard enough to bear, but it was not the only reason for her depression. She felt confused and disoriented, as she had been when Lincoln died. Nothing was lasting.

The family had many visitors that summer, and the boys had reunions with their friends, but Beth did not warm to any of the festivities. Only when she saw Pete Weatherly did she feel any emotion at all, and then it was pity for him, not joy over his return. The broken boy was returning to a world that had not wavered in its treatment of Negroes and probably never would. Half a million had died and the slaves were free and nothing had changed.

There was one other occasion that summer in which Beth thought of someone other than herself. Joe woke up from a nightmare shouting and screaming and she dashed down the hall to his room before her parents were awakened. She sat on the edge of her bed holding him until he calmed down and, thanking her, went back to sleep. She began to wonder if the war would ever be over for Joe or for Pat, who sometimes told her of nightmares in which the sound of cannon made him permanently deaf.

On the rare occasions when Beth felt like talking, she was comfortable with only two people: Kate and Diane. She didn't have to keep secrets from them or hide her depression. When Joe came home he was forced by convention to remain a discreet distance from the Widow Allister until enough time had elapsed to make frequent visits respectable. And so Diane spent most of her time with Beth, while Joe looked around for a suitable profession—he finally settled on the insurance field —and made secret plans for their future. Diane was supportive to Beth but disappointed that she could not seem to jolt Beth out of her torpor. She too began wishing that school would start, but she wondered if Beth would be of much benefit to her students in her current mood.

In late August Beth fell ill with a bad summer cold. It began with a fever that receded during the night, then shot up again, and finally exploded in a flurry of sneezes. She was asleep the next afternoon in her stifling humid room and in her dreams she felt a cool hand on her forehead. It was a man's hand, for it was larger and heavier than her mother's. She opened her eyes, expecting to see Pat. Kent was looking down at her.

She knew he would call when he returned to New York but she was surprised that he had come upstairs. He was smiling and seemed very happy to see her. She too was happy. Standing over her bed, Kent seemed hard and strong, like a stake driven deep into the ground.

"Kent, when did you get back to New York?"

"Yesterday. Are you feeling better? You seem to have no temperature."

"It's only a cold." She reached for a handkerchief and blew her nose. "Where are you staying?"

"In a hotel. I'm looking for permanent lodgings and also for an office."

"Why don't you stay at Aunt Louise's?"

"Does she have a vacancy?"

"I don't know. But she'd make one for you or know someone who would."

He was in civilian clothes: a light brown summer linen frock coat with a mustard-colored waistcoat and a dark brown necktie. He looked healthier than he had last winter, though he was still much too thin.

"Pat is at the hospital," she said.

"So your mother informed me. But I also wanted to see you."

"Oh." She smiled, certain now that the unpleasantness of last New Year's was forgotten. "You look very well, Kent."

"My first civilian clothes in four years."

"But I'm distressed that you had to find me looking so wretched."

"As a matter of fact you look very appealing, red nose and all. I've never seen you in a nightgown before or with your hair down and streaming over a pillow. Most attractive."

She blushed, thoroughly awake now. "I'm surprised that Mother permitted you to enter my chamber unchaperoned."

"Your mother made quite a ceremony of reminding me that you were ill and that I am a doctor."

Beth laughed. "She's a dear, isn't she?"

He nodded. Then he pulled up a chair, sat down, and cleared his throat. "Why didn't you tell me it was Gregory Allister?"

Her eyes widened. "How did you find out? Mother?"

"No," he said. "I was on my way here when I met Mrs. Kendall on the street. She informed me that Diane was in mourning, and I felt I ought to pay a brief condolence call. I knew Allister and respected him."

"So Diane told you."

"Yes. After a while we worked around to other subjects and she asked me about you. Diane has a way of extracting the most personal—anyway, I explained that there was a mysterious man in your life and she told me who it was."

"Did she tell you everything?"

"I would think so. You and he were planning to marry when she found herself preg—in a delicate condition."

"She did tell you. I wonder why?"

"She's a fine woman. Joe is most fortunate."

"So she informed you of that too. Kent, Joe knows nothing about the matter. Nor does Pat."

"You can trust me to be discreet. I don't need to tell you how sorry I am."

"Thank you, Kent."

Beth was astounded. For Diane to admit this to a relative stranger must mean that she loved Beth as a sister. She had always envied the strengths of friendships between men (Kent's and Pat's, for example), but she had not felt such a strong bond with someone of her own sex since she and Diane had been children.

Kent stood up. "You'll need time, Beth. When you've had it, I'll be back."

"Where are you going?"

"To Louise's. I've satisfied myself that you're going to recover." He smiled.

"Please don't go, Kent."

She wasn't sure she loved him—certainly not in the way she had loved Greg. But she was seized by a strong emotion that was partly physical desire and partly a warm feeling of satisfaction in being with a good reliable friend. It didn't matter at the moment that he was cryptic, didn't matter that she knew too little about him. She knew enough about him to judge him as a responsible man. And he had strength of character, of will. That was what mattered most.

He had once asked her to marry him. Suddenly she did want to marry him—and as quickly as possible. She must try to start living again.

"Please don't go, Kent."

"I want you to be sure."

"I am. I want to marry you. Unless you've changed your mind."

His smile was sudden and startled. "I never changed my mind." He sat down again, looking at her carefully. Then he said, "Beth, I don't want you marrying me on the rebound. I want you to be certain that—"

"Greg is dead, Kent. I did love him, but he's dead." She did not want to discuss him with Kent, but she found herself saying, "He died so horribly. I don't know if you can understand—"

"I've seen them," he interrupted. "Many of my patients in Virginia were rebels returning from Northern prison camps. I know of one who bit himself, then wrote his name on the wall with his own blood. To establish his identity, he told the guard."

"Oh, Lord!" She swallowed, remembering Greg's evergreen.

"Let's forget the damn war for a minute. Are you sure you want to marry me now?"

"Yes."

"You wouldn't prefer to wait?"

"Wait for what?"

"Grieving takes time, does it not?"

"Well yes, but—Kent, I'm very sure I want to marry you."

He touched her cheek. "When?"

"As soon as it can be arranged. Do you want a formal wedding?"

"Anything you wish, Beth."

"Church?"

"I'm an agnostic," he said.

"Yes. So am I. A small wedding, then, with a justice of the peace?"

"I don't care about the wedding. I want you."

She smiled. "Why are you so sure?"

"I'm thirty-five years old and I've been married. I know what I want."

"You're so strong, Kent."

"Strong?" He smiled ironically.

"Oh, yes. Very strong."

He bent to kiss her.

"You'll catch my cold," she said.

"I rarely get colds. But in any case it will be worth it."

As soon as she felt his lips she became aroused. But clouding her pleasure was the memory of last winter when she had practically told him she wanted to sleep with him. He had been stunned by her behavior then; she must be more circumspect now. She would permit him kisses and embraces but nothing more—until they were married. Having made that decision, she could yield joyously to the physical pleasure of his kiss. It was he who finally broke away, very agitated, saying, "Couldn't we just elope?"

"It would break mother's heart."

Just before dinner, Beth, still in a dressing gown and drinking sherry in the parlor with Kent and her parents, said to John that Kent wished to speak with him.

John said, "Does the matter concern your future, Beth?" He saw Kent grin. John walked across the room and extended his hand to Kent. "We don't stand on ceremony here. You have my blessing."

"Thank you, sir." Kent stood up and shook John's hand.

"I have no doubt you will support her more than adequately."

Kent nodded.

"Congratulations, then. You're getting the pride of our clan."

"I know that, sir."

Kate, who was utterly beside herself, dabbed at her eyes and began asking them questions about where they would live, what sort of wedding they would like. Then she stopped and said, "Goodness, you haven't had much opportunity to be alone. Come, John." And they vanished in twin streaks.

Beth began to laugh. "You'll have to get used to this family."

"I think I'm already accustomed to them." He took her hand.

"You like them, don't you?"

"Very much."

Beth looked up and saw her brother Pat standing in the

entrance to the parlor. He was grinning ear-to-ear, taking in the scene of his sister and his former comrade holding hands. He hadn't seen Kent since March.

Kent smiled and rose to greet him. "Well, Patrick."

Pat shook his hand. "Major Bombast. Are you home for good?"

"Ask your sister," Kent said.

"We're engaged," said Beth.

"That's bully!" He kissed his sister. "When did all this happen?"

"This afternoon. I proposed to him. I begged him. But I'll let Kent tell you about it. I want to ask Father to fetch Diane." Beth rose, sneezing, and walked down to the dining room.

Pat delivered a hearty clap to Kent's back. "She begged you?" he said, shaking his head.

"Not quite. She merely gave in. Consented. I seriously doubted that she ever would."

"You look good for a change." Pat sat down in a chair. "Beth works miracles that would impress Christ himself. Aren't you glad to be back where there are women to take care of us?"

"Yes, indeed. Have you found yours yet? The gentle soul you were looking for?"

"Not yet. I've been glutting myself on ample-bosomed ladies of easy virtue. I feel as though I've been let loose in a candy store. There's a girl named Ginger who looks like that woman you used to visit in the parlor house on Lafayette—" He broke off. Good Lord, Kent was to be his brother-in-law. They could never again discuss women the way they had done during the war. Kent was joining the ranks of the married men, and on top of that he was marrying Beth. There would be no more discussions of women. Respectability would now be laid on Kent's head like a lead crown.

"I suppose I ought to be getting married too." Pat sighed, visualizing his own transformation and that of his cursing former comrade into fusty, proper gentlemen. "But I'm happy for you, Kent." He paused. "Did you ever find out who that other man was?"

346

Kent hesitated, then said, "She was considering one of the officers at last year's New Year's party. She wouldn't tell me his name."

"I wonder who it could have been."

"It makes no difference, Pat. I'm glad she decided in favor of me."

Diane, who had been summoned over to the Shepherds' to hear the news, hardly looked like the grieving widow as she squealed her congratulations. Later Beth took her aside and whispered, "Diane, you not only look like a princess, you are one. Why did you do it?"

"Because Kent was uncertain. I do think he believed you were lying about there being another man."

"But to reveal your secrets that way!"

"He's a very understanding man. But I did it because I think you two need each other." She grinned. "Besides, I always felt sorry for you for not being as beautiful as I am."

"And you were dispensing alms?"

"I'm very generous."

"Even if you are simple-minded." She hugged Diane. "What did he say when you told him?"

"He was holding a cup of tea, and he set it down and said, 'She was telling the truth.' He tried not to smile. After all, Greg was dead. But I told him to hurry and go to you. *Then* he smiled."

Soon after dinner everyone left Beth alone in the parlor with her intended. They talked about where they would live and discussed the idea of buying a house. Beth also tried to introduce the subject of children, but each time she began Kent would interrupt her, usually with a kiss. Finally she asked impatiently, "Kent, you *do* want children, don't you?"

"Beth, right now I'm trying to adjust to the reality of having you. I've waited a long time."

"Yes, I understand that. But don't you want children?"

"If you do."

"I want them very much, Kent."

"I've no doubt you'll have them."

"*We'll* have them," she amended.

"We will."

She sensed a reluctance in him and wondered how he would adjust to fatherhood. Then she remembered that he had spoken of his little girl with pride. Perhaps the events of the day had overwhelmed him and he could only cope with one plan at a time.

There were long silences that evening in which Kent held her hand and looked at her wonderingly and in which Beth began experiencing twinges of guilt for having decided to marry Kent so soon after Greg's death. He had been dead only two months, and she could still hear his voice when he had said, "All that matters is you. And Laura." Was it right for her to try to smother the dreams and pretend that they had not existed? Yet she had said it to the priest automatically, without thinking, the night Greg died: "No, Father, I am no one." In the cemetery they had handed the flag to Diane. All Beth possessed was a piece of a print—a reminder of Greg's hell, not his glory.

She needed Kent. He would provide her with something that had been missing in her life for a long time: certainty, direction, solidity. To what extent was her feeling for him one of dependence, of wanting to lean against something that would not break as Greg had broken? She wanted to marry Kent. She wanted to marry him and drive away the memories of coughing and crying and caskets. The other memories—of Greg as he had been in the beginning—would never leave her. They would hide for a while and come stealing out at inappropriate times like naughty children. She must learn to live with that.

They planned the wedding for early October in the Shepherds' parlor. Kate had deplored the decision on a justice of the peace, but even this could not dampen her approval of the match. She had always liked Kent, seeing him as a lost young man who needed only the warmth of a large family.

Louise had dismissed all her boarders and offered to share

her large four-story house with the Wilsons. Beth and Kent agreed, but only after Louise consented to their paying a high rent. The main floor was to include Kent's office, which he planned to share with Pat. There would be two examining rooms, a small office or consultation room, and a waiting room. Part of the third floor would be a laboratory. Kent had told Beth of Louis Pasteur and the experimental work he was doing in France. He too wanted to study microbes and their effects.

"We'll have our own laboratory!" he exclaimed to Beth with uncharacteristic glee. "We'll get the best microscopes we can afford. I hope I have time to do the necesssry research." He paused. "Beth, would you mind if I asked you to help me? To manage the laboratory?"

Would she *mind?* Here was the answer to the dilemma of marriage: to have work of her own, and particularly work like this. She had not wanted to stand outside real life—men's lives—like a pretty carriage—necessary, but only on occasion. What power men had over life and death: Pat, who had the strength to heal in his long arms; Kent, whose mind would save many.

She had longed to share their power, and now Kent— without fanfare, without any qualifiers about her being a woman—was admitting her to the sanctum of men's work. In the laboratory she would be his equal. The idea thrilled her. The only woman she knew who felt the equal of a man was Sally. And Sally was very happy.

The weeks before the wedding were frantic. While Kate and Sheilah worked on Beth's wedding dress, Beth, assisted by Diane and Louise, went through the upstairs rooms of Louise's house selling old furniture, cleaning drapes, painting, and rearranging. In this they were aided by Louise's maid and cook, Theresa, and a contingent of Theresa's male relatives. Since neither Kent nor Beth had the time to shop for new furniture, the upstairs rooms looked very spartan by the time they were finished.

349

While this was going on, Kent and Pat were converting the main floor into an office. They treated their patients—mostly ex-soldiers from the regiment—in a small alcove while the carpenters sawed and hammered their way around them. Activities at Louise's began taking on the aspect of a Barnum spectacle.

The Pennsylvania Shepherds arrived at Louise's, seven strong, about a week before the wedding. Beth hadn't seen any of them but Bill since Lee's infamous campaign and there was a passionate reunion that fairly paralyzed Kent. Sally hugged him, Bill slapped him on the back, the children crawled over him and showed him their toys or paraded past in their pretty new dresses, and everyone shouted questions at him, not bothering to wait for answers. Looking desperate, he inched his way into a corner. Beth laughed and asked Bill to take Kent upstairs for a game of chess. As the two men walked off, John said to his daughter, "I daresay, he's acting like a trapped animal."

"He's always ill at ease when people come at him like a flood. It will take him time to adjust."

"Lord, I hope he will. This family is not what one would call reticent. What's the cause of his remoteness, do you know?"

"I'm afraid I don't, Father."

She did learn something about Kent's past, however, two days before the wedding, when his sister Anne came down with her family from Boston. Kent and Beth met Anne's train. She was an attractive woman, thirty years old, who looked something like Kent, though her hair was much darker. She offered Kent her hand but they did not embrace and Beth, accustomed to her brothers' bear hugs, found this lack of demonstrativeness strange. He shook hands with Anne's husband, then introduced them both to Beth, who followed Kent's cue and offered her hand. The boys, seven and five, and not at all reserved, tugged eagerly at their uncle's jacket and out shouted one another with accounts of the train trip. Kent seemed fond of them, and for a moment she could see how he might behave when he was a father. He would be good to his children but not physically affectionate. He would probably speak to them in the manner that he was now speaking to his nephews: in totally adult language. It would be Beth's task to translate his comments into words that children understood.

They accompanied the family to the hotel—they had insisted upon a hotel, though both Kate and Louise had offered to accommodate them—and helped settle them in. Then they brought them over to the Shepherds', where a welcoming dinner had been planned.

Later that evening Beth, on the pretext of showing Anne her wedding gown, managed to get her alone for a talk in her room.

"Anne, he never talks about his childhood. He did say once that he and his father didn't get on, but he didn't say why."

Anne sighed. "Beth, Kent does not approve of my discussing family matters."

"But I'm going to be part of the family."

"Yes, I know. But it must be his decision to tell you of these things."

"He won't, though. You must know him."

"Yes, and I understand how you feel."

"Can you tell me about his father?"

"Father was stern with Kent. He had very specific ideas about what men were supposed to be. He wanted Kent to be a scholar and an athlete. He would never tolerate any unmanly behavior like exaggerating a story or crying or failing to master some skill. At times I used to think he was pushing Kent too hard."

"That's awful. Did he treat you that way?"

"Goodness, no. My function was to do my lessons adequately and then help the housekeeper serve tea. Kent and I led very different lives."

"Were you close?"

"For years we weren't. After his wife died I did try to help him, and in recent years we've developed a sort of polite friendship. Nothing approaching the sentiment among you and your brothers, though."

"You didn't have that with Kent?"

"Never. As children we barely knew each other. I was always with the nurse or later with friends and Kent was either reading or out. He could read the *Aeneid* at the age of ten," Anne added, a hint of pride in her tone.

"In Latin?"

"In Latin. He also read Greek. Kent had private tutors in addition to school. He was accomplished at the piano at an early age. He was a fair athlete too, in the sense of running and jumping and feats of strength. But he hated organized sports, to my father's disgust, and was never very good at them. When they tried to teach him fencing, he fell on his sword like an ancient Roman. Fortunately it was upside down."

Beth laughed. "Oh, it's so good to hear these things. I could never picture him as a child." She paused. "And your mother?"

"I don't remember her, Beth. She died of pneumonia when I was six months old. Father rarely spoke of her. My aunts said that he had loved her very much and never wished to be reminded that she was gone."

"Does Kent remember her?"

"He must. But he's never spoken of her."

"What was his wife like? Nancy?"

"A bit like you, I think. In nature, not in appearance. She was very thin and fair."

"Tell me more about her."

"I have already told you too much, Beth. Kent would not like—"

"Why did he leave Boston?"

"He left after Nancy died. He had known her since they were twelve years old and it was a terrible blow."

"Oh yes, it must have been. Did he—"

"No more, Beth."

"But—"

352

"Does your family discuss you with him?"

"Every last undignified incident."

"Well, your family is different from ours. There's a great deal of love here. I'd like to tell you more, but Kent would be furious. I hope you won't give him a clue that we have spoken of these matters."

"Of course not. And I thank you for confiding this much to me. If Kent had lived near me or if he were less secretive, I would know him much better. I think it's only fair that I learn something, don't you?"

"Yes, I do. If I've helped at all, I'm pleased."

"You've helped a great deal."

Anne's revelations, though, disturbed Beth. Compared with Kent's history, her life had been joyous. Anne had said there was a lot of love in the Shepherd family. Beth had never seen it quite that way, but after hearing about the Wilsons she could understand what Anne meant. True, John lived in the clouds, Beth hovered just above earth, and Kate was sometimes at sea. All the members of the family had stationed themselves at different latitudes, longitudes, and altitudes but somehow they could shout to one another across the miles. Kate had tried to make Beth into a little woman as Mr. Wilson had forced Kent into manhood. But Kate had always been well-meaning. She could not imagine her mother driving her as Kent's father had done. Kate would sigh and say, "Oh dear," and hope that Beth would somehow see the light. And John too might be a distracted parent, a dreamer, but he accepted his daughter's individuality. And the children liked each other though they rarely saw eye-to-eye. They all sat around calling each other insane, but with pride in their voices. Yes, that was what Anne meant by love.

The bachelor party that Pat, as best man, gave for Kent was a disaster. Pat had selected a good restaurant but failed to take into account the fact that Phil and Pete would be among the guests. When they were refused admittance, Kent cursed in

353

language that would make an infantryman swoon, and Joe made ready to slug the owner but was forcibly restrained by the rest of the group. A jail sentence for Joe was the last thing they needed on the eve of the wedding. They ended up eating at an oyster bar and then went on to the home of Kent's fellow researcher, Ed Clark, where they drank heavily of his home-made wine. Ed tried to relieve the strain, which had been building all during dinner, by talking about the bride and recalling in detail Beth's handling of the wounded Gettysburg soldiers.

"A very intelligent woman," he said. "She summarized those case histories so capably that one might have thought she was the doctor." He turned to Kent and then to the men in Beth's family. They all nodded and smiled, but Ed's compliments did not generate further conversation. Everyone kept glancing nervously at Phil and his son.

Pete sat in a corner drinking steadily. One of his fists was tightly clenched. He had regained much of his strength and handsome appearance since his release from Andersonville five months earlier, but he remained very unhappy. Pat, who was Pete's doctor, had noticed the similarity between him and Gregory Allister. Pete too had seemed tired and defeated, obsessed with food, disinterested in such weighty subjects as prejudice and the future of the freed slaves. But now, with returning health, Pete was beginning to react to his society again. And tonight Pat could see that he was very angry.

At last Joe picked up a banjo and began singing the soldiers' version of "When Johnny Comes Marching Home"!

> In eighteen hundred sixty-three,
> Hurrah! Hurrah!
> Abe Lincoln set the poor slaves free,
> Hurrah! Hurrah!
> In eighteen hundred and sixty-three
> Old Abe he set the poor slaves free
> And we'll all drink stone blind,
> Johnny fill up the bowl.

He set down his banjo and said, "Seems we fought the war for nothing."

"That's not true," said Ed Clark.

Pete slammed down his glass of wine. "Yes, it's true," he said and turned to his father. "Pop, I'm going to leave the country."

"Pete, please—" began Phil.

"Come with me, Pop. Back to Africa."

"Back to Africa! What do I know of Africa? I helped build this country. And you fought for it. You and the one hundred fifty thousand Negroes who took up arms."

"Fought for what, Pop? To be turned out of a restaurant like animals?"

"Not every white turns you out, Pete."

"Pop, for God's sake. You bow, you scrape, you make excuses—"

"You will show me some respect, Pete!" Phil stood up, his eyes blazing, as the other men stared wide-eyed at this confrontation between father and son, "I'm sorry, Kent, "he said after a moment. "I had hoped that your party might be—"

Pete interrupted. "You're always so sorry. Stop being so damned sorry and start asserting your rights."

"You fool! This is not the time to—"

Joe said. "He's right, Mr. Weatherly. In his place I'd be shooting rifles all over the city."

"There, you see?" said Pete. "Even a white man can see—"

Phil sighed. "We do have rights, yes. We could assert them now and get shot through the head. Or we can effect changes slowly and stay alive."

"Or we can leave the country, Pop."

"*You* can. Go right ahead. Give up the rich land that's your birthright. Do what Lincoln wanted in the first place. Start a colony. But don't come crying to me, Pete, when you want your country again."

"I have a better idea," said John. "Stay here and write it all down."

"Write what down?" asked Pete, confused.

"Whatever you feel. Write about Andersonville or the treatment of Negroes in New York. Write about slavery. God knows you're more qualified than Harriet Beecher Stowe. What did she know about Negroes? What does any white know? It's the responsibility of literate black men to write their own experiences. The slaves can't do it until they've learned how to write. But you can, Pete. You've got talent, and not to use it would be an insult to your race and ours."

Joe looked at his father in some surprise. John's career suggestions were usually inappropriate to the young man being advised. But this one made sense.

"I'm no writer," said Pete.

Nate Klein said, "Oh yes you are. I read letters you sent to your father during the war. Why, you're a born writer." This from Nate, a literary snob.

"I don't know," Pete said. "I never thought about—" He broke off in confusion turned to John. "You're right about one thing, Mr. Shepherd. No white can possibly know how it feels to be a Negro. No white. Not even the poorest dreg in the slums. Put a fine suit of clothes on a poor man and he can go anywhere. But a Negro can be Oxford-educated, rich, and a philanthropist too; he can be a paragon, and still the lowest scum will call him 'nigger.' We live with that degradation day after day, Pop and I." He took a long draught from his glass. "And I, for one, don't intend to get spat upon for the rest of my—" He clapped a hand over his mouth and Ed Clark quickly led him through a doorway.

Pat rose and followed him. He returned in a few minutes and said, "He's all right. He's washing his face. Pete still isn't well enough to drink in the amounts that we do. I should have cautioned him."

"I think he's just upset," said Phil. He walked toward the door through which Pete had gone, hesitated, took another step, and stopped, his fists clenched. At last Pete appeared in the doorway. "Do you feel better?" his father asked.

Pete nodded and looked down. "I'm sorry, Pop."

"It's all right, son. It's all right," Phil said hoarsely, hugging him.

"I didn't mean to hurt you."

"I know you didn't." Phil patted his son gently on the back. "We have different ideas, that's all. Perhaps each should give the other a hearing."

Pete nodded. "I'd like to go home now. You stay and enjoy yourself."

"No, I'll go with you."

Pat, remembering that it was he who presided over this near-débâcle, said, "I'm sorry about the restaurant."

Pete said, "I'm the one who ruined the evening. I'll explain it to you some day. Perhaps in writing as Mr. Shepherd suggests." He turned to Kent. "Try to enjoy your last night of freedom."

"If you promise to be at the wedding."

And so the evening ended on a poignant note. Beth did not learn of any of this until after the wedding. She could understand Pete's rage, but she agreed with his father. Why indeed should a people who had helped create a nation, most of them toiling as slaves, permit themselves to be driven from it?

The wedding was small. Besides the family, there were the Kendalls, the Weatherlys, the Kleins, several neighbors, and five school friends of Beth's. Kent's guests included three doctors and their wives and Tim Kelly, his orderly during the war.

A chamber quartet played music. Beth was nearly in a swoon before the vows were taken but she managed, by taking deep breaths, not to faint. The bridegroom did not appear nervous at all. He simply looked happy.

After the wedding, when Tim was giving his good wishes, Beth whispered, "Do you remember the day of the migraine?"

"Yes, Mrs. Wilson. A lot has happened since then."

Tim was the first to address her by her new name. She heard it with a start. Mrs. Wilson! Mrs. Kent Wilson! Good heavens! As other guests congratulated her, Beth's mind was on the fact that with two words—"I do"—she had lost her name.

The subject of names came up again when John and Kate made a small ceremony of asking Kent to address them either as "Mother" and "Father" or by their first names. He opted for the second choice, claiming that at thirty-five he considered himself too old to be one of their sons.

Champagne flowed freely, and Diane, who had to affect a reserved behavior since she was still attired in unrelieved black, sat in a corner getting tipsy while Joe gallantly danced with the ladies, winking over their shoulders at Diane. Beth felt sorry for the two of them. It would be at least a year before they could even speak of marriage. But Diane, drunk for the first time in her life, was having a fine time watching the guests and fighting giggles at their antics.

Beth was reluctant to leave the reception. This was, after all, said to be the zenith of a woman's life. But Kent was growing restless. Kate noticed her son-in-law's pacing and delicately pointed out to Beth that men set more store by the wedding night than by the wedding and shouldn't they be off? So Beth had gone, nervous about the coming intimacy in the hotel room. When they were alone in their suite, she remained distant, and Kent wondered why.

"Do you remember what you said to me last New Year's? That I was too lustful for a woman?"

"I said no such thing. It seemed that you cared only for my body and were rejecting my sterling soul." He smiled.

"But you didn't object to my—carnality?"

"God, no! It was refreshing for a woman to admit to such feelings."

"Oh."

"And all this time you thought I was standing in judgment of your morals?" He paused. "Beth, if something else is troubling you, I want you to know that it makes no difference to me."

"I don't understand."

"I realize you would not have waited two years for Gregory had not the nature of your relationship gone beyond—uh—hand-holding."

"I still don't see what you—"

"I'm not a virgin, so I have no right to expect—"

"But I *am,* Kent."

He looked startled. "I see. I didn't mean to jump to conclusions, but I wanted to be certain you understood that I didn't mind."

"Why did you assume I'm not a virgin?"

"There were qualities about you. A sensuousness. But I suppose that was as natural to you as the way you walked. In any case, this is not the time to discuss it." He touched her arm. "Beth, I've waited a long time."

She felt the crimson blush. What would happen now? Should she slip into the dressing room first or should he? Obviously she should, for he was not moving. Why did books of etiquette never discuss situations like this? Wasn't this more important than the placement of silver and water glasses?

She began walking toward the dressing room, but he took her arm and led her over to the bed. He turned down the bedspread, then began unbuttoning her dress. She made no move to stop him but stood stock-still while he undressed her swiftly, draping her dress and petticoats over a chair. He removed the hoops and stays; then, leaving her in her chemise and stockings, he began to discard his own wedding clothes, dropping them carelessly to the floor. She turned away. There was a light on in the room and she did not deem it proper to stare boldly at him while he undressed. Besides, she knew how he would look unclothed: lean and sinewy. Soon she felt him lifting the chemise over her head, then tugging gently on her arm, easing her down to the bed. She closed her eyes as he removed her underclothing, then gasped when she

359

felt his lips on her breasts. In that instant all considerations of modesty were wiped from her mind. She was excited to the point of frenzy at the thought that at last—at last!—she would be able to complete the act of love. He kissed her breasts, lips, neck, and breasts again and his hands caressed other parts of her body. She was anxious now for the culmination and she tried to tell him this by embracing him tightly. She knew there would be pain, but a friend had once whispered that women who had straddled horses had an easier wedding night than others. She was glad she had ridden that way at Carlisle.

Kent had not spoken since he first began undressing her, but now he whispered, "It may hurt. I'll try to be gentle." Her heart began to pound wildly.

It did hurt for a moment. After that, pain gave way to a wave of sensation so acute that she lost awareness of everything but the feeling. She started to moan and she put a hand over her mouth to muffle it, but he said, "No, I want to hear you." Soon he too began to moan, but she heard it only distantly, for she felt as she did when she was about to faint—a falling through space slowly. That feeling passed in time, and then he was moving faster and faster—where did he get such energy?—until he went into several shuddering spasms and collapsed against her, breathing hard. After a moment he opened his eyes, turned over on his back, and looked at her, his face very serious. She fumbled for the sheet and drew it up over them. He did not comment or smile at this, but seemed to understand.

"How do you feel?" he asked.

"It was—I liked it."

"Did I hurt you?"

"At first. But later I—" She felt herself blushing again and asked, "Did you like it, Kent?"

"You were watching, weren't you?"

"It did seem as though you were enjoying yourself."

He smiled. "A classic understatement."

They did not speak for a while; then she asked, "Kent do you love me?"

360

He was taken aback. "What kind of question is that? Isn't it obvious?"

"You've never said the words."

"You know how I feel."

"Say the words, Kent."

"Of course I love you. Why else would I . . . Sometimes I think you're . . . Why must you . . ."

"You're sputtering like a steam engine. Goodness, but those words were difficult to extract."

He looked at her as though expecting her to tell him that she loved him too. But Beth was not sure that she did, and now she felt guilty about having demanded the avowal from him.

They had dinner sent to the room but they scarcely touched a morsel, so anxious were they to make love again. After the second time both of them fell asleep, exhausted and satisfied, Kent's arm around Beth. In the morning she was the first to awaken. Kent was sleeping soundly but his arm was still flung over her protectively. How wonderful marriage was! Kisses, hugs, exquisite transports to summits of sensation. She knew, of course, that there was more to marriage than this but now she could not imagine problems—not while Kent lay here, so appealing in sleep, his blond hair tousled, his face relaxed. She had never before known his countenance to be so serene.

And that was another pleasant aspect of marriage. One could know another human being in all his facets; find qualities in him that he never displayed to the rest of the world. She had seen a tense man in a moment of tranquility, a self-conscious man making love with utter abandon. And there would be more, for she would be with him always: in the morning and at night and in every season. So much time to discover and to share.

They decided to cancel their planned wedding trip through New England and remain here at the hotel. Kent was tired from the war and the following readjustment and didn't feel up to meeting train schedules. Beth was exhausted from the speeded-up wedding plans. So they stayed, attending concerts occasionally or shopping. Most of the time, though, was spent in bed: sleeping, talking, reading, making love. After several days, Beth began to wonder how she had ever gotten along without sex. She liked to lie back, eyes closed, feeling his body with her hands and lips and being explored in the same way by him. This sustained tactility was in such sharp contrast with their normally cerebral lives that she sometimes thought she was dreaming. These could not be the same two people who had discussed chloride of lime at a surgeon's table in Gettysburg.

She basked in her own pleasure; but she also enjoyed witnessing his helpless need of her. Kent's emotions, so lacking in his speech, were evident in the frantic grasping and moaning and thrusting. He was intensely physical, his hard body responding to stimulus like a finely tuned string instrument. This tension in him always excited her, even when he was finished and his body convulsed in sensual aftershocks. One afternoon he stretched lazily, turned to her, and said, "You're the fulfillment of my fantasies."

"Every one?"

"Well, almost."

"Which ones haven't I fulfilled?"

"We'll get to them. We have the rest of our lives."

"Will we get to mine too?"

"Do you have fantasies?"

"Of course I do. Can't women have them?"

He sat up. "What are they?"

"In good time," she said. He looked nervous and she began to laugh. "We have the rest of our lives."

They were finishing dinner one evening in the hotel dining room when she began looking at him in an intimate way. Even in public she was unable to conceal her desire for him. When the waiter cleared away the dishes she rose from her seat, but he didn't move.

"Aren't you coming, Kent?"

362

"I can't."

"What is it?"

"I can't get up just now, Beth," he hissed. "Sit down a minute."

Suddenly the reason dawned on her and she laughed.

"I'll get you for this," he muttered, and she laughed louder. The laughter was sufficient to dampen his erotic impulses and he rose suddenly and chased her out the door, mumbling in her ear that he was going to rape her. That night proved to be the wildest of their stay, and for a long time afterward they joked about it. After that, Beth never missed an opportunity to arouse him over dinner but he finally outsmarted her one night by exclaiming in a loud voice, "A baby, my dear? But what will I tell my wife?" On that occasion, happily the last night at the hotel, she ended up chasing him back to the room, gathering up her skirts and galloping up the stairs laughing hysterically. She had never acted sillier in her life. But this season, only six months after the war, everyone was behaving foolishly, and hotel personnel looked on with understanding smiles.

By the end of October, they were comfortably settled in Louise's large house. Louise was happy to have a family around her again. She and Kent got on well, and she cheerfully retired and let the Wilsons run the household.

In the first months of her marriage, Beth made an effort to act like the proper wife of a doctor. From early youth she had been told of the social requirements of marriage and she now tried valiantly to summon enthusiasm for her role. "At home" cards were distributed, dinner parties were held often, a maid was engaged to assist Louise's Theresa, and several pieces were borrowed from Kate to furnish the parlor. Because she had never mastered domestic skills, she now studied them and perused etiquette books as well. She would learn, once and for all, the differences among wines and where flowers were placed.

Kent was appalled with the change in his wife, and one

evening he said as much. He was looking over her shoulder as she was reading an article in *Harper's.* His eye caught a phrase and he plucked the magazine from her hand and began reading aloud.

> Our early mothers worked and trained their daughters to work and thus become healthy, energetic, and cheerful. But in these days young girls in the wealthy classes do not use the muscles of their body and arms in domestic labor or in any other way. Instead of this, study and reading stimulate the brain and nerves to debility by excess . . .

He handed the magazine back to her. " 'Debility by excess'?" He shook his head. "Could you summarize this opus for me?"

"It says that women should learn women's subjects in school to prepare themselves for their proper business. The schools as they're set up now don't address themselves to women's business but to men's."

"And what would 'women's business' be?"

"Oh—cooking, sewing, nursing, even doctoring, so long as we confine our services to women. It says, 'It is believed that the remedy for all these evils'—the evil of our sloth, they mean—'is not in leading women into the professions and business of men, by which many philanthropists are now aiming to remedy their sufferings, but to train women properly for their own proper business and . . .' "

"Do you subscribe to this idea, Beth?"

"Not exactly."

"Then why are you reading it so carefully?"

"I'm trying to understand this kind of thinking. You see—"

"You're what? Two months ago you were singing the praises of Lucy Stone. Can you have changed in so short a time?"

"I haven't changed, but I'll be expected to run a household, to entertain properly—"

"Beth, you're not doing this for me, are you? Because I cringe at the sight of a tray of calling cards. And Louise—well,

364

I think you're making her nervous. Your mother is certainly not urging you in this direction. Now for whom, exactly, are you changing your way of life?"

She shrugged. "I don't know any more who I am supposed to be. My friends are all settled, and they accept the order of things. I sometimes wonder what's wrong with me."

"Nothing's wrong with you. I suppose I should sit patiently by and wait until this phase is past. But I'm not a patient man, Beth. I married a woman. She has never been 'feminine' in the sense that this article implies, but she is no less a woman."

"Thank you, Kent. That's very—"

"Now will you please read something that will 'stimulate your brain to debility'? You'll be a lot happier."

By January she was herself again and she *was* a good deal happier. She still attempted to "keep up" socially, but her standards dropped, the dinners were fewer, and she abandoned all studies of "women's business." She came to admire Kent for not treating her like a glorified lackey.

They enjoyed their work in the laboratory. Pasteur's germ theory of disease, which had hit Kent like a heavenly revelation—"My God! That explains everything!"—had inspired them to conduct a series of experiments that did not always prove their hypotheses but generated an excitement that often reached the levels of their midnight moments in bed. It bound them together in a special way.

But there were difficulties in the marriage that sometimes overbalanced the benefits. Many of their romantic expectations evaporated within weeks of the honeymoon. Kent didn't change from the cynical terror of the field hospital into a sentimental husband. Nor did she remain the laughing bride of the hotel suite. The first shocks of adjustment were difficult because they were both temperamental, and they argued frequently as they had done at Gettysburg. And Kent could be downright depressing at times. The antiquated methods of the surgeons at the hospital drove him mad. When he sent patients there he ended up fighting with the staff and coming home in a mood so black that Beth was forced to tiptoe around him. Doctors dressed in dirty frock coats still performed operations with unclean instruments. She understood Kent's anger, but it was difficult to live with it.

He did not share many of her interests either—didn't like plays (except *Hamlet*), and wasn't much absorbed with literature, poetry, or politics. He did, of course, like music, and they sometimes attended concerts. He played every so often and he seemed to enjoy her playing too. But even his sensitivity to music had its irritating aspect. Over breakfast one morning he winced as Theresa, the cook, went in and out of the dining room singing, "The Minstrel Boy."

"How do you stand it?" he asked Beth and Louise.

"Stand what?" asked his wife.

"That note. The *be* in *betrays*. She always flats the damn thing." He was tense, waiting for the wrong note, and he gulped his coffee when she hit it.

"It's only that *one* note," Louise reasoned.

"Even so, it drives me crazy. Like chalk grating on a blackboard. And that's not the only song she wrecks." He concluded with his favorite remark, "All I ever wanted out of life was peace and quiet."

They didn't know what to tell poor Theresa. They couldn't very well tell her that Kent hated singing, because he himself sang on occasion. So they told her not to sing when Dr. Wilson was around because he often had headaches. Theresa sulked for days, oversalting the food and being late with meals, and Beth fumed. One miserable note and he had turned the household upside down. This was exactly the sort of thing she had feared when he had proposed last Christmas.

But Beth too had her sensitivities.

"A black frock coat and a navy waistcoat, Kent? Black doesn't go with navy."

"I like it."

"You used to have such good taste. Remember that summer outfit you were wearing when you come home from Virginia?"

"Oh, that."

"What about that?"

"I asked a tailor in Washington to put it together for me."

"I might have known."

"Why are you so damned preoccupied with these petty values?"

"Petty! Jarring colors are on a par with jarring notes, and you remember Theresa's singing."

"It's not the same."

"It is to me."

Louise, who had walked into the dining room during this exchange, commented, "If you want my opinion, I think you're both a little daft. You deserve each other."

Most of their disagreements were no more fundamental than this, but the arguments generated by them could be fearsome. Beth often criticized him for his careless disregard for the appearance of the house and, maids notwithstanding, she demanded that he keep things neat. ("Not fanatically; just ordered disarray will do.") But from such remarks grew great storms punctuated with much door-slamming on both their parts. There were nights when she lay awake, tears streaming sideways into her pillow, wondering how she was going to tolerate a lifetime of arguing. Sometimes, after one of their battles, she wouldn't speak to him. As the hours went by, her rage would gather impetus like an accelerating body. She was always taken aback when he suddenly spoke to her in a normal voice or reached casually for her as she passed. She would stare at him, speechless.

"We had a terrible argument, Kent."

"That's right."

"You do recall it, don't you?"

"Yes, I do."

"Aren't you angry?"

"I was."

Damn him! His short sentences and his monosyllables were infuriating. "Then why are you so calm, Kent? You're acting as though nothing happened."

"These things don't bother me as they do you."

"Why? People can't scream at each other the way we do and still like each other very much."

"Yes they can. Ask your brother about that."

She remembered Pat's account of their arguments in the army.

"I still don't understand you, Kent. The way you rant and rave sometimes, I believe you hate me."

"Consider your own ravings. Do you hate me?"

She did at times, but she wouldn't admit it. "No," she lied.

"Well then?" And that would be it until the next battle. She didn't understand him at all.

One afternoon when Beth was feeling particularly depressed about her marriage, Pat came down from the office for tea. He was in an expansive mood and didn't seem to notice at first how miserable his sister was.

"What ever happened to your friend Mary?" Pat asked.

"Mary?" This was the woman who had pined away for Pat at the New Year's party two years earlier. "She's married. She has a little girl two months old."

"Married, eh? And Emily?"

"Emily married two months ago. Why are you asking me about them?"

"They were so nice."

"Nice? Since when do you care about 'nice' girls? You were always chasing girls who treated you—well who took delight in putting you in your place."

"I've changed," he proclaimed in a resonant voice.

"But as recently as last month I saw you at a party making a fool of yourself over Ellen Larcombe and she's anything but 'nice,' Pat. I don't mean she's a tart, but I do think she likes to keep men on the string and I also think you enjoy it."

"You don't understand. It's time I became serious. I've known that since the war ended. My recent behavior was just a continuation of a bad habit. My heart wasn't in it."

"Are you joking?"

"Not at all."

368

"Will wonders never cease! Pat, three years ago there was a regular coterie of girls who worshipped the ground you—"

"Three years ago I was a child." He sighed. "Beth, all I wanted to know was whether those friends of yours were still free. You said No. Fine. I'll leave you alone to bask in your self-righteous—"

"Oh, hush!"

"What the deuce is wrong with you today?"

"Nothing."

"Well, I was just going to tell you that—"

"Tell me what?"

"That you and Kent served as a sort of model to me. I've stayed to supper enough evenings to see how pleasant marriage can be , how—"

Her mouth dropped opened. "How pleasant?"

"Kent's a different person. He's happy."

"Did he tell you he was happy?"

"No. But I ought to know him."

She sighed. No doubt Pat wanted the man he admired and the sister he loved to be happy together. He was bound to see things in the Wilson relationship that weren't there.

She smiled a false smile. "I'm glad we inspired you, Pat. I do hope you find someone too."

And within a month Pat had found her. She was Dr. Clark's cousin—a quiet, gentle girl. Beth and the family were speechless with the shock of Pat's transformation, though Beth was flattered that he had used her marriage as a model. What had Pat seen in Kent's attitude that Beth herself could not see? *Was* Kent happy? She doubted it.

Because she didn't understand Kent, she wasn't sure that she loved him. There were separate traits about him that she loved but she didn't know if they added up to a love for the whole man. Their physical relationship was excellent, however, and she always felt closest to him when they were in bed. He would say, "My God, you're beautiful," or "You feel so good," and she would be moved by his words. Once when they had made love in the morning and she had feared being

369

overheard by a carpenter working in the next room, Kent had said, "No, Beth, he won't be shocked. He will, however, envy me."

"Why?"

"Are you fishing for compliments? Because you're beautiful and exciting and enjoy intimacies."

She could love him so fully with her body that at times it was possible to believe that she loved him as intensely with her heart. But after the passion was spent and his feelings crept back to hide behind his words, she would ask herself: Do I love him?

By March, she still didn't know the answer to that question, but life had settled into a routine which, while not always pleasant, never lacked for activity. The caseloads of both Pat and Kent were built up quickly from among the soldiers of their old regiment (colonel down to private) and their families and friends. For all the endless days and sleepless nights and migraine headaches, Kent made little money. The wealthy were charged regular fees but the poor only nominal ones, and most of their patients were poor. They were proud people, however, and insisted on paying off fees with some service. Thus the house was always awash in part-time maids, part-time cooks to help Theresa, men who delivered free produce and poultry from their farms, dressmakers for Beth and Louise, tailors and barbers for Kent, and men to sweep chimneys. Many of Pat's patients helped ready the small house he had bought on Thirteenth Street with a loan from his cousin Bill. (Pat was to be married in April.) Everyone got along despite the short supply of money.

Some of the patients were also invaluable in assisting Beth with her laboratory work. They gathered the many specimens she was anxious to examine, from reservoir water to the saliva of pigs living in the Five Points. She did not yet have much to contribute to the field of medicine, but she loved to peer into the microscope and study these incredible one-celled organisms, some of them deadly (which ones?), who busied

370

themselves in life's endless race for food. She filled sketch-books with diagrams of these "beasties" (as van Leeuwenhoek had called them) and made an attempt to classify them by type. As Kent's caseload increased, he was able to visit the laboratory less often. She summarized her findings to him during his free hours, feeling very much like a university professor in consultation with a colleague. She loved her work.

As a doctor's wife, who had once assisted in operations, she often acted as nurse for Kent or Pat. Since most patients still believed hospitals to be charnel houses from which patients rarely emerged alive, many operations were performed in the office or in the homes of the patients. Some emergencies that should have been sent to the hospitals were brought to Kent's door by Tim, now a New York City policeman in the Sixth Ward, whose compassion for people prompted him to bring them to Kent rather than throw them on the mercies of hospital surgeons. And so it was that Beth came to assist in operations involving men beaten up by gangs, women with botched abortions, and babies who had been pummeled brutally by their parents. The horrors of New York slum life depressed her because conditions only seemed to get worse.

The city, aside from a few private charitable organizations, was almost totally insensitive to conditions in the slums. Even church officials claimed that the problems of the poor were owing in large part to "bad blood." It seemed to occur to few people that the immigrants would remain mired in squalor unless radical reforms were undertaken. Public schooling alone was not sufficient, for few immigrant children could remain in school. Still, Beth often wished that she could teach again. She could appreciate the need for her work now as she had not been able to do during the war, when concern for Greg and her brothers had preoccupied her. Today she would be a more dedicated teacher. But in New York married women were forbidden by law to teach—as though the loss of virginity was a condition so gross as to offend the morals of

371

innocent children, even those with "bad blood." How else to account for such an absurd law?

Changing this law was one of Beth's many causes. Others included setting up relief agencies in the slums and attaining suffrage for women. She joined a philanthropic group and she wrote letters to the newspapers that were sometimes printed. But elected officials, if they read the letters at all, never did anything. Most were too busy trying to conceal their involvement in Tammany corruption. She sometimes wondered what Greg would have done if he had lived. Would he really have organized a revolution?

With her laboratory, her nursing, and her various causes, Beth was always busy, but she could regulate her hours and maintain her health and spirit. Kent, on the other hand, was thin and haggard from being on call twenty-four hours a day. After a few weeks of coping with a very heavy schedule, he began alternating night calls with Pat and Ed Clark, the only two doctors he trusted. But even when he slept, Kent was tense. Only rarely was his sleep as peaceful as in the first days of their marriage. The nightmares that had afflicted Pat and Joe troubled Kent as well. Beth began to think of these dreams as a disease of war that was more serious than typhoid or dysentery. He would toss in his sleep sometimes, muttering words of which she could make little sense. She would ask him, if he woke up, what the dream had been about, but he would never discuss it.

One morning at about 5 A.M. he sat up straight in bed and said aloud, "It was the lint."

She had thought he was having another dream, but he was not, for he said, looking at her bleary eyes, "Beth, I'm sorry I woke you."

"Well, now that you did," she said ungraciously, "Tell me about the lint."

"The lint was responsible for the infections."

"Pray explain yourself," she sighed.

"I had a dream about Gettysburg," he said. "You were

coming toward me carrying your pile of sheets. They were bleached white. Bleach is a caustic agent like chloride of lime, so it must have killed most of the germs. The sponges were washed too. I doubt that they were completely free of germs, but they were washed thoroughly. And of course our hands were washed. We were at pains to wash everything in the contaminated area because we were thinking in terms of miasma spreading among the men."

"And the lint was never washed," she said, "because it came in from outside the contaminated area. Good Lord, it might have been scraped by someone with the plague!"

He said, "Yes. I dreamed I was standing at the operating table. You unfolded the sheets and laid them down. Tim and Johnny brought over a patient. You handed me a scalpel. I did the operation, tied the ligatures, and picked up a wad of lint. As I pressed it to the stump I woke up in a sweat. Something was wrong. Then I realized—"

"Wait a minute," she said. "The ligatures."

"Yes! They were never washed either. Or the bandages."

"Kent, do you know what else I remember?"

"What?"

"The flies."

"I thought about that the following summer. It occurred to me that whatever caused the disease might be carried from one man to another by flies. At Spotsylvania we managed to get mosquito netting. But the lint, the bandages, the ligatures —when I think of how many men died because I never considered—"

"You didn't know."

"I should have known. Doesn't it strike you as odd that we knew how to prevent decay in meat and vegetables but not in men? We could pickle cucumbers, salt and dry meat—"

"No one knew how it worked until Pasteur. It was a trial-and-error—"

"We were so inconsistent, Beth. We never used our heads. We had sense enough to boil water and treat sewage, and yet an awful lot of men are dead because of the lint and the ligatures."

They discussed other items that might have caused infection and made plans to see that everything coming into the office was washed thoroughly. The were still talking when the sun came up.

"The next thing we have to determine," Kent continued over breakfast, "is *how* the body kills germs. Do you suppose there's a caustic chemical in the blood that burns up small amounts of germs but can't handle a major assault? What do you think, Beth?"

They talked on and on, oblivious of Louise's turning green over the pancakes as they used explicit medical terminology. When he went up to the office Beth sat at the table smiling, feeling very good for a reason that could be summed up in one phrase: "What do you think, Beth?" If they could share more interests like this, she thought, they would have a very happy marriage indeed.

EIGHT

Oh Shenandoah, I love your daughter
Away, you rolling river!
I'll take her 'cross that rolling water
Away, I'm bound away
'Cross the wide Missouri.

In April, 1866, Pat married Eileen Connell at a very Irish wedding that was lively enough to compensate for Eileen's reticence. The reception was the occasion for much speculation as to why Pat had chosen such a retiring bride. Beth explained to close friends that Pat had changed. Later she asked Kent if he agreed.

"It was the war," said Kent.

"What do you mean?"

"He should have waited until he was over the war."

"You didn't wait."

"I didn't have to."

She questioned him that night and afterward, but Kent would make no further comment. It was one of the qualities about him that she detested: the terse phrases mumbled with no explanations following them.

More and more often she began asking herself why she had married him. And at the same time she could not imagine living with anyone else. Kent was grouchy, overworked, antisocial, and eleven years older than herself, but he seemed right for her in a way she could not define and she felt that love for him, if not apparent, was there beneath the surface waiting for something he would say or do before it came out and declared itself. Then again, perhaps married love was different from the excitement of courtship, where the very thought of a lover set one's heart pounding. Perhaps ideal marriage was friendship with sex added, and since the physical part of their relationship was gratifying she need only work at friendship and then love would come.

One night when they were sitting in the parlor reading, she said, "Kent, the Martins have asked us to a whist party."

"Can't you make excuses?"

"Why?"

"I don't like parties. You know that. I'm accustomed to being alone."

"Then why do you need me?"

"You're my wife."

"You mean my body is available any time you need it?"

"Oh, for God's sake!" He slammed down a book.

"It's the truth, isn't it?"

"Beth, bodies are available all over New York for a lot less money than the cost of keeping you. What the hell is wrong with you?"

"Do you love me, Kent?"

"Of course I do."

"Why don't you ever say it?"

"You should know me by this time. I don't repeat the obvious over and over again like some goddamn romantic poet. But since you're so anxious to hear the words, I'll say them. Yes, I love you!" he bellowed.

"Me? Not just my body?"

"Why do you take such pleasure in provoking me, Beth?"

"I don't."

"Oh yes you do. You dig at me like a miner, for what reason I can't fathom."

376

"You force me to dig, Kent. If I didn't, you'd never tell me a thing. Did Nancy tolerate this?"

"My first wife?" He looked incredulously at her.

"Of course your first wife. Whom did you think I was talking about?"

"I don't care to discuss her, Beth."

"Why?"

"Because she's irrelevant to this discussion. If one can go so far as to call it a discussion."

"Do you still love her?"

"I *don't* care to—"

"Do you?"

"Damn it! Do you still love Allister? Shall we sit here and talk about loving the dead? Is that how you like to amuse yourself?"

Beth started to cry and ran out of the room. He caught her in the hall and turned her around, grasping her arms. "I didn't mean it, Beth."

"You never 'mean' any of your remarks. What kind of a man raised you, Kent? I know he treated you badly, but I didn't realize he'd made you totally insensitive."

"Did Anne tell you about him?" He was angry.

Beth stopped crying at the sight of his face. "No," she lied, "I guessed it. Anne told me almost nothing, though I asked her about you."

"Beth, have you been feeling well lately?"

"Why?"

"Your behavior."

"*My* behavior!" She shook free of his arms and turned away. "I can't even dignify that remark with a reply. I'm going to bed."

"How long has it been since your last menstruation?"

She swallowed. "I don't remember. I was never—uh—periodic. A long time, though."

"You're fuller," he said.

"I'm what?"

"Your breasts. I've felt them."

She blushed.

He asked, "Do you feel ill in the morning?"

"No. That's why I haven't said anything to you."

"The missed menstruation, the fuller breasts, the mood-iness—"

"Just because I'm angry you think I'm with child. Of all the evasive ways of dealing with problems!"

"I know I'm difficult. Give me time to talk about these things, will you?"

Suddenly he was placating. When she stood back and looked at his face, she could see that he was very disturbed.

"What's wrong? When I said I wanted children, you agreed."

"You want them very much, don't you?"

"What is it, Kent? Aren't you happy about it?"

"Very happy," he said in a monotone.

In the last four months of her pregnancy, Kent was impossible. He was nervous and cranky—short with the cook, with Pat, and with Louise. He felt that the doctor Beth had engaged was careless and he questioned Beth at length about the prenatal examinations. He insisted on doing an internal examination himself and she refused.

"My hips are wide enough."

"That means nothing."

"You think you're the only doctor who knows anything, don't you?"

"Let me examine you."

"No."

"Why?"

"Modesty forbids."

"Modesty! I'm your husband."

"We should preserve some mysteries."

"Oh, for Christ's sake!"

In the evenings he wouldn't sit still for ten minutes at a time but paced about, bristling whenever the street noises were too loud or the conversation (especially when they had guests) too tedious. In bed he tossed restlessly far into the night. At first she thought this to be frustration over the fact that they weren't permitted sex, but later she realized that something else was troubling him. She was certain that he did not want children and she could not understand why. Whenever she questioned him, he insisted (too loudly) that he *did* want children but she knew he was lying. Many nights she fell asleep crying at the thought of her little child being neglected by a cold, resentful father. The tension remained high for weeks.

One evening in October she began having sharp pains during dinner.

"I think it's started," she told Kent.

He dropped his spoon. "Are you sure?"

"I've had discomfort before, but this time is different. The pains are definite and regular. Yes, I think this is it."

Louise set down her napkin, and Kent roared for Theresa and the other maid. "Prepare the room, and please be quick about it."

"Kent, they just started," Beth said. "These things take time."

"I want you in bed immediately."

"Can't I finish my coffee?"

He sighed. "Very well. I'm going upstairs to supervise arrangements. I'll be down in ten minutes." He stood up and left the dining room.

Louise winked across the table at her niece, who was nervously gulping her coffee. "Don't worry," she said.

The procedure for the delivery was to be unusual. Though most middle- and upper-class women no longer used midwives, they still delivered babies in the nuptial bed, while female relatives hovered about them and a doctor in a frock coat did the necessary without too much attention given the cleanliness of his hands. Beth's delivery would be different. There was a small room down the hall from Kent's office. Patients who had had minor operations sometimes rested there for a few hours before going home. This room had been selected for Beth's labor and recovery. The baby would be delivered in Kent's office on an examining table which had been fitted with straps. The doctor, however, would be not Kent but a man Beth had chosen on the recommendation of several of her friends. There would be no agitated friends and relatives in the delivery room, only the doctor, a nurse, and a man to administer ether. Kent wanted to be present but Pat had talked him out of it, asserting that since Kent was something of a fanatic he would be apt to question Dr. Anderson's procedures, distract the man, and make him angry. Pat depicted a scene in which Kent and Dr. Anderson were at each other's throats and poor Beth was begging them to stop fighting and deliver the baby. The scene was so vivid to Kent that he reluctantly agreed to stay away.

The pains continued all night long. Kent sat next to his wife but spoke little. A cot had been set up in the room so that he could be near her before and after the delivery, but he refused to lie down. The long hours of her pain and his silence were torture for Beth. At dawn she asked Kent to send for her mother and for the doctor.

"It's too soon for the doctor," he said, feeling a contraction and frowning.

"How do you know?"

"It's obvious."

"Get the doctor, Kent."

"I'd rather deliver it myself."

"Damn it, Kent! I'm in pain. Dr. Anderson has agreed to use chloride of lime. He's agreed to scrub everything. Now for God's sake don't be difficult." She bit her lip, suffering a contraction. Then she said, "Go, Kent. Please."

"Very well. I'll send for the doctor and your mother. I imagine the whole family will arrive with her."

"I *want* them here," she said indignantly.

"Yes, I understand that. But you can't have them all in the room."

"I want them all in the house, though. And I want Mother in the room." At least her mother would *talk* to her. And mother had been through four pregnancies and could reassure her. She was frightened. She well knew the mortality rate of women in childbirth. All through her pregnancy she had dreamt of all the awful things that might happen. The labor might go on for days and she might die with the child inside her. Perhaps she would bleed to death. These thoughts went through her head now, but she did not share them with Kent. She had been told time and again that women ought not distress their husbands with such fears. Then she decided that her fright was foolish. She had a strong mind and that mind would compel her body to expel the baby. She would not permit herself to die.

Dr. Anderson arrived about 8:30 A.M. Kate came in soon afterward, but the doctor would not permit any other women in the room, including Louise and Diane. Kent, however, was in and out continually, upsetting everyone, complaining about everything. He informed the doctor that the pelvic examinations were not being done frequently enough and he felt most of the contractions himself, his usually steady hand trembling and his brows knit. Beth, whose pains were now severe, was furious, and when Dr. Anderson stepped out for a moment and Kate went out to speak to him, she raged at her husband.

"I think you want to add to my suffering. These pains are bad enough. Do you have any idea what your behavior is doing? It's making them excruciating. You're upsetting Dr. Anderson, my mother, and me. Especially me. I rather think you enjoy it. Now please, please get out of here!"

He left quietly, which was odd. Normally he would have slammed the door. She cried in frustration. She had wanted him to sit by calmly, stroking her hand, telling her that everything was going to be all right. And now, on top of this godawful agony, she had to contend with his histrionics.

Kent went downstairs for some coffee and John offered him a drink instead.

"No thank you, John. I have to stay sober."

"Why, for heaven's sake?"

"No drink, John. Thank you."

Later Kent walked into his consultation room. They had canceled appointments today, but Pat was there trying to work at the desk, though he was too nervous to ccncentrate. His own wife hadn't come down today because she was in her fourth month of pregnancy and plagued with bouts of nausea. He had looked in on his sister earlier and shuddered when he saw her wincing in pain. What a price women had to pay in order to propagate the race!

Kent sat down in a leather chair. "Your sister kicked me out of the room."

"Well, you're acting like a madman, Kent."

"I don't like it, Pat. It's been twenty-one hours."

Pat nodded. "It's a long time, but it's not unusual. Many women—"

"I *knew* this would happen. I *knew* it." Kent pounded his fist on the arm of the chair. "It was the same way with my first wife. I didn't want Beth to have children. I've been dreading this moment for months."

"Did you tell her that?"

"No. She wanted them so badly that I thought she'd divorce me if I took preventive measures. Hell, I wanted children too, but not at the risk of losing her."

"Don't worry. She'll come through it."

"I shouldn't have let Anderson handle it."

"Kent, you know that few doctors deliver their own babies."

"No, I didn't deliver my first one. But I will deliver this one."

"Have you taken leave of your senses?"

"Damn it, Pat, I won't stand by and watch her die. I don't trust Anderson."

"You checked his credentials. They're good, Kent."

"I'm going to study a few cases. Will you administer ether?"

"Anderson has an assistant for the ether."

"Whether you help me or not I'm going to deliver that baby."

382

"I have no choice then, do I? I ought to be around anyway to pick you up off the floor when you pass out."

Kent ignored the remark. He took a pair of reading glasses from his jacket pocket and began studying some illustrations in an obstetrics book. Pat skimmed through a similar work. After about twenty minutes Pat looked up. "Do you think we'll need forceps?"

"I don't know. She wouldn't let me do an internal. But I did tell Anderson that all my instruments were scrubbed and ready, including forceps." He paused. "God, if we were only able to do a safe Caesarean. I might avoid fatal infection but I wouldn't know how to avoid shock." He removed his glasses and rubbed his nose where they had pressed against it. "Still, if it looks as though she can't deliver any other way—but by that time she'd be too weak, wouldn't she, and she'd die anyway." He placed the glasses on his desk, shaking his head and muttering. "What can I do? I don't know what to do, Pat."

Pat was about to suggest that the two of them sedate themselves with alcohol and let Dr. Anderson do his job, but Kent was on his feet striding toward the door. He was thinking it could not happen again. He would not accept the loss of Beth too. But he felt hopeless, and his expression was not lost on John, Joe, Louise, or Diane, who were standing in the hallway when Kent hurried past them.

The baby was to be delivered on the examining room in Kent's office, and Beth wondered why Dr. Anderson wasn't transferring her there. She was in acute pain now and she began asking for Kent, but the doctor would not call him.

"He's much too disruptive, Mrs. Wilson. Don't you agree, Mrs. Shepherd?"

Kate said nothing and bit her lip, but Beth chastised herself inwardly for having been so short with her husband. She wanted him badly now. Dr. Anderson was so complacent that she didn't think he would care if she died here in bed. Kent would care. If he could see her now, he would be doing something to help her, not sitting here with a self-righteous smirk on his face.

A few minutes later the door opened and Kent walked in. As soon as she saw him she remembered that women must be stoic for their husbands' sake, and much as she wanted to scream "Help me!" she tried to look brave, muffling a cry with her hand. She heard him murmur something to Dr. Anderson. Then he was standing over her. At this point another contraction came—they were very close together now—and she reached up and grasped Kent's hand, pulling herself up almost to a sitting position and moaning. The pain passed, and for a moment she was ashamed because she had not been brave and had alarmed him. She could see the beads of perspiration on his brow and the helpless look on his face. She was able to relax only for a moment before the pain was stabbing at her again and she was tearing into his arm with her fingernails. When the next pain hit, she forgot all about Kent's sensibilities and tore at his arm, moaning, "I can't stand it!"

She heard Kent say in a shaking voice, "I'm taking her to my office."

"She's not ready," said Dr. Anderson.

"I want to examine her."

"I'd like you to leave, doctor. Immediately."

Kent bent down, picked up his wife, sheets and all, and carried her out. Dr. Anderson followed them, muttering under his breath. To the group in the hallway the scene might have looked comical if it were not so frightening. Kent looked like the hero in a bad play. Dr. Anderson was the pursuing villain and Beth the rescued maiden. But her piteous moans prevented them from seeing anything humorous in the situation.

"All right, gentlemen," said Dr. Anderson to Pat and Kent when Beth was on the examining table. "Now will you leave?" He stood before them with his arms folded.

"I want to examine her," said Kent.

"I asked you to leave. She's my patient. You came in there like a pirate—"

"Goddamn it, I *will* examine my wife!"

Dr. Anderson stormed from the room and Beth, no longer caring whether she lived or died, continued to gasp. Kent did an internal examination. He said to Pat, "Dilating all right but no engagement." To Beth he said gently, "We're going to ask you to stand, Beth. I'm sorry." Each of them holding an arm, they helped her to stand and made her bend her knees several times, then again lifted her to the table. Kent scrubbed his hands once more and examined her. He ruptured the amniotic membrane.

Kent said, "Try to bear down, Beth. Push."

"I can't!" she screamed.

"Please! Please try." She bore down feebly and he felt her abdomen, waiting. "Good. That was fine. Relax now." He waited. "All right. Again. Push." He repeated the commands over and over, watching her writhe as he listened to her moans and to the sound of his own voice, hating himself for its harshness: "Push . . . Push . . . again . . . again . . . again. . . ." Fifteen minutes ticked by. Kent, with mounting panic, felt for the baby. Beth's moans became shrill and Kent grew so pale that Pat thought he was going to faint. What would he do if Kent collapsed? At the end of twenty minutes Kent said, "I'm not going to wait. Get the nurse."

Pat strode toward the door and shouted for the nurse. He washed his hands, picked up the forceps and handed them to Kent. Then he reached for the ether.

"Push, Beth," said Kent for what he hoped would be the last time. Her scream was ear-splitting. He shuddered. "It's almost over," he said hoarsely. "Let's go, Pat."

Pat placed the ether cone over her nose and said, "Breathe deeply, Beth."

"Take it away, Pat!" she screamed.

"That's right. Deeply."

"I'm suffocating! Stop! You—"

"That's right. Good." said Pat soothingly.

After a few moments of this Kent asked, "Is she under?"

"I think so."

"Nurse, will you wash your hands in that solution? Yes, that one. And don't dry them. Ready, Pat?"

"Ready."

Kent had done only three forceps deliveries since the war. He edged the forceps in, clamped them around the baby's head (to bruise his child's cheeks before he could see them!), and pulled.

It was a little girl. He held her securely by the feet and slapped the first breath of life into her. She began to cry furiously, healthily. He tied and cut the cord and handed the baby to the nurse, glancing briefly at the baby's face and then at Beth's. Tears filled his eyes, blinding him for a moment. He blinked them away and turned to deliver the placenta. That done, he pressed on Beth's abdomen. Then he stood up and took a deep breath.

Tears of relief streamed down Pat's face. "Congratulations, Pop. A healthy baby." He paused. "It was just a prolonged labor, wasn't it?"

Kent nodded.

"Do you think she'll need forceps next time?"

"Don't talk about next time," said Kent.

"What will you tell Anderson?"

"I don't know. He may have known what he was doing, but—"

"Tell him you panicked. He'll understand."

"I don't give a damn what he thinks."

Pat sighed. "I've delivered my share of babies. But my own sister. Jesus, I'm—it was like the first time I ever saw a woman in labor. I couldn't stand the—"

"Don't talk about it," Kent snapped.

"Yes, you're right. I think she'll recover nicely, and there's no point in dwelling on—"

Kent's eyes widened. "Pat, do you really think she'll recover?"

"Well, of course. Look at Beth. She's obviously going to be all right. What's wrong?"

"It's nothing. Nerves. Here, help me move her down a bit, will you?"

As they were preparing Beth to be moved, Kent glanced over at the baby, now being weighed. He had wanted a little girl. He had been smiling at his first little girl when his wife had begun to hemorrhage. After that, he had scarcely seen her. There was a dim memory of a thin wailing and a wet nurse being summoned and a tiny coffin being laid next to a full-size one, but his only clear memory of her had been that first look at her, the overwhelming pride of fatherhood when his wife said wonderingly to him, only moments before she began to bleed, "We're parents, Kent." He had heard those words over and over in the years since. "We're parents, Kent." They had been her last words.

The first thing Beth felt as she swam upward into consciousness was a hand encircling her wrist. She was slow to realize that the hand was Kent's and that he was feeling her pulse. She was lying in bed and no longer in acute pain. Then she knew that she had given birth.

"The baby—" she murmured weakly.

"She's right here," said Kent.

"She?" Beth smiled.

"A girl. Eight pounds six."

"Oh, where is she?" Beth tried to raise her head, but Kent told her not to move.

"Nurse?" he commanded. A raw-boned woman appeared next to Kent holding a small pink bundle. Kent raised Beth's head slightly, propping pillows behind her, as the nurse rested the sleeping infant beside her mother.

"The purple marks on her cheeks are temporary," Kent said hastily. "They'll disappear."

Beth's eyes widened. "Forceps?" Such extreme procedures often did harm to the baby.

"Yes, but she's fine. Pat and I did a thorough examination."

Beth studied her daughter curiously. She was swaddled completely; only her tiny face was visible—red, wrinkled, and marred. This was her daughter and she ought to be feeling love for the child. Yet she felt only amazement at this creature who had for so long been invisible. She studied the baby's features. The only distinguishing characteristics she could see were a turned-up nose and a wisp of blond hair peeking from under a cap.

"I think she must look like Mother," she said to Kent. "My nose is straight and so is yours, but Mother's is turned-up. And both Mother and the baby are blonde."

At this a muffled sob was heard somewhere in the room and Beth said, "Mother, are you here?"

"Right here, dear." Kate walked over to the bed. "She's beautiful, isn't she?"

Beth did not think the child was beautiful, though she wanted desperately to think so, wanted love for the child to come flooding over her like a warm rain.

Kate smiled. "I know you can't picture her as she will look," she said, as though reading Beth's mind. "But when you've had other children you will better be able to judge their potential."

Beth said, "Is it normal if one doesn't love a baby right away? Oh, I don't mean I don't love her. I—"

"She's a stranger to you, dear. You don't yet see her as a person."

"But I *must* see her that way!"

"You'll love her to distraction within a few weeks," Kate said. "I can guarantee that."

"We plan to name her Katherine after you, Mother."

Kate dabbed at her eyes. "Kent told me, yes."

Kent said, "Everyone wants to see you now, Beth. But only for a moment. It's imperative that you rest."

She said to him, "I'm glad you brought the baby, Kent."

He cleared his throat but said nothing.

"And I'm sorry I said all those dreadful things to you. It wasn't that you didn't want children. You were worried about me, wasn't that it?"

"I was concerned," he said.

"And you did want Kathy?"

"Very much."

"I wondered about that for a long time. I should have realized that you would be worried about childbirth." She smiled wistfully. "Kent?"

"Yes?"

"We're parents. Can you believe that?"

Kate looked over at her son-in-law, expecting to see a proud smile, but he was staring at Beth strangely and his face had gone deathly pale.

"Did you hear what I said?" asked Beth, who could not, from her supine position, see Kent's face as clearly as Kate could.

"Parents," Kent repeated. "I promised everyone that they could come in for a minute—" He walked toward the door, weaving slightly as though he were drunk. It was obvious to Kate that he was suffering from the strain of the day. She too felt unsteady on her feet and she returned to her chair in the corner while John, Joe, and Diane filed into the room. Each spoke briefly with Beth and then looked at the baby. Everyone cried but the father of the child, who stood woodenly at the door staring across the room at his wife.

John came over to where Kate was sitting and kissed her on the cheek. "Hello, Grandma."

Kate said, "I think I would prefer *Grand'mère*. It has a nicer lilt to it."

"But the baby's not French."

"What does it matter?" She smiled. "You look smug."

"I'd like to render Shakespeare's 'Seven Ages of Man.' "

"Spare us, dear, just this once. And besides, that child will be a woman and those lines do not apply."

John smiled and looked over at Kent. "The new father needs a drink," he whispered to Kate.

"The new father needs a night's sleep. But you go downstairs and have a drink with him. I'll join you by and by. John, where are Pat and Louise? They wanted to see Beth."

"They're in the office. Kent didn't want everyone in here at the same time." He paused. "Kate?"

"Yes, Grandpa?"

"Tonight when we get home we'll have a toast to the new arrival?"

She winked. "I should like that very much." But she wondered if she would have the energy for one of John's toasts.

Soon everyone except Kate had left the room. In the hall Kent directed the nurse as to how he wanted the child to be cared for. The nursery upstairs too, had been scrubbed today, under Kent's barked directions. When he entered the room again, Kate, looking up from her spot in the corner, was shocked to see that the expression on his face was one of raw terror. Surely Beth could not be in danger! Pat had assured them of that immediately after the delivery and Kate herself could see that Beth had come through it very well. She looked over at her daughter, who had dropped off to sleep. Then she turned again to her son-in-law. What on earth was wrong with him?

He walked over toward the bed. Beth was lying too still. He moved swiftly over to her. Then he saw her chest rising and falling and he took a deep breath. She was sleeping. He grasped the bedpost for support. She was only sleeping. She wasn't dead.

Kate came over and stood next to him. "She looks good, doesn't she, Kent?"

He nodded.

Kate touched his arm. "You were afraid, weren't you?"

He didn't answer but began to shake. His teeth chattered.

Pat came in with Louise and they smiled down at the slumbering Beth.

"How is she?" Pat whispered to Kate.

"I'm not sure."

"What do you mean?"

She nodded towards Kent, and Pat looked at him. He whispered to Kate, "I half-expected this." Then he looked at

390

Beth again and whispered, "Beth is fine, Ma." He took a step over to Kent and said, "Go up to your room and get some sleep."

"No."

"You're shaking like a leaf."

"I won't leave."

"Go down the hall to the office then. But for God's sake get out of this room and sit down."

"Yes. Go, Kent," said Louise. "All three of you go. I'll stay with Beth for a while." She looked at Kent. "If she wakes up she will not want to see you so frightened."

Pat caught Kent's shirt collar in his hand. "Do I have to steer you out of here?"

"Very well. But please check her, Louise. If her color changes the least bit—move the lamp close so you can see—"

"I've attended my share of lyings-in," said Louise. "I know what to look for. Now off with you! The three of you."

They sat in the office waiting room, Kate and her son-in-law on the couch and Pat in a chair facing them.

Pat said, "I should never have let you deliver that baby. You told me once that you couldn't operate on people unless you saw them as machines. And I let you do a forceps on your own wife. Jesus Christ, what a fool I was!" He turned to his mother. "Excuse my language, Ma."

"I'll just say a novena for you every time you take the name of the Lord in vain," Kate said.

"I'll need them, Ma." He paused. "The average man would have a hard enough time delivering his own infant. But a doctor, who knows things can go wrong, who has seen them go wrong time and time again, should never do it. And particularly Kent, who lost a wife in childbirth." He stopped short and looked at Kent. "I'm sorry. I didn't mean to remind you. But Anderson was a perfectly competent doctor who intended a forceps all along and was waiting for the right moment—"

"How do you—how do you know?" Kent stammered, his teeth still chattering.

"The nurse just told me. You should have let him do his job. Look at yourself. You're in pieces. And for what? She's healthy. She can have more children if she wants them—"

"I impregnated her." Kent shuddered. "I put her through that hell. Christ, I nearly killed her."

"Killed her!" Kate exclaimed.

"Nancy and now Beth . . ."

Pat said, "Beth's alive, you idiot. And you didn't kill Nancy."

"She was so thin," said Kent.

Kate said, "Kent, you didn't kill Nancy. Many very slender women are able to carry—to bear—children. As a doctor you should know that."

"He does know it," said Pat. "I'm afraid your son-in-law has lost his mind. Tell me, Kent, whom else did you kill besides half the soldiers in the army?"

Kent looked down, rubbing his shaking hands together. "My mother," he said.

Kate was wishing she had her smelling salts with her. "Your mother!" she exclaimed. "How did you—"

"I was building a snowman in the back yard. I asked her to help. She—she caught cold. Three days later she was dead." He paused. "Pneumonia."

"Why do you think you killed her?" asked Kate, puzzled but relieved. For a moment she had imagined a slaying.

Kent shook his head.

Pat always kept a bottle of whisky in the office, and now he brought it out and poured Kent a jigger. "Drink this."

Kent picked it up and downed it in one gulp. Then he drank another. And with the third he began to relax.

"Good?" Pat asked.

"Yes. Good and drunk. No more, Pat, please."

Kate had been staring at Kent ever since the snowman revelation. Now she asked him, "Do you remember your mother well?"

"My mother," Kent repeated dully, feeling dizzy.

392

"What was she like, Kent?"

"My mother. Let me see. Well, I heard her tell people that she was sorry she had ever had children."

Kate and Pat exchanged quick glances. Kate said, "Did you believe that, Kent? After all, she did enjoy playing with you. The snowman—"

"The snowman. I pestered her to come out in the back yard. She was annoyed, said she was tired. But, no, I had to insist."

"She didn't enjoy playing with you?"

"No."

"What kind of sentiment did exist between you?"

He raised an eyebrow. "Sentiment?"

"Don't you believe your mother loved you?"

"She didn't want children."

"Nonsense. Mothers often say such things when they're angry, tired. You weren't old enough to put such statements in perspective, Kent. Isn't it possible that you're forgetting how much she did love you?"

He shrugged.

Kate said, "But I suppose what matters is the way you remember. And you don't remember the love."

"No."

"But how did you come to the conclusion that you killed her?"

Kent pressed a hand to his temple. "God, this whisky—"

"Did someone *tell* you that you killed your mother, Kent?"

"What? Oh. Yes, my father did. He said, 'Why didn't you drag me out into the snow so that I could die with her!' Classic line. Worthy of Edwin Booth."

Kate thought: his father could not have meant that. He was obviously out of his mind with grief. To make a statement like that to a young boy!

"Did you believe him, Kent?"

"That I killed her? I no longer believe I did it intentionally."

"But you believed it at the time?" she persisted.

Kent nodded.

"When did your father explain the truth?"

Kent laughed shortly. "He explained nothing. He didn't talk to me until spring."

Kent was slightly inebriated, Pat thought, but mere liquor had never before induced him to speak about his family. The strain of the day had so drained him that he was no longer concentrating on keeping his secrets. Kate, appalled by what Kent had told her, wanted to know more. Kent answered her questions as candidly as he had answered the others, at times with bitter sarcasm. Often Kate could scarcely make out what he was saying. But the story she and Pat pieced together from Kent's mumbled ironies and the fragmented recounting of his childhood was very depressing.

His father had eventually resumed speaking to Kent, but his conversation was limited to commands and criticisms. He hired tutors for the weekends when Kent was home from his strict Latin school and made certain that his son was kept busy. And when he heard from a friend that Kent was being taunted as a coward by his schoolmates, he berated the boy for failing to take up challenges. But when 10-year-old Kent tried to explain that he found fist-fighting barbaric, his father would have no such excuse. Finally, in a blind rage, Kent did strike back at a classmate and succeeded in pummeling the boy unconscious. Fortunately there was no brain damage, but Kent had been so sickened by his own violence that he never touched anyone again except for a man in the army named Gilbey. Even then he had been careful not to strike his head.

In his childhood years he had apparently been close to no one. Anne, who was five years younger, was doted on by a loving nurse who didn't understand Anne's strange older brother and so kept her charge busy with pursuits that excluded Kent. Various housekeepers had tended to Kent's clothing and meals, but apparently none had established a motherly relationship, for he could not now recall the names of any of them. When his father was home, he used the occasion to lecture Kent on manners, grades, and—until the schoolyard incident—cowardice. His mode of instruction eschewed physical punishment but relied on unrelenting sarcasm.

When Kent was twelve, a lively girl of the same age moved into the house next door. They became close friends in the teasing insulting manner of young adolescents. Her name was Nancy. Kate gathered that they had been devoted to one another.

By the time they worked around to the subject of Kent's marriage to Nancy, he was becoming more sober and considerably less candid. Suddenly he looked from Pat to Kate and said, "Why am I telling you these things? How did I—"

Kate said, "It's good that you can talk about it, Kent."

"Christ, I never thought I'd sink this low. The thing I most despise: a maudlin drunkard." He shook his head. "I'd better be getting back to Beth."

Kate said, "But Kent, there are so many things troubling you, and I think—"

Pat said quietly, "Let him be, Ma." He stood up. "I'll check on Beth and the baby, Kent. Relax for a while longer." His eyes met Kent's a moment. He nodded slowly as if to say, "I understand now." There was so much empathetic pain in Pat's face that Kent had to turn away. He looked up just as Pat was closing the door behind him and raised his hand slightly as though he had wanted to tell Pat something.

"What did you want to say?" Kate asked.

Kent swallowed and shook his head, unable to speak. He leaned back and closed his eyes, wondering for a moment what sort of person he would be now if his father had been a man like Pat.

Kent could remember Pat running at him through the woods: "Like it or not, Kent, I care about you and I won't let you blow your brains out."

Kent's late father would have said, "Don't be histrionic. You know you're incapable of aiming straight."

Kent thought: capital fellow, Henry Wilson, staring down the length of a long mahogany table watching him eat. How old had he been then? Thirteen? Fourteen. His father's eyes piercing, unwavering, from appetizer (appetizer?) to dessert, and then, "Your table manners are atrocious, Kent."

Indeed, father. Indeed, pater meus qui est in domo miserabile. Mea culpa, mea culpa, mea maxima—

Kent would think these things but never say them aloud. Had he done so, the penance would have been worse.

Henry Wilson. How his eloquent words rang down through the years. "I do think the ivories would respond more lyrically if you tried a lighter touch, Kent. Your hand is much too heavy. Use it on enemies, not music."

This is my beloved son in whom I am well pleased.

He would never cry. Not over the crime, not over the punishment, not over anything. One day he would leave, never return. Meanwhile, he would go next door to see Nancy.

Nancy. Laughing, teasing, stubborn, loving Nancy. A boy who had her could stand Henry Wilson. A man who had her could stand all the Henry Wilsons of the world.

Someone had heard him think that. He didn't believe in God or the devil, but someone must have heard. He'd been too happy that summer, too content. He was a respected doctor, a soon-to-be father, and he had Nancy. A man who had Nancy could stand anything. He had thought the thought too loudly.

Kent leaned forward, shuddering, and put his head in his hands. Kate touched his arm, but he was unaware of her gesture. He pressed his palms against his temples as though to crush out thought.

Hot. Liquid Boston-hot. Nancy pale and exhausted. But a perfect delivery, an exquisite baby daughter. "We're parents, Kent." Silence. Nancy? Silence. Nancy? Nancy? Two doctors—colleagues. Two doctors and no remedy.

Nancy still, serene. Nancy sleeping. Doctors murmuring, "Sorry," women sobbing. An icy wind whipping into the sweltering room. Nancy cold. Cover her and keep her warm. Awful wind. Never anything like it. Have to tell Nancy about it. But Nancy won't wake up. Not now. Not ever. Nancy will never wake up.

Crazed, crying and crying, friends over day after day. "Get hold of yourself, Kent. Nancy wouldn't have wanted . . . must try . . . new future . . . new beginning . . . new . . ."

Shut them up. Shut them all up. Stop crying. Stop caring. Stop.

Diving down and down—the floor of the sea. Living under water, pressure in the head. New York. Clattering city, loud and crushing as the ocean. The weight of it. Bellevue. Good. Good, numbing work.

Lincoln—Sumter—war. His truth is marching, ultimate truth is marching. Men no longer men. Walking with Pat, stumbling over bones.

"Fought here a year ago, Kent."

"Here?"

"This very spot."

"Yorick."

"Yes."

"Knew him, Horatio."

"Wouldn't be surprised, Kent."

Regiment dying, laid out under trees. Don't cry, Pat, Tim. These aren't men, no. Skin, bone, blood, nerve, muscle, humerus, radius, ulna, tibia, femur, adductor longus, adductor brevis, adductor magnus . . .

Pat's sister. Pretty young thing. Nice breasts. Flirtatious, silly. Know the type. Shouldn't be here. Death, amputations, no place for simpering belles.

Pat's sister. Not a belle at all. Clipped, defiant. Nancy. Sarcastic, witty, delightful. Nancy. You-can't-push-me-around Nancy. Ignore her. No one can ever be Nancy. No one. Understood?

Dark liquid eyes. Not Nancy. Full breasts, brown hair. Not Nancy. Want her. Ignore her. Want her. Not Nancy. Nancy and not-Nancy. Beth.

"Kent, I like you, but there is someone else. I swear it."

Fight for her. Can't move. Frozen. Cold granite January February. Soldiers dying. Graves and more graves. Requiem. Good idea, relieve pressure, relieve the head. Requiem. Peace and quiet.

"In the woods, Kent? You're examining revolvers in the woods?"

Don't tell Pat. Fidus Achates, never forgive. Keep bullets in coat pocket. Go help him, for God's sake. Cruel to leave him with responsibility for all those men.

Beth. Elizabeth. Elizabeth Wilson. Long tangled hair, soft breasts, clasping, moaning, caressing. Beth. Won by default. He's dead. Intervention of the gods. Prefer a fair fight. Nevertheless he's dead. Is he?

"Kent, do you love me?"

Don't tell her too much. Ruin everything.

"We're parents. Can you believe that?"

Don't say it, don't say it, Nancy said it—

Kate's voice at the end of a tunnel. "Kent?"

"Um."

"Kent?"

"Yes?"

"Are you all right? You're trembling again."

"Oh." He raised his head and sat up straight. "Yes. I'm all right."

"I think I'll go downstairs and ask Theresa to fix you something. You should eat."

"I can't eat, Kate."

"Don't worry about Beth. I'm her mother, and if I'm not worried—"

"She's my life," he said hoarsely.

"Yes, I know."

"She's everything. Nothing must happen to her."

"I understand that, Kent, but you must be sensible." She paused, thinking. "Kent, does Beth know anything of what you told us tonight?"

"No."

"You ought to tell her."

"I can't."

"May I tell her?"

"No."

398

"Why, Kent?"

"If she knew what sort of life I've had, she'd realize that I'm not the man she thought she married."

"I don't understand."

"She considers me strong."

"But you are strong."

He shook his head. "No."

"But Kent—"

"If she knew about any of this, she—"

"She what?"

"Kate, I can't talk about it any more."

"Very well." Kate sighed heavily. It had been an exhausting day. She had experienced the gamut of emotions: fear of Beth's dying, joy over Beth's safe delivery and the birth of a grandchild, sadness for her troubled son-in-law. She was very tired and she did not wish to argue.

The door opened and Pat walked in. "I've checked Beth. She's sleeping soundly. Breathing regularly and her color is good. As for the baby, she's as feisty as her mother and father put together, and I fear for the sanity of the man who marries her."

"You have Kathy married already?" exclaimed Kate. "I need my salts, Patrick! I'm still trying to adjust to the idea that I'm a grandmother, and you—" She began to laugh helplessly. "I'm a poor old woman who ought to be calming herself with a quiet cup of tea, and I feel as though I've been barreling up and down the mountains all day long. I no sooner confront one problem—" She broke off, wondering whether Kent would be offended by her complaint. But Kent was smiling. She noticed too that the trembling had diminished. She said, "Patrick, please fetch Theresa and ask her to send up some sandwiches for Kent and a brandy for me."

"A brandy, Ma? You don't drink."

"I'd like to get drunk. The brandy please, Patrick, before I swoon."

Pat laughed. "I don't believe you've ever fainted in your life."

"I have indeed. You've never seen me is all."

"Are you bragging about it, Ma? Do you have to prove that some things shock you? Nothing shocks you."

Kent looked from one to the other. Could Beth really be in danger now if these two people who loved her could joke like this? He sat back and lit his pipe. When Theresa came up with the sandwiches, he ate three and asked her for some coffee and fruit. Then he returned to Beth's room and sat by her bed until, fully satisfied that she would recover, he went to sleep on the cot beside her.

The months following the birth of Kathy were good ones for Beth. She had nurses to cushion her against the more tedious aspects of motherhood and could therefore take full advantage of the glories of that exalted state. She worked every day in the laboratory for a few hours, relishing the quiet. The dual career of science and motherhood satisfied her appetite for variety and, she felt, made her a better mother.

Kent, amazingly, proved to be a good father. As she had once predicted, he was not as demonstrative as she, but he took keen note of the baby's progress and from time to time could be found in the nursery, his foot rocking the cradle as he hummed a song—rarely a lullaby—and read a textbook or *The Scientific American*. With his reading glasses perched on the end of his nose, he looked and sounded like a mad professor. Sometimes he held the baby awkwardly and talked to her. He never chanted nursery rhymes and shunned any form of baby talk, but he quoted from Virgil, Homer, Shakespeare— anything he had ever memorized in school, including a list of the bones of the body. Kathy would gurgle with pleasure, just as she did when Beth recited "Ring around the Rosy." But eventually Kent began using simple English with his little girl, and Beth was surprised and relieved. It seemed that he could communicate with children after all.

Beth adjusted to her marriage and settled into its rhythms.

She still sparred often with Kent, but after a time Beth found herself feeling better after a healthy airing of grievances. Because Kent could not share many of her interests, she began pursuing them independently. If she wished to be with people and he did not, she either visited them alone or had them over when he was working. If there was a play or a lecture she wanted to attend, she went along with another couple. One evening they had a discussion of the differences in their interests.

She had recited Wordsworth's "She Dwelt among the Untrodden Ways" and had asked, "What do you think?"

He nodded but offered no opinion.

"You don't like it, do you?"

"Beth, is there a clause in the marriage vow that says we must share the same tastes?"

"No, I suppose not."

"You're always searching for beauty in the world, for good-ness—fairness—and I respect that quality in you. That is, I wish you well in the quest. At the same time, I can't always share your enthusiasm."

"But you're searching for something too, Kent: truth."

He shrugged. "We're getting away from the issue. I don't understand why you're so hellbent on creating problems where they don't exist."

But she continued to wish that she and her husband could share more than baby, bed, and laboratory.

Finally she answered with a philosophical "It doesn't mat-ter" that old nagging question as to whether or not she loved him. Whatever it was that kept their marriage from being the panacea she had wished for was not so important any more. She learned to live with Kent, to accept him. By the time Kathy was seven months old she could tell herself that the marriage, while not inspired, was a good and enduring one. She was proud of her realistic appraisal and believed that she had finally matured.

Kate did not tell her daughter about the incident in the

waiting room on the day of Kathy's birth, partly because Kent had asked her not to. Pat had also objected: "We can't tell her, Ma. There are things that happened in the army that I've never mentioned to her because it isn't my place." For a long time Kate agreed. But in May, on the day of Joe's marriage to Diane, she abruptly changed her mind.

It had been a quiet wedding but a happy one. Kate was pleased. That Joe and Diane would probably have a good life together in part made up for the distressing fact that Pat's marriage was not very happy. He said little to the family, but it was obvious from his tone and from the despairing look on his face that the gentle Eileen was too retiring a wife to suit him. His marriage, Kate felt, had been a casualty of war, as had those of many boys who had come home wounded in spirit and ready to marry the first girl who could apply any kind of salve. But mistake or not, Pat now had a son, and a divorce was not likely. He would probably seek a mistress, as so many men did, and the thought of her eldest son's being condemned to a furtive life was depressing.

She was sitting in the library after the wedding thinking about her children and listening to the music downstairs. Several wedding guests—ex-soldiers from Joe's old company—had drifted over to the Shepherds' with Pat and Kent and were now drinking and singing lustily. Pat's wife and two other women had left for their homes, sensing that this reunion was something they could not be a part of but also realizing that the men wanted to be together. Beth had stayed to watch the Grand Army of the Republic relive past glories. She had often longed to be part of such a reunion, but she had envisioned a more sober and reflective gathering, not a raucous group of hard drinkers who looked askance at her every time they began to launch upon an indelicate tale. She was disappointed too because the music was flashing too many unhappy memories back to her. She watched them all sing and she wondered how they could seem so cheerful. Were they remembering only the glint and the glory? Finally Beth went up to the library, where she found her mother sitting comfortably near the fire and starting off into space.

"It was a beautiful wedding."

"Yes," Kate said, "I think they'll be happy. Are you as tired as I am?"

"Every bit. But the men aren't. You should see them. You'd think they missed the war and were anxious for another one. They're all drinking, and I suppose some will have to be carried home."

"They can sleep wherever they fall," said Kate.

"Are you serious?"

"Let them have their fun. Lord knows they fought hard enough for it."

"Yes they did." Beth smiled, surprised at her mother's attitude. She sat down and leaned back in a chair. The strains of "Kingdom Coming" drifted up from the family room. "Even Kent is happily pounding away at the keyboard, and he loathes war songs."

"But he understands the feelings of comradeship that they evoke," said Kate. "He's a sentimental man."

"*Kent?*" Beth laughed. "Hardly, Mother. This is unusual."

"Kent is very sentimental," Kate repeated. "Especially about you."

"No he's not, and he's the first to admit it. You can't expect everyone to be as romantic as Joe."

Kate remembered Kent's words: Beth was his life. One couldn't say anything more romantic than that. Beth had a right to know how he felt, and if he wouldn't tell her then she would. She would tell her daughter everything that had been said that night because she was certain that such revelations could only benefit the marriage. Kate could do nothing about Pat's unfortunate situation but she could help Beth, and if this made her a meddling mother-in-law she didn't care. She loved her daughter too much not to speak up now.

"Beth, how much do you know about your husband's life?"

"Very little, I'm afraid."

"There's something I have to tell you, and I hope Kent will forgive me."

Half an hour later Kate walked out of the library and asked one of the veterans loitering on the stairs to fetch Dr. Wilson. She heard the singing stop and then start up again with a new piano player, who wasn't as skilled as Kent but made up for it in sheer exuberance. Her son-in-law appeared in the hall and bounded up the stairs to the landing, his hair flying. Ashes from the pipe he held fell on his silk waistcoat. Even in elegant wedding attire Kent managed to look disarrayed.

"You wanted to see me?" he asked, smiling.

"Yes."

"Is the party getting too rowdy or is it just my piano-playing?"

She looked away from him. "No, it's—I've been talking to Beth." She took a deep breath and said, running her words together, "She's in the library. I betrayed your trust and told her what happened the night Kathy was born because I felt she had to know and because I love you both and I had to do what I felt was right. I know I meddled but perhaps some day you'll understand—"

He touched her arm awkwardly. "All right, Kate."

"You're angry."

"I wish you hadn't done it, but I know you meant well."

"Please talk to her, Kent. She wants to see you."

"Yes. All right." He opened the library door. She couldn't begin to guess what he was thinking, but he hadn't been angry and she was relieved. She called down the stairs to another veteran and asked him to fetch her husband. With three children married and one away at school, she had a need to share her feelings with John.

Kent entered the library. The war songs accompanied him into the room. Beth, standing beside her father's desk, saw Kent and walked swiftly over to him. Her eyes were red-rimmed. He closed the door, but it didn't snap shut, and the

404

lyrics of "Marching through Georgia" could still be heard.

"I don't know what your mother said to you," he began, "but let me assure you that it was exaggerated. Not because she is given to hyperbole," he amended loyally, for he was very fond of Kate, "but because we were all very agitated that evening and said things that—"

"I love you!" she interrupted.

He sighed. "Pity is what you're feeling. Not love." He walked over to the couch and sat down.

"Who are you to tell me what I'm feeling?" She rustled across the room in her coral silk dress and stood before him looking very much as she had that first Christmas, when he had stopped at the Shepherds' during his furlough. Her hair was up and she was wearing long golden earrings. She had been Diane's matron of honor and had never seemed more beautiful to him. The baby had made her figure even fuller than before. She said she was too plump, but he thought she was perfect.

She said, "I learned some very important facts tonight."

"I suppose you did."

"I'm glad you were married to Nancy."

He was startled. "You are?"

Beth sat down next to him. "Nancy kept you whole. I doubt you could have endured life without her. And there's something else, Kent. She explains why you argue so passionately and forget so easily. You teased and insulted each other as adolescents, and I assume that didn't change with marriage."

"I see. No, it didn't."

"Now that I understand that—" she grinned—"I shall look forward to screeching back at you without getting too upset about it. And don't say that all you ever wanted was peace and quiet. You obviously hate peace and quiet."

"Not true. It depends on what sort of sound is coming at me."

"Well, I won't argue the point now. I have more to say."

"Can't we forget it?"

"No. Oh no, Kent. This is one time when I will finish what I've begun." She paused. "Do you recall a conversation we had a long time ago about cowardice?"

"It was when Joe—"

"Yes. I said that refusing to murder and maim was not cowardly, and you said something enigmatic about wishing you'd told that to someone. It was your father."

"Yes."

"Why didn't you tell me how brutal he was?"

"There was no reason to tell you."

"Yes there was. I might have spent the last year and a half convincing you that you weren't a murderer."

"Your mother told you that?"

"She told me everything."

"Good God. I had hoped she would leave me with some dignity."

"She did the right thing. Don't hate her."

"Of course I don't hate her, but I insisted that she not mention this!" He clenched his fists.

"Kent, please!" She waved her hand impatiently. "I wanted to tell you—there were so many things I'd planned to say to you, but if you're going to sit there glowering and clenching your fists—"

"I'm sorry." He relaxed his hands and then, not knowing what to do with them, folded them together tensely. He turned to her. "Go on, Beth."

"Well," she began hesitantly, "right after we were married I remember watching you while you slept. I was thinking that I wanted to know as much about you as possible because— because I wanted to love you fully—that is—oh, I'm not expressing this very well, Kent."

"I understand what you're saying," he said softly.

"I so looked forward to knowing you, sharing your dreams. Sharing your disappointments too. Everything. But you didn't seem to need me." She cleared her throat, remembering her mother's description of Kent that night. She said to him, "Now I've discovered that you need me very much."

"Yes, I do. But I never realized that my dependence would please you so much."

"Dependence? No. You're very strong, Kent. Considering what you've overcome, I think you're incredibly strong. But you still need me and it isn't dependence. It's love." She touched his arm. "I've never been certain that I loved you, but I am now. You see, I've always wanted a man who had the ability to distinguish between me and the million other women in brown hair and hoop skirts. I wanted someone to choose me for a reason. Do you understand?"

"I'm not sure—"

"I didn't know why you chose me. You never gave me any reasons. I know you found me attractive, and perhaps bright enough to amuse you, but there seemed to be no other reasons. And tonight I discovered one. I have many of Nancy's qualities—"

"I didn't marry a second Nancy."

"No. But I was like her in some ways, and you did love her. You also married me because of my family and because I was interested in medicine and—well—because you loved me. Knowing the reasons makes all the difference."

"Didn't you have reasons for marrying me?"

"Yes. But I wasn't aware of them at the time."

"What were they?"

"I'm not certain I can explain exactly. Since I was a child I've wanted a special kind of husband. I suppose I wanted him to be my friend. That word is inadequate, but it will have to serve. Friends meet each other on the same plane. They give to and take from each other, but neither is higher or lower. Neither is too important to need the other. Many men don't really need their wives, Kent. Oh, they use them in bed or display them like jewels, but they don't especially need them. When they want advice they ask other men. They don't consider women capable of adult observations on business, politics—anything. So it's impossible for them to respect their wives, or indeed any woman." She stopped and looked at him. "You were different, though. You accused me of having feminine wiles, yes, but you never implied that you considered me your inferior. That must have been why I was attracted to you even when I was convinced I disliked you." She turned away and murmured, "Still, I wanted to hear you say that you needed me."

"Yes, I think I understand," he said.

"But you were ashamed to admit it. I suppose it was pride or perhaps the thought that if I ever found out how much you loved me I would take advantage of you in some way. You were afraid I would gloat, weren't you?"

He colored. She was right.

"And all I can say to reassure you, Kent, is that I don't consider love to be a game of teasing each other to see who cares the most. I know some people call that love. Pat used to thrive in those advance-and-retreat relationships. I think he rather enjoyed the anxiety of never knowing how the woman felt about him. But I love you and I admit it right out loud because I think it's more romantic to say it than not to say it and it's most romantic of all to mean it."

He was moved by her frankness and was about to tell her how much he did love her, but she began to speak further.

"And as to the rest of it, Kent, I used to think it a great problem that you and I were so different. Greg used to say that people loved most fully when they were alike, but I question—"

"Must we discuss Greg now?" His voice shook.

"Please. Hear me out. If he and I had spent a lifetime nodding agreement to each other's remarks we might have nodded ourselves into walking sleeps, whereas—"

His eyes widened. "Then Allister is dead?"

"But of course he's dead. What do you mean?"

"I used to wonder if—when we were in bed—if you thought of him."

"Do you mean when we—oh my God, no! You didn't think of Nancy, did you?"

"I didn't have to. I wanted you."

"Well, I wanted you too. And all these months you've

408

wondered if I might be unfaithful in my mind? You've accused me of many things, Kent. But this—" She glared at him and he turned away, his lower lip trembling. He looked very young in that instant. She could picture him in his father's library suffering that crazed man's diatribes. And then it occurred to her that Kent had not been able to trust his own father.

She said to him, speaking softly, "You've never had reason to trust anyone, have you? Not your father, not your mother. Not even Nancy and the child. Lord knows they didn't want to die and leave you, but they did. No, and you couldn't trust the soldiers you saved not to go off and get themselves killed. Even now you can't trust the surgeons at the hospital." She laid a hand on his. "I think I understand why you might have doubts about everyone, including me. But you'll learn to trust me. You will."

She had not been looking at him as she spoke. Now she turned her head and saw that he had covered his face with his hands and was crying. She caught her breath. Someone—it must have been Pat—had told her that Kent never cried. Awkwardly she placed a hand on his shoulder and felt his lean body convulse as though trying to shake off hurt. Beth was very distressed. It was painful to witness tears, and when the person was someone very dear, it was unbearable. Her impulse was to soothe him with platitudes and admonish him not to cry. But she knew she must not do that. In one brief statement she had reminded him of all his losses and betrayals. The memory had cut into him like a bayonet. There was no way to right the ancient wrongs. He could achieve release only in this way, and to distract him with meaningless words would be almost cruel.

He had slumped forward. Gently she drew him against her, leaning back against the armrest of the couch and drawing his head down to her shoulder. He was crying hard, in gasps. She held him tightly and he clung to her, his arms around her waist and his hands gripping the silk of her skirt.

After a few minutes he murmured her name, raised his

head with effort, and blinked several times, as though trying to remember where he was. "I'm sorry."

"You mustn't be—"

"I've ruined your dress."

"I don't care about the dress." She was looking with compassion at his haggard face and red, swollen eyes. Seeing her expression, he sat up and turned from her, pulling a handkerchief from his pocket.

After a while he said in a low voice, "I never quite believed I had a family."

"What do you mean?"

"Until now I was never sure."

It took only a moment for her to understand his meaning. Then she reached for him again. He settled into her arms, laid his head against her breast, and closed his eyes.

She knew now that all through their marriage he had been afraid. At first he had feared childbirth. She had survived that. But he had not relaxed even then for he had never been certain of her loyalty. She must have convinced him tonight that she would not hurt him, betray him, or leave him, for he had at last opened himself to her.

She, who had grown up in a loving family, took loyalty for granted. But Kent was different. How wary and frightened he must have felt. How alone. And how grateful now to have a family.

She stroked his hair. He did not open his eyes and she was certain that he had fallen asleep. She tried to sort out the facts that had been revealed to her tonight and to piece them together. But the facts were scrambled in her mind. She was too drained to think clearly, and it was not really necessary that she determine exactly why he was the man he was. What mattered was that she loved him.

After a while she again became aware of the music downstairs. The songs they were singing now were not war songs. They were gentle pieces. Earlier this evening she had been led, almost step by step, from the screaming hell of Gettysburg, to the riots, to Greg's death and the bleak summer following. She was profoundly affected by music and most of the singing had depressed her.

But now they were singing a song that spoke not of "The Union" but of a land. She and Kent both liked the ballad. Kent often sang it to Kathy in lieu of a lullaby. It was the story of a white trader who asks an Indian chief named Shenandoah if he might marry his daughter. Beth found the song far more evocative of her country's avowed purpose than were the patriotic pieces that sent men marching to their deaths with images of terrible swift swords and bombs bursting in air.

> Oh Shenandoah, I long to hear you,
> Away, you rolling river.
> Oh Shenandoah, I long to hear you,
> Away, I'm bound away,
> 'Cross the wide Missouri.

A white man had loved an Indian maiden and she had loved him. They were married and they went away. Without war. Without treachery. Without cavalry stampeding through the West massacring her people.

> Farewell, goodbye, I shall not grieve you
> Away, you rolling river.
> Oh Shenandoah, I'll not deceive you,
> Away, we're bound away,
> 'Cross the wide Missouri.

The weathered veterans down in the family room sang all the known verses and then repeated them. They would not let the song go. Beth, wishing to hold onto the warm emotion she was feeling, did not want them to.

The music rolled up to her as the Shenandoah River still rolled, as the Missouri and the war-torn Potomac rolled, as the ocean rolled against the island of Manhattan, as the tortured hills of Gettysburg rolled into the Appalachians. It rolled slowly, as the wagons had rolled—over the prairies, over the Rockies, over the Sierras and down to the sea.

Her country was in that music. She could feel the crunch of it beneath her feet, smell its honeysuckle scent. Years ago she had criticized Whitman for failing to use structured rhythms and controlled imagery in capturing the feel of the land. Now she could understand his reason. The rhythm of this land was not measured in iambic pentameter, and its imagery was boundless.

It was natural, then, for her to wonder how a land so majestic could produce a people as capable of brutality as of nobility. The truth, she knew, was that the land could sometimes be ugly, and the people, being part of the land, reflected that quality. The people imitated nature which, having slashed a countryside in storms of gray and black, then streaks a sunset with color or offers a grainfield sustenance.

No, the music did not tell the full story, but it was the half of the story she wished to hear tonight. She had heard the other half too many times.

Kent stirred and pulled himself to a sitting position. His face still looked ravaged but there was a calmness in his eyes.

"Were you asleep?" she asked.

"No. Just thinking."

He sat for a moment, fumbling for his pipe, listening to the song.

> Oh Shenandoah, I love your daughter,
> Away, you rolling river.
> I'll take her 'cross that rolling water,
> Away, I'm bound away . . .

He set his pipe down and reached for her hand. He lifted it to his lips and kissed it. Kent had never done that before. He said, "I wanted to tell you earlier, Beth—I do love you."

"I know you do. You needn't say the words."

"I want to say them."

Kent had changed. He had actually changed. Suddenly he was the calm and demonstrative man she had wanted him to be. But how would they now behave toward one another? She

412

was accustomed to the old Kent. Happy as she was, she didn't quite know how to respond to the new one.

"I love you too," she said.

Later when they were walking home, awkward in their new intimacy, a carriage careened around the corner and into their path, the horse missing them by inches. Kent at once denounced the driver with his usual colorful invective. Beth, herself true to form, criticized him for swearing in public. He asked her if she had expected him to praise the idiot, and she said of course she hadn't but he could have murmured his epithets rather than shouting them. He told her that the driver wouldn't have *heard* him, and what would have been accomplished if he couldn't hear? She suggested that nothing had been accomplished anyhow. He grunted. Suddenly she began to laugh.

He hadn't changed at all. And she hadn't changed either. This evening they had touched each other, but their natures had not been altered. Instead, the moment of sharing had created a home. It was based on love and mutual need. It had four walls and a roof and there was room in it for both of them and Kathy to grow. It would be a good home.

ACKNOWLEDGMENTS

There were hundreds of historians who wrote about Victorian life and the Civil War and I am indebted to each of them. Among these were Bruce Catton, whose remarkable books made life in the Union army comprehensible to a woman living more than a hundred years later; George Worthington Adams, whose *Doctors in Blue* clarified many otherwise confusing accounts of medical procedures in the army; and Richard Bales, who compiled music for a record titled *The Union*—music that so effectively created an atmosphere of the times that I conceived an entire chapter and added to several others after hearing it.

In addition to my immediate family, cited in the dedication, several relatives and friends assisted me by bolstering my confidence during the writing of this novel. They are Leona and Ernest Thompson, Agnes Fedus, Mae Vaccaro, Barbara Puskar, Susan Baker, Lucille Krejcik, Robert Krejcik, Edwin Ritchie, and Kathryn Ferraro.

The final draft of the book was submitted to James Seligmann, a literary agent who has a combination of kindness and good sense. And then one afternoon a woman with a gentle voice called me and said, "I'm Julie Garriott over at St.

415

Martin's and we like your book." Julie was to become my editor.

Primary- and secondary-source research was done at the New York Public Library; the Museum of the City of New York; the public library in Carlisle, Pennsylvania; several museums at Gettysburg; and the Floral Park Public Library. This last, located a block from my home, was able to provide me with rich and varied sources of material that made my task infinitely simpler than it might have been. To Mrs. Frances Kaminer, who followed every step of the writing with enthusiasm, I am grateful.

I am thankful also for the comments of those people who read portions of the manuscript and offered their comments. They are Valerie Dowdell, Frances Wostl, Terry Sciacco, Evelyn Hart, Barbara Gurmo, John Fox, and Peggy McHale.